THE STONE IN MY SHOE

R I C K   B U R K H A R T

A
Burk's History Publication

The Stone in my Shoe
First Edition, Paperback-Published 2015
A Burk's History Publication
Published and Printed in the United States
ISBN: 0692615695
ISBN 13: 9780692615690
Library of Congress Control Number: 2016900500
Burk's History Publications, Temple Terrace, FL

10 9 8 7 6 5 4 3 2 1

CONTENTS

FORWARD

The Stone in My Shoe by Rick Burkhart is a thoroughly researched historical novel that seeks to tell the real story of US and Cuban history from 1952 – 1964 minus the propaganda from the US, Cuba, and the Soviet Union. The book is also an entertaining read with complex, interesting characters ranging from the innocent to Mafiosi. The *Stone in My Shoe* describes the relations among Castro, Kennedy, and Khrushchev dispassionately and gives an account of the Kennedy assassination completely at odds with the official version. Another noteworthy hero is the man whose last second decision averted nuclear catastrophe if not oblivion. In all of this is interwoven a touching love story.

Dr. Victor Peppard, Author
Professor of Russian,
University of South Florida

DEDICATION

History is written by victors. This has been the convention since the beginning of the written record, and it sometimes may only contain shades of the truth. This book is dedicated to the investigative reporters who risk their freedom as well as their livelihood to find and record the unabridged truth, and to the professionals whose conscience demands they reveal their secrets regardless of the risk. This fictional tale revolves around these disclosures, and the author's ability to see through the propaganda of the times. This book is not intended to replace what is known, or to rewrite history; it is intended to entertain and to differentiate propaganda from truth. In other words, this is raw History as it happened without any nation's propaganda told in a fictional story that is entertaining and easy to read.

I want to thank Don Gettner who undertook the first reading and edit of this book. He is a brave sole. I also want to thank my pre-readers Jack and Virginia Balthus, Bonny Cofone, Marie Hornbrook, Kay Davis, my wife Dawn Burkhart, fellow author Brandon Currence, and Dr. Victor Peppard who after reading the draft authored the Forward. Thank-you all.

ammo, and diesel fuel the men were slow to react. Seeing this, El Jefe untied himself, ordered Juan Almeida to take the helm and steer directly into the wind. This was no easy task as the wind was continually swirling in all directions. El Jefe then began throwing much needed supplies into the sea and continued to shout encouragement to the men. Rafael joined in, as did several others. Most were too sick to even move except to throw up. The waves washing over the men saved them from their own expulsions. Their boat, named the Granma, was living up to her moniker as Grandmother to her children. She had protected them the best way she knew how, but now her age was a factor. It was now just a matter of survival and El Jefe had chosen to discard his precious ammunition and supplies. If they survived, they could get more but he had to help Granma keep the men safe. The doctor was one of the few who were physically able to help throw supplies overboard. El Jefe had spent his last dime on these supplies and they were extremely important to him but the men came first. While the Doctor and El Jefe worked in the bow, Rafael worked in the stern to lighten the load. Rafael had seen this strange behavior from El Jefe before. He would choose people over anything else in the world. Maybe that was why he did not choose baseball. What would that have done for anybody else? An idealist, he always wanted to make life better for everyone, not just himself. Stupid, stupid thought Rafael. Wasn't it easier to get men than supplies and ammunitions? How do you fight a war without ammunition? As the men made progress with the supplies, the deck inched higher off the water. Maybe this would work.

The doctor was helping throw a crate overboard when he lost his balance. He was going overboard with no chance of survival. He was not scared to die; he could accept that as long as he made every effort to stay alive. Just as he regained his balance, a large wave broke over the boat and insured that he washed over. At the last minute, a large hand grabbed his arm and threw him back to safety. Only El Jefe had the strength to do this. However as El Jefe grabbed and thrust the doctor to safety, his momentum carried him toward the side. In horror, the doctor watched as El Jefe left the Granma. Juan also saw this from the helm. This frightened him more than the storm. Without El Jefe, they would not survive the storm and the revolution would never begin. Rafael saw El Jefe leave the boat from the stern and knew he had to act. This band of brothers may be doomed anyway he thought but without El Jeffe they were definitely going to die. As a member of the Tampa College swim team, he was a very good swimmer and did not hesitate to grab a life buoy and leap toward El Jeffe as his body approached the back of the boat. Swimming in a flat pool was not the same as swimming in a violent ocean and Rafael's confidence immediately evaporated as he hit the water. Struggling to just hold on to the buoy and occasionally breathe air instead of salt water, he had no hope of grabbing El Jefe as he went by. Not only would he not save El Jeffe he would also die because of his foolish action. What made him think he was the hero and could save El Jefe? On the contrary, he was going to have his Waterloo in the middle of the Caribbean Sea. Rafael found it impossible to maintain a hold on the buoy. The sea pulled at him with a strength that frightened Rafael. He had always been at home in the water; he learned to snorkel as a kid and always-loved being in water. However, he did not love this water. This water was savage and had a mean intent. As a massive wave hit him, he lost his grip. He knew he would never avenge his loved ones but would soon meet them in the afterlife. As he resigned himself to his inevitable fate, he

Prologue
THE STONE IN MY SHOE

What is the stone in my shoe? It could be a pebble, a small stick, or maybe a clump of debris. We know it when it's there, that's for sure. And the sooner we remove it the better we feel. Organized crime also has a concept for a stone in one's shoe. This is someone, an individual that needs to be removed from the living. If the boss asks "who will remove this stone from my shoe?" He is really asking for a volunteer to kill someone. Now the term is no longer literal but metaphorical. The stones in this book are metaphorical. One man's stone may be another man's hero or maybe if not a stone or hero, someone of no consequence. This book is a fictional work surrounded by historical facts whenever and wherever possible. When the facts are not known the most feasible account in this writer's opinion has been used. You may not agree with me as to who is the stone and who is the hero in this story. There are several to choose from. You may even decide the stone with the sharpest edge may not even be a person. It may be propaganda or misinformation. I don't really care who or what you choose as stone or hero, as long as you enjoy the walk. And may all of your shoes remain free from stones.

Chapter 1
CARIBBEAN 1958

On a sixty-foot wooden boat built for a maximum of twelve people, eighty-two men were trying to survive the night. The storm had been sudden and unexpected, but then this is the Caribbean where storms are always a possibility, and in late summer a probability. The boat was so overloaded that the waves were easily breaking over the side and sweeping anything not tied down into the sea. These eighty-two miscreants had departed Mexico yesterday and were to rendezvous with more of their group in Cuba tomorrow. That would not be possible because of the storm and the decrepit condition of the boat. The *Granma's* engines were desperately in need of a major overhaul, belied by the massive amount of smoke churning from her stacks. In this condition, she could not reach cruising speed in calm water, and the Caribbean was anything but calm as the late summer storm whipped the water into a frenzied caldron of crests and valleys, each one threatening to engorge the craft.

El Jefe, their leader, stood proudly at the helm of his doomed boat. He wore fatigues and a soldier's ball cap on top of his six-foot frame. With his wavy black hair, dark eyes and Roman nose he presented a picture of confidence to his men who now only wanted to stop the sickness. Somehow, he clenched a wet cigar between his teeth as he shouted orders and encouragement from inside the pilot's cabin. Although he was inside, he was just as wet as the men who had escaped to the outside. As the men had been sick for sometime, the outside was the only area that did not reek from the stench. How could anyone maintain a positive attitude in such an impossible situation as this, wondered Rafael. Was he trying to emulate Napoleon? He was easily the tallest man in the group unlike Napoleon who would have been the shortest. El Jeffe did not have Napoleon's inferiority complex but he certainly had his drive and determination to succeed. He was a natural athlete and had been a great baseball pitcher. The New York Giants baseball team had offered him a contract and a signing bonus to pitch in the United States, but he turned it down to study Law at Havana University. How stupid thought Rafael. Rafael had been educated in Tampa, Florida and he knew how revered baseball players were in the United States. In Cuba, they are admirable, but in the United States, they are heroes. Rafael thought Joe DiMaggio could probably be elected President of the United States, if he wanted to take a cut in pay.

A violent wave broke over the boat interrupting Rafael's thoughts. The bilge pump, the one that was working, could not keep up with the water that was swamping the boat. The boat, overloaded with excess passengers, guns, ammunitions and supplies, was beginning to flounder. The heaviest items were the barrels of diesel fuel needed to make the trip from Tuxpan, Mexico to the southeastern coast of Cuba. The tank only contained 1200 gallons. To make the trip another 2000 gallons were stored in barrels on deck. Every man on board was or had been seasick except of course for El Jefe. Therefore, when he ordered everything thrown overboard except for the guns, minimal felt something pushing him toward the buoy. As the wave that had broken his grip moved on without him, two large hands surrounded him and latched onto the buoy. His intent was to save El Jeffe, but instead El Jefe had saved him. Just as Rafael grabbed the buoy, the rope tied to the Granma reached its full length and the buoy ripped out of his hands. However, the sudden jerk was not too much for the stronger hands of El Jefe. Again, El Jefe grabbed him and brought him close enough to grab the buoy. The doctor and two other men who had temporarily forgotten they were sick pulled Rafael and El Jefe back to the *Granma*, and helped them climb the rope ladder that was thrown over the side. El Jefe thanked Rafael for his courage and told him next time just throw the buoy in and stay on board the Granma.

The Granma with the lightened load saved the eighty-two souls that day just as a Grandmother would by cradling them to her bosom and not letting go. However, when they left her care and landed in Cuba only twelve would live long enough to make the rendezvous in the Sierra Maestra Mountains. Of those twelve, only five would survive the next year. Included in the five was Rafael Diego Moreno Suarez, the son of a tobacco farmer who would later plot to kill John Fitzgerald Kennedy, President of the United States, and would save Fidel Castro from Central Intelligence Agency (CIA) assassination plots numerous times. The doctor, Ernesto Rafael Guevara de la Serna (Che), would always follow his nature as a friend of the people until his death at the hands of the CIA. Juan Almeida Bosque, the first Blackman in Fidel Castro's Government, who would be honored as a hero of the revolution and was later used by the Kennedy administration in a plot to kill Fidel Castro. Raul Modesto Castro Ruz whose Communist views would influence his older brother and El Jefe, also known as Fidel Alejandro Castro Ruz.

Chapter 2
THE DEVIL'S DOGS SIERRA MAESTRA MOUNTAINS 1958

Jesús heard the soldiers before he could see them. They were coming up the hill that leads to the creek. He did not get many visitors this high in the Sierra Maestra Mountains and he was anxious. Are they from Batista's army, or Fidel's rebels? He could not tell, but he hoped they were from Fidel's rebels. He had heard about the severe beatings and sometimes murders by Batista's men. He cursed his bad luck for sending his sons to market this morning with his only gun. However, transporting their goods, tomatoes, bonitos and garlic to market required the show of a gun. They had never had to use it but it was necessary to show you could defend your produce. He warned his wife to stay in the house and not let their daughter come out of her room. The wood frame two-story house set into the hill and had three rooms. Once it may have been painted white, it was hard to tell now, as the boards were mostly grey. The downstairs contained the kitchen and eating area with a curtain separating the boys sleeping area. Upstairs included two rooms; one for Maria and him and the other for their daughter Anita. The roof was grass thatch and was adequate for heavy rains but not for hurricanes. In the ten years he had farmed the land, he had to rebuild the house three times. They were happy here; they had enough to eat, the land was hard, but the dirt was rich and grew enough food for them and some extra they could sell at market to buy the things they needed. They had even been able to buy a pig, which was almost ready to butcher and would help feed the family for many months. His daughter had been caring and feeding the pig and had even named it. He knew he would have trouble with her when it was time to butcher. "Please God let them be from Fidel," Jesús said aloud as he watched them come over the horizon.

As the three men crested the hill, Jesús could see that they were not heavily armed. Only the one in the middle had a rifle, the other two had handguns in their belts. They were dressed in fatigues and flannel. Obviously, these were not Batista's men, and Jesús began to relax.

"Buenos Dias" said the one in the middle who obviously was the leader.

"Hola and welcome. I am Jesús Hermoza, and this is my farm."

"Gracias Jesús, I am Dionisio. My comrades are Juan LeBrigio and Eutimio Guerra. We are from the 26th of July Movement and represent Fidel Castro."

"Viva la Revolucion!" exclaimed a relieved Jesús. "Fidel's men are always welcome here."

"Mucho gracias Jesús. Do you have any food or arms we could buy?"

"No señor, I only have one rifle and all of my extra food has gone to market. My wife and I would gladly share a meal with you. Please come, we have fresh bread, rice and black beans."

"Much appreciated señor, if permitted we will eat outside."

"Si, I will let Maria know."

As Jesús went inside Dionisio gathered his friends and whispered, "What do you think?"

"I think I see a fat pig in the pen and who knows what might be in the house," said Juan. Eutimio added," I think we take what we want. And if the woman is nice we take her too."

"Si, I will go first," ordered Dionisio.

Juan and Eutimio looked at each other and acquiesced to Dionisio, after all he had the rifle. Dionisio and his two friends were from Santiago de Cuba. They could not read nor write and had never gone to school. What they could do was fight. When the Revolucion started Celia Sanchez, the daughter of a doctor that made house calls, recruited them. Now there was a woman, thought Dionisio. I would sure like some of that! He had thought if he volunteered and brought two others he might be able to get some, but she had been a snob and rebuffed him. Uppity bitch he thought. Probably wanted someone with all or most of his teeth he reasoned. He had lost many in his fights and drunken brawls. The three men were some of the first to join and were confident they had autonomy of actions. After all, Castro needed fighters and they were the best in his army. If you could call it an army, thought Dionisio. It was more like a few men got together to raise hell rather than fight a war. He thought a war was big and they were small. Castro had told them to be kind to los compensinos. He had instructed them to pay for everything they took from the locals. However, that did not apply to traitors.

When Jesús and Maria brought out the food, the three shared a look of confidence and lust. Dionisio appraised the short woman and her long black hair tied in a ponytail. She had raven black eyes, a small nose and generous mouth. She wore a sack dress that displayed a full bosom and a proportional figure that was both feminine and rugged. She was suited to this life in the mountains and would be very satisfying in bed. She was obviously shy and did not look at, nor speak to, the three guests as she brought each one a bowl of rice with black beans, onions and bread. Dionisio almost drooled when he thought she might put up a fight. Nothing excited him more than the spirit of a woman that said no. He could feel his manhood react just thinking about what was going to happen.

As the three ate, Jesús broke the silence, "How are Fidel and the Revolucion?"

"Fidel is well and we continually make progress. Batista cannot find us, but he is easy for us to find. We continually harass and retreat. Fidel is a brilliant leader" Dionisio replied. "We have little to eat though and this meal is delicious. My compliments and thanks to Señora Hermoza."

"Bueno, we don't hear much up here but are hoping for his success. He is truly a friend of the people. If we had known you were coming we would not have sent everything to market." Jesús was becoming more and more uncomfortable with his guests as they continually looked at each other and his wife. Juan was almost snickering as he ate and sneered at Maria.

"Eutimo, Juan take Jesús and tie him to a tree, I will take Maria inside. If she is nice we will not kill him."

Maria screamed "Nada!!"

All three men turned their guns to the door when it opened and were stunned. There in the doorway stood a beautiful young girl with wide black eyes and her mother's long wavy hair. Although sheathed in a loose flannel gown, her young and firm body was evident.

"Madre!" she yelled.

"No Anita, I told you to stay in your room," yelled Jesús.

"Ain't you the pretty one Anita? You stay right there," said Dionisio, "I will have fun with you."

"Comrades, you can have the Madre, I 'm taking the senorita."

"No señor, I beg you don't do this! You can take anything you want, just leave my family alone," exclaimed Jesús as he crossed himself and added, "This is not God's way, this is not Fidel's way."

"This is exactly Fidel's way. You are obviously a traitor to the Revolucion and a Batista supporter; otherwise you would have sold that fat pig to us when we offered to buy supplies."

"No, please you can have the pig and anything else that might serve the cause. Please señor, we gave you our food. Please, please leave my family alone!"

As Dionisio slapped Jesús, knocking him to the ground, both women screamed.

"And gag him also, I've heard enough."

Dionisio turned to the girl and laughed" Come pretty one, show me your room and I'll teach you the dance of love. How old are you, Anita?"

"Thirteen" she said as she shook with fright.

Dionisio could not contain his excitement or his erection as he went toward her. God knew he and his men needed this as it is not natural for a man to go this long without release." Have you ever been with a man before, Anita?"

Anita, as her face turned red from embarrassment, turned her back on this man with his protruding erection. "No señor, mi Madre says that it's God's way to wait until you are married to do that."

"Who is your Madre to think she knows God's way? Shit, it's God's way for a woman to please a man. You will know how after we are done. You are lucky to have me as your first, and your teacher. "

Anita could not imagine how this smelly, bearded man with bad teeth could teach anything but terror. His breath was the worst odor that she had ever encountered. It was worse than the horrible stench of her pig's defecation. His hands were rough and he scratched her with his nails as he tore off her dress. When he threw her on the bed, she was already crying. "Why God? What did I do that was so wrong to deserve this punishment? It must be my fault but I do not know what I did?" When he thrust into her the pain was so great she screamed, "Don't do this!"

He slapped her hard on the right side of her face, "Shut up or it will be worse."

As he moved back and forth, her pain was so bad she began pulling at her hair as hard as she could. She must have done something wrong for God to punish her so. This man must be from the Devil to hurt her this way. Why has God allowed the Devil to do this? What did I do she asked herself? The Devil grabbed her young breasts with his nails and began to squeeze them like a cows utter. He drooled on her belly as if he needed milk from her young breast.

"I am cursed, "she screamed, "Why God? Please tell me, I won't do it again!"

When this Devil's messenger grunted and stopped another was there to take his place. He grabbed her and flipped her over. His thrust was so hard and violent she passed out.

When she again became aware of her surroundings, the pain was so bad that she again starting pulling her hair so she could think of that pain instead of what was happening. She pulled harder until she felt hair pulling out of her scalp. This helped, she thought. The drool on her back was so heavy she thought the Devil must have been foaming at the mouth. She screamed again and heard only a sadistic laugh. She had thought the stories of the Devil's Dogs were not true and were just to frighten little girls, but now she knew they were real. Unbelievable to her the pain increased as the drooling and groaning intensified. She knew the Devil's Dogs were punishing her for her sins. Her name meant 'blessed' according to her Madre, she thought it must really mean 'cursed.'

"Oh God please forgive me" was all she said as she passed out again.

"Che, do you think these three have deserted, or are they searching for food?" asked Ramon.

Che Guevara thought about that before he answered, "They left their assigned guard posts before the end of their shift. They put us all at risk. They are deserters."

"I know but food has been so scarce, Dionisio said he had not eaten a full meal in three days."

"You have not eaten a full meal in three days and yet you are still here. None of us has eaten a full meal in three days yet the struggle must go on. We have made some wonderful progress of late, food, guns and ammunitions will follow. "

"Si, you are correct, but the airlift is late, and we are starving."

"We will survive, as always Fidel has a plan. Fidel would not have sent the six of us out here if he did not think they had deserted. We will find them; they have to account for their actions."

As the squad cleared the crest, they could see an unconscious man tied to a tree. As they cautiously approached, they could hear a mixture of male grunting and women crying from inside the house.

"Ramon, release this man and see to his needs. The rest, come with me." Che slowly opened the door to see a man holding a woman on the ground while another was on top of her panting and grunting.

"Stop this now!" he said as he rifle butted the man on top. As that one fell to the floor he looked into the eyes of the one holding her, "Bastante, let her go now!"

Che bent down to the crying woman as she curled into a fetal position, "Please Señor my daughter!"

"See to the commotion upstairs, Lalo. Andale!"

After a few minutes, all were outside, except for the two women. Maria was trying her best to help Anita who was crying and kept saying over and over, " Please God forgive me" before she passed out.

"Dionisio, Lebrigio and Guerra you are charged with desertion, rape, and terrorizing this family. You will be taken back to camp and tried for your crimes. Do you have anything to say?"

"Si Che, you know me; I am a fighter. We were only searching for food to bring back. When the family turned out to be traitors and friends of Batista we were interrogating them. I know we do not torture but it seemed like the best way to get the women to confess. That is all."

"Si, Che we were just hungry, and trying to protect the troop from traitors," said Juan.

"That is not true!" said Jesús. "My family fed these three, and we are not traitors to the Revolucion. We support Fidel and all those that honorably fight for him. But not these three!"

"Señor Hermoza, will you come with us to testify against these men?"

"Señor Che I cannot leave my wife and daughter."

"Señor I am a doctor and can treat them here before we go. I will insure that they are ok. Do you three live here alone?"

"My sons are at market and have my gun, or I could have stopped this."

"You also could have died if you had tried. I will treat Maria and Anita and then first thing in the morning we will leave for camp. I will leave two men here for their protection until you return tomorrow night. They will not go inside the house. We will leave them enough food so that Maria and Anita will not have to see them at all unless there is trouble. You have my personal guarantee that they will be ok. Now, let me see them as a doctor."

When Anita came around again she could not believe her eyes. Her Madre was helping one of the Devil's Dogs as he touched her and she screamed. It was a scream unlike anything Che or Maria had ever heard. The anguish, the shame, the utter disassociation with life stunned them both. As the scream ended Anita softly uttered, "God I know I've offended you but no more, no more" and she became unconscious again.

During the march to camp the next day, it took all of Che's willpower to keep from shooting Dionisio and his companions. Damn Fidel and his insistence on a trial before any executions, it is a waste of time. These three deserve to die now and not live a minute longer. Che went to Fidel immediately upon arriving at camp and explained everything that had happened and that Señor Hermoza had agreed to testify.

"Muy buen Che, we will have the trial now."

"I will be the judge," said Che.

"No, you will be the prosecutor, Che."

"You will be the judge Fidel?"

"No, I will defend them; Rafael Moreno will be the Judge."

"What?" However, by the time he said this Che could see the wisdom in Fidel's choice. "You don't think he will be overly persuaded because you are defending them?"

"If Moreno is the man I think he is, it is time he became invested in the cause of doing what is right and not just revenge. I think this will serve that purpose."

"And if you are wrong?"

"Then the Movement will have lost a potentially valuable asset. However, I am not wrong. Moreno will prove to be a man of the people and will do the right thing."

Che was still not convinced. "We shall see," he said.

Chapter 3
THE TRIAL
SIERRA MAESTRA
MOUNTAINS
1958

A rectangular wooden table was set at the top of the rise and covered with a white sheet. Rafael sat along one side with Che at one end and Fidel at the other. Behind Fidel, the three prisoners were in chairs with their hands tied behind them. An open chair was across the table from Rafael for the witness. Rafael could see the rest of Fidel's men sitting on the ground or on the rocks down the slope from the table. They were very quiet and seemed very concerned. Dionisio Gonzales was the troop's best fighter. He had proven that he was brave and was always willing to be the first to engage Batista's men.

Rafael cussed to himself for allowing Fidel to assign him as judge. He had complete autonomy to decide guilt or innocence, punishment or acquittal. However, he did not want this responsibility. It should be someone devoted to the Revolucion, and committed to 26 July Movement, not him who is only here for revenge against Batista. Fidel argued that as a member of the fighting group everyone had a responsibility to insure discipline, morale, and to protect the group from unnecessary risk. Everyone knew Fidel's rules: no desertion, no treason, and no mistreatment of the Cuban people. Hell, Castro would have Che treat injured Batista soldiers and then when they were well, release them unharmed. Fidel or his men never tortured prisoners. If Batista captured one of them, the torture would not stop until he had told them everything, or died. Some of their captives confirmed the rumors; the prisoners they knew about first hand were all dead. Fidel would always say if you do the right thing it will lead to the right outcome. Rafael also believed that, but damn if it was not frustrating at times. That is ultimately why he agreed to serve as Judge. It was right for all members to share the burden of responsibility and group safety without regard for why they were there. Damn.

The trial began with Che calling Lieutenant Sardinas to the witness chair. He established that the three accused were assigned guard duty the night they disappeared, and were not at their posts when relief arrived. Fidel established that Lieutenant Sardinas did not know when they had left their post and it could have been just before relief arrived, thus not putting everyone at risk. He ended with, "Lieutenant Sardinas, every one of us is hungry, and is it not reasonable that if they were starving that they would want to get food as soon as they could?"

"Si, that would make sense but they should have waited until they were officially relieved from guard duty."

Next, Che called Jesús Hermoza to testify.

"Señor Hermoza, please tell us what happened at your farm yesterday afternoon when these three defendants visited."

"Si, Señor Guevara. They came to my farm and asked to buy supplies. I did not have any to sell, but I offered to feed them. They ate two helpings each, and then called us traitors and tied me to a tree while they raped my daughter and wife."

"Are you a traitor Señor Hermoza?"

"No señor, I have never even seen a Batista soldier and I do not want to see one. So far, they have not come to this part of the mountains. It is difficult land and it is hard to travel anywhere quickly."

Next Fidel addressed Señor Hermoza. "Señor Hermoza, I am very sorry that this has happened to you and your family. No father, no husband, should ever have to endure such a happening. I sincerely hope that Doctor Che is right, that Maria will recover physically. Anita's injuries are more severe and she needs the help of specialists in Santiago to insure that internally she is ok. Doctor Guevara is also concerned about Anita's shock suffered during the attack, and suggested that Father Sebastian should visit her when she is in Santiago for treatment. Please be assured, I will assume any cost. Now, as to that day, did you give Señor Gonzales any reason to believe that you were a traitor?"

"He said it was because I did not offer to sell him our pig, but that is Anita's pet and cannot be sold. I am not a traitor and support only your cause. You are the champion of the Cuban people."

"Gracias Señor Hermoza, that is all."

Next, Che called Ramon Rubina. "Señor Rubina what did you see when you arrived at the Hermoza farm?"

"We saw Señor Hermoza gagged and tied to a tree. He was unconscious, and had a whelp on the side of his head. We also heard moaning and crying from inside the house. When we entered the house Señor Hermoza was on the floor with Eutimio raping her while Dionisio held her on the ground. Upstairs Juan was still sodomizing the girl, even though she was not conscious."

Fidel asked, "did they say why this was happening?'

"Si, Dionisio said the Hermoza family was traitors and they were questioning the wife and daughter."

Che asked, "Did they appear to be questioning the wife and daughter?"

"No, they were raping them, and the girl was not conscious."

Fidel then called Dionisio to speak for the accused. "Tell us why you left your post and what happened at the Hermoza farm."

"Juan, Eutimo and me, we decided to look for food as soon as our shift was over. We waited until it was time, and left. We were starving. I know we should have waited until the relief got there, but they are never on time, and we were so hungry we could not. When we got to the farm, we asked to buy supplies. They said they had none but we saw the pig and thought they must be Batista supporters. We ate their food, that is true, but we only intended to talk to the women. The best way to get them to talk is to take their clothes from them. Therefore, we did that, and just got carried away. It had been so long since we had a woman; we couldn't help it. The wife wanted a real man, you could tell. She had that look you know. We were only trying to get food and supplies, and return to camp. We were not deserting!"

Che's closing remarks were short and to the point. "These three are guilty of desertion, rape, and sodomy of a thirteen year old girl. They have disgraced the Movement and must be executed."

Fidel, who could never give a short speech, said much more. "Hunger can make you lose all sense of reason. It can drive you to do things that a well-fed man would not do. Dionisio and his companions have proven to be strong fighters and brave in front of the enemy. This does not excuse them from accountability for their actions. This court will decide if their actions merit the ultimate punishment, and execution, or some lesser punishment to repay the Hermoza family for their abuse. Remember they cannot repay the Hermoza family if they are dead. It is clear these people are not traitors. They did not merit what they received. However, were the circumstances such that soldiers acting in good faith could have been wrong at the moment of decision due to their extreme depredation? Or, should they be held accountable to the letter of the law? This court will decide and all of us will accept that decision as just, because our system is fair and it is right to accept the court's decision."

"Viva la Revolucion," exclaimed the men.

As the judge, Rafael had a front row seat to everything that happened. He was amazed that every side conversation ended, every cigar held and not smoked, and everyone and everything stopped when El Jefe spoke. His charisma was infectious. These men would follow him anywhere. Now he thought it was his turn and he questioned if he was prepared to decide the fate of these men. "We will have a one hour recess, and then this court will render a decision."

Rafael walked down to the creek, sat on a rock and lit a cigar. His inner dialogue was a debate with himself. He wanted to do the right thing, He wanted to do what Castro expected, but what was that he asked himself. Did he want his best fighter executed or to do some kind of penance to repay the Hermoza family? He realized he did not know what Fidel really wanted. He did not hear Fidel as he walked up beside him. "Are you ok Rafael?"

"Si, just trying to decide what you want done."

"Young Moreno, do not disappoint me by worrying about what I want or don't want. You must make the decision on your own based upon the information given at trial. All you need is there. You must ask yourself only one question. What is the right thing? What decision provides justice? You cannot worry about consequences of doing what is right. The consequences will take care of themselves. When you have right on your side, history will absolve you."

When Rafael reconvened the court, there was total silence from the men. Every eye, every ear was tuned to his next move. Rafael began, "Dionisio Gonzales, Juan LeBrigio and Eutimio Guerra you have been charged with desertion and with terrorizing the Hermoza family which included rape of the wife and daughter. The moral compass of any successful Army is determined by the rules that govern the Army's actions and the administration of appropriate consequences when those rules are broken. Our rules represent a very high expectation and at the same time are very simplistic. One, no desertion is allowed. This applies when assigned a duty on and off the field of battle. No exceptions, if one wants to leave 26 July Movement, all one has to do is tell his commandant. This has never been refused and has happened more times than we would like. Our Leader is adamant; if you do not want to fight for our cause, and are not willing to die if necessary for that cause, then you should leave. Second, treasonous acts against the movement are punishable by death. If you betray us to Batista, you will be executed as a traitor. Third, we will not mistreat the Cuban people for whom we fight. This is also very simple; we fight for the poor of Cuba. How can we justify any malfeasance against the people we represent? If we do not have the support and trust of the Cuban people, we have no cause. Furthermore, we cannot offer any excuses, any hardship claim, or unusual circumstance to justify breaking our laws. We all share the responsibility of and accountability for holding these rules sacrosanct. Therefore, Señor Gonzales, Señor LeBrigio, and Señor Guerra this court finds you guilty of deserting your assigned post and for terrorizing the Hermoza family, which included rape and sodomy of Señor Hermoza and Señorita Hermoza. You will be executed by firing squad immediately."

As the convicted men were prepared for execution, only Dionisio had any last words. He yelled "Viva La Revolucion!" just before the squad leader said "fire!"

Chapter 4
RAFAEL'S STORY
1958

After the execution, Rafael returned to the same rock by the creek for a cigar. Cigars were the vice of choice for the movement. Che joined him with cigar in hand shortly thereafter.

"Very well done young Moreno; I think you have a new status within our group."

"You mean the one that executed our best fighter?"

"No, I mean the one that upheld the law in a difficult circumstance. You have a new status as a leader, and as such will be expected to be a role model."

"Is this 'no good deed' goes unpunished?"

"No, it is a reward for doing your duty as a revolutionary and champion of the 26th of July Movement."

"But I am only here for revenge."

"Maybe at the start that was your only reason for joining us but it is clear to Fidel and to me that you have embraced our cause and are a true champion of the poor and mistreated. Tell me your story; why is a college educated man marching around in the Sierra Maestra Mountains?"

As Rafael contemplated why Che wanted to know his background, he said, "It's a long story Che."

"We have time," said Che. "I don't mean to pry, but I am interested in why people put themselves in harm's way voluntarily. To fight for the rights of the poor is commendable and honorable. For an honorable man, such as you, to put yourself in harm's way for a different purpose makes me curious. Tell me only if you don't mind telling your story."

Rafael thought about that for a moment before he said, "I don't mind. I also think it is important to know the person guarding your flank in a battle of life and death. And so should you." Rafael thought the place to start was when his padre sent him to Tampa four years ago.

His Padre sent him to study at Tampa University in 1953 to learn agriculture and business administration. He earned a degree in both and after the war, he planned to use this knowledge to grow and sell tobacco. The University was a magnificent collection of buildings with silver Moorish minarets, domes, and cupolas surrounded by ornate Victorian gingerbread in downtown Tampa. They were the most beautiful structures Rafael had ever seen. They have domes and spirals that culminate in long slender almost needle-like tops that are magnificent. Henry B. Plant originally constructed the main building as a hotel in the 1890s. However, more importantly to the students, it is only a short ride to Ybor. Ybor is a vibrant city, and is the home of hundreds of Cigar factories. Most people think factories are huge buildings that support many workers; however, a cigar factory only needs four workers if they have access to good tobacco, someone who knows how to sort the tobacco, and at least one experienced roller. Big is not always better. Ybor is also home to thousands of Cuban immigrants that have come to work in the factories, or to escape the ruthless dictator that is in charge of Cuba. It has a Cuban style and elegance that instantly cured Rafael's pangs from being away from his family and the farm. It is the Latin quarter of Tampa and is home of the Spanish, Italians and Cubans that have settled in west central Florida. Ybor was also where his Madre's Uncle, Manuel Suarez, settled in 1890.

Rafael's Padre sent him away to study because of his friendship with Isabel Mendez. Isabel was his younger sister Pilar's best friend. As kids, she and Pilar would get together a lot, and Rafael always seemed to be around. He thought she was the prettiest girl he had ever seen, and the attraction seemed to be mutual.

At the time, Rafael knew that his Padre and her Padre thought the better match would be for her to marry his brother Alfonso. However, nothing formal had been announced so they still had time to change their minds. His oldest brother Fernando was married to Alicia, and he was in line to inherit the family business. His second brother Alfonso was to inherit the tobacco fields, and his Padre wanted Isabel to marry him, and tie her father's tobacco lands to theirs. That would not happen if she married Rafael the third son. As the third son, he was not part of the future family business. It was his role in life to make his own way either in something else, or on a different farm. His Padre had offered to help him find suitable land if he still wanted to be in the cigar business post college. His Padre was afraid that the University of Havana would not be far enough away to discourage their relationship.

Rafael felt nothing would have changed or diminished their love for one another, only death.

Ybor is a magnificent place and wonderful playground for young college kids such as Rafael. Ybor was forever changed when his Tio Abuelo Manuel Suarez brought his game Bolita to town. Manuel Suarez was his Buelo's oldest brother in his Madre's family. Out of respect, Rafael called him Tio Don. He was the black sheep of the family. As the oldest, he should have inherited the family business, which was sugarcane. He hated farming. He loved gambling, and the excitement that went along with the life of a gambler. When Manuel faced a long prison term because of his numerous arrests, he immigrated to Miami to avoid prison. From there he went to Ybor and found his calling, running Bolita games. Bolita, under the supervision of organized crime, changed not just Florida, but the East Coast of the United States and all major cities west of New York to California. Rafael's Great Uncle established the first games by walking the streets in Ybor and selling numbers to any Cuban that wanted to play. Eventually, as organized crime took over Bolita or "the numbers," it became their prime source of income. Bolita out- grossed prostitution, loan sharking, extortion, insurance fraud and all other illegal gambling activities by a large margin. In the 1920s, prohibition, narcotics trade, and Bolita were the trinity of illegal income.

Bolita is a simple game. Law enforcement calls it an illegal lottery game. A Bolita bag contains balls numbered from one to 100. The object is to bet on which number will be pulled. Rafael's Great Uncle was delighted with the overnight popularity and instant success of his Bolita games. He made enough money to purchase a grocery store as his front, and sold numbers in the back of the store. At his meat counter you could buy pork, lamb, beef, prosciutto, spalla, a single lunch offering that rotated between moros y cristanos(black beans and rice), lechon asado(slow roasted pork), arroz con pollo(rice and chicken) or that sandwich that was invented in 1890 Ybor called a cubano, a mixto, or a Cuban sandwich. At the same time, you could buy a number between 1 and 100. On Saturday, at 6pm, he would conduct the drawing, with the winners receiving a 90 to 1 jackpot if they had the winning number. By the time Rafael reached Ybor, his tio abuelo was a moderately wealthy man. For a young college student he was a great resource, and he gave Rafael the knowledge he needed to survive Ybor.

Chapter 5
UNIVERSITY OF TAMPA
1953

By 1953 when Rafael arrived in Tampa, Bolita was still a main-stay, not only in the Latin society of Ybor, but also in Tampa. Don Italiano was gone; Wall had defeated Antinori for control and Santo Trafficante Sr. replaced him in 1947. Rafael's tio abuelo was now 84 years old and still owned and operated a successful grocery just off 7th Avenue in Ybor. It was successful in part because of the Bolita tickets he sold from his meat counter. The University of Tampa was an expensive private school with students from wealthy, mostly southern families in what is called the Deep South part of the United States. For Rafael, money was short as his family was on a tight budget since his Padre had recently purchased land next to his farm that the family was cultivating to produce tobacco. Land in the Pinar del Rio province of Cuba was not cheap but worth it, as it is the best place in the world for tobacco. In addition, the valley called San Juan y Martinez where Rafael's family farm was located was the best of the best. Occasionally, Rafael would hear the students talking about going to nightclubs and casinos in Ybor, and about the gambling games, which included Bolita. Ybor was not far from the University but it was not close enough to visit regularly, if you did not have a car. To get a car Rafael needed a job, and he thought what better place to start then with his tio abuelo Manuel Suarez. He met him at his store. Manuel watched this young strapping boy, no, young man walk from the front of his store to the back and he began to smile.

"Señor Suarez, I am Rafael Diego Moreno Suarez your...."

"Of course I know who you are!" he interrupted. "Look at my eyes. They are the same as yours. Have you ever seen our eyes outside of the family?"

"I have never seen my green eyes outside of me. Yours are the second pair that I have ever seen! Mi Madre did not tell me they were from her side of the family. To have olive skin and not brown or very dark eyes is rare. I thought I was an anomaly."

"You are not an anomaly, as you can see, but we were blessed by God! The angels, Rafael, touched our eyes. Welcome to Ybor by the way. It's about time you paid your respects!" Manuel continued through his smile," Your Madre sent me a letter telling me you were at the University of Tampa. How do you find the US?"

"It is very exciting here. I did not want to like it and was determined not too, but Ybor is magnificent. It is just like a Cuban city, you can smell the roasted coffee and freshly baked bread; it is just like being in Cuba ...that is except for the people I left behind. I miss them."

"The streets may look and smell like Cuba, but the dangers are much greater here. And the girls? Very pretty si?"

"Si, very pretty, very forward also, and so sophisticated."

"Yes and very warm, very exciting, no?"

"Si."

"Is school interesting?"

"Si, the school is a modern marvel. I have never seen buildings like the ones at school. The architecture is Moorish and Victorian and the main school building used to be a Hotel. The classrooms are large with only about twenty students in each class. The professors are very wise, and I will learn a lot from them."

"And your family? Is your Madre well?"

"Si, everyone is doing fine and the cigar business has never been better."

Manuel liked Rafael from the start. He was definitely his Madre's son he thought. However, the dangers in Ybor are real and he knew it was his responsibility to teach him and keep him safe. "Bueno, Rafael, your Madre is my favorite person in the whole world. She was always the inquisitive kid that wanted to know everything. I saw the hotel not long after it was built, it truly is a wonder. I am glad you came by to let this old man see you. You have made my day."

Rafael knew this was the time to sell his idea. He said, "I have noticed that the students at the University like Ybor for lots of reasons; the nightclubs, the girls, and also for the gambling, especially Bolita. I was hoping that since you brought Bolita here, you could help me start selling Bolita tickets at school. This would save the students a trip to Ybor. Is this possible?"

Manuel immediately began shaking his head. He is definitely his Madre's son, no fear and so adventurous, just like her. He knew his job was now twofold; protect this kid not just from Ybor but from himself as well. With this in mind he said, "Si, it is possible, but it is not going to happen. I promised your Madre to not allow you to get involved in any illegal activities. You don't understand Rafael, all gambling especially Bolita, is run by a ruthless group of gangsters. They think nothing of killing anyone that gets in their way or diminishes their income. Competition is not allowed. You would have to work for them if you sold Bolita numbers at school."

"You sell Bolita numbers here, so you must work for them, why not me?"

"Nada, I promised your Madre. You cannot work for them. It is too dangerous. Do you need money?"

"I want to buy a car. It is not necessary, as I can always take the bus, but a car would be nice."

"And a car is always nice for the girls too, si?"

Rafael blushed before he said," Si, it would be nice for the girls too."

"Your Madre said it would be good for you to find a smart Spanish girl while you are here." Manuel could see in Rafael's face that he had hit a nerve and new that his Madre had tried to diminish Rafael's feelings toward Isabel. Therefore, he was not surprised when Rafael said, "Si, I know that is what my family wants. Most of the girls at school are from the US and are not Spanish. Do you think she wants me to bring home one of them?"

"No, I don't think so. Your choices are better here in Ybor. Just stay away from the Spanish girls that work in the casinos. They are to be played with, but not to keep. The Italians own them. Besides Bolita, what kind of work can you do?"

"What I know is the cigar business. It's too bad none of the factories use lectors anymore."

"Si, the radio is so good here, readers aren't needed, and are too expensive anyway.

What is your knowledge of the cigar making process?"

"I was the best in the family at sorting and grading tobacco, and also in cigar rolling. I really liked working in our nursery to insure Criollo and Corojo seedlings were always ready for planting. Making the cigars is a talent, which I enjoy; cultivating a new strain of tobacco is an art, which I love."

That is it then thought Manuel. I'll get him a job in a cigar factory. He will love it and they will love his knowledge of tobacco.

"Only a Cuban could have a love affair with his tobacco, Rafael. Give me a week and I will find you a legal job. There are no tobacco nurseries here, but cigar factories are everywhere."

"Muchas gracias Tio Don, it would be wonderful to work in the cigar business at any level."

"You are just like your Madre, bright, inquisitive, and a true romantic. It would give me pleasure to help such a man. Especially a man with my green eyes."

Manuel knew that jobs in Ybor in the tobacco business in 1953 were not in demand. Although Ybor still made more cigars than any other place in the world, automation had taken a toll on the premium handmade cigar factories. There was still a demand and the demand was large but some of the art had diminished. Progress, he thought. It was always about money. The bosses also wanted to make more with less people and more profit. A fine cigar was made to be admired, to roll in your appreciative fingers and to enjoy slowly like a beautiful girl. Ah, damn, he thought to himself, maybe Rafael and his Madre aren't the only romantics in the family.

When Rafael returned the following week, Manuel had him a job and a car. It was a beautiful 1948 Chevrolet convertible. It was light green with a white top, three speeds on the column, and perfect for a young student on the prowl. He told Rafael he would have to make payments but with his new job at the Flor de Lis Cigar Factory, payments would be easy. The factory was located in a two story wood frame building on 22nd Avenue next to the railroad track. It was a perfect location for receiving and dispensing product. Ybor was no longer producing 500,000,000 cigars a year as it did in 1929, but in 1953, it was still the cigar capital of the world. The big players included Hav-A-Tampa, which had invented the machine-rolled cigar, and Arturo Fuente, a Cuban family that had immigrated to Tampa in 1912 following the Spanish American War. The company, originally known as A. Fuente and Company, had a disastrous fire in 1924 and stopped producing until 1946. The Fuente brand quickly reestablished itself as the finest Cuban cigar company outside of Cuba.

"Rafael you report tomorrow morning at 4:30am. Your supervisor will be waiting. Drive your car and be on time."

"That won't be a problem, I promise!" said Rafael between smiles. He could not stop looking at the car. "Can I .....?"

Laughing Manuel said, "Here are the keys, the tank is full, enjoy."

"Gracias, mucho gracias!" he said as he walked as fast as he could to the car.

Manuel watched him go with great pride and only slight concern. The car would not be a problem nor should the job, but it was not without some risk. The only job he could fine Rafael was in the factory owned by his boss Santo Trafficante Sr.

The Flor de Lis Factory was small in comparison to the mega factories with only twenty rollers (torcedoras), and produced between 4500 and 5000 cigars a day, six days a week. They specialized in corona and half corona, the most popular sizes for marketing. The factory contracted with a distributor to supply the cigars, which they retailed. In other words, they were a wholesale plant that furnished a finished product for a distributor. The company did not have bundlers so each roller used three stacks of tobacco sorted by purpose. The first stack contained the filler, the second contained the binder, and the third and most important contained the wrapper. Rafael's job was to arrive early, and stock each of the twenty stations with the appropriate tobacco according to which size the roller was making. Therefore, the roller could work continually, maximizing his effective production of cigars. Each roller received a bonus for any cigars made above their minimum quota. Rafael's supervisor Senor Jose Benal was very pleased Rafael knew immediately which leaves were fillers, binders, wrappers, and the grades of each.

"Señor Moreno, where did you learn about tobacco?"

"I was raised on mi padre's Cuban tobacco plantation in Pinar Del Rio. I have been tending to plants, harvesting, drying, fermenting, and rolling tobacco for as long as I can remember. In addition, I have been smoking cigars since I was 12. I don't know why padre had a rule that no one could smoke until his or her 12th birthday, but that was his rule. What a party that was. It was like a right of passage in our family."

"I'm sure it was, Rafael," he said laughing. "Until you learn each roller's capacity it is best to give them more than they can use to insure they don't run out. They tend to bitch a lot when that happens."

"Si, of course, gracias."

"Manuel Suarez is your Great Uncle right?"

"Si, señor."

"Because he vouched for you, I 'm going to give you a key. Since you have to come in before anyone else is usually here, you will need it. The only other person that sometimes comes in at four-thirty in the morning is the owner. His regular day is

Wednesday. I have no idea why he wants to come in that early but he does. He won't bother you as he mostly just stays downstairs in the back office and reviews the books. By the way, don't piss him off. He is a reasonable guy but his enemies tend to have unhappy endings. Capisce?"

"Capisce? I don't understand this word. Is it English?" asked Rafael.

"No, Rafael it's Italian. If you are going to be in Ybor very long, you will need to learn a few things about Italians. The Spanish, Negroes, and Cubans do all the work here and the Italians have all the guns, and collect the money. Get Manuel to tell you about this for your sake. Ybor is not safe for the uninformed."

"Really? It seems like a northern Cuban city with its architecture and food."

"Believe me amigo, those things are here, but this ain't Cuba."

After Rafael's first two days, he stopped by Tio Don's grocery to thank him.

"Que bola Rafael, todas bien?"

"Si, muy buena. I love my job. It is easy and pays well. Muchas gracias for the job and the car. They are both great. I just have one question. Jose said something about the Italians running things in Ybor. He also said to ask you what that meant."

The smile left Manuel's face as he said, "Let's go in the back and I'll tell you about how I met them and I think you will understand."

Chapter 6
BOLITA
1953

Manuel and Rafael remained silent until they reached Manuel's office. Manuel was the first to speak, "Rafael, when I was selling Bolita from the street, some of my regular customers started asking questions about my connection to Don Italiano. At the time, I did not know Don Ignazio Italiano. And I was warned to be discreet or I would meet him in a most unpleasant manner. Initially, Bolita was no threat to the Don, but as it grew, it affected the Don's casino business. When I bought the store, I became a sitting target. Thinking that it would be better if I initiated the meeting with Don Italiano, I did just that. I let it be known that I wanted to meet him, and pay tribute as they call it. Finally the day came when I was told to be at his wholesale grocery business."

The back of Italiano's wholesale grocery business contained several rooms used as staging areas for deliveries and the business office. Next to the business office was a hallway with two chairs and another door that led to the Man's office. It was in one of these chairs that Manuel waited. Standing on each side of him were Charlie Wall and Ignacio Antinori. Both were constantly smiling and sharing comments in Italian that he could not understand. He was very nervous and his legs were visibly shaking. He tried to ease the tension he felt by talking, "Does Señor Italiano know about Bolita?"

Charlie cuffed him on the side of his head, "Shut the fuck up, Don Italiano will tell you what he wants you to know. Until then, shut the fuck up. Capisce?"

After that not so nice warning, Manuel remained quiet until he was called into the office. He knew this was not going to be pleasant. His only mission was to leave there alive. Don Italiano was seated behind a desk, which was on a foot high platform. Three chairs were in front of the desk, the one in the middle slightly in front of the other two. The result was whoever sat in the middle chair could not see the other two behind him and had to look up at Don Italiano. Manuel was told to sit in the middle chair. Don Ignazio Italiano, an immigrant from Villabate, Sicily and good friend of Joseph Profaci who also came from Villabate, effectively controlled life in Ybor and West Tampa. Some even said he controlled all of Tampa and Central Florida. The unusually large man on the elevated platform instantly intimidated Manuel. The light that emanated from the window behind the Don further exaggerated this affect. The light cast a shroud around the man, which reminded Manuel of a picture of Jesus he had seen in a book. Several immigrants had told Manuel that Don Italiano was considered to be God. At this moment, he looked that way to Manuel as well. He seemed to be omnipotent to many locals, and nothing went unnoticed on his streets. Manuel knew this included his Bolita action. At this moment, Manuel would give anything to have approached him from the beginning. Italiano did not look like God in the face with his dark hair and large black mustache; however, he certainly acted as if he thought he was God. In addition, the people around him acquiesced to him as if they thought he was a walking manifestation of the Almighty. Everything was his until he said otherwise.

"Suffice it to say Rafael, I was beat up and thought that I would die in that room. I had disrespected the Don in his view by starting Bolita without his blessing and without giving him his cut or tribute as they call it. I don't remember exactly what he said, but it was something like this."

"You know this is my town or you would not have asked to see me. You know the gaming houses in Ybor are either mine or a tribute is paid to me in order to stay open. Everyone pays for my protection from the unsavory scum that would otherwise make doing business impossible. There are no other options! And now you, you motherless cocksucker, dare to open a gambling game in my town without a word! Think carefully Suarez, why should I allow you to live?'

"I knew I needed to deflect his anger from me so I mentioned that I had brought a tribute for him. You see when Wall searched me, he took it and had not given the envelope to Don Ignazio. Once I mentioned it, Wall handed it over and received a scowl from the Don. To live I had to give Ignacio my game and all rights to it, and to convince him that I could best run it for him. Since it is a simple game anyone can run it, but not everyone had figured out how to control the winners."

"How did you tell him to control the winners?" asked Rafael.

"Rafael, there are two ways that I used in Cuba to control the winning numbers. One adds lead to the balls that if they win will mean the smallest payout and they will go to the bottom of the bag, easy then for the catcher to latch on to them and pull them out as the winning numbers. The second is to put the desired ball or balls on ice before the drawing and the catcher would be told to pull the cold ones. Again assuring the smallest payout. Both of these methods can be used in front of the patrons to insure they believe the game is fair. Both of these methods are still used in some games today. The Dons have changed over the years but the greed and the desire to make as much money as possible always remains. From that day to this, I have kept a low profile and paid tribute to whoever was at the top. Ybor is a place of adventure, opportunity and hidden danger. That is why I promised your Madre to keep you safe and out of any illegal activity."

"Gracias Tio Don, Ybor is not the sleepy little town it appears."

Manuel hoped he had been strong enough with his story to insure Rafael would stay out of harm's way and not accidentally step in a pile of Italian crap. He knew in Ybor your life depended on knowing and abiding by the rules." So you see if you insult the Italians, the head guy, or Don, who is now Santo Trafficante, you don't always live long enough to say you're sorry. In my case, I had something they wanted, and only I knew how to control it. Otherwise, I would not be here. Bolita represented a new money stream outside loan sharking, insurance fraud, casinos, prostitution, illegal drugs, and people trafficking. I was lucky, but I was also prepared for my initial confrontation with them, and knew my only option was to give them my game and help them control it. In Ybor, the smart man always has an escape route planned ahead of time. These organized gangsters don't usually kill anyone outside their business, but mistakes happen, and the innocent die just as easily. Behind the friendly grocery store owner, the baker, the successful cigar company, the friendly restaurant, lurks the shadow of an Italian. Do you have a key to the Flor de Lis Factory?"

"Si, but it is closed today."

"I know that's why you needed a key and why today is the day to show you Ybor's greatest secret. A secret that if it's known you know, could cost you your life. You must promise to never tell a soul. If it is discovered we will both die as I am the only one that could have told you."

"You're serious? The look on your face tells me this is no joke."

"No it's no joke, but you may need this knowledge, and I trust you to maintain the secret and never to go near it unless you are in danger. Come, let me show you." Manuel knew he was taking a huge risk with Rafael, but he didn't know any other way to protect him from what always happens in Ybor if you are around long enough. Sooner rather than later someone always gets greedy, wants more of the action and makes a play at the boss. He didn't want Rafael to be collateral damage. He would never forgive himself if that happened.

As the two went into the factory using the side door Rafael always used coming to work, Manuel made sure no one else was in the building. He then directed Rafael to the business office on the first floor. Looking at the west wall, Manuel asked, "What do you see?"

"I see a desk, several filing cabinets and a metal wall cabinet that contains office supplies."

"Go to the far side of the wall cabinet and push it toward the side wall," directed Manuel.

As Rafael did this, he noticed the outline of a concealed door about four feet tall and four feet wide. He pushed on the inside of the cutout and it sprang inward away from him and into the darkness. Behind the opening was a large hole with two flashlights on either side. He took one of the flashlights flipped it on, and went down the steps. At the bottom, the shaft took off as far as the light would shine toward the south. The tunnel had a brick arched roof and concrete sides and floor. "What is this? This is amazing!"

"Don't get too excited, young nephew, this is the most guarded secret in all of Ybor. Tunnels run underneath certain restaurants, businesses, warehouses, and at least one home that connect to a main shaft. The main shaft leads to the warehouse area at the docks. These tunnels have been escape routes for some, but are used mostly for bringing in what is not supposed to be here. Drugs, people, and contraband of all types have all used these tunnels as their Port of Entry into the United States. There is nothing that cannot be smuggled into Ybor through these tunnels. That is why knowledge of these tunnels outside of the family, and I don't mean our family, I mean the Trafficante family, is forbidden. This factory is owned by the family, and is a favorite of Santo's. If a power play occurs this is a logical hit point for his enemies. If you happen to be here alone in the mornings, you may need this tunnel as an escape route. And you should know when a family member needs cash flow or to remodel his factory, the factory has a habit of catching fire. These wooden buildings burn very quickly. The door opens inward. With care, you can slide the cabinet back into place using the built-in recessed handles. You must never let anyone know you are aware of the tunnels. You also must never go into them again unless it is to save your life. Do not travel far from this entrance, as you will certainly be discovered, and you will die. Rafael, I hope that you will never have reason to use them, and I am probably obsessing thinking you might. But, I promised your Madre to take the best possible care of you and because of that I had to tell you this secret. Listen to me Rafael when I say, having lived in Ybor during what was called the era of blood, I know how ruthless the fight can be over control of organized crime. There is too much money in what they do and eventually someone always wants a bigger share. When the shooting starts, it is time to duck and run. You will not be the target, but if you are in the wrong place at the wrong time, the easiest thing for them to do is eliminate you as well. So never tell, never show, and never take anyone with you if you have to escape. Let others take care of themselves. If you take someone else, you will both die. Agreed?"

"Agreed. And muchas gracias."

As Rafael went back to school, he could not help but think about the tunnels, and what an adventure it would be to explore them. All kinds of pictures went through his head as to what things and what people may have come through those shafts unknown to the rest of the world. And the construction included brick arches and concrete sides, not dirt and timber. These tunnels were built to last, and to support a lot of traffic. He wondered how many people passed through these tunnels. And the bootlegging, the slave trafficking, and probably illegal drugs and arms were all possible tenants of the Ybor tunnels. The tunnels would be a good way to get anything unseen either to the docks or from the docks. The possibilities were endless. Endless that is, as long as they were a secret. What other secrets lie in this quant little Ybor wondered Rafael?

He knew he would never again look at the quant little overgrown Cuban village in the same way. America the beautiful, home of the free and land of secretes! His classmates, especially the girls, were fond of saying that behind every successful man is the woman that really runs things. Now he knew behind every successful Cuban in Ybor is an Italian that really runs things! He thought with a chuckle that the most efficient way would be for a Cuban male to marry a connected Italian female. Then both would be covered! He was equally sure this never happened in Ybor. Segregation of the different ethnicities was required. For example, every ethnicity had their own Club. El Centro Espanol catered to anyone with Spanish ancestry, El Centro Asturiano, Spaniards from northwest Spain; Circulo Cubana, any light skinned Cubans; La Union Marti-Maceo, dark-skinned Cubans; the Deutscher-Amerikaner, for German Americans, and of course the L'Union Italiana, the Italian Club. Not only were these social clubs, but membership to the big ones (usually about a dollar a month) entitled the member to free medical care. And since the El Centro Espanol, and the El Centro Asturiano also had established hospitals, membership included free hospitalization. The Great American melting pot seemed to include dividers so mixing did not occur. The Club Managers told Rafael this was to maintain ethnic purity. But, he knew it was just discrimination. One of his best cigar rollers had two members of his family at the Marti club because their skin was dark; while the rest were light-skinned members of the Circulo Cubana Club, which would not take any dark-skinned Cubans even if they had the same parents as some of their lighter skinned members. This was unique to the United States for Rafael, as in Cuba no one cared about one's skin color. At least not on the farm. If you could work, you were respected, if you couldn't or wouldn't, no one liked or respected you. Color was not relevant.

About three weeks into his job, Rafael met the Italian that ran the Fleur de Lis Cigar Factory. He came up to his floor about an hour into his shift, "Hola, habla usted Ingles, Italiano?"

"Si Señor, I speak English."

"If you are going to stay long in Ybor you should learn Italian as well."

"I have heard that Señor. It would appear that Italian is Ybor's business language."

"No, English is the language of business, but Italian is the first language of most of Ybor's businessmen."

"Gracias Señor, that is a subtle but important difference."

"I'm glad you get it, I was told you were a smart college boy from Pinar Del Rio Province in Cuba yes?"

"Si Señor, that is my family's home. We have a small tobacco plantation that produces tobacco for the Cohiba Company."

"Cohibas are my favorite. We produce a good cigar here but it is not as flavorful. Can you tell why? Our Cuban tobacco is not cheap but even our best rollers cannot make a cigar as fine as a Cohiba."

Confused, Rafael wondered why would the owner ask him such a question. He must know this is not Cuban tobacco. "Ah, señor, this is a test right? Anyone with tobacco experience knows this is not Cuban tobacco. The color is wrong, the veining is not right, the texture, the oiliness, and the feel are all not Cuban. If you burn a leaf the smell also will tell you, it is not Cuban. My guess would be Mexican, although I can't be 100% sure, as some Guatemalan growers use this same seed."

Santo stared at Rafael, looking deeply into his green eyes until Rafael became uncomfortable, but he would not look away. Finally, he said, "Well done young Rafael. Yes it was a test and you are right, this is Mexican tobacco, but we will be changing that soon, very soon." As he said this, his face became very serious and very stern. "Rafael, my name is Santo Trafficante. I have enjoyed talking with you. You are what I heard you were. I very much like Manuel. Bolita has been a great success all across the country, although in other parts of the country, it is known as the numbers game and not Bolita, but it is the same, and it did not exist before Manuel. My family will always be grateful for this. If you need anything while you are here, come and see me, ok?"

"Si Señor Trafficante, gracias."

"Call me Don Santo, Rafael."

"Si, Don Santo, gracias."

The next week Rafael received a shipment of tobacco that was obviously Cuban. The quality of the cigars increased dramatically as a result. Rafael wanted to share this with Jose Benal his supervisor and plant manager but he was told Jose no longer worked there. When he asked why, he was told that he had retired from the cigar business.

"I heard that he had pissed off the boss in some way and was permanently retired Rafael. If you know what I mean. The proof was what I heard the boss say to one of his goons. He asked him to remove the stone in my shoe that is Jose," said Margareta Prello, one of their best rollers. Everyone gasped when she said that. "You know Rafael that is Don Trafficante's way of saying he wanted Jose retired permanently. And he has not been seen since," said Margareta.

Rafael no longer thought of the Ybor tunnels as an adventure waiting to happen, but as a death trap that he wanted to avoid. When he explained everything to his tio abuelo, he asked him, "Am I responsible for Jose's disappearance and possible death?"

He replied," No, you are not responsible. If Jose had been buying cheap Mexican tobacco and passing it off as Cuban to Trafficante, and skimming the difference, he got what he deserved. You do not fuck with the Italians."

Rafael's Tio Don was a very wise man.

Chapter 7
DINNER AT THE COLUMBIA
Ybor 1956

More Wednesdays than not Don Santo would make a point of stopping at Rafael's work location. Rafael was very nervous about this at first but soon relaxed as Don Santo mostly wanted to talk tobacco and about what made the Cuban cigar the best in the world. Rafael tried to educate him the best way he knew how: "The seed, the land, and minerals found in the land, and the climate are all very important Don Santo but I think it's the Cuban farmer. No one loves tobacco plants like a Cuban. A Cuban will caress and talk to his plants and I think he even reveres them. It takes passion to grow the best tobacco."

"Yes, Rafael, the Cuban is passionate. But you are a dreamer. Italians are more fatalistic. If we see something we want, we take it. There are only two things the Italian farmer can grow, grapes and olives. It is our God given right to grow the finest wine grapes and the best olives. Passion is reserved for women. The Cuban cigar is the finest as you have taught me and if it takes Cuban passion to make the best, so be it. The cigars you gave me from your home are indeed my favorites. Did you roll them yourself?"

"Si, my family sent me a care box with tobacco and a knife. Every few months they send more tobacco so I am always well supplied. I enjoy rolling the cigars. I see it as an art form when done correctly with the finished product as something to be savored and enjoyed slowly."

"Like a woman eh?" Don Santo asked with a smile.

"Si, like a woman," Rafael said shyly. "Like a Cuban woman."

"Ah, you don't like American girls?"

"American girls are sophisticated and smart, but lack the Latin passion of a Cuban."

"And Italians?"

"I don't know any Italian girls, so I can't say."

"Well, beware of the Italians young Rafael. They are smart, sophisticated and passionate. Also, know whose daughter you're trying to fuck. Some dads have no sense of humor, capisce?"

"Si, Don Santo."

Rafael vowed then and there to stay away from all Italian girls in Ybor. Giving Don Santo some of his cigars had been a mistake. Manuel had warned him about never asking for a favor from Santo, as he would own you after that. It seems once the Italians have done you a favor you are indebted for life to do them favors, as they deem necessary. Rafael thought it would be ok to give him something, and maybe turn the tables, so to speak. Unfortunately, it didn't work that way. Once he gave Don Santo a sample he made from his Pinar Del Rio tobacco, he liked them and he asked for more. Rafael knew he was trapped. You can't tell the Don, no. So every month he gave him 20 of his precious works of art. It seemed to Rafael that it really didn't matter if you received a favor from the Don, or did a favor for the Don you were obligated from that moment on to acquiesce to the Don's desires. As Rafael pondered his situation, he said to himself, "damn, how did I get into the very situation Manuel warned me to avoid? Damn stupid of me!"

After work, Rafael always went to the Molino Coffee shop on 7th avenue. He loved to sit and sip cafe con leche and smell the coffee beans roasting in the factory. The smell would be so strong, it seemed all you had to do was open your mouth and the flavors would pour in. Mix in the smell of fresh bread from Le Segunda Central and he would instantly be transported home to Cuba. Next, it was breakfast time for Rafael. His favorite place was just down the street, the Columbia Restaurant. The Columbia was a true Spanish delight. The restaurant was the largest in Ybor, covering most of a block. It had three stories including the semi basement floor. Rafael often wondered if it also had a secret door. What he did know was it had the best food in town. From seafood to steaks to Spanish and Cuban favorites, one could not go wrong with any choice. It even had a salad named for the year the restaurant started, 1905. Although not invented at the Columbia but certainly perfected there was a sandwich called a Cuban. Rafael laughed to himself about the name since there is nothing similar to it in Cuba. A 'Mixto', as it was originally called, was invented in the 1890's so factory workers could eat without leaving their work stations. As different immigrant factions joined the Ybor population, ingredients were added to the sandwich reflecting those cultures. For example, the Cubans are responsible for the mojo-marinated roast pork; the Sicilians, the Genoa salami; the Spanish, the fine ham; the Germans and Jews, the Swiss cheese, pickle and mustard. Put it all together on freshly baked Cuban bread pressed for crispness and you have a 'Cuban sandwich.' Casimiro Hernandez founded the Columbia in 1905. In the last few years, Caesar Gonzmart, who married Adele Hernandez, had been running the operation. Unknown to

Rafael, Santo Trafficante also owned part of the restaurant. If it was profitable to own, the safe bet in 1960 Ybor was Santo, if he didn't own it outright, he at least owned part of it.

Rafael and his classmates heard about a Cuban revolutionary that was going to be speaking in Ybor at the Vicente Martinez Ybor Cigar Factory building. He was following Jose Marti's agenda who had solicited donations, and eventually military support, to fight the Spanish American War in the late 1890s. Because of this war, Cuba gained its Independence. One of Marti's most impassioned and successful speeches was delivered in 1893 at the VM Factory. Rafael brought a date, Sue Ann Cummings, to the Columbia for an early dinner before the Fidel Castro speech. Sue Ann was a classmate of Rafael's at the University of Tampa.

"Thanks for bringing me here Rafael; I have always wanted to eat here. What is good?"

"Everything is good. Are you in the mood for seafood, steaks, traditional Spanish or Cuban food?"

"I think I want something traditional. Would you mind ordering for me?"

"Of course not, Sue Ann." Rafael thought the Southern tradition of having two first names was cute. Of course, the fact that Sue Ann had light red hair, blue eyes and just enough freckles to be endearing didn't hurt. As was her custom Sue Ann had her hair in a long ponytail that reached to the middle of her back.

"Joe, we will have 1905 salad, frijoles negros, and arroz con pollo. And to drink select a good Italian white, perhaps an Orvieto or Frascati por favor. "

"We have an Orvieto Classico that would be nice, Mr. Moreno."

"Muchas gracias, Joe."

Sue Ann, a senior, came from Tupelo, Mississippi. Her family had a large cotton plantation, which gave them something in common; however, Rafael found out she knew very little about growing crops or running a plantation. It seemed to Rafael, the Southern girl's job was to marry someone who could provide so she didn't have to worry about 'men things.' Sue Ann was a little different from the Southern mold in that she wanted to teach high school history when she graduated. She thought history had not been kind to the South following the Civil War and was sometimes bitter. She was a racist and was afraid of Negros. Rafael thought his Spanish ancestry and brown skin represented an adventure for her, sort of like forbidden fruit but not quite. She was always quick to point out that he was Spanish to her friends. In other words, Sue Ann was safe to date for Rafael without fear that she would get too serious. As Rafael had thought, many times his heart belonged to Isabel and always would. However, an occasional fun evening was a pleasant diversion, and he hoped tonight would be the same.

"What did you order for me, Rafael?"

"It's a Spanish casserole with chicken, ham, green peppers, artichoke hearts, olive oil, and Valencia rice. It is one of mi Madre's favorites."

"Wow that sounds terrific. What do you think of this Castro guy? I think it's wonderful that he is trying to overthrow the tyrant Batista, don't you?"

"Well, my family has not had any trouble with Batista. We have heard stories of his cruelty and that you had better not cross him. But he has always been respectful of mi padre. Mi padre has even shared some of our hybrid seeds we produced in our nursery. Batista also owns tobacco lands but they are not in the Pinar del Rio region like ours. His lands are in the Sancti

Spiritus area of central Cuba. Mi padre says that even with our hybrid plants that area cannot rival Pinar del Rio for the finest tobacco. It doesn't have the soil or the same favorable weather. Tobacco from his area will always be second best in Cuba but certainly still some of the best tobacco in the world."

"You have met him?" she asked.

"Si, my brothers and I met him when Batista visited our area to discuss issues with the tobacco growers from Pinar del Rio. He came personally because of his interest in the tobacco business. He was still in the military at that point but was going to run against the current President Prio in the 1953 election. Of course, that did not happen as Batista conducted a bloodless coup prior to the election and assumed power. Batista had the support of the United States so there was no resistance that he couldn't eliminate by threats without the necessity for blood. Many organizations speak out against him but no one before Castro at the failed Moncada Barracks raid in 1953 dared face his soldiers in combat. Castro spent 18 months in prison for that one. Batista considered him such a minor threat that he was released as part of a general amnesty."

"What else do you know about Fidel Castro?"

"I know what is common knowledge to all Cubans. Castro was an outstanding athlete in school in all sports. His best was probably baseball. The New York Giants offered him a professional contract that included several thousand dollars in bonus money. He declined the offer so he could study law at the University of Havana. Before he graduated, he began making speeches against what he called Latin and South American tyrants that controlled their country through brutality and the support of the US government. One of these was Batista; another was Rafael Trujillo of the Dominican Republic. He heard about a group that was being organized to invade the Dominican Republic and take down Trujillo. Trujillo is another dictator that has the blessing of the United States. As he had been elected President of the 'University Committee for Democracy in the Dominican Republic', Castro couldn't resist and joined the invading group. As Trujillo was well connected to the CIA and US politicians, he was informed of the raid and was ready. The raid was a disaster and Castro had to jump into the sea between the Dominican Republic and swim home to Cuba. Some say he swam the whole way, others say he was picked up by a Cuban fishing boat when he got close. Either way he swam a very long way in the ocean before reaching safety, but I doubt he swam the entire 140 miles. But he did swim a long way in open ocean waters."

"That is incredible to escape that way. He was lucky to escape the Moncada raid alive. Fidel Castro is a hero of Cuba because of his efforts on behalf of Cuban's oppressed population!"

"Hero? Bullshit. He was just lucky both times and he failed both times. He also failed when he joined the Bogotazo riots in Bogotá Columbia. He was visiting with a student group sponsored by Argentine President Juan Peron when he joined the riots and stole guns from a police station. More than 3000 people died in the riots. Castro was arrested, cleared from being involved in any of the murders, and was released. He failed again to achieve anything of value. Instead of a hero I would say he was a fuck up that can't get anything right and is damned lucky to still be alive."

"Yes, but Rafael, isn't it romantic that he fights for his beliefs and is willing to risk his life in their defense? It's like the Latin version of Southern Chivalry to risk all for principle! I can't wait to hear his speech tonight."

"You and your Southern pride. Sue Ann, you do realize the South lost the Civil war right?"

"Only too well do I and my family know, Rafael. We suffered horrible atrocities at the hands of the Northern Carpetbaggers that invaded Mississippi after the war. "

"Buenas tardes Señor Moreno," said Santo Trafficante.

Rafael had been so engrossed in his conversation with Sue Ann that he did not see him approach and was startled. He immediately stood up.

"Buona sera Don Santo, what a pleasant surprise." Rafael stood and replied in Italian, as was their new custom. Don Santo always greeted him in Spanish and Rafael reciprocated by greeting him in Italian. "May I introduce Señorita Sue Ann Cummings from Tupelo, Mississippi? She and I are students together at the University of Tampa."

"Ah, an American and a very pretty one too. Welcome to the Columbia. I hope you enjoy your evening with Señor Rafael. And Rafael, thanks again for the cigars, I have never had better." As Joe arrived with their main course at that time, Don Santo added, "Joe, we will comp this table tonight, anything they want. And also sing this pretty girl a song."

"Of course, Don Santo, as you wish."

"Sit down, Rafael. Enjoy your evening." He said as he left without waiting for a reply.

Rafael was momentarily stunned, as he sat down. He had vowed to stop the interchange with Don Santo at conversation, and giving Santo cigars. Now he would owe him dinner! How did he let this happen? "Joe, how is it that he can comp our table? I thought only the owners can 'comp' a table."

"Santo Trafficante is an owner along with the Casimiro Hernandez's family. Casimiro's son-in-law, Caesar Gonzmart, is the proprietor. Casimiro was the founder in 1905 and all of them can, of course, 'comp' a meal if they wish. Don Trafficante does not do this often; you have his blessing for some reason."

Rafael knew Joe was fishing for an answer as to why but he said nothing. Damn it he thought. He felt trapped with no way out. He was consumed with his thoughts and even forgot Sue Ann was there.

After Joe left, Sue Ann asked," Was that really Santo Trafficante, the mob boss?"

"Si, and don't ever use that term 'mob boss' in here again. There are consequences for rudeness that we don't want."

"Sorry, I meant nothing by it. I had no idea you knew these people."

"What one means is not important. It's what one does that will get you in trouble. And I don't know these people. He owns the factory where I work is all." Rafael's tone and demeanor had definitely changed from confidence to distress, all because his dinner was on the house. Welcome to Ybor he thought.

Sue Ann noticed the change but could not imagine what had happened. At first she thought she might have done something, but that was ridiculous, she was always the perfect Southern lady, just as she had been trained. "Ok, don't be so defensive. I 'm just impressed is all. There seems to be a lot to Rafael Moreno that I didn't know."

Sue Ann's obvious admiration snapped Rafael from his trance as he embraced the additional attention from this girl because of knowing Don Santo. It just might lead to a happy ending tonight he thought. He knew he would feel guilty because of Isabel but that wouldn't happen until tomorrow and besides she was in another Country and engaged to his brother. Enjoy he told himself.

After the meal and as they enjoyed flan for desert, Joe Ramon, as requested, sang them a song. He choose "Again," a very popular love song written by Newton in the 1940s. Joe had only been at the Columbia for two years but he was already known as the "singing waiter." Sue Ann was completely enamored by the end and Rafael thought about skipping the speech so that her mood wouldn't change, but she insisted they here this Castro's speech.

A large crowd was already present when they arrived at the VM Factory building where Castro was to deliver his speech. This was the building where José Martí delivered a speech in 1893 to gather support for Cuba's fight for Independence, which later became known as the Spanish American War. The 1886 factory was one of the area's first and was built and operated by Ybor's founder Vicente Martinez Ybor. The Factory covers an entire city block between 8th and 9th avenue and 13th and 14th street. It is a four story brick building that has a raised step entrance on the front, which provides a natural platform for impassioned speakers to deliver their speeches. The raised front area is covered by a white portico, which provides shelter from the sun and rain, both of which are plentiful in Tampa.

Chapter 8

CASTRO'S YBOR SPEECH 1956

As the 300 plus people gathered, Sue Ann could see that most were Hispanic. There were a few others in blue suits that looked very much out of place. They were spread out among the crowd and had some kind of earpieces that seem to allow for communication.

"Oh dear Rafael, is he going to speak in English or Spanish?"

"I suspect Spanish."

"Oh my, would you be a dear and translate for me. I am so interested in what he has to say, I don't want to miss a thing. I know you don't like him but I really want to know his thoughts and why he would continue to risk his life for others."

"It's not that I dislike him Sue Ann, I just don't share his need to fight other people's battles."

"That's not very chivalrous Rafael. If you saw a damsel in distress would you not intervene and help even if she was being beaten by her husband?"

"Of course I would. The strong should not be allowed to beat the weak just because they can."

"And you would be a Southern hero to me if you did. Now if this were happening across the street, would you cross it to help? And if it were a block away would you go that far to help? How far would you go to right a wrong, Rafael?"

Rafael did not like feeling defensive with this southern belle. She seemed to have a perspective of right and wrong with which he was not familiar.

"Well, I guess you have to weigh the depth of the wrong and compare it to the cost of correcting it before you act."

"Spoken like a true business man. In your opinion then a wrong should only be addressed if it is cheap enough to do so!"

"Nada, I didn't say that. Mistreating people should never be allowed, but I was only trying to be practical. You can't correct all the wrongs in this world. It's too complicated."

"You did say that Rafael. You put correcting a wrong in terms of dollars, which leads to total inequality between people that have and people that have not! My family lived this before and after the Civil War. We only saw our own transgressions, after the war when the carpetbaggers did the same things to us that we had done to the slaves before the war."

Fortunately, for Rafael, Castro came to his rescue and began to speak but Rafael sensed the mood of the evening was gone and with it went the happy ending he had envisioned. Sue Ann became absorbed with Castro's speech as Rafael translated. He began by quoting from José Martí's speech delivered 64 years earlier on these same steps:

"Like stones rolling down a hill, fair ideas reach their objectives despite all obstacles and barriers. It may be possible to speed or hinder them but it is impossible to stop them. We are

all free, but not to be evil, not to be indifferent to human suf-
fering, not to profit from the people."

After a pause to contemplate Marti's words Castro began, "Cuba is in the grip of a dictator that usurped power in 1952 when faced with a losing election bid. Knowing he could not win the election, he took control in a coup that many call bloodless because no one died before he took control. Thousands have died in the last 4 years because they dared to oppose Batista's betrayal of the Cuban people to US big business such as The United Fruit Company. Batista has sold out Cuban mines to companies that exploit the Cuban worker to enrich themselves and the criminals in the Batista Administration. And they are not the worst. Elements of organized crime have bribed Batista to allow open prostitution, drug smuggling, and casinos to further rape the Cuban worker. Intimidation, loan sharking, and murder have all been used to enforce Batista's rules. The Cuban worker has been lied to and threatened anytime objections are raised as to the humanity of their treatment. Currently, United States businesses own 90% of all Cuban Mines, 80% of the public utilities, 50 % of the railroads, 40% of the sugar production, and the telephone company. Batista, in cooperation with these companies, determines the cost of these services to the people of Cuba. The telephone company was so happy with Batista that they presented him with a solid gold telephone paid for by the company's outrageous fees. More than 66% of the population is considered illiterate. Less than 50% of the homes in Cuba contain telephones, electricity and indoor plumbing. More than 33% of the people live in absolute poverty with no hope of a better life except for this revolution. Medical care is beyond the reach of most Cubans. Social and economic reforms must take place in

Cuba. Everyone should have access to free education, free medical treatment, and the opportunity to own land. Agrarian reform is necessary to achieve these goals. By this, I don't mean taking away land without compensation. I believe a limit of 1000 acres should be imposed except where larger tracts are needed to maintain agricultural efficiency. By this, I mean selling unused government land to individuals willing to work it and make it productive. Cuba, like the U.S., is a nation of cultural diversity. Slaves were imported by US companies to work the land for hundreds of years. Slavery in Cuba is no more and so must discrimination be a thing of the past in Cuba. Everyone in Cuba, and I don't mean just males but everyone, men and women, will be treated with equal opportunity. As Martí said:

> *The struggles waged by nations are weak only when they lack the support in the hearts of their women. But when women are moved and lend help, when women who are by nature calm and controlled, give encouragement and applause, when virtuous and knowledgeable women grace the endeavor worth their sweet love then it is invincible. Famous men, and women of much talk and few deeds, soon evaporate. Action is the dignity of greatness.*

The 26th of July Movement, named for the date of the Moncada Barracks attack, asks for your help so we can light the Cuban oven so everyone can bake bread and live free!"

It seemed the applause might last as long as the speech, which was two hours long. After it was over Castro asked everyone to sing the anthem of the revolution, which went like this:

Guantanamera, guajira Guantanamera
Guantanamera, guajira Guantanamera

Yo soy un hombre sincero
De donde crece la palma
Y antes de morirme quiero
Echar mis versos del alma
Guantanamera, guajira Guantanamera
Guantanamera, guajira Guantanamera
Mi verso es de un verde claro
Y de un carmín encendido
Mi verso es un ciervo herido
Que busca en el monte amparo
Guantanamera, guajira Guantanamera
Guantanamera, guajira Guantanamera
Cultivo una rosa blanca
En julio como en enero
Para el amigo sincero
Que me da su mano franca
Guantanamera, guajira Guantanamera
Guantanamera, guajira Guantanamera
Con los pobres de la tierra
Quiero yo mi suerte echar
El arroyo de la sierra
Me complace más que el mar
Guantanamera, guajira Guantanamera
Guantanamera, guajira Guantanamera

Rafael translated the song for Sue Ann who just loved it. She thought it was the second most romantic choice for a revolutionary theme song that she had ever heard. Second only to her beloved South's Dixie during the Civil War. Rafael never understood why so many Southerners obsessed about the Civil War even though it was almost 100 years ago0. When is it time to move on he wondered? Or is it they feel so passionate about their homeland and the way of life it represented that they can't forget? Is the sense of loss so profound that it doesn't diminish with time? Rafael knew he felt that way about Cuba and Isabel. Maybe those feeling were similar. Ah, he scolded himself; don't get so melancholy for Home, not with such a pretty girl sitting beside him.

Girl from Guantanamo, my peasant girl from Guantanamo
Girl from Guantanamo, my peasant girl from Guantanamo
I am a truthful man
From where the palm tree grows
And before dying I want
To let out the verses of my soul
Girl from Guantanamo, my peasant girl from Guantanamo
Girl from Guantanamo, my peasant girl from Guantanamo
My verse is light green
And it is flaming red
My verse is a wounded stag
Who seeks refuge on the mountain
Girl from Guantanamo, my peasant girl from Guantanamo
Girl from Guantanamo, my peasant girl from Guantanamo
I grow a white rose
In July just as in January
For the honest friend
Who gives me his open hand
Girl from Guantanamo, my peasant girl from Guantanamo
Girl from Guantanamo, my peasant girl from Guantanamo
With the poor people of the earth
I want to cast my lot
The brook of the mountains

Gives me more pleasure than the sea
Girl from Guantanamo, peasant girl from Guantanamo
Girl from Guantanamo, peasant girl from Guantanamo

For those, Rafael included, that did not know, Castro told the crowd that the verses of the song were written by José Martí. Rafael noticed that the men in blue suits with the earpieces neither clapped nor sang nor made any facial expressions at all. This surprised him. How could anyone be neutral after this amazing speech? You would have to either like him or hate him; to remain neutral was impossible, such was the conviction of this man.

As Rafael and Sue Ann drove toward campus neither spoke for a while. They were both deep in thought about the words of Castro, although for different reasons. Finally, Sue Ann broke the ice, "That was awe inspiring. I now know what it must have been like to hear Robert E. Lee speak. Of course, he is wrong about the Negroes being equal but he'll learn. I mean they should be treated properly, but equal? Not hardly. "

"Who?"

"Why Robert E. Lee silly, the greatest general this country has ever had."

"You mean the South in the Civil War?"

"Of course, the North never had the best leaders, everyone knows that silly."

How ironic Rafael thought; Sue Ann, the Southern Belle, and Trafficante (Mob Boss) shared racial beliefs. Of course, for Trafficante, if you weren't Italian you already had two strikes. Three and you became a stone in his shoe. Well, that sealed it, thought Rafael, with his melancholy and her dreaming there would be no happy ending this night!

Chapter 9
YBOR FIRE
1957-1958

After graduating from the University of Tampa, Rafael decided to continue his education and get an advanced degree. This would not only strengthen his ability to run a cigar factory but would also relieve his parents of the upcoming confrontation. In 1956, Rafael's Padre and Isabel's Padre had agreed on a marriage pact. Rafael's brother Alfonso would marry Isabel on her 21st birthday. She would turn 21 in 1958. Everyone had agreed to this except, of course, Rafael and Isabel. He and Isabel reasoned that her marrying him would also unite their families and allow for continued cooperation between the two biggest tobacco plantations in the Pinar del Rio province. Why were they the only ones that thought so? Nothing could be said to them that made sense. They had been in love since they could walk. The kids in the two families always went to the school built by Rafael's Padre on their plantation. His Padre opened it to everyone in the valley, peasants' or landowners' kids, it did not matter. He thought everyone should be educated and that knowledge was a gift from God and should be shared.

As the wedding drew closer, the letters between Rafael and Isabel became more frantic. They could not disobey their parents. At least Isabel could not. Rafael would have if she had agreed, but for her and most Spanish children, to disobey the head of the family was a sin that could not be forgiven. If she did, her family would disown her and never speak to her again. It was just unthinkable, at least for her. There was nothing Rafael would not sacrifice to be with her. During Rafael's yearly three week visit at Christmas in 1957, they racked their brains trying to find a solution to this impossible situation. There was nothing they could think of that did not mean being ostracized by their families. Rafael even offered to take her to Ybor when he went back to school, but he knew she would suffer too much. This would have destroyed her. When he returned to Ybor, he did not think he would see her again until after she was married. For him to attend the wedding was too painful a thought for them to even consider.

In January of 1958, Manuel Suarez died suddenly at his grocery. Rafael's Padre and Madre traveled from Cuba to Ybor to attend his services. Witnesses said he was talking one minute and then stopped, stood for second longer, and then fell over. The doctor indicated he had a massive heart attack and was probably dead before he hit the floor. He was buried in the Spanish section of the L'Unione Italiano in Ybor. Rafael tried to talk to his Padre about the marriage announcement between Alfonso and Isabel, but he would not discuss it. Alarmed by the official announcement, Isabel had written Rafael as soon as she was told. His Madre just shook her head and said, " Nada, Rafael, she is not for you." The finality of her words hit like a ton of bricks. Rafael felt life without Isabel would have no meaning and no happiness. Was God punishing him for sowing his wild oats in

Ybor? He didn't know, he just knew he felt terrible and couldn't think of anything that eased the pain. When his parents went home, Rafael thought he would never smile again, such was the depth of his depression. The sadness turned to anger as he refused to accept that any legitimate reason existed that should keep them apart. How could their parents be so stupid and so cruel! And for what? Greed, and only greed! To refuse and deny their love because it wouldn't be the best business decision? How selfish and cruel they were! At that moment, Rafael hated them and the whole world!

It was Wednesday and Rafael was distracted about Isabel and their dilemma when his thoughts were interrupted by some kind of noise. He stopped his daydreaming and realized it was hammering. That's odd, he thought, it was not even light outside. Who would be hammering in the dark? As Rafael explored the factory, the smell of gasoline became stronger and stronger. What the hell, he thought. When he reached the door that he normally used to enter the Factory, it would not budge. He ran to the side door, no difference. Suddenly the walls outside burst into flames. "Mierde, me cago en la leche!" he yelled. From outside he heard in Italian, " Chiddu arrusti u so pesci nte cianmi di l'incediu, Trafficante, madone de mia iarrusu!" He understood some of the words like fire and fuck-you so he knew this was a take-out move directed at Don Santo. He was collateral damage and of no concern to anyone but himself. He knew his only exit was through the tunnels. He said aloud, "Gracias, Tio Don. May you rest in peace; the Ybor tunnels will save my life."

When he got to the office, he found Santo on the floor, unconscious with blood on the side of his head. He was alive but not moving. He would die in the fire that was rapidly consuming the factory. He stepped over the body and moved the cabinet to descend to safety. "Mierde!" He knew he should leave him but he could not. At almost 6' tall and a strong 195 lbs, carrying the old man of maybe 5'8", 150 lbs would not be a problem. The problem would be when he regained consciousness and realized they were in the Ybor tunnels. As Rafael hesitated, he reasoned that if his uncle were still alive, he would leave Don Santo but since he was dead, he should save him. To save him or leave him were both punishable by death if it were known that he could have saved him. And the family would want to know how he had survived while Santo died. Either he was in on it and would die, or he knew about the tunnels and would die. "I'm fucked!" he yelled. His only choice was to save Santo and hoped that meant something. Would the family see it that way and give him a pass? After all Santo would be dead if he didn't know about the tunnels. Or would they see him as a gavone trying to take advantage of the situation for his own benefit. Since he was not family, nor even an associate or a worthless babbo, he was not bound by the omerta code of silence. Rafael was still mumbling as he went back and picked up Santo and brought him to safety. He mumbled, "Mi Padre can be heartless and cruel but I refuse to follow in his footsteps!" After collecting Santo from the office, he stopped a safe distance down the tunnel and put Santo on the ground. He had taken two flashlights, one he still carried as he paced back and forth trying to decide his next move. The other flashlight he placed next to Santo shinning on his face so he could see when he woke up. One option, leave him here and venture down the tunnel until he found a way out. But Tio Don warned him not to do that, as he would surely be caught before reaching an exit. And what did the exit look like and where would it be? He had no idea. "Mierde!" he said to no one. Even without Santo, he would have the same problem, but not quite.

The plan with Suarez was to wait long enough for the crisis to pass and exit the same way he came in. If Santo did not wake up, he could still do this. He would just have to wait maybe 24 hours for the fire to be put out and the rubble to cool and he could leave that way. He immediately felt better having reached this decision to just wait it out. As he walked back toward Santo, he was not aware of the person sneaking up behind him. The pain was fleeting as the world turned black.

Rafael woke up in a room that he had never seen. He was naked and tied to a chair in the middle of a room with all of the light directed on his face. He could not see anyone but he could here murmurs of conversation around the room. His head hurt and he could tell that his hair was matted on the right side from his own blood. One of the shadows approached and threw a bucket of ice water in his face. He didn't know water could hurt so much. But it didn't hurt nearly as much as the slap across his head that followed. Before he passed out another bucket of water insured that he would not escape into the sweet oblivion of unconsciousness.

"Who paid you, cocksucker? You will tell us shekoo!"

"Paid me for what," Rafael croaked.

"The hit on the skipper, shithead," someone outside the light said before another slap.

"Is Don Santo dead? I tried to save him."

Another smack followed by "We will ask the fucking questions baboo. You will answer or we will feed you your own piseddu, capisce? You have 30 seconds"

"Oh let me do it Franco. It would give me great pleasure to feed this aricchi du porcu his own educated dick, that is if I can find the little thing! "

After the laughter, "Ok talk asshole unless you want to eat your own dick"

"All I know is my Great Uncle Manuel Suarez showed me the tunnel entrance in 1952 when I first went to work at the factory. He swore me to silence and I was only to use it for emergencies. I have told no one else. When someone tried to kill Don Santo by nailing the doors and windows shut and burning the factory, I found Don Santo on the floor of his office unconscious. I carried him into the tunnel to save him. That's all I know, that's all I meant by taking him into the tunnels. I tried to save him, not kill him. If I wanted him dead, I would have left him there to burn. If he is dead I am sorry, I liked him as mi Tio Don did. Now release me and fight me like a man you poor excuse for a stuppaghiara or kill me and…."

Franco's fist caught him flush on the nose, knocking him and the chair on its back. Rafael was sure his nose was broken. Since he had boxed in school a broken nose was not unfamiliar, but it still hurt like hell. He had deliberately provoked him as the embarrassment of the situation overrode his fear. He didn't know exactly what stuppaghiara meant but he knew it had something to do with sucking the cork out of a wine bottle so he knew it was not flattering. If he were to die, he would not go begging or whining to this goon. Already mad at the world because of Isabel, he felt no fear; living or dying was the same.

"Stop!" came the order from the back. As Santo walked into the light he said, "Sit him up, untie him and give him his clothes."

"Skipper, he insulted a made man. He has to suffer for that. And he knows about the tunnels, he has to die for that."

"And he saved my life, I owe him for that!"

"Ok, we can give him a nice gravestone skipper, but he has to go."

"Franco," Santo said as he patted him on the check, "A full accounting will be made, when I say it will be made, capisce?"

"Of course Don Santo I meant no disrespect, you are my godfather and will decide."

"Get word to my son as soon as he gets in from Cuba to come here immediately using the tunnels. And do it discreetly. As long as young Moreno and I officially died in the fire, there is no rush to action where he is concerned. No one outside of this room is to know we are alive until I say otherwise, capisce?"

"Of course, Don Santo," the three goons answered as one.

"Now leave us and bring back food for us both. As we are in the Columbia, Rafael, we will at least eat well until a decision is made. I like you Rafael. You work hard, show respect, and gave me some of your precious cigars every month without asking for anything in return. But that only goes so far. I'm going to miss your cigars most of all. Regardless of what decision is made, your life in Ybor is over, and maybe mine too. We will talk until my son Santo Jr. gets here, then we will decide. Say if you still have a tobacco stash in your room, maybe we can smuggle it out!"

Chapter 10
FIGHT FOR LIFE
YBOR 1957

As he waited in the room Rafael's thoughts vacillated between Isabel, Don Santo, and his situation. If he died here, he knew Isabel might morn, but a marriage to his brother might turn into a consolation. For su Padre and su Madre, they would grieve and probably blame themselves for sending him away; however, the Plantation would continue, and the family would recover. Maybe they would name a cigar after him, who knows? The Rafael Reserva! Nada sounds more like rum than a cigar. When Don Santo talked, it was about the "good old days in Ybor" and included some of the plots and murders that had taken place during his watch. He talked about Bolita and how Rafael's great uncle had changed Ybor forever with his game. Rafael guessed he felt safe talking to him since he was not likely to leave this room. By the next day, Santo's men had figured out who started the fire. It was a mafia style corporate takeover bid. Payback would occur when Santo Jr. arrived tomorrow. Rafael knew his fate would also be settled at that time. It amazed Rafael that within two hours of Santo asking, Rafael's tobacco, cigars and leather pouch with his cigar knives and paste arrived at their room.

He was able to make about 50 cigars with the tobacco, all of reasonable length and shank. Don Santo was most appreciative, as Rafael knew they now belonged to him. He and Santo talked about everything except Rafael's future. Rafael told him about Isabel and the family conflict and was rewarded with a scolding for dishonoring his father's wishes. To Santo that was the most important element of Rafael's story as obedience was a son and daughter's first obligation. The fact they were in love was rude and unworthy of respectable children.

"A son should always honor his father and obey without question his wishes. In this family to do otherwise is punishable by death. In an Italian family, such a thing as you consider would never happen. It is a matter of duty and honor and cannot be violated. You are young and will know the truth of this when you run your own family." The last statement hung in the air for a long time before either spoke. "Rafael, you saved my life but you have knowledge that only made men are to know. To know about the tunnels is not permitted outside the family. If someone outside finds out by accident or for any other reason, that person has an accident. This has never been questioned. These tunnels have served my family for many years and represent so much in future profits. They have never gone out of service and never will as long as they remain a family secret. All manner of things from people, arms, and drugs have successfully and secretly been moved because they are only known to family members. The tunnels must be protected. But, you were able to save my life because you knew. Do you want to join our family? This would save your life."

"Don Santo you honor me with that question. However, I am not Italian, and I would not fit into the family. I am a cigar maker who loves the land and the challenges of growing the best tobacco and making the best cigars. That is my passion, that is the only life I want. You know this from our talks at the factory. It would be a mistake to join your family. And to do so would be to go against mi Madre's wishes that I not get involved in your questionable Ybor activities. Did you not tell me to obey mi Padre and Madre?"

"I do know this Rafael, but I had to ask you because you saved my life. I agree with you that it would be a mistake. I respect the fact you would not dishonor us both by accepting this offer. The offer that was obligated since you saved my life. Now that obligation is gone. You are an honorable man in spite of this Isabel thing. I sincerely hope my son and I can find a solution that does not require a headstone."

"Me too," and they both laughed. At least on the outside Rafael laughed. To die was one thing, but to live in a world with Isabel married to his brother was not any better. Rafael enjoyed talking to Santo who had always treated him fairly. However, in his thoughts about his situation and Isabel's, he was a very angry man.

Santo Jr. arrived around lunchtime. The resemblance between father and son was striking. Both about 5'8", both about 150lbs., both with glasses, light complexion, and the same nose in the middle of the face. Jr. did have more hair, at least for now. They hugged and kissed each other's cheeks Italian style.

"Welcome home my son."

"Thanks, it is not often I come for a funeral and hug the corpse," he said laughing. "And you must be Moreno." He turned back to his father without waiting for a response. "Lunch is on the way. Eat here or in another room?"

"Let's eat here, have a cigar, then we can talk in private. What do you know?"

"Franco picked me up at the airport and filled me in. It seems Moreno has given us quite a problem. A debt of honor and a business obligation at the same time. Not to mention his insult to Franco. I would like to have seen that!" For some reason they both thought that was extremely funny.

Lunch arrived. They ate mostly in silence. Once the plates were removed, they all lit one of Rafael's cigars and contemplated one another. Santo Junior's eyes were even more intense than his father's were. They shared the same penetrating stare which said 'you can't hide anything from me so don't try.'

"This is a fine cigar; Dad says you made these, Moreno?"

"Si, mi Madre sends me tobacco from our farm and I rolled them here. It's the Pinar del Rio soil that makes them special."

"What's new in Cuba, son?"

"Business is booming. Batista will do anything required to keep his pockets lined. Lansky and his family, along with ours, now own most of the profit centers." Looking at Rafael he added, "I will tell you more later. I do enjoy this cigar. Let's have some Buca sent in as well."

The Sambuca with the requisite three coffee beans arrived within two minutes of Santo opening the door and issuing the order.

"Salute"

"Salute"

"Salute"

"What about the insurgents? Are they causing trouble?"

"Not really, Batista keeps his thumb on any asshole that poses a threat."

"What about this Castro bum? He was just here to raise money and I heard he was a damn good speaker with training troops in Mexico."

"Batista has a spy in Mexico and will know when he leaves and where he is going to land. It shouldn't be much of an issue. If Castro somehow surprises Batista, we of course will donate money and arms to insure our world does not change. We owned Prio before Batista and we will own any fucker that takes over after Batista. Money always talks and insures the bastards don't disappoint. They are all greedy monkeys."

"Sounds about right. Let's take a walk."

They were gone for more than an hour. All Rafael could do was pace back and forth, in what seemed like a small room. Rafael's thoughts were about family and Isabel. Would he ever see them again? He wondered. He was still angry, but now he wanted the opportunity to tell them of his anger. The longer they were away the less scared he became. Instead, he let his anger extend into his current situation. He was angry that someone else would control his future as his parents were doing in Cuba. And by doing a good deed and saving this gangster's life, his was now in jeopardy. He thought about trying to escape. How many guards were outside the door? At least one, maybe two. Where exactly in the Columbia Restaurant was he? He didn't know that for sure either. Near the bar room he suspected based on how quickly the Sambuca had arrived. There were no windows in this room so there was no frame of reference. He searched every inch of the room looking for an entrance to the tunnels but it was not here. They were not stupid enough to make that blunder. When they returned a guard entered first so his plan to overpower the son and take the father hostage was not possible. His only option was to listen and maybe try to escape when or if he was taken somewhere else.

"Sit down Rafael," Don Santo said. "Here is the plan. We will both remain dead to the world."

"I don't understand that Don Santo. Why were we presumed dead when no bodies were found in the fire rubble?"

He laughed at that one. "Of course two bodies were found. They were burned beyond recognition. The assumption was made that we were dead and that will never be reversed. For me this is a great opportunity, one that usually does not present itself, but I am happy for the opportunity to retire in peace. I will leave this country and Santo Trafficante senior will be dead. You love to grow tobacco, I love to grow grapes. I thank you for making this possible. We know who set the fire and my son will see restitution is made along with a healthy vic. As for you, you are also dead and will remain so. Whether you get to grow tobacco, we will soon see. Franco as a made man demands restitution for your insult and he will receive it. You also asked to be untied and to fight Franco one on one and you will receive that as your wish for saving my life. Therefore, all traditions and all debts are paid. You will fight Franco in a ring with no weapons. We will conduct the fight sort of like a boxing match, but I wouldn't count on a ref to enforce any rules. The fight will be until one of you can't get up or answer the bell. If Franco wins, he gets to kill you. If you win, we will smuggle you into Cuba with certain restrictions that we will cover if that happens. Capisce?"

"Capisce. And if I don't want to fight?"

"You die."

"I will fight"

"You will also wear a mask; we do not want anyone at the fight to know who you are. Franco is a bull of a fighter but you are taller and have reach. We should be able to get a lot of action on this fight. Besides, we don't want anyone that bets on you seeing your broken nose. Eat well, and rest today, Rafael, the fight will be tomorrow night."

Father and son left the room laughing with an arm over the other's shoulder. They were obviously proud of their solution. Had Rafael known he had a favor owed him for saving Santo's life by tradition and their code he certainly would have chosen something else. But, the tradition and the code were always subject to Trafficante review. He knew he really didn't have a favor other than what the Trafficantes wanted. Alone to contemplate his future as much as it was, he thought about the fight. How ironic, instead of a flight for life he had a fight for life. The best way to win a fight was to know your opponent's weakness. What was Franco's weakness, Rafael wondered? He certainly was strong. Only about 5'9", but almost just as wide with shoulders like an ox. He had a gut from too much pasta but he was not fat. He was not overly quick and telegraphed the punch before he broke Rafael's nose. It would have been easy to avoid the blow, had he been free. With no rules in this fight, Rafael knew he couldn't allow it to become a wrestling match. Rafael knew that if Franco tied him up in a bear hug or trapped him in a corner he would surely die. He also knew there would be no chance of him leaving the ring alive if he didn't win, Franco would see to that. Rafael's chances lay in his quickness, stamina and his superior athletic ability. Maybe he could use Franco's dislike of him for embarrassing him in front of his crew. In other words, Rafael thought a little trash talk during the fight might help.

Rafael was escorted to the fight through the tunnels with a hood over his head. The smell of dead fish indicated they were near the docks. Rafael's hood was replaced with a ski mask that covered his head with slits for eyes and mouth. He could see that he was in a warehouse. The ring, if you could call it that, was outside the building in the dirt. Lights were strung above and across the top. Wooden posts defined the fighting area with ropes attached to restrict the fighter's movements. It was obviously a converted cock-fighting ring made larger to accommodate men instead of chickens. The crowd was allowed to circle the ring and even lean on the ropes for the best view. Franco and Rafael were stripped to the waist, with taped hands, but no gloves. Rafael could see that Franco was indeed more ox than man. A viewing stand was raised to one side to accommodate the crowd. The bell to identify the start and finish of each round was located on the stand next to Santo Jr. Santo Senior, since he was dead, was nowhere to be seen.

Stools were placed in each corner. As the two fighters sat, Rafael studied Franco. In return, Franco glared at Rafael with a smirk. He was looking forward to inflicting as much pain as possible to this outsider who had insulted him in front of his crew. Death would not be quick and would not be painless. His smirk morphed into a sneer. Rafael noticed Franco was not sweating, which meant he hadn't warmed up properly. That's good, thought Rafael, a shot to the temple could end this quickly. Surprisingly, Rafael was not nervous. He was confident in his boxing skills but he had never faced anyone in this type of controlled street fight. If this stayed a boxing match, he had a chance to win through movement and counter punches. His broken nose was a concern, but he had boxed with a broken nose before. In one of his first fights at school, he was careless and allowed a right hook to hit flush, knocking him to the canvass and breaking his nose. The adrenaline rush that followed allowed him to continue and win. This would be different because the break had occurred a few days ago, but as his coach said, sometimes you just have to suck it up and be tough. The nose would hurt, but it would not kill him. He had to force himself to think strategy and ignore the pain. As both fighters were consumed with their individual thoughts the man with the bell began to speak, "Gentlemen welcome to our little cock fight. We have Franco 'the bull' Stunadi, our un-defeated local champion, against the ferocious masked Bandito, also undefeated. As a special promotion by Don Trafficante, this fight will last until one of the fighters is knocked out or can-not answer the bell. We will have three-minute rounds with 90 seconds in between rounds. I will be the referee and time the rounds from here."

Oh, fuck Rafael thought, no ref inside the ropes and Franco is a seasoned ring fighter.

"You have 3 minutes for any last bets and then we begin. Franco is a 5 to 1 favorite."

When the bell sounded Franco immediately ran at Rafael intending to make this a quick contest, as Rafael sidestepped he hit him full on the temple. Franco shook his head side-to-side and grinned. The crowd was very loud and very close as they leaned into the ring over the ropes. As Rafael maneuvered to avoid Franco's charges, boos expressed the crowd's reaction to his tactics. The crowd had obviously bet heavily on Franco and didn't want this to last long. They wanted their winnings and then to go back to the bar to spend them. While a few may have been on Rafael's side, the Franco supporters drowned them out.

The first round ended with more running by Rafael than fighting. The second round began in the same way as the first, another charge by Franco and another temple shot by Rafael. As Rafael shuffled out of the way he came close to the crowd leaning on the ropes and received a kidney punch as his reward. Rafael didn't know who did it but obviously, it was someone that was betting on Franco. The second and third rounds ended with a few punches exchanged but no serious damage by either. In the fourth round things changed. It began like the others with a charge by Franco, only this time as Rafael sidestepped, Franco stopped and lunged toward him. Franco grabbed Rafael and pinned his arms to his side. A head butt to Rafael's nose came next, and then another. Rafael dropped to the ground like a sack of potatoes with mostly black for vision with only a few stars adding light. Rafael new there would be pain when his nose was first hit but he was not prepared for this intensity. He could not hear the crowd but he was sure they were cheering loudly. What Rafael could hear were his own groans every time Franco kicked him as he rolled on the mat. Franco finally kicked him so hard he fell through the spectators and found the dirt floor just outside the ring. Unfortunately, Rafael was still being kicked as he lay on the dirt floor, not by Franco but by the Franco supporters. Without warning, the kicking stopped as two goons intervened and picked him up. Rafael recognized them from the Columbia and knew they were Santo's men.

"G-get back in there and fight m-maggot. I have money on you," one of them yelled.

As they pushed Rafael back into the ring, someone else doused him with a bucket of water. The crowd laughed at this, not realizing that the water cleared away the darkness and stars from Rafael's vision. With a glimmer of hope, Rafael looked up just in time to see Franco grab him in another bear hug. This time, however, he was able to place his head next to Franco's and avoid the head butt. Franco walked around the ring carrying Rafael as he walked, trying to get at his nose. He too knew his opponent's weak spot and meant to exploit it to the end. When this didn't work and Franco couldn't hit Rafael's nose with his head, he became impatient and threw Rafael to the mat and tried to kick his nose. Rafael anticipated what Franco would try, grabbed his right foot between his left arm and side, and immediately hit him in the cojones as hard as he could. Franco was not wearing a cup and the effect was immediate. He grabbed himself and fell to his knees. Rafael was still too dazed to follow up his sudden advantage and by the time he could stand, Franco was recovering enough that a mutual cease-fire occurred. The round ended with no more damage by either fighter. As Rafael sat on the stool he looked and felt like beaten fighter. He was in better shape than Franco was but not by much. He was quicker but in a bear hug that didn't matter. Rafael conceded to himself that the next round would be his last. He would live or die based on the next few minutes and there was nothing he could do about it. When the bell rang, Rafael anticipated Franco's stop after faking a charge and hit him flush in the face. Franco stood his ground and smiled although his teeth were bloodied, he was not fazed. After shuffling around, Rafael tripped over an extended foot near the ropes, and a bear hug ensued. Rafael again put his head to the side of Franco's to avoid his head butt and this time whispered in his ear, "You fight well for a stuppaghiara. By the way your sister was a good fuck last night, baboo."

Franco's rage was audible. He released Rafael, stepped back to coil his blow in an attempt to dislodge Rafael's head from his body. The attempt to inflict the intended damaged made the coiling a relatively slow process, allowing Rafael one desperate move. As Franco coiled, his neck became exposed just enough for Rafael to hit him in the throat. If the crowd had not been cheering expecting Franco's *coup de grace* they would have heard the crack that announced Franco's windpipe was shattered. As Franco grabbed his throat, Rafael used his last ounce of strength to hit him in the temple. Franco fell to the ground in a heap. His body was in spasms even though he was not conscious. The crowd was stunned to silence and then began to cheer. At least some did. Rafael looked at the platform and saw Don Santo Jr.'s standing ovation.

When Rafael's escort arrived to take him back to the Columbia, Franco was still on the ground. His spasms had stopped and he was not moving. No one had even bothered to check on him. In the warehouse, the mask was replaced by a hood and Rafael was taken back to the Columbia. At least he thought it was the Columbia. As he thought about it, he had been told it was the Columbia but how could he be sure. Being around these people was making him paranoid. In the room was Santo Jr. and someone introduced as a doctor. He checked Rafael and treated several areas. Broken ribs were added to his broken nose but both injuries were expected to heal. He didn't think Rafael had permanent liver or kidney damage but told him to expect blood in his piss and stool for a while. Rafael didn't know how to take this news, as he couldn't feel any part of his body that did not hurt. The doctor again pushed on Rafael's nose to straighten it and laughed saying, "the Signoritas like a war wound and that's a good one. I think he will live Don Santo."

After he was gone, Rafael asked Santo Jr., "Did I complicate things by winning?"

"A little, but the most important thing is you made me money. My father said you would win. But I didn't know. I knew you would have to kill him to win and I really didn't think you had the stuggots. But Dad reminded me you had Suarez blood and you would do what you had to do to win. By the way what did you say to him at the end?"

"Actually I'm not sure since I don't know the exact translations of the Italian phrases. But I do know I complimented him on his ability to suck and his sister's ability to fuck."

Santo acknowledged Rafael's words by laughing so hard he had to bend over.

"Bravo Rafael that was the key. You didn't know it but rumor had it he was a fanook or at least a mezzofinook, and his sister is a pucchiacha that fucks anything that moves. Win or lose, he was dead. You just saved us the trouble. He was giving dad angina anyway. Now what to do with you. Are you sure you don't want to work for us?"

"I'm positive that is not my future. My future is tobacco and cigars. How is your dad by the way? I did not see him at the fight."

"He's dead. He died in a fire. No one will see him again in this country. However, if he were alive, he would be pleased that you won. This is also the last time you will ever see me. As soon as you are well enough to travel, you will be smuggled into Cuba and will never return to the U.S. I mean anywhere in the U.S. If you do, you are a dead man. You cannot return to your school to get anything before you go and you will not write or communicate with anyone in the US. If you do, you will die in Cuba. You have my father to thank for this; I would have had you whacked, as you are a threat to him. For some reason he trusts you and is willing to assume that risk. Don't disappoint. All in all, it has been a piacere."

Three days later, Rafael was on a boat headed to Havana, his family and Isabel. He realized that living and dying were not the same. He was very happy to be alive. As long as he was alive and the marriage had not taken place, there was still a chance. Maybe it was a small chance, but it was still a chance. Dying would have to wait, and if he had anything to say about it so would Isabel's wedding. Rafael was definitely a glass half-full type.

Chapter 11
HOME SWEET HOME
1957

Rafael had a lot of time on the trip to decide what to tell his parents. He didn't want to scare them with the truth but knew he didn't have a choice. His green eyes always gave him away. His Madre could always see through any lie he told as a kid. It was those green eyes of his, that he had never seen until he met Manuel Suarez, had always made him different. The rest of his family had the same olive complexion with the traditional dark brown eyes. Rafael received a lot of teasing from the other kids in the area. That's probably why he learned to fight so young. He was also fortunate that he was big for his age.

Rafael rode the bus from Havana to Pinar del Rio since he had not notified anyone that he was coming. He was happy to come home but all he could think about was Isabel. Her marriage to his brother was less than a week away. How could he allow this to happen? He wondered this and at the same time wondered how could he not allow it to happen? Neither Isabel nor Rafael wanted her to be ostracized by the families. And for her to refuse would cause just that. That's more than anyone could ask of a Cuban girl. Maybe he thought his brother, Alfonso, would refuse. Why should he? Isabel is beautiful, smart, and represents their padre's wishes. And Alfonso always does what su padre wants. There was a time when Alfonso thought little Isabel was an ugly nuisance, but then so did Rafael. When Isabel was a child, she was always hanging around. She and Rafael's sister Pilar would follow the boys to play baseball and hang around when they were doing chores in the fields, or in the nursery. She was always asking questions about the plants and why one was better than another and why certain leaves were used instead of others for the cigars. Rafael's older brothers would not bother with her. He was always the one to answer her questions. He also had more free time than his brothers had and would often take the girls exploring hills and large rocks that support a large number of caves surround the Pinar del Rio valley. Some are easy to find, others more remote. When the three playmates discovered a new one that was hidden by a large boulder with overgrown vegetation hiding the entrance, it became their place. The cave had a small opening that expanded onto a massive cathedral ceiling with a vertical exit that allowed fire smoke to cascade upward. They discovered this the first time they started a fire and watched as the smoke rapidly disappeared upward. This became their favorite picnic spot and the three of them, Rafael, Pilar, and Isabel, vowed to keep this place a secret known only by them.

At first Isabel was just a friend of the family, Rafael's sister's best friend and nothing more. To Rafael both girls could be pests, always under foot and intruding into his tobacco nursery time. Isabel was tall for her age, and very thin. She had long black hair to the middle of her back that she always wore in a ponytail. Her dark eyes and light skin were a pleasant contrast. Her family was from the Galicia region in northern Spain. Rafael's family was from Andalusia in the south. In Spain, the further north one goes the lighter the skin, with the olive complexion being most prevalent in the southern areas along the coast. When she became a teenager, things changed. On Rafael's fifteenth birthday, Pilar and Isabel wanted to go to their cave, which they now called Alcazar. They named it Alcazar after Queen Isabella's Alcazar de Segovia where she ruled Spain in the time of Columbus. Although everyone called her Isabel, her true name was Isabella in honor of the Queen.

"Isabel, when are you going to smoke a cigar? Your namesake Queen Isabella was the first European to smoke cigars, which were given to her by Columbus. Since she was instrumental in the early success of the Cuban cigar don't you see it as a blaspheme for you to be named Isabella and not smoke?"

"No, I don't, Rafael. You know I tried one on my 12th birthday and didn't like it."

"As I remember you were sick as a dog," Rafael said with a smile.

"You shut up brother," said Pilar "Or she won't give you your special present!"

"That's right I won't if you're going to be a bully. I don't like bullies!"

"Ok, sorry, I'll start a fire. What is this mystery present that can only be given here?"

"Patience brother."

"And why are you calling this Isabel's present when you both are obviously involved?"

"Brother, do you know how to be patient? Just wait. And it is not a present from me, just Isabel."

"Caca, you kids."

"Stop swearing brother and we are not kids; we are thirteen now! We are young women and don't you forget it!"

"Si senorita, I didn't mean to hurt your feelings," he said.

"You are indeed old maids."

As Pilar smacked him on the shoulder she said," Brother if this was not your birthday we would hate you forever! Now for the last time be nice or you will ruin this."

As Rafael looked at Isabel it seemed she was about to cry. "I am sorry Isabel. You know I would not hurt you for anything. I was just teasing."

"It's ok, Rafael. I know you are excited because you are fifteen now," she said as she patted his arm.

What's gotten into these two? Rafael wondered. He had never seen them so serious. He knew brothers and sisters are supposed to fight and not get along, but that did not happen with Pilar. Pilar is truly a great person, he thought, kind to everyone and to everything. And Isabel although different in appearance with her light complexion, was otherwise her twin. They can be mischievous as they certainly had something percolating here. What are they up to? A special cigar? No, that can't be it; we make the best on our plantation. A new baseball glove? Perhaps that's it. Or maybe new tobacco knives? That could be. Tickets to a game in Havana! That would be amazing. That has to be it. As he thought this Rafael smiled. These two are certainly precious, exquisite and beautiful in their own ways but they are just kids and so easy to read.

"Ok. I'll be nice. Is the fire ok? Is there anything else I need to do?"

"Si, please sit there and face this way. We want to blindfold you."

"Blindfold? Are you serious?"

"Yes we are serious. This only happens once."

"Ok." Only happens once? Rafael said to himself. What in the world is going on? What have they planned? I've been to Havana to watch a baseball game before. The first to give a new glove? That didn't make sense either. And why blindfolded? Maybe it's a present not wrapped and they want to have it in place before I see it. That's possible but only happens once? Kids, young girls and their dramas!

As Rafael sat blindfolded trying to figure this out he heard one of them move. He could tell by her smell, it was Isabel. The soap she used left her with a clean fresh smell that was always pleasant. Its funny how being blindfolded made the smell more intense and perhaps even more pleasant. As he pondered this, he felt the wind touch his lips, ever so slightly, ever so pleasant, ever so gentle. The wind intensified and pressed just a little. What a wonderful feeling Rafael thought. He had never experienced that sensation before. And as suddenly as the wind pressed it was gone. He felt cheated, why did it stop?

He took off the blindfold, "What just happened?" He looked at Pilar and she was smiling, he looked at Isabel and she was crying ever so softly and her face was beet red.

"Isabel, what's wrong?" Rafael said as he went to her and tried to comfort her by putting his arm around her. As he did this, she leaned into him. The warmth of this intimacy was something Rafael had never experienced before. It was not like hugging his Madre or Pilar. That was always nice but this was different in a way he did not understand. This was two people not blood related that wanted to hold each other. Rafael didn't understand this feeling, but he knew he wanted it to last forever.

"I have given you my first kiss and it was wonderful. I have wanted to do that for a long time now. Pilar and I thought this was the time, and this was the place. I am crying out of relief that you did not reject it and because there can never be another first time. Thank-you Rafael."

Rafael was awestruck and didn't say anything for a long while. To kiss a boy on the checks is no big deal and men, women, boys and girls do that as Spanish custom. To kiss a boy on the mouth is a very big deal, and sometimes does not happen until a marriage has been arranged. Even though, this was the 1950s and things were sometimes very progressive. Rafael knew in their families things were not progressive, as they still practiced the old customs of arranged marriages. Even though she had quit crying and was no longer upset, Rafael still held her and didn't want to stop. She's not a girl anymore he thought. He can't treat her as a girl ever again. With absolute clarity, he realized he didn't want to. "No, thank-you Isabel that was the best present I will ever have in my life."

As Pilar joined in the embrace, overcome by the emotions of the moment, they all began to cry.

Alcazar became their sanctuary. A place where they could be alone. Where they could hold each other and kiss without the blindfold. When Rafael closed his eyes, he could still feel the wind caress his mouth with such tenderness that he became weak in the knees. He knew her smell was more than just the soap. He didn't understand why but other people he knew who used the same soap did not smell the same. Another uniqueness about Isabel that he couldn't explain was her skin. Her skin radiated warmth that he did not feel when he touched anyone else. He had no idea what could cause such a thing, but it was there.

"Isabel, I love to look at you, you are so beautiful, but to smell you and touch you are indescribable to me. Your smell is the most exciting thing I know except for your touch. Your touch is almost electric with the warmth of it radiating from my head to my toes. I have no idea why this is so, do you?"

"No, Rafael, I do not know for sure," she said with absolute seriousness. "I have wondered the same thing as I too experience those feelings. I think it must be God's way of telling us we are meant for each other, but I'm not sure."

"Maybe," he said, "All I know is it is wonderful and I can't get enough. I never want this to end. We must be together forever. I will talk to mi Padre to see if he will approach your padre to arrange our marriage."

"Rafael, that would be so wonderful, I love you so much!"

"And I love you Isabel. You are a beautiful woman that I will love as if we are part of the same body. Our kids may have green eyes like mine. Does that matter?"

"No, Rafael, I hope they do. They are beautiful eyes that are so expressive and can never lie. They will be unique to our family. What could be more wonderful?"

"Muy bien. I will talk to mi Padre."

"I love you my treasure."

"I love you, my Queen Isabella. I will forever be your vassal."

As appropriate, Rafael waited until his seventeenth birthday to approach su padre. "Padre, I don't understand. How can she be promised to Alfonso as wife?"

"Don Mendez and I have both noticed the way you two have been acting lately. The subtle glances, the winks when you think no one is looking. An alliance between the two families is satisfactory only if it's to Alfonso. Alfonso will own and operate the fields and nursery, your oldest brother Fernando will operate the factory and business end. With Alfonso and Isabel married, the two plantations can operate as one. This is a benefit to both. As the third son, I will help you get land of your own when the time comes, but a marriage to Isabel is out of the question. Don Mendez and I both agree on that. Have the two of you been intimate, don't lie Rafael!"

"No of course not. We would not do that until we are married. That is only right, and God's way."

"True, Rafael, and very good. I know you and Isabel will get past this and move on. Alfonso will make her a good husband."

"Padre, we love each other! We can't not be married!"

"I know it seems that way now, I should have stopped this much earlier but we thought it would just pass. A childhood crush that eventually would turn into a fight and that would be that. Unfortunately, that did not happen and now it is time for college. I have decided the best way to help you both is to send you to the University of Tampa. It's a fine business school and it is next to Ybor where your Madre's uncle lives. Don Mendez and I are not cruel and to insure enough time passes have decided to honor Isabel's wish to also attend college. She will learn to be a teacher as is her wish at the University of Havana. On her 21st birthday, she and Alfonso will be wed. By then I'm sure you will have met a fine Spanish girl in Ybor and will wish Isabel and Alfonso well."

"Is Alfonso ok with this?"

"Is that important, Rafael? He will do his duty to the family as you will do yours. Enough! Both families have decided it. It is done. Get over it. Everyone has some kind of childhood crush. It passes! You will leave in a month."

Su padre was wrong back then. It did not pass for either one of them. As many times as they could they snuck away to Alcazar. They held each other, they kissed, they vowed that their love would never end. And they cried.

"Come away with me Isabel. We will leave this place and make a place of our own."

"To go against our families is to go against God, Rafael. How can we do that and survive? To disgrace our families, to disgrace God would destroy our love. I cannot be responsible for you doing this, as you could not live with yourself if you caused me to do these things. We are in God's hands. Your touch tells me God wills us to be together, but I don't know how it will happen. Have faith; go to school, as I will. It is more than 5 years before my 21st birthday. God made the world in 7 days, what can he do in 5 years? We will write, we will pray, and God will tell us what to do. You will come home for visits and we will escape to Alcazar. Alcazar is our true world. When we are there, no one exists but us. Do not despair my love, my treasure."

"And I thought I would be the smart one in this family. As always I am your vassal my Queen Isabella the wise."

Five years later, they were still waiting for God to do something. It was unfortunate thought Rafael that he was kicked out of Ybor or he would not have had to endure the wedding. His visits had been limited to Christmas only. The rest of the year, he worked and went to school. They did write weekly and would always find a way to visit Alcazar when he was home. Their love was just as true, intense and exhilarating as their first kiss. As Rafael walked toward his home, he was absorbed in his thoughts. "God has not done his part. Why would a God torment us like this? Were we so bad? Maybe I was. I had taken a life in the Ybor boxing ring. But, if I had not he would have taken mine. Doesn't that count? But, Isabella has never hurt anyone. I knew that without God's intervention she would do her duty and marry Alfonso. She would be a good wife and do what a good wife does, but she would never be a happy wife. How, why, should God want that for her?"

As he approached the plantation, he saw only workers in the field so he walked to the nursery. There he saw Alfonso bending over a seedling. "Hola, Alfonso"

"Rafael! Hola," he said as they embraced. "How? When did you get here? Why are you here? Last, I heard, you were staying in school and would miss the wedding. I am so happy that you decided to be here. The whole family should attend a wedding!"

"Wait until we get the family together and I will explain why my plans changed brother. Are you happy with Isabel as a future wife?"

"Such a question, Rafael! Of course, she has grown into a beautiful young and smart woman. I am lucky that Padre planned so well. The marriage works well for both of our families. We will become the largest Cuban owned tobacco plantation in the Pinar del Rio Province. As she and I have discussed, we will do our duties as our Padres desire. I do wish she were more into it though. She seems to always be distracted when we talk of our marriage. I have no doubt she will be a good wife and mother and will always do what is right by God and our families. I hope that someday she will also be glad to have me as a husband. She is not an affectionate girl and is always restrained with me but maybe that will improve with time."

Rafael thought to himself, 'If you only knew brother, with the right person, she is very affectionate and loving with a warmth that has no end.' He then said, "You are a good man brother; I'm sure all will work out. Will the wedding be at the Church?"

"No, Isabel's Padre has built a small outdoor chapel on his plantation just for this purpose. Father Greco will perform the ceremony. It is very nice. Come, brother, let's go inside the main house. Su Madre will be so happy! "

"Muy bien."

The first things Rafael's Madre noticed after the initial greetings and hugs were the remnants of the facial bruising and cuts and the slightly bent nose from the Ybor fight. Rafael downplayed the fight. He didn't tell them it had been a life or death situation. He couldn't lie, but he didn't want to scare them either.

"The fight was just a way for Don Santo to make money on the situation. He would have sent me home anyway as long as I promised not to tell Ybor's secret."

"Imagine Fernando, tunnels under the whole city. And masonry tunnels too, not just dirt and timbers!" exclaimed su Madre.

"And Manuel told you about them?" su Padre asked.

"Si, he wanted me to have an escape route just in case."

"He put you in danger Rafael, and should not have done that! You could have worked somewhere else!"

"Jobs in the cigar business in Ybor were not that easy to get Padre. The cigar business is not as large there as it used to be. I was grateful for the job and happy there, until the fire. I don't know how it started but I was afraid I couldn't get the door open so I used the tunnels. Knowing about the tunnels saved my life, Padre, even though it meant I had to leave Ybor. I missed Cuba anyway. The United States is ok but it's not home. Cuba is where my heart is."

When Rafael said that his Madre and Padre exchanged looks that silently said, "I hope he is not going to cause trouble with the wedding." After the quick glance, Rafael's Padre looked at him with his stern expression that Rafael had seen many times as a kid. The clincher to Rafael was when su Padre rolled his cigar. This had always been a sign that at the very least a lecture was about to commence. "Rafael, come into my study, I want to talk in private."

"Fernando, he just got home, can't business wait?" asked su Madre.

"Business does not wait for any man. Either a man meets business head on or it will pass him bye. Come, Rafael," he ordered.

For Rafael's Padre, his office was his favorite room in the house. No one was allowed to enter unless he invited him. It was always locked if he were not there. Rafael thought he guarded his sanctuary as much as Santo did his tunnels. The room was mahogany trimmed with a large mahogany desk in the center. On the walls surrounding the desk were mahogany bookcases with all of the books he had ever read. He never sold or gave away any book that came into his possession. "Books were knowledge and knowledge was the key to a man's success," he would always say. On the far wall, the family photos were hung and included some of their ancestors from Spain. The Moreno ancestors grew grapes for sherry in southern Spain. They migrated to Cuba in the 1920s to learn the tobacco industry and never left.

When Rafael entered the sanctuary, su Padre was staring at his Padre's picture.

"Sit down, Rafael," he ordered. "Have you seen Isabel?"

"Nada, Padre."

"As you know the wedding will take place on her Padre's plantation in two weeks."

"Alfonso has already told me."

"You will not interfere, you will not make a scene, and you will respect the decision."

"Padre, I will not intervene because I can't. I will not make a scene because it would do no good, but I will not respect the decision because it does not have to be this way! A marriage between us would serve the same purpose!"

"No it would not. It is Alfonso's birthright to inherit the fields, not you! You know this and I have already promised to help you get your own fields."

"You are putting business ahead of everything Padre including your sons' happiness, mine and Alfonso's! And Isabel's happiness as well!"

"Rafael, you do not understand without business there is no happiness. You are so young. You will learn this one day. I had hoped it would be before now, but no matter. You will accept this now, and accept that one day you will learn the ways of business always supersede the ways of the heart. The ways of the heart will conform as needed. My marriage to your Madre was arranged for business purposes. Happiness followed. So too will this be for Alfonso, Isabel and you. Times have changed and not all marriages are arranged for business. As the third son, I can either arrange yours or let you choose. Either way it will not interfere with the family business."

"No thank-you, Padre, I will make my own way!" Rafael said as he tried to shield the contempt he felt.

"Very well, Rafael. Know that Isabel and her Padre have discussed all of this and she will do her duty. Your presence only makes this more difficult for Isabella."

"I know that padre, the only reason I am here is because I can't be in Ybor! And you should know this, if Isabel would have agreed to run away with me, neither of us would be here!"

Staggered by the blow that was those words, he said very softly, "Isabel is very wise, son. You should be ashamed for tempting her to go against her Padre's wishes. You would never be happy going against both families."

"That is what she said."

"Again that was wise. I really had hoped that being away would cause your infatuation to die."

"No, Padre haven't you heard absence makes the heart grow fonder?"

"No, son, I have not heard this. Perhaps it is an Ybor term. I know you are hurt by this. But it is only temporary. You and Isabel will move past this and learn that the families did the right thing."

"I hear what you are saying, but I do not believe it is true. Like I said before I will not make a scene, and I will not intervene not because I respect the decision, but because it would not do any good!"

During the next two weeks, Rafael saw Isabel only a few times. They were never in a position to have a private conversation. It was driving Rafael crazy. Several times, he had gone to Alcazar at night hoping she would come, but she never did. He would ride home on his horse just before daylight so his absence would not be obvious. He really didn't care if someone knew; he just didn't want to answer any questions. On the last day before the wedding, it was a madhouse. Everyone had something to do to get ready. Rafael declined to be in the wedding, telling Alfonso that he did not want to since it had not been planned for him to be home. Alfonso accepted this although Rafael didn't think he really understood the logic. There was no logic in it to understand, Rafael thought he just couldn't bear it.

When everyone left for the rehearsal, Rafael rode out to Alcazar to be alone with his thoughts. He made a fire and lay down on the blanket like he and Isabel had done so many times before. Alone with his thoughts he pondered why the cave was always cool even when it was very hot outside. He didn't know the answer and his thoughts turned to the wedding. The wedding was scheduled for mid morning tomorrow. He decided he just couldn't endure being there and would go home tomorrow and make up some reason for his absence. He berated himself as he thought, "I cannot witness their marriage. I just cannot do it! I am not strong enough. I was strong enough to kill a grown man but I am not strong enough for this. This was ten times harder. Why had God not saved us? We prayed he would everyday, but it had not happened. Why, God, were we made for each other? Why did our touch ignite the other when this did not happen with anyone else? Why, God? Mi Padre is just stupid and has never experienced a love like ours. He has no frame of reference to understand our feelings. But God, you made us. You made us for each other, and now you turn your back to us. Are you asleep? Do you sleep? I don't know. The world, my world is not ok. It was like being kicked in the stomach 1000 times."

Rafael could not find any relief even in Alcazar. For him their was no relief from the hurt. He knew Isabel must feel the same. He had no idea how she could compartmentalize her feelings in such a way to permit her to do her duty. Was her faith that much stronger than his? As he pondered this question, he fell asleep and dreamed of Isabel and her velvet touch. He dreamed she came to Alcazar and they made passionate love for the first time. The love was so real he could feel the warmth, he could smell her smell, and he could feel the wind in her kisses like the very first time. He caressed her body. Every inch was perfect. Her hair smelled so clean it was erotic. The essence of her love was nirvana. This was something that could only be dreamed of because no man could survive such beauty and richness of life, if it were real. He thought no living man deserved to feel the way her love made him feel that it could only be experienced if he were in Heaven. When Rafael awoke before dawn, Isabel was in his arms snuggled deep into his shoulder.

"Isabel, are you real or am I still dreaming."

"We are both dreaming my love because I cannot be here. You know that."

"Isabel you are here, this is not a dream. Did we make love?"

"Rafael, I will always love you and cannot imagine another man in my bed. But that is not our life. I once thought it would be. I once thought God willed it so, but I was wrong. I wanted it to be so strongly that I could not think of any other reality. I don't know why God did not allow it. Could it be we wanted it too much? It seems our love will have to be only in our dreams like this night. For us to make love before my wedding to another is unthinkable. So do not think about it. Instead, and for the last time hold me a while longer. I will have to leave before daylight."

And he did. He was afraid to sleep for fear she would vanish, because maybe it was a dream. But he slept anyway. When she got up to leave, he held her so tight it hurt.

"Please leave with me, Isabel"

"Shusshh my love go back to sleep and let this dream end as it should. We have been over this so many times. There is no solution, only our duty to God and our families, which we will perform. Stay here and be my strength. Do not come to the wedding. I could not bear it now. Promise?"

As she rode away, Rafael stood in the opening until he could not see her shadow anymore in the full moon. When she was gone, he went into the cave laid down and cried. The last few hours were the happiest of his life and now the hurt was the worst in his life. He could still smell her scent.

He stayed in Alcazar until mid morning. Only her smell told him it wasn't a dream. But then can't you dream smells as well? He asked himself. Maybe this was all a dream. Maybe she was never there at all. He did not think he could feel any more sadness. But he did. It was time to go. Isabel and Alfonso would be married by now. He had to pull himself together. He knew the only thing he could do to recover was to once again embrace his beloved tobacco. He still knew how to grow tobacco, to hybridize the best plants to make them stronger and clone the results for perfect reproduction. That would be his life now. He would absorb himself with the land. He didn't feel any better but at least he had a direction and a place to start. Maybe he would create a new strain and call it the Isabella line. As he went outside, he could see the smoke before he heard the screams that were hidden inside.

"Fire!" someone yelled.

The valley was covered in pockets of fire and smoke as far as he could see. Smoke was bellowing as high as the mountains. His horse was gone. Rafael didn't know if the horse had been stolen or if the fire had scared him. He ran toward the plantation. As he passed other farms, he couldn't see anyone trying to put out the fires and a few workers were running away. What the hell, he thought. Why aren't the compesinos putting out the fires? He asked himself. Then he saw a soldier riding toward a peasant. As he reached him, he sliced into his neck and shoulder with his saber, so hard his head almost came off. He was dead before he hit the ground. The soldiers weren't helping put out the fires, they were starting them! The smoke allowed Rafael to avoid the soldiers as he made his way home. As he passed a neighbor's plantation, he tripped over a peasant in the field.

"Get down, Señor Rafael, or they will kill you."

"Gonzalo, what is going on, I don't understand this?"

"Neither do I, Señor. At daybreak Batista's soldiers began torching the fields and killing everyone in sight. Except for the women. They raped the girls first and then killed them. I heard them say kill everyone in this valley because they are traitors to Cuba. Stay down Señor there is nothing we can do. There are too many!"

"This cannot be, Gonzalo, we are friends with Batista. Mi padre helped him with tobacco seedlings from our plantation. He cannot believe we are traitors."

"Maybe, Señor, but I think your plantation was the first they burned."

Rafael got up immediately. He knew he had to see to his family first and then Isabella's. He ran as fast as he could and still avoid the soldiers. The immense smoke that lingered on the ground effectively shielded him from the soldiers' search for survivors and strays. There was little wind and most of the smoke just hung in the air like a funeral shroud. When he arrived home, Rafael could see that Gonzo had been right. His fields were fully engorged with fire and the buildings were almost totally leveled. His heart ached as he approached the main house. He first saw Gabriella, one of su Madre's maids, crawling away from the fire off to the right.

"Gabriella, are you alright?" As he ran to her, he could see that most of her clothes were gone. She was bleeding from every opening in her body. Her head was badly misshapen because of the hideous lump on the left side. A lot of blood was running down the side of her head onto the ground. She was whimpering and moaning at the same time. She could not live long.

"Señor Rafael, you are safe!" she uttered between whimpers. "Everyone is dead. Most were killed before they were put into the house and burned but not all. I could hear Alfonso scream as the house went up in flames. I think it was him. I could not tell for sure with the soldier that was in my face. They thought I was dead so they didn't bother with me after that." Her strength dissipated her last words were whispered, "they took Pilar out back, you must hurr....."

Rafael closed her eyes and hurried to find Pilar. He found her naked body behind where the nursery had been. Dried blood was covering her from her navel to her knees. He didn't see any other injuries except for some bruising on her arms where she had been held. Her death had not been pleasant. Rafael's temper raged as he contemplated his families slaughter and rape by Batista's soldiers. His padre had helped Batista and considered him if not a friend a valued associate. His family did not deserve such treatment from an enemy much less a friend. Rafael did not know why this had been done but he knew they would pay with their life. As these thoughts raced through his mind he ran to Isabel's home. The scene was repeated there, as it was throughout the Pinar del Rio valley. The crops were burnt and the owners and most of the workers slaughtered. According to a survivor who had hid near Isabel's home, a group of soldiers had taken her family into the main house. Since he knew the family, he knew Isabel had been among them. The soldiers had stayed in the house for quite a while before they came out adjusting their clothes and torching the house. The survivor had been afraid to look into the window so he had not seen what was done to the family but they both knew. All Rafael could do to control his rage was to grip his fists as tight as he possibly and yell as load and threatening as his lungs would allow.

The survivor looked at Rafael in alarm before he said, "senor please be quiet some of the soldiers may still be around."

"I hope so!" As Rafael uttered these words the fog muffled the riders approach but Rafael was ready when he emerged. The soldier laughed the laugh of someone lost in the lust of killing. As rode straight toward Rafael he raised his sword in his right hand. As the survivor ran Rafael stood his ground and did not move. Finally, he crouched into an athletic posture and waited. The soldier intended to ride to Rafael's right which would expose him to the saber. He was not bothered that this peasant had not run, he had already killed dozens that had frozen in terror and didn't move until he chopped them into oblivion or severed their heads from their bodies. He decided to bury his sword in the top of this one's head. When Rafael dodged to his right he was so close he could fell the breath of the charging horse. The rider was caught by surprise by the sudden and reckless move and was unprepared as two hands grabbed him as he rode by Rafael. Rafael immediately slammed the soldier to the ground as hard as he could and pounced. Before the soldier had time to react Rafael had kneed him in the sternum with all of his weight. The sword was forgotten as Rafael hit the soldier in the face until his strength ran out. The face on the ground was barely visible when he stopped. A bloody pulp belayed the fact that the soldier was still a teenager. As Rafael looked at himself he saw blood covered his arms and had splattered his chest and face. As he looked at the dead soldier on the ground he gritted his teeth and uttered, "It's not much but it's a start."

His world in Ybor had ended abruptly and now his family and Isabel were also gone. As he lay in the field from exhaustion and his sense of loss, his inner pain began to surface. The realization that he had lost everyone that had been important in his life came to the front of his thoughts. With his adrenaline subsiding the magnitude of the loss hit him in his gut and it hurt. His will and intestinal fortitude saved him from the debilitating grief that wanted to absorb him. He would not succumb, he would hold Batista responsible and he would see to it that he paid for the needless destruction of this day. Batista had chosen to kill innocent Cubans and destroy valuable Cuban resources. Rafael had to hold him accountable. He knew he could not do this alone. Before he could stand, he knew he had to find Castro and his rebels. He needed a man of action not talk. As Don Santo had told him in Ybor, "the enemy of my enemy is my friend." For Rafael, Batista had become a 'stone in his shoe' that he had to remove in as painful a way as he could arrange. Only Castro and his movement offered that opportunity.

Chapter 12
SIERRA MAESTRA MOUNTAINS BASE CAMP 1958

That's a very sad story Rafael. I have been told Batista killed more than 300 people in the Pinar del Rio valley that day. I am very sorry your family and Isabel were part of that. Did you find out why?"

"I heard rumors but I don't know for sure."

"Fidel was told it was not because he thought anyone was traitorous. He was frustrated that his tobacco could not compete with the tobacco from the Pinar del Rio. With Pinar out of business, his tobacco became a lot more valuable. That's why the crops were burned. If he were eradicating traitors, there would be no reason to burn the crops. And with the families gone, production will be down for years perpetuating his inflated tobacco profit."

"That was one of the rumors, Che. But how can a man kill that many people and destroy that many healthy plants just to make money?"

"Rafael there are times when you are wise beyond your years, but this is not one of them. This is capitalism applied by a dictatorship that values dollars above people. The sad part was Batista did not need this money as it was small compared to his share from the casinos. It was just greed. The vilest evil in the entire world."

"Mi Padre told me I didn't understand business. That business comes before the happiness of people. It would appear that he was a capitalist also."

"Capitalism without the greed is not a bad thing. It's just no one has figured out how to separate greed from the capitalist system. No matter how much money is made it is never enough to satisfy the thirst for more money and more power."

"You know why I joined Fidel, why did you, Che?"

"My story is not nearly so long, Rafael. I had almost finished medical school and a friend, Alberto Granado, and I decided to travel to South America. We planned to work along the way as doctors to pay for the trip. We worked in several leper colonies; we worked for the miners in various countries and had a very educational experience. We saw firsthand the evils of American imperialism. We learned the CIA would arrange a coup in any country that would not cooperate with American business. It did not matter if the country was democratic or a dictatorship to the CIA. The only thing that mattered was if the American mining companies could control the mineral extraction, and if the United Fruit Company could control the produce industry. Utilities and telephone monopolies were also guaranteed or the government would be overthrown. And it did not matter if the government had been democratically elected. They would still be overthrown through a coup with a dictator taking over who would be pro-American. The new leader would be expected to offer sweet deals including monopolies to U.S. companies that wanted whatever was of value in the particular country. The poor would be expected to provide the physical labor in horrible conditions, and for little compensation. What better way to control the poor? Keep them hungry, uneducated, and indebted to the company store. They can't complain for fear of losing their pitiful job because they have debt, and it's the only job in town. The US technical workers and supervisors were well compensated to keep the peasants in line and to insure no unions would interfere. More than one labor organizer would simply disappear on his way to work with little or no investigation by the local police who received compensation from the companies for not looking too hard. The workers would be told that the union organizer had just moved on to somewhere more promising. This is the same Imperialistic plan that the US has implemented in the Dominican Republic with Trujillo and in Cuba with Batista. Rafael, Trujillo is one of the cruelest dictators in South America second only to Francois 'Papa Doc' Duvalier of Haiti. Senator John F. Kennedy is also Trujillo's godson. The Kennedy patriarch was not only a capitalist but was also connected to organized crime. He and Trujillo were friends.

Sorry, Rafael, you asked why I was here and not to listen to my political rants. After my motorcycle trip in South America, I finished medical school and traveled again. I traveled to every Latin American country except for Haiti and the Dominican Republic. I traveled first as a student and then as a doctor. I met poverty, hunger, disease, and the inability to cure a child only because I lacked resources. I saw how the numbness of hunger and continued punishment reach a point where the death of a child is an unimportant incident. It is sad to see human beings almost indifferent to losing a child. This happens often in our Latin American homeland. Life is so difficult that people are almost consoled to lose a child and spare him life's difficulties. These people have no hope and no dreams of anything better than the misery they endure each day. I was in Guatemala in 1954 when the democratically elected Jacobo Arbenz was attacked and overthrown. The United Fruit Company, the US State Department, and the CIA, under the direction of Foster Dulles, orchestrated the coup. Arbenz was replaced with Castillo Armas whose only qualification was his promise to allow US Companies to rape the land and enslave the people of Guatemala to do their bidding. You see it is easy to find a greedy dictator willing to sell out his country for a profit. We are all children of our environment. Fidel's made him a socialist, and mine made me a Communist. On this, El Jefe and I can agree to disagree. We both demand true independence for Cuba from the Cuban dictator, Batista and from the imperialistic stranglehold of the American companies that are raping the Cuban natural resources and enslaving the Cuban 'compesino' to do their required labor. When I first met Fidel in Mexico, we talked through the night. At breakfast, I was ready and pledged my allegiance to Fidel and the 26th of July Movement in order to free Cuba and the Cuban worker from imperialism. For this I am willing to sacrifice my life to insure its success."

"No, Che we will not sacrifice your life to the cause," interrupted Fidel. "We will help the Imperialist sacrifice their lives trying to defend this system of slavery and profiteering. We will capture Batista alive, if possible, and put him on trial for his crimes. Lieutenant Moreno you will be assigned to my column for future engagements. I can use your wisdom and ability to see the big picture. Nice work on the trial. You reached the only moral verdict possible that serves our cause and you defended it with aplomb. Well done indeed."

"Gracias, El Jefe, but I did not do it for you or the Movement. My decision was based upon the morally right thing to do given the nature of these horrendous crimes. And I am not a lieutenant."

"You are now lieutenant, and you will learn that the morally right thing to do is exactly what the 26th of July Movement is all about. If you make all your decisions accordingly you will be a servant and promoter of our cause."

"Well, that's what the 26th of July Movement is all about if you win. If you lose, it was an insurrection, not a 'Revolución', and we are traitors to Cuba, not heroes of the revolution. That was true when the American colonies revolted against Great Britain. If they lost, they would be hung as traitors, but since they won, they were heroes of the American colonies and founding Fathers of the United States. History says there have been many more insurrections than 'Revolucións' with a few coups, successful and unsuccessful, thrown in for fun. Also, I am not sure I share Che's opinion of the US. Certainly there is a bad element in all societies but I found the majority of Americans to be honest, educated, and willing to make sacrifices for their fellow man. Of course, to some this did not include the Negro population. However, even most Southerners meant them no harm, as they were valued property. That sounds so, I don't know, wrong I guess, to refer to people as property. Many, many civilizations have been under that misconception throughout history, that people, slaves could be property. Hell, some even considered women and wives as property even after slavery was abolished."

"I don't disagree with your assessment of the American people," said Fidel. "They are for the most part great human beings that believe in Democracy and a free way of life. Even though some still see the Negro as a slave instead of a valuable addition to their society, except in times of war. They have no problem sending Negroes to war to fight for their country. Unfortunately, it seems the American government is moving away from representing and serving the middle and lower class of their population. Perhaps it never did represent these classes since it was formed by the elitist of their day. Now it only represents the rich and the companies owned by the rich. It does not care about human rights disasters as long as the bottom line, the company profit, is maintained. They tell the US population that they are represented and have their best interest in mind when decisions are made. However, this is not true. Look at the design of the American government; it is not a democracy it is a republic. This means that if the majority does not rule, the laws of the land passed by their government rules. In a true democracy the majority rules. The US elitist does not trust the majority to decide what is right, or perhaps they know that what is right is not always in their best interest. Socialism is an economic system like capitalism and does not prevent the government from being democratic. Communism is a radical form of socialism with the government usually run by a dictator but it does not have to be. It is possible to have a country with a communist economy and a democratic form of government. Why are the Americans as afraid of Communism and Socialism as an economic form? The reason is it becomes much harder to control the population. If the lower and middle classes do not have debt, do not have to worry about medical care, and are well educated, then they have time to think about how they are being governed. This would create instability in the U.S. as it is currently being run. As a result, the US picks its socialized elements very carefully. They have socialized education, military, police, fire departments, and for the most part their utilities are socialized with price controls by the government. I believe the US government fears socialism because once a population experiences the higher quality of living associated with socialized medicine they will never be content with any other system. If you compare the cost of medical care, the United States has the most expensive. If you judge the quality of care by infant mortality rate and the population's life expectancy, the US is in the middle of the pack behind many so-called third world countries. The worst part of the US's system is human rights. The government advocates for human rights, yet the Negro is considered a second-class citizen not fit to use the same drinking fountains and restrooms as whites. In addition, the Americans ignore the human atrocities that are perpetuated by the CIA's dictators. Trujillo in the Dominican Republic, and Batista in Cuba are just two of the many in South America who are brutal in their human rights violations. President Roosevelt characterized the US position when he said about the Nicaraguan dictator Somoza 'he is a son of a bitch, but he's our son of a bitch!' As long as the US companies get what they want, almost any atrocity is acceptable. And if the international complaints get too loud then that dictator is assassinated and another clone takes his place."

"I hear what you are saying, Fidel, however if the American people don't like someone in government they can be voted out of office at the next election. This has happened many times in the past."

"Yes, it has Rafael. But who controls the candidates?"

"Well anyone born in the US who is 35 years old, has lived in the US for the last 14 years, has never been impeached by the Senate, and has never fought in a revolution against the US, can run for president."

"Money decides who gets to run for president, Rafael. In the US, only the Democratic candidate or the Republican candidate can become president. An independent can run but he has no chance of being elected. How are the candidates selected for these two parties?"

"They are chosen by the members of each party in primary elections so anyone that meets the qualifications and is a member of that party can be elected."

"In theory yes, in reality, no. The companies that donate the money choose them. If a candidate does not have the ability to raise funds, he cannot win in the primaries and will be cast aside. The money-people control who the people get to vote for and they only choose those candidates that they can control."

"There are always fundamental differences between the Republican and Democratic candidates so there is always a diverse option."

"On certain topics, taxation, abortion, minimum wage, and gun control for example that is true. On other topics such as government support of the military industrial complex, government interference in business, the free enterprise system, and opposition to further socialization of anything, especially medical care, there is no practical difference. This is because the representatives of these interests donate to both parties. They may give more to one over the other but both candidates are obligated to the financial support of these interests. As a result of keeping both parties competitive with each other, the influence of the money people remains high. As soon as a candidate is elected his primary goal is re-election. To insure that he will have the money for his re-election bid, the elected official will cater to the lobbyists representing the money sources. These are primarily oil, medical, insurance, and the biggest, the military industrial complex. If they control who gets to be a candidate and then who gets reelected they control the government. And what controls the money men?"

"I don't know."

"Unfortunately, greed! As a result, the rich get richer and the poor get poorer. That is why this system cannot be part of this revolution. Power must be given to the people, all of the people. Cuba will be a true democracy where the majority rules."

"You make an interesting point Fidel. I don't think most of the Americans are aware of this. Or have even considered this as a possibility. They have faith in their government to do the right thing, to stand up for human rights both in the U.S. and abroad."

"The US government says all the right things; their actions abroad say something else. For example, the Government is anti-crime in the US, however; in South American, it is difficult to tell the difference between the CIA and organized crime. Both are into gunrunning and illegal drugs. Organized crime is in it to make money. The CIA is involved to create a source of money that is not accountable to any oversight committee and serves to pay for their black-ops such as supporting the overthrow of governments that aren't cooperating with American imperialism. It creates a secret slush fund that can be used for anything. And I mean anything. With this money source the CIA can operate totally independent of anyone else in the government, including the President."

"Fidel, are you implying that the US people will have to revolt to correct this?"

"I do not think there will be another US revolution as in 1765, or even the civil war of 1860. As least not in our lifetimes.

As long as big business can abuse third world countries, they can afford to appease the US middle class. The middle class in turn will help keep the poor down so there will be no organized revolt. As the rich get richer, too rich to have to pay, and the poor get poorer, too poor to pay, the middle class, the only ones left to pay all of the costs, will get squeezed and become smaller and smaller. When the middle class is no longer comfortable, complacency will end. When this happens a revolt is possible but not until that time. A strong enough president could reverse this trend, but he would have to be willing to oppose the status quo. That will require an extraordinarily strong individual that would be willing to remove the harness that still yokes the American Negro. Education would then become the key. An educated, and I mean a truly educated, population not one that has just been fed propaganda is a strong voice that cannot be ignored indefinitely. That is why we will have socialized education in Cuba open to everyone. With that education the Cuban people will no longer tolerate anyone trying to take away their freedom nor any foreign nation that tries to reintroduce imperialism."

The soldiers that had gathered around listening to Fidel and spontaneously began to sing the anthem, "Guantanamera." As often happened at base camp, a conversation with Fidel had turned into an opportunity for him to teach. He never disappointed.

Chapter 13

HAVANA
1946

In the main conference room of the Hotel Nacional, Santo and Santo Jr. talked quietly as the rest of participants gathered.

"How in the hell did Lucky get out of prison?" asked Santo Jr.

"In 1942 The Department of the Navy had the CIA ask Meyer Lansky if he would help control the New York City docks against possible German sabotage. Meyer immediately seized the opportunity to help his boss Luciano get out of his 50-year prison term and told the CIA that the only person that could control the docks was Lucky. The CIA talked with him in prison and brokered a deal between Lansky, Naval Intelligence and New York Governor Dewey. In exchange for his cooperation in controlling the docks Lucky was granted a full pardon after the War and deported to Italy."

"God bless the CIA, best fucking partnership ever!" exclaimed Santo Jr.

Both men laughed, continued to smoke their Cohibas, drink their brandy and waited for the room to fill. At the head of the table was Luciano and Meyer 'The Little Man' Lansky, the top financial and gambling operations guy. To Lucky's right were the New York and New Jersey delegation, Frank "The Prime Minister' Costello, Luciano family boss; Quarico 'Willie Moore' Moretti, Luciano underboss; Albert 'The Mad Hatter' Anastasia, Mangano underboss; Giuseppe 'The Old Man' Profaci, Family Boss, and seven other underlings. Among them was Vito Genovese. To Lansky's left were Sam Giancana, Chicago Boss with two of his associates as well as Carlos 'Little Man' Marcello, Family Boss of New Orleans and several members of the Jewish Syndicate delegation.

As he watched everyone take their seats, Santo knew he and his son were given preferred seats at the opposite end of the table directly opposite Luciano and Lansky. It was not his way to draw attention to himself or his son but this was a special occasion. He was announcing that his son would be taking over their family's work in Cuba. He was going to stay in Ybor from now on to insure a smooth distribution of the drugs smuggled from Cuba to Tampa utilizing the tunnel system. Both the Cuban business and the Ybor business were important to everyone in the room as the profits were shared. Not always equally, and not always fairly, but the ones in control always got at least their share.

Meyer Lansky began "Salute Don Luciano, cento di questa giorni!"

"Salute", everyone said in unison as they stood and lifted their glasses to Lucky.

From the side door Frank Sinatra who had entertained the night before came in with a briefcase. "If I may interrupt for just a second before the meeting starts, I would like to present Don Luciano with a present from his West Coast friend." Frank opened the briefcase, which was filled with stacks of money.

"Don Luciano, please accept this 2 million dollar tribute as a show of respect."

"Millie grazie, Frank. Please express my gratitude to our friends."

As Frank left the room, Lucky continued. "Our first order of business, I bring up not because I want to but because I have too. In my absence on the street, certain parties that I will not name have been less than cooperative with other members in this room. It has been expressed to me in private that the only way to make this right is to reinstitute the position of Capo dei Capi. This is not something I want but something that I will do for our business. Having said that, is there anyone that is opposed to this?"

When no one said anything Santo stood up, raised his glass, and said," Salute, Capo di Tutti Capi, the boss of all bosses! Godfather Luciano welcome back and may I be the first to show my respect!"

"Salute," everyone said in unison as they stood and raised their glasses.

"Grazie. I will receive each of you in private before we resume the meeting. We have much to discuss but tradition dictates I receive you each individually first. Don Santo, I will see you first as you rightfully requested."

As Santo and his son entered the side room where the newly minted Godfather waited as if on his throne, he said, "Godfather you do me an honor by receiving us first. I am not worthy of such importance."

"Nonsense Santo you are the backbone of our little thing, our La Cosa Nostra. You always do your part, accept your share without complaint, and maintain order in your areas with a strong hand. You are the most worthy."

"Grazie, Godfather," he said as he kissed his hand. "May I introduce my son Santo Trafficante Jr.?"

Santo Jr. followed his father's lead and kissed his hand.

"Welcome," said Luciano.

"Grazie, Godfather."

"Godfather it is time for my family to share responsibilities in order to maintain absolute control and to maximize our business. In order to do this Santo Jr. will be taking over our Cuban operations and will spend almost all of his time here and I will oversee everything in Tampa, if that is ok with you, Godfather?" he asked.

"Of course, Don Santo, that is very wise. Meyer can use a full time hand in Cuba and I believe your son is perfect for that job," replied Luciano.

"We will take our leave then. Mille grazie Godfather."

As each in turn paid their respects, Santo watched the faces as they entered and as they left. He noticed a red-faced Genovese enter the room and a white-faced Genovese leave. Ah, he thought, this is not over. Santo knew that Genovese was the cause of Lucky's move to become Capo dei Capi. Genovese had recently returned to New York from exile in Italy and was openly challenging Costello as family boss. He obviously had been threatened by Lucky to get in line or else. Or else he would become a stone in his shoe.

When the conference resumed that afternoon the first topic was the Flamingo Hotel in Las Vegas. Benjamin 'Bugsy' Siegel along with his girlfriend had been overseeing the construction of the Las Vegas Flamingo Hotel and Casino. Since gambling was now legal in Las Vegas, Siegel had convinced Meyer Lansky to invest in Las Vegas as a back up to Havana, just in case anything went wrong there.

"We have confirmed reports that on numerous occasions Virginia Hill, Bugsy's cunt, has been taking frequent trips to Zurich to deposit money in an account of Bugsy's. This fucking Siegel has turned a 1.5 million dollar proposal into a 6 million dollar fuck-up. I propose that Charles "Trigger Happy" Fischetti be given the honor of removing this stone from my shoe." The vote was unanimous.

The next order of business involved the drug trade.

"While on vacation in Sicily, I met with Nicola Gentile and Antonio Farina and arranged to ship heroin to Cuba. As you know, heroin is legal to make in Italy and this would be pharmaceutical grade. We can cut it to street level to maximize our return. Any questions?"

Frank Costello, who controlled large gambling concessions stood up, "Godfather I would like to ask again if narcotics is where we should be. Drugs bring unnecessary risk and scrutiny to La Cosa Nostra that we don't need."

"Frank, we have discussed this before, if we don't do it someone else will, like the fuckin' spics or mooleys. With this serious money, they could try to reduce our influence. This we cannot allow. The drug money allows us to own politicians, police and other city officials. As long as we pay them they will look elsewhere to make their quota," responded Luciano.

"Si, Godfather, but I own that fuckin' Hoover already. He will not be able to deny La Cosa Nostra is real forever with drugs involved," answered Costello.

"You have done a great job controlling that fucking fanook, and I'm sure you will continue. Hoover is a fuckin' empty suit that will never touch us no matter what. Enough said. The drugs will come to Cuba. From here, a small amount will go to New York and New Orleans and the rest to Tampa for distribution by Santo. Let's vote."

Again, the vote was unanimous.

"The last agenda item is our local business in Cuba. Things could not be going any better. Batista is our goomba. He will do fuckin' anything and allow fuckin' anything we want. Rumor has it he may be replaced soon by Carlos Prio Socarras. If this happens, Batista will be in exiled in Florida on his ranch. I have talked with our CIA connections and they are ok with this. It would seem Prio is just as greedy as Batista and should maintain business as usual. Of course, if this does not happen the CIA with our help will return Batista to power. We could try to keep Batista in power but that could get messy without active CIA cooperation. We might be able to force cooperation but I don't think it's worth it at this time. So the recommendation is to let Cuban politics run their course this time. Discussion? No? Let's vote."

Another unanimous vote followed. It seemed no one wanted to challenge Luciano on anything. At least not in front of everyone else. Following the meeting, Genovese asked Luciano for a sit down. This was granted the next day in Luciano's room at the Hotel Nacional.

"Buon giorno, Godfather, grazie for this meeting," said Genovese. "I am sorry to bring bad news but I thought you should know. Some fuckin' rat, I don't know who, tipped off the fuckin' feds that you are in Cuba."

"Son of a bitch! Mother fuckin' scumbag!" yelled Luciano.

"I know, Godfather, I had angina when I heard."

"What are they going to do?"

"I think they will ask Cuba to send you back to Italy."

"Mother fucker! Are you sure they know?"

"I am sure Godfather. There can be no mistake."

"Batista will never agree."

"I think he will, Godfather. The US will pressure him until he folds. To go against them will guarantee Prio takes his place as President. Given the situation, I think you should consider transferring your control now while you can to insure no break-down occurs. I am prepared to take this burden from you if you prefer."

"You mother fuckin' rat prick, you did this!" Lucky yelled as he leaped for Genovese. "I will kill you rat."

"No Godfather I did not do it!" he said without moving.

Luciano hit him and kicked him until his guards pulled him off. Genovese had three broken ribs, a broken nose and one eye completely shut.

"Take him to a doctor. And you listen to me prick, if you ever tell anyone of this, you're dead. If I find out you tipped off the feds you're already dead, capisce?"

"Si, but I did not tell them."

Within two weeks, Batista was at his door.

"I am sorry Lucky but I have to deport you to Italy. I told them no at first and they stopped sending needed medicines to us. I countered with stopping all sugar shipments to the US. They don't care. They want you gone and trade must continue or I cannot stay in office. Prio will not treat you as well as I do. You can still be in charge but from Italy."

Luciano knew this was an empty gesture. He knew that as soon as he left, the power in Cuba would be shared between Lansky and Trafficante. Cuba had to be controlled from Cuba. At best, he would be able to control US operations.

"Mother fuckin Genovese! I know how to handle a stone in my shoe!"

Chapter 14
HAVANA
1952

Despite Batista's cooperation with the US over Luciano, Carlos Prio Socarras became president in 1948. By 1952, Meyer Lansky and Santo Trafficante had had enough of Prio.

"This fuckin' prick," said Lansky, "is bad for business. He says one thing does another and then says he didn't understand. His goons are interfering with Bolita and our girls. He even busted a heroin shipment. I know the fucker promised to curtail our activities but this is not acceptable. The fucker is stealing from the country right and left and is thought of as the most corrupt president ever, and he wants to deflect by harassing us. I don't fuckin' think so. We are nobody's scapegoat!"

"I agree, Meyer, I think we should consider bringing Batista back. We can pre negotiate with him for an even better deal than we had before. Can you check with the CIA to see if they have any issues with Prio? If they do, he can disappear, if not Batista, with our help, and no interference from the CIA, can be put back into the presidential palace."

Within three days, Meyer had the answer. "The CIA does not care who is in charge between Prio and Batista as long as it does not get bloody. They do not want collateral damage."

"Since when do they give a rat's ass about collateral damage? Never mind. I will visit Tampa next week and arrange a visit with Batista at his Daytona Beach ranch."

Batista's ranch was located on 1000 acres of cattle land just outside Daytona Beach. The compound's main house was a large single story stucco house with clay colored tile roof. The house surrounded a central courtyard that was open to the house on all four sides. In the courtyard was a fountain and small swimming pool. The entire central area was covered with screening to eliminate mosquitoes. It was in this courtyard that Santo voiced his plan, as both men puffed on a Cuban cigar and sipped frozen daiquiris.

"Fulgencio, we miss you. Have you considered a return to Cuba?"

"Everyday I consider it, and everyday I think it would be foolish," he answered.

"It would be unless you had the right friends."

"Do you know where I can get those friends, Señor Trafficante?"

"I think you already have those friends. To activate them some future concessions might be in order, but that would be little compared to a return to the presidential palace. Don't you agree?"

"Si, Señor. And what concessions do you think they would be?"

"Perhaps if Cuba would match any 1 million dollar investment in new Cuban Hotels and casinos and also donate a gaming license that would be a start. That and a promise to never interfere with the activities of Cuba's friends should be enough to insure your return."

"Will the CIA also approve my return?" he asked.

"If we approve they will approve," Santo said even though he knew it wasn't exactly that way. In this case, it was pre-approved.

"Of course, I would agree to those concessions as they are nothing I wouldn't approve anyway, especially for my friends."

"In that case I would prepare myself for a return, if I were you. Send word to me when you are ready and we will begin. It should not take long. We will have everything ready in Cuba."

"Muchas gracias, Señor Santo. I will not forget this."

"Neither will we, Presidente!"

Within a month, Batista executed a successful and bloodless coup ousting Prio and establishing himself as the new Presidente of Cuba. He had thought he might be able to win an election and become president that way but that was not in the cards. All estimates indicated he would finish third. The bloodless coup sufficed as Prio was not inclined to fight. Batista had been a very popular member of the military and had most of them on his side.

"Well done, Santo, everyone is happy with the job you did," Meyer said.

"It could not have worked out better. No blood, no collateral damage, and we have our partner back. It's time for another building boom with the concessions you arranged. We will make millions!"

Chapter 15
APALACHIN NEW YORK 1957

Santo Trafficante Jr. and Roberto Mendoza, a Cuban associate, sat in the Waldorf Astoria dining room eating quietly discussing their upcoming meeting with Albert Anastasia, head of the Mangano family. "Anastasia," said Santo, " is the worst kind of boss. He gained his position by assassinating the Mangano brothers to whom he had sworn allegiance. The cocksucker is part of the liberal New York sect, along with Costello, that is trying to gain ultimate power over the conservative Sicilian led families of Genovese, Lucchese and Gambino. They will do anything for power without regard for our traditions. Sooner or later they will overreach and that will be the fuckin' end."

"What does he want to meet with you about tonight, Boss?" asked Mendoza.

"Something about Cuba and our business there. He may want to buy in a larger share or start a new operation. We'll soon know."

"Are we meeting here, Boss?"

"Yes, we will meet here in the dining room. It's more secure than a private room. I don't trust anyone that murders his boss.

If you are willing to kill someone to whom you owe allegiance then you have no honor and will murder anyone for any reason."

Santo and Roberto were smoking a cigar and drinking Sambuca when Anastasia came in. With him was only one guy, Nick Parise, his underboss.

"Buona sera, Santo, who's this with you?"

"Buona sera, Alberto. Buona sera, Nick. This is Roberto Mendoza, one of our guys in Cuba."

"Buona sera Don Anastasia, Don Parise," replied Roberto. He did not mistake the insult when he was not acknowledged by either man. It was an insult to him and disrespectful to Santo as he was his man.

Santo chose to ignore it for now, "Cigar gentlemen we have Cohibas, Brandy, Buca?"

"We have our own cigars Santo, and I prefer Sambuca," replied Anastasia. He obviously does not trust our cigars are not poisoned, thought Santo. Asshole, poison is a woman's weapon.

After the Sambuca arrived, Anastasia got right to business. "I want to address the Cuban casino business that you and Lansky have working."

"You want to invest, or start a new one?" asked Santo.

"Neither. I want 50% as tribute for allowing you to continue in operation."

"Have you lost your fucking mind, Anastasia? You don't come in here and demand tribute from me!"

"You better think that one over little man. You are old school, your kind's on the way out. Yours can be sooner or later, your choice. My associates and I will be in Cuba next week. We will meet you and Lansky at the National on Wednesday at nine. If you are not there and if you do not agree with the tribute, there will be restitution. We will come heavy! Thanks for the Buca. See ya."

Santo did not respond as the two left.

"What do you want to do, Boss?"

"I want you to contact your Puerto Rican friends as soon as we leave here. I want you to find out where Anastasia will be tomorrow, if he has any routine things he does, like visit his mother, hang out at a particular strip joint, see his gumba, anything like that. I also want you to get an untraceable sawed off shotgun and two 9-millimeter Browning's. We will give the cocksucker his tribute."

"You got it, Boss; I can get everything from Manny. I'll have it by morning. This rude motherfucker is do a proper tribute indeed."

After Anastasia's routine was reported to Santo, he decided the best opportunity was at his barbershop. Anastasia also had a gumba that he kept in a nice downtown high-rise, but it was too crowded and he had quickly ruled that out. Santo also knew nothing would be expected this quick. The barbershop was ideally located in Anastasia's old neighborhood with easy access from the front. Manny came with Roberto and Santo to act as the scout. He would walk into the barbershop, identify how many players were present, identify where Anastasia was, and report to the car.

"Roberto Anastasia is in the second chair. The first chair is empty. The third chair is also empty. The fourth has a civilian. Anastasia's driver is reading the paper in a side chair facing the door. There is a bathroom in the back with an emergency exit that leads to the ally."

"Manny, we will get out of the car here away from the front door. I want you to drive the car around back and pick us up there. Let's go. Roberto, you take the shotgun and take out the driver. I will take Anastasia," ordered Santo.

As Santo and Roberto entered the barbershop, ski masks in place, Santo couldn't believe his luck. Anastasia had a hot towel on his face and did not see them. The driver did and was blown off his feet by Roberto. He was dead before he hit the wall. Anastasia jerked the towel away as Santo shot him in the chest knocking him to the floor. The barber raised his hands in the air. "Back away barber!" Santo ordered.

"Yes sir, no problem."

Santo calmly walked over to Anastasia who was lying on the floor, not dead, but barely moving. "How's this fucking tribute!" he said as he shot him in the head.

Santo and Roberto calmly walked to the back and out the exit door. The car was not there. "Fuck," said Roberto. The car was not in sight.

"There he is, 100 yards away behind the dumpster." He was blocked by the dumpster and a car parked across from it. "Let's go," said Santo as they calmly walked to the car. As they passed the dumpster, the weapons went inside. Their gloves and masks came off as they got into the car. "Well done, Roberto, well done."

"Thanks Boss, that was fun. I did not like that rude cock- sucker. And you asking him how he liked his tribute was per- fect!" said Roberto as Santo smiled.

As the driver delivered them to LaGuardia airport Santo gave Roberto his ticket to Miami and then to Havana. Santo's ticket was to Tampa. He would be going on to Cuba the next day. "Thanks Manny" Santo said as he handed him a fat white envelope filled with Benjamins.

"Thank-you Señor Trafficante. It is always a pleasure to be of service."

"What the fuck were you thinking, Santo?" asked Lansky the next day at the San Souci Hotel and Casino in Havana. "I agree the fuck had to go, but why whack him yourself?"

"He deserved it and after his insults I deserved the right to do it. Fucking tribute my ass!"

"Now we have another problem. This only makes Genovese stronger. Now he has to be taken down a notch to maintain order. This thing of ours is becoming more and more unstable and with that comes more scrutiny by the feds. We cannot let these new bosses destroy what has been, and should continue to be lucrative with plenty for all and minimum interference from the feds. Roselli and Giancana are already here and Marcello will be here shortly. We want to discuss Genovese and this emergency meeting he has called for next month at Barbara's place in Apalachin New York."

"We already had a meeting there. What the fuck, having it at same place as last year is not smart."

"Genovese is guaranteeing security for the meeting," added Lansky.

The meeting with Carlos Marcello the New Orleans boss; John Roselli, underboss of Chicago; Sam Giancana, Chicago boss; Meyer Lansky, and Santo Trafficante Jr. was held at the San Souci after lunch. "Thanks for coming on such short notice. I trust everyone has everything they need and has been made comfortable?" asked Lansky.

"Yeah, yeah, cut to the chase Meyer. What's up?" asked Giancana.

"With Anastasia out, the balance of power has once again been upset. Genovese is now in position to be Capo dei Capi, which we all know he wants. Santo and I believe this Apalachin meeting is for that purpose. If that happens Genovese will not be content to stay in New York. We believe he will want more control in Chicago, New Orleans, Tampa, and Cuba."

"Fuck that. He can't have a damn thing in Chicago. It's my fucking playground," said Giancana.

"Yeah, and New Orleans to Texas is my fucking yard!" said Marcello.

"We feel the same about Cuba and Tampa," said Santo.

"Lucky should have killed him when he had the chance," added Meyer.

"We can't take him out now; it would cause a total war. We would all go down. Business would go to shit. Everything would be crap. You brought us here, Meyer, you must have something in mind," said Marcello.

"If we all agree taking him out is not an option, then we have to discredit him in some way. This meeting where he has guaranteed security may be the way."

"I don't follow," said Roselli.

"It's never a good idea to repeat a meeting location. That's always risky. Many bosses are already jumpy because of it. If this meeting is raided, Genovese will be shit with everyone coming down on him. He will be held responsible."

"That's too risky, Meyer. If there is a major raid like that of a top-level meeting, not only will a lot of guys get charged but the Feds will have to acknowledge us. Our fucking Hoover will have to target us," said Marcello.

"I can still control Hoover," said Giancana. "He may have to make some noise but I can control that noise. He has no choice. Hell, we taught him how to keep files on people and control them by threatening exposure. The fanook has no choice but to play ball. We have pictures of the cocksucker in action with Clyde Tolson, his asshole fuck buddy. Eisenhower's 1953 executive order, which bans gays and lesbians from having federal jobs, fucking guarantees his cooperation. He sees himself as the king of US government. He thinks he can get anything from anyone thanks to his secret files. He would kill himself before he would give up his throne in disgrace. We have made him a commie fear monger. He doesn't have fuckin' time for us. He even publicly denies we exist."

"That's fuckin' great, Sam, but if there's a raid of a major meeting that might all change," said Marcello.

"Maybe some things will change. But we still can control it. We have him by his fanook stuggots and he knows it. He will behave or else. I say we do it."

"I think it's the only shot we have to keep Genovese out of our territories," added Meyer

"I agree," said Santo.

"Ok, we in Chicago will go along but I'm not going to the meeting. I don't need the grief a possible arrest will cause," said Giancana.

"I don't think none of you should go," said Santo. "I'm the only one that has to be there because of Anastasia. Genovese wants to make sure there is no retaliation that will start a war and ruin his bid for Capo dei Capi. Make up an excuse to not be there. I will have a false identity and will be released. Everyone knows I do that all the time and that won't cast no suspicion on me."

"Agreed," said Marcello.

"Agreed," said Roselli.

"Agreed," said Lansky.

"Agreed," said Giancana.

The Apalachin meeting occurred as scheduled on November 14, 1957 at the home of Joseph Barbara. The 53-acre compound easily had room for more than the 75 black Cadillacs, Lincolns and various limousines that arrived that morning. Barbara's banquet room was set up with a stage for the bosses and special guests from Italy. Over 100 members, that included Bosses, Underbosses, Consiglieres, soldiers and associates attended. In the center of the stage was a podium for the speaker. Tables were set up on stage and in the audience so everyone could eat comfortably before the start of the meeting. The waiters served the bosses and stage dignitaries first, and then two servers per table insured that everyone else would be served simultaneously. As the servers left the room and closed the doors, Genovese went to the podium and began the meeting that he thought would at last make him Capo dei Capi. Something he thought that fucker Luciano should have done for him in Cuba long ago. "Don Civello, Don Colletti, Don DeSimone, Don Zito, Don Sealish, Don Ida, Don Valenti, Don Trafficante, Don Profaci, Don Gambino, our host Don Barbara, and to all of you, welcome to this meeting. We have some vital areas we need to discuss to maximize our business, but first we need to make peace. Recent events have indicated that certain factions of our family have seen the necessity of settling differences of opinion on their own without asking for a sit-down. This risks a major war, which is bad for business. The reason for this individual action is understandable, as we have not had a central base in a long time. It is time we formally united with a Capo dei Capi."

Simultaneously the Genovese supporters stood and cheered. As they settled down a voice from outside the room began knocking on the locked door, "Cops! It's a raid!" Most jumped up and began scrambling for the doors. A few, including Santo, were more cautious and slowly made their way to a window to look out. Sure enough, dozens of uniformed officers were charging the building. They almost waited too late thought Santo. He was almost crowned. Santo went to a back window and laughed to himself, assholes and elbows were all he could see as a number of guests fled to the woods.

"Don't move, you are all under arrest!" shouted the first cop in the door as the others began to round up those that had not escaped. In all 53 were arrested. Louis Santos from Tampa was one of them but he was later released. In all, 20 were charged with 'Conspiring to obstruct justice by lying about the nature of the meeting' which included Genovese and several of the other bosses. As Santo flew back to Cuba, he smiled. He knew this would be the end of Genovese's try for ultimate power. He also knew the price would be more heat from the feds. Now he and Meyer could concentrate on what was happening in Cuba. This fucking Castro was creating a lot of support, but could he really win against Batista and the US? He didn't think so, but it wouldn't cost much to support both just in case. It really didn't matter, as all of these monkeys were the same. There was too much money to be made for anyone to change Cuba now. We can offer anything that is required to separate a man or woman from his money. Life was good.

Chapter 16
REMEMBERING THE GRANMA 1958

As Rafael waited for his next deployment, he thought about how far they had come since the boat ride from Mexico. What a disaster that had been. The revolution almost died the first day. Batista had been tipped off by a spy in Mexico and knew the general area where Castro would land. The expected meeting with a group from Santiago did not happen because the Granma was two days late. The entire crossing took more than 30 hours longer than planned. They left Tuxpan, Mexico at two in the morning in bad weather. They did not have any seasickness pills and almost everyone got sick. Men were collapsed in clothes drenched in vomit. If that wasn't enough El Jefe went overboard and had to save Rafael who tried to save him. When they finally landed, the boat hit a reef and the men had to swim ashore, leaving the remainder of their heavy gear that had not already thrown overboard in the storm. Then within an hour of landing, Batista's planes began strafing. They scattered in the swamp. No one knew what to do. After seven miserable days at sea, the force was divided into small groups trying to hide in the swamp to avoid Batista's air force. Without radio contact one group was unaware of any other as each desperately tried to reach the rendezvous point in the mountains.

After three days of wandering, Rafael's group of seven came to Alegria de Pio, which means happiness. Here a small group of Batista's soldiers ambushed them. They were outmanned and out-gunned. With only farm rifles to defend themselves, they lost more than half of their men before they could get away. Now the group was down to three, Rafael, Juan Benitez and Ramiro Valdes. After three more days of marching, staggering really, they managed to find Fidel at the farm of Mongo Perez. A compesino that they encountered, sympathetic to Castro, led them to the farm. He had heard that Fidel was there. All totaled, 12 men remained of the original 82 that left Tuxpan only 11 days before. Without El Jefe's constant encouragement, most would have quit. Twenty men arrived from Santiago de Cuba two days later and Fidel was ready to fight. He laid out his strategy of guerrilla warfare, ambush and retreat, which had been his tactic for most of the war. His first victory occurred at a small barracks on the La Plata River in the Sierra Maestra Mountains.

"Look, Fidel that is Chicho Osorio on that mule. He is one of the cruelest foremen to ever work the fields," said Caesars, one of our compensinos who was both a friend and guide. "He is so drunk he's going to fall off!"

As El Jeffe ran down to the road he said, "Come on." As he approached Osorio he said, "Stop! I am Colonel Mendez and I demand to know why the Army has not killed these rebels. The Army here is doing nothing and I aim to stop that."

"It's true, Colonel', slurred Osorio as he teetered on his mule, "The men in the barracks do nothing. They drink; they play cards, and do nothing against these fucking rebels. The compesinos are getting uppity too! I had to beat two of them just now for that. The army does nothing and lets the compesinos talk back to them. It is disgraceful. The rebels on the other hand do wear nice boots. Look," he said, as he raised his feet and showed Fidel his Mexican made boots. The same boots Fidel and his men were wearing. "I took these off one rebel I killed who was trying to sweet talk one of my compesino girls."

"And if you caught this Castro, what would you do?"

"Why, I'd cut his dick off and feed it to the pigs," he said laughing.

"Come Chicho, let's go to the barracks and surprise them. We want to demonstrate how unprepared they are. You lead ok?"

"Si, Colonel, follow me."

As the men followed Chicho to the barracks, a small group headed by Raul left the main group and surrounded the overseer's hut, ready to cut down anyone that exited when the shooting started. Fidel started the shooting. The first to die was the murderous informant Chicho Osorio. Fidel asked for surrender and was met with heavy gunfire as a response. The rebels fiercely responded with the desperation of an army running out of ammunition. If they did not capture the barracks and take needed supplies, they would not be able to attack again. Fidel was always in front, always impervious to the danger as he led his men on the attack. Not wanting to disappoint their brave commander, the rebels fought bravely and fiercely. When they reached the door, Batista's soldiers surrendered. They had two dead, five wounded, and three were taken as prisoners. The weapons and ammunitions were confiscated and for the first time every rebel had his own gun. Fidel questioned the prisoners and had Che attend to their wounded. The rebels did not have a single wounded soldier. After Che was finished Fidel said, "We will leave the three prisoners to attend to their wounded, let's go." The three prisoners couldn't believe they would not be tortured and killed; such was the fate of any rebel that fell into Batista's hands.

"Fidel, are you not concerned that we will just have to fight these same soldiers again when they recover and are re-armed?" asked Camilo Cienfuegos, one of 12 remaining from the Granma.

"Camilo, we are not Batista's men. We do not torture, we do not threaten, we do not withhold medical attention, and we will not take a life unnecessarily. This is our morality; this is our creed. Si, we may fight the same soldiers again. However, for some of them that have their own sense of the moral high ground, Batista's torture and senseless murder will prove to be intolerable once they know they have an alternative. Some will refuse to fight for him and go home. Some may even ask to join us and fight against him. As with everything we do, history will be the judge of what's right and what's wrong." Fidel's precedent of releasing prisoners unharmed and trying to save any wounded combatant would continue throughout the Revolucion. Never before or since have enemy soldiers been treated in such a manner. For Fidel, his brother Raul and Che Guevara it was only right and humane. None of them considered doing it any other way.

After the battle of La Plata, word of Fidel's willingness to fight to resist Batista's tyranny spread and recruits followed. An air raid by Batista was also forthcoming as he attempted to end the 26th of July Movement. In an attempt to stop the recruits, Batista announced that the Movement and Fidel had been killed.

In an attempt to counter Batista's misinformation tactic, Fidel allowed his supporters in Havana to escort a US reporter to his camp. His name was Herbert L. Matthews. After ham sandwiches made with crackers, and coffee in tin cups, they talked and smoked Cohibas. Fidel used Rafael as translator.

"With no food grown in this area of the Sierra how do you eat? asked Matthews.

As Fidel talked, Rafael translated, "We have food sent in by courier along with arms and ammunitions. We buy from local stores and sometimes we buy from farmers as we move. The result is sometimes we eat, and sometimes we don't."

"Batista said you were dead. Obviously, you are not. Why would he do that?" asked Matthews.

"We have been fighting for 79 days now and we are stronger than ever. His soldiers are fighting badly. Their morale is low, and ours could not be higher. We are killing many but when we take prisoners, they are questioned, we take their arms and equipment, talk kindly to them, and release them. They are never tortured or shot. I know some of them have returned to fight us again; some have been questioned and tortured by Batista and in some cases shot as examples to others. They really don't want to fight us and their leaders really don't know how to fight a mountain guerilla war. We do. The Batista controlled press talks about Algeria but never about us. Batista wants us dead but he can't find us while we know where they are at all times. You will be the first to tell the truth about what is happening here."

"How do you expect to win against the government when it has the backing of the United States?" asked Matthews.

"It's true the government is using arms from the United States not only against us but also against the Cuban people. They have bazookas, mortars, machine guns, planes, and bombs, but we are safe in the Sierra. They must come and get us but they can't."

"What does the 26th of July Movement stand for, and why do you fight? asked Matthews.

"The Movement is named after the date of the Moncada barracks attack which began our efforts to overthrow the illegal government of Batista. He took control not through an election he was destined to lose, but through a military coup. We fight to correct this wrong, we fight for Nationalism, anti colonialism, anti-imperialism, liberty for the Cuban people, and democracy. We mean a true democracy where the majority rules, not a republic like the United States. We fight for social justice where every man is equal not just the white man, or in some cases, only the rich white man, and the need to restore the Cuban constitution. We are socialists, but anti-Communist. We believe every man should own his own home and work his own fields. We hold no animosity toward the United States and the American people. But above all our fight for a democratic Cuba and an end to the Batista dictatorship. There is no hatred of the Cuban Army for we know the men are good and so are many of the officers. Batista has 3000 men in the field against us. For obvious reasons I will not tell you how many we are. Batista's army works in columns of 200, we work in groups of 10 to 40, and we are winning. It is just a matter of time and time is on our side. Why should soldiers die for Batista's $72 a month? When we win, they will make $100 a month and will serve a free democratic Cuba. You have taken a great risk by coming here. You have my personal guarantee that we will get you safely back to Havana."

"Thank-you Señor Castro, you have been more than generous with your time," said Matthews.

Matthews' *New Your Times* articles were a big help to the movement. For the first time the Cuban people heard the truth about the 26th of July Movement and that Castro was still alive.

Shortly thereafter, the Rebels received their most unusual recruits. Three American youth from Guantanamo Bay: Charles (Chuck) Ryan, whose father was a Navy medic stationed at Guantanamo Bay, age 19; Mike Garvey, age 15, and Victor Buehlman, age 17; both were also sons of United States sailors stationed at Guantanamo.

"Hola, gentlemen welcome to M-26-7. I am Lieutenant Moreno; did you get a sandwich and something to drink?"

"Yes," they all replied.

"Do any of you speak Spanish?" Rafael asked.

"No," they all said.

"Ok, no problem. I need to ask you all some questions for security reasons. As I am sure, you can imagine we constantly have to be on guard against Batista spies. That's why we have all kept our beards even though we now have razors. Because of that, we are suspicious of anyone without a beard."

"Yes sir, we have all heard about the 'los barbudos,' the bearded ones. And we are not spies. You already know me as I have been bringing guns and supplies from Guantanamo Bay for weeks now. I can vouch for my young friends too. We have all decided after listening to the Cuban workers on the base that the dictator Batista has to go and we want to help. And I want to help more than just bringing in supplies. I want to fight," said Ryan.

"We want to help as well," said Buehlman.

"That's right, we couldn't just sit back and do nothing," said Garvey. "We have read in the *New York Times* what the movement stands for and we wanted to help make that happen."

"Have any of you had any military training?" asked Rafael.

"I have had two years of ROTC," answered Ryan.

"I have not," said Buehlman.

"Nor I," said Garvey. "But we are fast learners and will be useful. We have brought our own rifles. And we are all good shots!"

"Thank-you, my friends, I will talk with Fidel and see where we can best use you. Chuck thank-you for your service already in bringing much needed supplies to us. You have already been very valuable."

"It is the least I could do for the cause, Lieutenant Moreno."

"El Jefe, I have talked with the boys, I do not think any of them is a spy.

The oldest Chuck Ryan has already been helpful by smuggling supplies from Guantanamo Bay. He wants to increase his role and is here to fight. The other two are very young with no experience but genuinely want to help. My concern is if an underage American is killed fighting with us. That could be very bad for us and could hurt our ability to recruit. Worse, it could be used by the Americans to enter the war openly with troops, which would be devastating. My recommendation would be to not use the young ones and to send them back as soon as possible. For Ryan we could use him only sparingly until we find another use without risk."

"That is wise council, Rafael, gracias. Celia Sanchez will be bringing another reporter up here in a few weeks and we will send them home then. I will explain to them that the risk is too great to be a part of the Revolucion until they are at least 19. As for Ryan, we will give him as safe a position in the next battle as we can. Then I will send him to the United States to help raise support for our efforts as a combat veteran."

Celia Sanchez arrived with Robert Taber, an American producer with the Central Broadcasting Company, and Wendell Hoffman, a photographer, on April 23, 1957. They would film and publish a documentary, *Rebels in the Sierra*, for CBS. The three Americans were a central part of the production and became valued contributors to the movement through this work. It was arranged that when Robert Taber left, Victor Buehlman and Michael Garvey would go with him to Guantanamo Bay. Fidel had convinced them of their contribution to the movement and that it was too dangerous for them to stay. Reluctantly they left.

In June, Charles Ryan got his baptism by fire at the Battle of Uvero. Eighty revolutionaries attacked a fortified compound with 53 well-equipped defenders. As always, Fidel fired the first shot. Charles volunteered to cut the telephone lines to minimize reinforcements. He conducted himself bravely and gained much respect from his comrades. The battle lasted two and half-hours with advantage going back and forth. Finally, the Commanding Officer of the garrison was wounded and he raised a white flag. Both sides had substantial losses with more than a quarter of the participants "hors de combat." The rebels had six dead, two severely wounded and thirteen others wounded. The Army had fourteen dead, nineteen wounded, fourteen that were prisoners, and six that had run away during the battle. Fortunately, one of the Garrison survivors was a doctor and he and Che treated all of the wounded, on both sides, addressing the most serious first regardless of side.

As Che pondered how to deal with Leal and Cilleros, the Army doctor said, "Doctor Guevara, Leal and Cilleros cannot be safely moved because of their injuries. If you will leave them here so I can attend them I give you my word they will not be shot and that they will be given the best possible chance to survive."

Che after studying the Army Doctor and judging his sincerity replied," Gracias Doctor, I will leave them in you care and trust your word of honor as a soldier and a doctor."

The rest of their wounded and the prisoners left with the rebels. They all knew they would never see Leal and Cilleros again. After Fidel talked with the two they were leaving behind, he came to Rafael.

"Rafael, I don't see the American. Is he all right?"

"Si, El Jefe he is not wounded. He cut the telephone wire and fought very bravely. He has gained the respect of all that saw him."

"Muy buena, Rafael. I think it is time to consider sending him to the US as a combat veteran to report on our mission."

This was a great victory for the Rebels that set the stage for future battles. The morale was very high and everyone could sense this was a turning point in the struggle. When the planes came as they always did after any sizeable fight, it was easy to hide in the forest and they did not fire. After they left, the prisoners were questioned and released unharmed, as usual. As soon as they reached base camp Fidel talked with Ryan, "You fought well, Chuck, I am very proud of your courage and your willingness to be in harm's way for our cause. My English is limited but I will try to speak it because of the importance of this talk."

"It felt right El Jefe. The movement has right on its side and will triumph in the end. And your English is way batter than my Spanish."

"I believe right is on our side also Chuck. However, to win we will need everyone doing their best for the movement. Without that commitment we cannot win."

"I believe you have that from every one here and from your comrades that supply us both on the ground and through airdrops."

"Si, things are improving every day but much still remains and I think you can be a major factor in helping us win this revolution."

"Gracias, El Jefe, for your confidence. I will do whatever is asked of me."

"I am glad to hear that Chuck, as I have a special mission in mind, if you are interested."

"Of course anything I can do I will do."

"Perception is always a vital element in a successful revolution. Everyone here knows why we fight and what we hope to achieve. The reporters have helped by telling the truth. However, unless the truth is constantly reinforced, negative propaganda from Batista will be all that is heard. As a result, donations of money and arms will dwindle. As a fluent English speaker and an American citizen, you are in a unique position to help us in this regard. If you would be willing to go to New York and work on our behalf and spread the truth, the value could be without measure."

Immediately deflated by the thought of leaving the fighting men, Ryan replied," I do not want to leave these men that I have come to respect and trust." Hesitating as he looked into Fidel's eyes he read the necessity of his wish, "But I will go if you think it is for the best."

"Si, Chuck, it is best this way. I don't want to lose a fighter in the field such as you, but you alone can be successful in New York. If you are successful, and I know you will be, it could mean the difference in winning or losing the Revolución. It is that important."

Charles Ryan, the last of the American volunteers, left the next day. Ryan's fundraising was so successful he was able to buy a merchant ship full of munitions. However, the United States blocked the ship off the coast of Texas and it never reached Cuba.

Chapter 17
VICTORY
1959

By May 1, 1958, the war movement was taking its toll on Batista's forces. Fidel's strategy of surprise attack, fall back, and attack again was undermining the enemy morale. To exacerbate their discomfort the rebels had interrupted their supply lines, deprived them of support from the large landowners, and sabotaged transportation routes and communications. Other factions of resistance were also lining up to join M-26-7 as they made life difficult for Batista and his army. By May, the war expanded from central Sierra Maestra to the west toward Santiago and at the same time to the east toward Las Villas. As the Rebels gained land, Batista became desperate. Batista and the army decided to make a major offensive to stop the momentum. He needed to stop the Rebel momentum and if he could crush them forever, that would be even better. Ten thousand soldiers were sent to the Sierra Maestra to overwhelm the revolution and annihilate M-26-7 with overwhelming firepower. Batista sent 14 battalions with artillery, tanks, air support and 3 naval vessels through Santiago de Cuba. Since Castro had sent Che and his forces east, they were too far away to recall. That left the Rebels with 200 men ready to face Batista's Army of 10,000. In advance of the fight, Fidel received a letter from Batista's General of the Army Eulogio Cantillo. By reputation, Cantillo was known to be a fair man and did not use brutality, torture and indiscriminate murder, which made him an anomaly among Batista's Generals.

"Rafael, listen to this," said Fidel. "Cantillo is sending 10,000 men to crush M-26-7. Once the fighting starts there will be no quarter except for me. I am to be arrested and tried. Everyone else is to be murdered on the spot. However, if we surrender now all of us will be arrested and sent to Havana. They are in route now toward our outpost at Las Mercedes. We must assemble the men immediately."

"Si El Jefe, I will put out the call."

Within an hour, all of the available 200 men were assembled. In addition, Fidel made the shortest speech of his life. "Soldiers of the M-26-7, soldiers of freedom and democracy, soldiers of a free and Democratic Cuba, soldiers against tyranny, soldiers against imperialism, soldiers against the illegal Batista government, my friends, my colleagues, my comrades in arms, my fellow free Cubans. I bring to you exciting and terrible news. We are winning our revolution." Massive spontaneous cheers rang out. Some started to sing the Anthem "Guantanamera." "Please wait, let me finish. Success is always followed by increased risk because of the enemy's desperation. Batista has dispatched a massive army of 10,000 soldiers toward Las Mercedes because he is losing. We cannot dodge an army of that size. We will be forced to fight until we are dead or until we are victorious. General Cantillo has given us a third option to surrender now, and we will be spared and taken to Havana for trial."

"Viva La Revolucion! We win or die, we never surrender!" yelled one of the Rebels.

"Viva La Revolucion! Viva La Revolucion! Viva La Revolucion!" others added their voices until the noise was overpowering. It did not stop until Fidel raised his arms. With tears in his eyes he said," Comrades, I would go to war with you anytime. I am so proud of each one of you. We will be victorious! We will free Cuba! We will win over tyranny. We do not have long to prepare before we will meet the Army head on. We will begin now."

After the meeting Rafael asked Fidel, "Fidel what is your plan for 200 to defeat 10,000?"

"The fight will be 200 lions against 10,000 sheep. Our morale could not be higher. Theirs could not be lower. Many of their comrades have left the Army. Some have joined us; some have just gone home. If our initial resistance is fierce, their will to fight will diminish. If Batista had done this the first year of the revolution, we would have lost. Now we may still lose but we have a chance. Our men are seasoned veterans willing to be in harm's way. Our cause is strong and is still a great motivator in spite of the danger. Batista's army does not have our commitment to a cause. They fight for an illegal government and a brutal dictator. They fight because they are forced. We fight because we want to serve our cause. We have a chance and we have time to prepare our defenses. We can force them to fight in a small area by fortifying and structuring the surrounding area to funnel the attack into as small an area as possible. We will have three to four fallback areas if it gets too hot. Nevertheless, the cost of forcing us to retreat will be severe and test their moral conviction to the extreme. Initially, it will be a fight of arms and numbers, we will lose that, but the longer it takes the more it will become a war of intestinal fortitude and in that we will triumph! Anticipating that this might someday happen, a lot of the infrastructure we needed to funnel their forces had already been put into place. The rest we can do now. Let us begin!"

Everyone watched Fidel and his brother Raul prepare for the upcoming battle. It was as if they had anticipated a massive attack and instead of fearing the confrontation, they welcomed it like a Sunday picnic. Their mood and demeanor were infectious. It was obvious in their faces and in the vigor with which they prepared that that totally embraced this opportunity to overcome this challenge. Everyone knew this battle would decide the war. It would not end it, but what would follow would be clean-up action no matter which side gained the advantage. This one battle would decide if the clean up included the remaining revolutionaries or if it included the remaining soldiers who had not given up in defeat. One way or the other the Revolución would be won or lost in the next few days. Led by the Brothers Castro, 200 men prepared for battle with a calm enthusiasm, and a determination rarely seen in the history of war and never by a force outnumbered fifty to one.

When Batista's army finally arrived, the Rebels were ready; at least they thought they were ready. The Revolutionaries were accustomed to hit and run and had never before faced a major force head on. They resisted, they fought like lions and they lost fighters. However, they held their ground much longer than expected for such a small number. They forced Batista to use everything he had to get them to fall back. After seventy straight days of fighting, they had fallen back several times but they still fought with a determination that belied the fact that before this they had never fought an engagement that lasted more than a few hours. If the Brothers had really thought the Batista forces would not be committed, they were wrong. They too fought like lions. Once, twice, three times the Rebels retreated, and Batista's forces pressed forward, immediately claiming the ground the Revolutionaries vacated. With tireless efficiency, the Batista forces gained the upper hand. After a third and final retreat, the Rebels were in their fourth and final redoubt. The four lines of trenches with logs protruding from the front to discourage all out charges had served the rebels well. Now the Rebels were in their last. Batista's army could see that the Rebels had nowhere else to go and were encouraged. The fighting intensified as both sides knew the end was near. With desperation, the Rebels had mined the third fallback line with explosives. Fidel thought the army by this point would be losing its will to fight. He was wrong; they were more determined than ever to finish the Rebels for good. There was no way for the Rebels to know if the fierce fighting had reduced the Army's numbers as there were always enough to fill the redoubts and press forward. It was obvious that they were assembling as many as possible in the third redoubt in anticipation of the final charge and destruction of Castro and his Rebels. Fidel knew they would check for booby traps when they occupied the first two redoubts that the Rebels vacated. Desperation was apparent on the Rebels' faces as they prepared for the army's charge. Their only prayer was after finding nothing in the first two redoubts they would not check very closely in the third. The revolutionaries would know their fate when the detonator was engaged. If the ground shook, if the blast moved men and dirt and they heard screams and shouting, they just might have a chance. If the explosives were discovered and disarmed the war was over. They could not retreat any further. To leave the forth redoubt was to die. They would be in the open and slaughtered like ducks on a pond. El Jefe had the detonator and was waiting until as many soldiers as possible were in the third redoubt. The time was now. Fidel lowered the detonator's plunger. His men had one eye on Fidel and the other on the soldiers. As Fidel lowered the detonator's arm, his men involuntarily held their breath. They all knew what was at stake. When the plunger was all of the way down, nothing happened. He raised and lowered it again; nothing was the response. As the men processed the meaning and the inevitable outcome, a few curses could be heard above the gunfire. After a momentary lapse, the Revolutionaries renewed their attack with vigor. They would die, but they wouldn't die alone. Fidel moved away from the detonator and returned to firing toward the army, which was fully entrenched in the fallback number three redoubt. Rafael had helped wire the detonator and the thought occurred to him that maybe they had wired it incorrectly instead of what everyone feared, that Batista's army had disarmed the explosives. He crawled over to the detonator and looked at the wires. They were properly connected; it should have gone off unless they had discovered the explosives. Sergeant Angel Verecia had also helped with the wiring and came over to the detonator. He must have had the same thought as Rafael. "The wires here are ok Angel; Check the wires as far back as you can, perhaps a wire is cut or broken."

"Bueno, Rafael."

They had laid the wiring to the east side of the line of retreat so no one would accidentally trip on it. As Angel made his way to the east from the redoubt the firing was intense but he had some cover. At least for the first ten yards, after that he would be fully exposed with no chance to repair the wire. Suddenly he exclaimed, "Me parecio!"

"That's it Angel. Cut both wires there and I will bring the detonator to you," yelled Rafael.

"Bueno."

As Rafael crawled to his location, he heard Angel scream. He knew he had been shot. As Rafael reached him, he saw Angel's leg was disfigured and bleeding profusely. Angel helped Rafael reconnect the detonator with gritted teeth. They saw that Batista's men were coming out of the third redoubt and were starting to charge the fourth. They had no time for formality and as the wires were set, they raised and lowered the plunger as fast as they could. At first, nothing seemed to happen. Before the shock of failure could register, the earth shook so hard they were flattened on the ground. The blast was so strong the debris field radiated for a hundred yards in every direction. The enemy firing stopped. The ones unaffected began running away from redoubt number four. There were still enough soldiers to defeat the Rebels but they no longer had any will to fight. Fidel and Raul's battle plan had once again saved the Rebels from certain death. Two hundred had just defeated ten thousand. The history of Thermopylae had been rewritten. This time, Fidel, their King Leonidas, defeated the vastly superior Persians. As the Rebels cautiously walked toward the hole that had been redoubt number three, they saw first hand the devastation created by the blast. The entire redoubt was gone along with most of the men that had only minutes before knew their victory was at hand. Just behind the hole in the ground, they found a group of soldiers holding a white flag. There were at least 10 of them for every one of the rebels but they did not attempt to resist capture. They knew they would be treated fairly. Some of them joined M-26-7 once the cleanup was completed. The rest were stripped of their equipment and let go. The rebels were fortunate in many ways that so many defected. They had captured several Sherman Tanks but none of the Rebels knew how to operate them.

It took several days for the Rebels to reconnoiter the newly acquired resources and men. As Fidel had envisioned this one victory insured that his group would be successful. Batista had not given up, at least not formally, but the result was inevitable. Batista still had almost 17,000 soldiers in Oriente Province under the leadership of General Eulogio Cantillo, the same one who had offered to accept Fidel's surrender before the Battle of Las Mercedes. With his new troops and resources, Fidel was able to surround Batista's troops. When Cantillo asked Fidel to meet face to face to establish the terms of surrender; Fidel agreed to meet him at a neutral site near Palma Soriano. General Cantillo flew to the meeting in a helicopter. Just him and the pilot, unarmed and unafraid.

"Buenas tardes, Comandante Castro."

"Buenas tardes, General Cantillo. I want to thank-you for your letter prior to the Las Mercedes battle. In it you expressed regret that the M-26-7 was going to end in that manner as we were brave, courageous men who fought for what they thought was right."

"Thank-you Comandante, I meant what I said. I could not imagine a scenario that would enable you to escape alive, much less to win the battle. I felt the only way to save you and your brave men was to offer surrender with safe conduct to Havana. You surprised us all."

"Si, General. It seems we surprised everyone but ourselves. Contrary to King Arthur's original thought, might does not make right; instead right makes might as we have proven time and again in this revolution.

"So it would seem Comandante. I know we have lost the war. You and M-26-7 will win. There is no will on the part of the army to resist but they will fight, as is their duty. That is unless we can create a formula that will end it."

"Well, we can save a lot of officers and men who committed no crime. I suggest that you have the garrison in Santiago de Cuba revolt in order to give shape to a civilian-military movement in cooperation with the rebel army. When this happens, within 24 hours Batista will no longer be in power."

"I will agree to this of course. I would also like to personally go to Havana to arrange for my brother and his troops to also surrender so that when you arrive it will be peaceful."

Rafael leaned over and whispered in Fidel's ear and he responded to his plea.

"And if you go to Havana I want you to guarantee that Batista will not escape. You are not to talk to the United States Embassy or anyone in the United States Government. We do not want a coup. Those are our conditions to let you go."

"I give you my word as an officer that it will happen as you wish."

The surrender was to happen in seven days. They used that time to prepare to march and to make contingency plans if something went wrong. As the day of the proposed surrender in Santiago came and went, Fidel knew Cantillo had lied. To have someone you respect, even if it's the respect earned as a worthy opponent, lie to you so blatantly causes one to lose confidence in his fellow man. Fidel was very disappointed by this betrayal. It meant the war would go on for another three months and many lives would be lost on both sides that could have been preserved. Raul, Che and Camilo Cienfuegos were sent west to sever the island in two parts before traveling on to Havana. Rafael went with Fidel to Santiago de Cuba with 1200 well-equipped men. In Santiago Batista had a force of 5000, by far the best odds the Rebels had in the war. The best equipment went east with the other three columns. As always Fidel had a strategy that included plan A and plan B. Plan A would minimize casualties, plan B included taken by force.

First Fidel tried plan A, "Before we initiate a battle I want to meet with the commander in Santiago, Colonel Rego Rubido. Maybe he will prove to be more honorable than Cantillo."

Fidel sent an emissary to the barracks to arrange a meeting. Colonel Rubido agreed and met Fidel on the road leading to the town.

"Hola, Colonel Rubido, May I offer you a Cohiba?"

"Gracias, Comandante Castro, I didn't know you were so well provisioned in the mountains."

"We have found many useful things after some of our battles. We try to make use of everything and waste nothing, especially the finest cigars in the world."

"Of course. You did not ask to meet to discuss cigars, I am sure. What do you propose?"

"I do not propose anything Colonel. But I thought you should know what Commander Cantillo had proposed to us."

"Go on, por favor."

"General Cantillo had agreed that the war was lost for Batista. He asked if I knew a way to preserve as many officers and soldiers as we could. I proposed to him that if he could persuade you to revolt, others would follow and the war would be over in a matter of days. Unfortunately that option has passed."

"Why has that passed? If we surrender would that not bring about the end for Batista?"

"Of course if you surrendered it would preserve your officers and men but the coordinated military and civilian revolt is no longer possible. It would help end the war sooner but not as quick as it would have as a joint effort."

"Would you allow me and some of my men to join M-26-7 if we surrendered?"

"We would interview them and if they wanted to be part of the revolution for the right reasons we would welcome you and your men."

"It is done. We will honor the dishonorable Cantillo's agreement and revolt. Santiago de Cuba is yours, Comandante Castro."

Fidel knew this would end his fighting in the Revolucion. His troops could not possibly catch up with Raul, Che and Camilo before they arrived in Havana. Conceding that fact, Fidel consigned himself to meeting as many of his followers as possible as he traveled to Havana. It took Raul, Che and Camilo another month before Che led the way into Havana. At the last minute Batista, several members of his government, and $300 million dollars left Cuba in three aircraft. Cantillo was found at the Presidential Palace attempting to take over in a military coup. His supporters abandoned him when Che appeared and he was arrested. It was several more days and many speeches before Fidel could reach Havana. When he finally arrived, more than one million supporters cheering in the streets greeted him. The easy part for Castro was now over. Socializing and protecting Cuba from outside intervention would prove to be the most daunting task of the Revolución and M-26-7.

Chapter 18
A NEW BEGINNING
HAVANA
1959

Rafael had never seen Fidel this mad, and to make it worse Rafael was the reason he was mad. His eyes and brows were slanted and there was not a hint of a smile on his face. His immediate reaction was he was letting his leader down but Rafael still had unfinished business. Fidel continued, "What do you mean you don't want to be in government, Rafael? Cuba needs you. I need you. You have served Cuba very well in the last two years. If you do not want to have a cabinet post for which you are very qualified, then at least stay and help me with the design and organization of the government. It is not an easy task to organize from nothing into something worthwhile that serves all of the Cuban people, not just the privileged. I know you want to hunt for Batista, but that can wait. Cuba is more important. "

"El Jefe, I do not want to disappoint you. However, you know I joined to see Batista pay for what he did to not only my family but also 20,000 other innocent Cubans. It is true that I also adopted M-26-7 and its desires for a better Cuba, but I can't let Batista go."

"I also wanted Batista to stand trial, and if not for Cantillo's lies he would have. However, to waste energy for revenge when so much can now be done for Cuba is too selfish. Cuba needs an education system, Cuba needs a medical system, Cuba needs to shutdown the casinos, the drug trafficking, the prostitution, and stop being the bordello for the rich. Pinar del Rio and the tobacco plantations have only partially recovered from Batista's attack. They could use some help and you are the perfect choice to head the Ministry of Tobacco."

"I'm sorry, El Jefe, but I cannot go back to Pinar del Rio; it is too soon."

"Then stay and help me directly. My English is not good enough to use in a public forum. A trusted interpreter would be invaluable to me. Someone with your perspective and knowledge of the United States can help with stabilizing Cuba's relationship with the Super Power."

"I am surprised you would consider that, Fidel. The Americans supplied Batista and tried to defeat you during the revolution and yet you want to make peace?"

"Rafael, it is the way of the world. In order to survive, a third world country such as Cuba must be aligned with either the United States or the Soviet Union. To protect Cuba from the other super power, this must be done. The Communists also supported Batista in the revolution. They controlled the major labor unions in Cuba. The general strike that helped motivate Batista to give up was done in spite of the Communist leaders urging people not to strike. I have to choose the Soviet Union or the United States and I choose the United States. I have received an invitation from the American Society of Newspaper Editors to come to the United States and give several speeches. It is customary for the United States President to invite traveling dignitaries from other countries to a meeting at the White House. I want to use this meeting to sign a document that I will furnish to stabilize our relationship and to agree to aid and support each other in any struggle with the Soviet Union. I will need an interpreter that I can trust. I need you for that. I am a socialist, Rafael, not a Communist. I believe a treaty of support with the United States will give Cuba its best chance to survive as an independent and free country. I do not want anything for myself, I want only for Cuba to be a free country with opportunities for everyone, not just the elite. I want all children to be educated, not just the children of the elite. I want all Cubans to have access to medical care, not just the elite. I want all homes to have electricity, telephones and inside plumbing, not just the richest. I want all Cubans to have the opportunity to be landowners and own the fields they work, not just the big American companies. This is my dream, Rafael. This is my vision of the new Cuba. Help me; help Cuba achieve these things, Rafael, as you helped make her free. I am not asking for a lifetime commitment; at least stay for now. Revenge can wait, Cuba cannot."

"El Jefe it is impossible to tell you no. I will consider this and let you know tomorrow."

"Gracias, Rafael, I will see you at your convenience tomorrow. As you always have, I know you will do the right thing."

Rafael knew he was just delaying the inevitable. He had gained too much respect for Fidel Castro to reject his request. He also loved Cuba and wanted only what was best for her. He hated Batista for killing his family and his love, Isabel, but he had no plan that would fulfill his need for revenge. He had been told the US would not let Batista land so that was something.

In addition, he knew Castro would not let Batista escape justice if that were feasible. Rafael knew he could not replace his loved ones, and to help Cuba in any small way was his duty, and what they would have wanted him to do if they were alive. With or without his revenge, he promised himself that eventually he would return to Pinar del Rio to grow tobacco, but not yet.

As both men knew he would, Rafael acquiesced to Fidel. "I will do whatever small part I can contribute for now, El Jefe. I will go with you to the United States if that is your desire as long as we do not visit Tampa. As you know I am not welcome in Ybor, but I reserve the right to go after Batista later, if there is any possibility that I can get to him. Agreed?"

"Agreed. As an added precaution when we travel to the United States, you will use the name Rafael Gomez, which is also your legal name. After two years of fighting and struggle the bearded Rafael Gomez does not look anything like the young Rafael Moreno from Ybor."

"Thank-you El Jefe. Will you take the position of President in Cuba's new government?"

"No, Rafael. Now that the revolution is over, military commanders cannot be allowed to occupy political office. We have to remain the moral guardian of the revolution. Our duty is to ensure that the promises to the people are kept. Our primary responsibility is to re-establish democracy. To adopt economic and social reforms to benefit the Cuban people; agrarian reform, urban reform need to be established within the rule of law. I will be in charge of the Army and defenses for Cuba. We, M-26-7, have appointed Manuel Urrutia to be president. Manuel had been a magistrate that was against Batista and had actually acquitted revolutionaries that came before him. We, M-26-7, have chosen the lawyer and my former teacher at the University, Jose

Miro Cardona, to be Prime Minister. I believe that if we created an army with twelve men, which never abandoned a wounded fighter nor struck a prisoner, then we are the ones who should lead in the affairs of Cuba. However, we want only the best men, the most qualified men, in these important positions. Of all our compañeros only Raul, Che, and myself will have positions in the new government. The people of Cuba will have the true power."

El Jefe's statements made Rafael recall what happened when they had first arrived in Havana after the war. Fidel was informed that guns and ammunitions had been stolen from the Havana Armory. "I remember the way you handled the stolen guns and armaments from the Havana armory when you arrived in Havana. You asked the people who would steal guns and to fight whom. The revolution is over; there is no need for guns and armaments. The people were so outraged they demanded the return of the armaments. You were able to get them returned with no bloodshed by appealing to the people."

"Like I said, Rafael, the people will have the true power in Cuba. We have to listen and meet their expectations or they should replace us in the same manner we replaced so many before us that only wanted control out of greed. It will be hard for some to believe, but I did not fight this revolution for personal benefit, I fought this war only for the people of Cuba."

The first three months of the new government were very tough. Before leaving Cuba, Batista had raided the State Treasury. It was estimated that he stole at least $300 million dollars from the government, plus all of his monthly payments he had received from the casinos through Lansky and Trafficante. In his seven years of power, it was estimated that he could have received as much as $700 million that he put into Swiss accounts. The tax system was left in place so that helped some, but times were hard. The casinos had been closed and the money confiscated, but after three days, they were allowed to reopen as long as they only employed Cubans and that no Cuban would be allowed to gamble. The confiscated money was not returned. The Casinos didn't really care as this was still less than Batista demanded as graft.

All of the high-ranking members of the National Crime Syndicate such as Meyer Lansky had left with Batista or at the same time, except for Santo Trafficante Jr. Santo thought he would not be touched since he had contributed to Castro's Revolution. To his surprise, he was arrested, his money confiscated and his drug pipeline was shut down. His personal loss was over $13 million dollars. Systems were set in place to make education not only available but also mandatory for every child in Cuba. The University was ramped up to educate enough doctors to support Cuba's new socialized medical program. Many Cubans were going to school for the first time in their lives. Castro's system allowed everyone in Cuba, citizen or not, to receive free medical care. The agrarian land reform consisted of making previously unused government land available for ownership to anyone that would work the land. For the first time peasants who had only been able to work someone else's land were now able to own and work their own land. With everything that was changing and all of the planning required to make the changes effective, the time to travel to the United States came very fast. Even so, Fidel, Rafael and the rest of the party thought they were ready and prepared. It was time, Fidel thought, to enlist the US into a partnership that he envisioned would protect

Cuba from any possible invasion initiated by the Soviet Union or its allies. All he had to do was get President Eisenhower to sign the treaty he would bring with him and Cuba's autonomy would be insured for the next 100 years. The very thought made Fidel Castro smile. He could not imagine any scenario that would cause the US to reject his offer of friendship and unity against the Soviet Union.

Chapter 19
UNITED STATES
1959

"God damn it! Ike, you can't play golf in North Carolina with a Head of State coming to visit. You have to invite him to the White House for at least a talk if not a dinner," said Richard Millhouse Nixon. Ike, you're not a politician and never will be, he thought to himself. What would you have done without me? You may have been a great general but in politics, you don't know your ass from a hole in the ground. You're all spit and polish with no stomach for hard political fights. I don't know how you became a five star general. You must have been a great soldier to get there with no will for political infighting.

"Bull shit, Dick. He isn't Head of State officially. He made himself head of the army not president. Urrutia is president of Cuba. I want you to put him in his place. His agrarian reform talk is not good for US business interests in Cuba. We have spent a lot of money to control Cuba's oil and sugar industries, not to mention telephone and utilities, and he threatens to take it away. I don't care if he has a law degree from the University of Havana; he is still a peasant! Of course, if you don't think you can handle him, I'll get someone else," replied Dwight D. Eisenhower. He should have eliminated Nixon when he had the chance and not agreed to allow him on the 1956 ticket as the Vice Presidential candidate, he thought to himself. He had never liked him and his underhanded politics. He will say and do anything to win. The truth matters not to him. If he had not campaigned so hard in the 1954 Congressional races for the Republicans it would have been simple to remove him from the ticket, and Eisenhower would have too. Nixon has too many questionable friends with questionable tactics and questionable ethics for him to ever be comfortable.

I know he wants me to endorse him as the Republican presidential candidate for 1960, but I just don't know if I will. If I don't it will piss off many of the Republicans he has done favors for, but so what, it's my decision. I think I'll just wait a little longer. Give him enough rope; you never know what he might do. Hell, I should have dropped him in 1952 when it came out he had an illegal slush fund that he had maintained throughout the California elections. He proved worthy of Helen Gahagan Douglas' nickname of 'tricky dick' when he gave that damn 'Checkers speech'. I should have stuck to my gut and divested myself of 'Tricky Dick Nixon'. Not doing so may yet blow up in my face.

"Of course I can handle him, Ike. However, I will not invite anyone to the White House that wears fatigues as his dress clothes. And wrinkled ones at that! I will invite him to the Senate building and it's only appropriate that if he wears his fatigues, and I have no reason to think he won't, when he leaves he'll think he has been dressed down by the toughest drill sergeant in the Army! If he doesn't want to play ball with us, his administration will be short lived."

"I'm fine with that. We already have the Trujillo thing that should end his government anyway. If he is a Communist, we let Trujillo invade Cuba; he hates Castro anyway. If he's not and you think he will work with us, we will call it off with Trujillo. That son of a bitch has become an embarrassment with his brutality in the Dominican Republic anyway. We don't need the association unless there is a positive gain. Call Dulles and either push him on Trujillo's invasion or tell him to back off. Tell him I would like to have Castro gone while I'm still President if that is our direction."

Painting him as a Communist shouldn't be hard for you, Ike thought. After all, that's how you won your Congressional seat and you did it again when you ran for the Senate. Neither one of your opponents was really a Communist, but it didn't stop you from saying they were, and that was enough for you to win both times. I really hate that politics is played that way. I guess I wouldn't have won if you hadn't attacked the Democrats so vigorously in our campaigns. I wouldn't do that type of negative campaigning, but for you it was no problem. I hate that kind of smear politics. I hate even worse that it is effective with the American public. Elections should be won on merit, not slander.

"On second thought, Ike, this will be fun. It's time someone told Castro the facts of life in our backyard and how to play our game. If he wants to play here, he has to play by our rules or he will go the way of every other dictator in Latin America that did not accommodate us. That should be easy for Dulles and Trujillo, if need be. After all, I think Dulles invented the term 'plausible deniability' and with Trujillo, we need that. No matter what we cause to happen, we must maintain plausible deniability. If you can't positively prove we were involved, then we weren't!"

"Fine with me Dick. Make it happen, but insure our position of plausible deniability of course," Eisenhower said as he left the room. Ike knew he was tired of Washington. His two heart attacks had really sapped him of his energy to play the political game. Politics were important in the military. However, it seemed different then. Merit was just as important. A degenerate gambler like Nixon could never have made it in the Military. He thought the 'Cuban Mystique' has enveloped him. Hell, he was even down there a week before their first election. In addition, that Cuban friend of his, Charles 'Bebe' Rebozo. What kind of name is 'Bebe'? It sounds like a pole dancer's name. For all Eisenhower knew they both might be associated with Meyer Lansky and his Cuban thing. He knew he was chummy with Batista.

"Enjoy your golf, Ike; I'm going to enjoy my round also. By the time I'm done, Castro won't be able to sit down for a week!" he said with a laugh.

The first stop on Castro's eleven-day trip to the United States and Canada was in Washington D.C. At the Cuban embassy, where the congregation stayed, a message from Assistant Secretary Rubottom indicated that Vice President Nixon was inviting Fidel to a meeting in the Senate Building on the 19th at 10:00 am.

"What do you think this means, Rafael?" asked Fidel.

"It means the President is snubbing you and passing you off to the Vice President. This is not appropriate protocol. It is always customary for any visiting dignitary to receive an invitation to speak with the President unless he has been called away on matters of State. We can look into this and see where he is," said Rafael.

"Not the start we wanted, but we can still work with the Vice President on the agreement for military assistance in the advent of a Soviet threat to Cuba or the United States. Am I right in thinking he has the ability to negotiate on behalf of the government?" he asked.

"I believe so, I'm not sure though."

"I'm sure if we convince him of the benefit, he can convince Eisenhower.

Now let's visit the Lincoln Memorial. I want to pay my respects to the great leader. Has someone picked up the wreath?"

"Yes, El Jefe, we have it."

After Fidel left the wreath at the Memorial, reporters had gathered for an impromptu news conference. As planned, Fidel wanted to try his English and see if it were possible to effectively communicate in English. He and Rafael had been practicing, but Rafael was afraid he would not be able to express himself with the same level of charisma in English that he never failed to have when he spoke in Spanish.

"Mr. Castro are you enjoying your visit to the United States?" asked one reporter.

"Yes, very much," Fidel answered.

"Are you a Communist?" asked another reporter.

"What?" Fidel was surprised at this question. He had never indicated he was a communist.

"It's a simple question, Mr. Castro, Are you a Communist?"

"No, I am a socialist and believe in democracy for Cuba," Fidel said.

"Aren't Raul Castro, your brother, and Che Guevara, Communist? And aren't they in your government?"

"Yes, but I don't understand your line of questioning."

"As communists, Raul Castro and Che Guevara being in your government would indicate to us that you have at least communist sympathies, wouldn't you agree?"

"No, I am not a Communist. I am a Socialist and believe in democracy for Cuba," Fidel said again and began to walk away. He was not comfortable with the questions and his inability to converse the way he wanted in English.

"I will practice my English so next time I will be able to speak more freely," he added as he continued to walk away.

"I don't blame you Mr. Castro, I would be uncomfortable with communists in my government too," added one reporter.

After they returned to the car and drove away from the Lincoln Memorial, Fidel said in Spanish, "Ok, my English has to get better before I engage in that kind of rhetoric with reporters. Why do they think I'm communist? The Cuban Communist party has never been a supporter of mine and I have never supported them."

"That's true El Jefe, but you have been talking agrarian reform and you did lower the cost of electricity and telephone service in the first weeks after the revolution. Both of these things indicate, at least to the United States companies that own the power plants and the phone service, that you are indifferent to their profit margin. Ever since McCarthy and his witch hunt for communists in government the term 'red baiting' has become an acceptable and successful attack that opposition parties in the US can use to diminish the popularity of any politician. Even if it's not true, it has worked. Communism in the United States means the Soviet Union and is considered treason to the United States citizen."

"Do the people understand, Rafael, that Communism is an economic system like capitalism or socialism and not a government? The United States has a problem with the Soviet Union because, like them, they want to dominate third world countries with the same type of imperialism. It would not matter what type of economic system the Soviet Union had, they would still be opposed to the US because they are competing with them for world domination. Even if the Soviet Union were a capitalist block instead of a communist block, the mutual desire for world domination through third world imperialism would be the same and therefore they would still be enemies," said a clearly frustrated Fidel.

"No, Fidel, the American citizen does not understand this. The United States government has convinced them that the Soviet Union is bad because it's communist, not because of the competition over third world countries. To explain it that way would require the United States to admit that they also covet the third world's resources and want to exploit them with their brand of imperialism. You have upset the apple cart, El Jefe. You want Cuba to belong to Cubans. How selfish of you!"

"I still believe that a third world country must be aligned with either the US or the Soviet Union for protection from the other. Cuba cannot defend itself against either one without the protection of the other. At least not right now, perhaps someday, but not now. An alliance is imperative, Rafael. Furthermore, the alliance must allow Cuba to be free of imperialism, by either super power. Otherwise the revolution is a failure."

"Let me explain the US concept of communism that I was taught living in Ybor," said Rafael. "It might help you to understand the US politicians' and reporters' perspective. Following World War II, Russia acquired several countries in Europe out of fear the Allies would attack them; they needed a buffer to avoid a direct line of attack from Europe. The countries they acquired offered that buffer. The Allies, led by the US

and Britain, condemned this action, even though they would
have probably done the same if they had been in Russia's position. Sixty million people died in WWII, 30 million were
from the Soviet Union. They had a reason to fear the West and
another war. By contrast, the US lost 420,000, Great Britain
lost 450,000, and Germany, who started the war, lost 7 million. In direct contrast to what one might expect after the war,
the bad guys, according to the US and her allies, were not the
Germans who started the war, nor the Japanese who bombed
Pearl Harbor; instead, the Soviet Union became a target of fear
and hate. Communism and anything associated with it became
a source of distrust, fear and a target of politicians and the media. To be communist was tantamount to treason in the United
States even though it's an economic system and not a government. According to the mongers, if one were Communist, he
surely was anti American and worthy only of contempt and
ridicule. The attitude of the times was that you could not
be American if you tolerated anything Communist. In other
words, anything American was good and wholesome, and anything Communist was bad and unholy."

"That is ridiculous, Rafael. The American people would
never believe such a preposterous notion."

"I'm sorry El Jefe, but that is the propaganda that was spread
after the war and is still being promulgated by today's US politicians. That's why those reporters asked you about Raul and
Che. To associate with Communist is to be Communist in this
Country. Americans are wonderful people, but I'm afraid they
are also gullible and believe everything their government tells
them. This is no different from you and the Cuban people;
they will believe anything you tell them at face value. The
only difference I see is that you tell the people of Cuba the

truth regardless of outcome, while the US Government tells the Americans what they want them to believe to suit their purposes, indifferent to the truth. It seems to the American politician not getting caught in a lie is the same thing as telling the truth."

"That explains a lot, Rafael, gracias. I have always thought that for a country to do evil things its people must believe it is doing good. Without the acceptance of the people no government can survive for long and no Revolución will be successful."

Fidel decided that from then on, his speeches would be given in Spanish and he would keep his English to a minimum, only using it in less confrontational settings. The reporters at the Lincoln Memorial served to alert Fidel to the possible confrontational attitude he might receive from the US Government. He enjoyed himself at the Bronx Zoo in New York and at the baseball game he was able to attend. He ate hotdogs and hamburgers at Yankee Stadium and seemed to interact well with the fans and vendors at the park. The press enjoyed taking his picture and he seemed to relax. He gave speeches at Harvard, the Council on Foreign Affairs in New York City, and one in Washington to the American Society of Newspaper Editors. In all of them Fidel was quick to point out his desire for a democratic Cuba and made it a point to reiterate that he was not a Communist. He acknowledged that he was a socialist but differentiated between the two for emphasis. Fidel acknowledged to himself convincing Nixon to accept his treaty might be harder than he first thought. He had no idea that the US was so manic and seemingly paranoid about Communism. Were they so insecure about Capitalism that they were afraid it might not stand up to an even fight against Communism? They can't be, he thought. Communism is no good. Capitalism has its disadvantages also in that greed usually leads the way instead of need or reason. A socialist democracy is by far the best mix for any country, including the US and Cuba. Maybe that is the fear. If the people compare the different types of economic systems they just might decide for themselves that Capitalism is not the best. Better than Communism but not better than Democratic Socialism. He knew what his goal had to be for all of his remaining speeches. He had to teach the US people that he was not Communist and hope it reached Nixon before they met. Otherwise, he was in trouble.

Castro's best speech on the trip occurred in Washington at the American Society of Newspaper Editors.

"In the Cuban socialist state the people are the agent of change; in a Communist society the government is the agent for change. In a Communist state, no religion is allowed; in Cuba, we have freedom of religion. In Cuba we invite private investment; in a communist state that is forbidden. In Cuba, we believe in a democratic state that can coexist with socialism, like in most of Europe and in Scandinavia. In Communism, a dictator is usually in charge and makes all of the decisions for the people. In Cuba, the people will always have the control. In a communist state, no one can even own the house they live in; in Cuba, we want everyone to be landowners and to develop their house according to their needs. In reality, all developed countries have some form of socialism, even the United States. In America you have socialized military, police, firefighters, voting system, justice system, the FCC, food stamps, parks and recreation services, public schools and public libraries, just to name a few. Cuba wants all of these socialist programs along with free medical care for everyone based upon need, not the ability to pay."

Apparently, not all Americans thought of the United States as a socialist country even in these programs, as some boos were heard when Fidel pointed out the United States socialist programs. At the end of his speeches and explanation of socialist Cuba, he would also say that in the event of hostilities with the Soviet Union, Cuba would always side with the United States.

The reason Fidel accepted this trip so early after the fighting was over, with so much still needed at home, was the opportunity to meet with the President and solidify this position with a formal commitment. The fact that President Eisenhower had not been called away out of need but had chosen to play golf in North Carolina to avoid Fidel's visit was disturbing. It seemed that the press enjoyed covering the President's golf outings, which made his choice obvious. As scheduled on 19 April 1959 Fidel met with Vice President Nixon in his old office in the Russell Senate Office Building. As the two entered the office, Nixon put his arm around Castro for a picture. That was the last friendly thing Nixon would do.

"Please have a seat, what should I call you?" asked Nixon.

"You may call me Fidel, what should I call you?"

"You may call me Mr. Vice President," replied Nixon. Raising a folder, he began, "I have an FBI report that indicates you have two communists in your government, your brother Raul and Che Guevara. We don't appreciate communists in government. This would imply that either you are also a communist or you at least are a communist sympathizer. Is this true?"

Rafael was noticeably uncomfortable as he translated the conversations back and forth. He could tell from Fidel's facial features that he was angry at these insults and that his English allowed him to understand Nixon's statements before Rafael said anything.

"No, neither is true. I am not a communist; I belong to the Ortodoxo Party. I have never been supported or endorsed by the

Communist party in Cuba. I believe in socialism and democracy for Cuba."

Without acknowledging Castro's statements Nixon continued, "Your recent price cuts of the Cuban Electric Company would seem to indicate that might not be true."

"The Cuban Electric Company is owned by the American Foreign Power Company and has extorted the Cuban people with exorbitant pricing condoned by Batista. It is time that all Cubans have access to electricity, indoor plumbing and telephone service, not just the elite."

"And you expect American companies to absorb these costs?"

"I do not expect the companies to sell for a loss, nor do I expect the Cuban people to pay more than is fair for these services. Batista may have allowed American companies to rape and pillage Cuba but I will not! In the US, government sets the electricity price for all citizens, is this not the same?"

Again, Nixon ignored Castro's comments and question, "You claim to want democracy. Do you intend to hold elections anytime soon?"

"I will hold elections when political parties have been developed and the electoral process established."

"America wants to help Cuba because of the condition in which the country has been left."

"And when would you send this aid?"

"Right after your first general election."

Fidel knew Nixon was intentionally provoking him. He also knew the results of this meeting were determined before he entered the room. He concluded with, "Democracy is more than just a word; there can be no democracy where there is hunger, unemployment, and injustice."

After three hours of insults and threats, Castro had the message. He didn't even bother to discuss mutual defense. There was no need to show the treaty Castro wanted. Nixon made it very clear that he wanted Fidel gone. Nixon's hostility gave away his agenda. He was the axe man and wanted nothing less than the extinction of the Castro government. Well, thought Castro, the meeting definitely let him know where he stood with this super power and what they think of the current Cuban Government. It might as well be a sewage plant with a broken mixer.

After the Cuban party left, Nixon contemplated the meeting. He knew Castro had gotten the message, but would he do anything about it? Hell no, he thought, the man is too ideological. There is nothing more dangerous than a man who can't be bought. How dare Castro interrupt his casino investment with his friend of many years Bebe Rebozo. Not to mention the loss that he will have from The United Fruit Company. Hell, Allen has his own financial reasons to hate this peasant, since he sits on the United Fruit Company's board. He picked up his phone and called Dulles.

"Allen, Dick Nixon here."

"Hello Dick, how's the golf game?"

"Never good, you know that. Listen I'm calling for Ike. This Castro bum is a problem. Ike doesn't care how it's done but he wants his government gone from Cuba before he leaves office. Can you do that with Trujillo and our contingency plan? Covert funds only with plausible deniability of course."

"I don't see why not. Let me look into it and I'll get back to you."

"I know you can do this. We are looking for something like we did in Iran in '53 and Guatemala in '54. We want Fidel and Raul gone and a suitable replacement that will follow our rules. Castro is talking agrarian land reform that will hurt United Fruit, which we cannot allow. Instead of a straight invasion by Trujillo, let's see if we can't get some counterrevolutionaries involved and create a new Cuban government that Trujillo can recognize and come to their aid."

Dulles knew exactly what Nixon wanted. In Iran the CIA had Mohammad Mossadeq arrested and put into prison until his death and replaced him with Faziolla Zahedi. The 1953 CIA led coup was called Operation Ajax. The new Shaw was brutal but acceptable because he stopped the nationalization of American oil companies in Iran. In Guatemala, Jacobo Arbenz was going to create an agrarian land reform that would have hurt the United Fruit Company so Dulles had taken a direct interest in the outcome. Even though Arbenz had been democratically elected, he had to go and was replaced by a military dictator, Colonel Carlos Castillo Armas. Both plans had worked and could easily be duplicated in Cuba, thought Dulles.

"I got it Dick, no problem. I'll let you know when I have a plan."

"Thanks, Allen."

"Anytime, Dick, best regards to Ike and tell him I said Castro who?"

"He'll like that Allen."

Chapter 20
CUBA AND COMMUNISM 1959

"Rafael, no one can know about the meeting with Nixon; the rudeness, the insults. If people were to know, they would think I can be bullied. I cannot allow this. Because I now have to make nice with the Soviets. The Soviets cannot know they were second choice. Nixon and Eisenhower have made it clear they want me out because I will not play American ball. They don't know me; they don't know what I want or what I'm going to do. From now on, it will stay that way. Once I have a pact with the Soviets, they will make life very uncomfortable for Cuba. However, I must do this without falling victim to Soviet imperialism. One is just as bad as the other. The world knows what the CIA did in Guatemala and in Iran. They will now try to do that here with me. Cuba will have an intelligence service also. Nevertheless, it will be a long time before it is effectual. I must have another source into the CIA and what they will plan."

"The secret to being a good translator is not remembering what was said. I remember nothing of importance about Nixon, El Jefe, sorry."

"It's ok Rafael I forgive you, but next time try harder," he said with a smile.

"How do you feel about a deal with the Devil?" Rafael asked.

"I don't believe in the devil, Rafael. What are you thinking?"

"You have someone in Cuba that I know has connections with the CIA, but I don't know if you can trust him."

"Go on."

"Santo Trafficante and his associates have had several dealings with the CIA that I know about. How extensive and how much information he could give you, I don't know. "

"What kind of dealings?"

"Drugs and arms dealing are the two I know about. When I was confined to a room in Ybor awaiting their decision on what to do with me, I overheard father and son discussing a drug and arms delivery that involved the CIA. If they knew I heard them, I would not be here today. They take keeping secrets very seriously in that family."

"Why would he help us?"

"The only motivation I can think of is money."

"When you talk to him find out, if you can, what it would take. When we closed the casinos, he was arrested and we confiscated several million dollars of his. He was only in jail for three days. When we decided to reopen the casinos, he was released but we kept his money. You can decide when you see him if you want to tell him he is going to be arrested again for drug trafficking. This will not be changed but he can receive favorable treatment if you see fit. You have full autonomy in dealing with him."

"Me?"

"Of course you, you have met him. I imagine he trusts you as you are an honorable man. I, of course, cannot be seen having any contact with him. That's obvious and to do otherwise would compromise his ability to get information."

"Very well. I'll see him tomorrow."

Rafael knew the logical place to meet Trafficante was in Santo's San Souci Casino. The casinos had been closed by M-26-7 for three days after the Revolucion and then reopened. The labor unions complained that many workers would be out of a job if the casinos closed; so Fidel agreed to reopen with certain restrictions. Only Cubans could be hired, and no Cuban was allowed to gamble. Arms and drug trafficking were closed down, as well as the bordellos, loan sharking and other graft controlled by Organized Crime. Rafael told the guard in front of his office that he was there to see Santo.

"What is your last name?" the guard asked.

"My last name is not important. Don Trafficante knows me as Rafael from Ybor."

"Wait here and I'll ask if he has time for you."

As he waited Rafael contemplated what he was about to do. He had promised his Great Uncle, he would never accept anything from Trafficante, as it would forever put him in his debt. Now he was voluntarily going to propose just that. He knew the deal would be made; it was a good deal for Santo. Would it be equally as good for Castro? He hoped so. Especially since it was his idea. Unlike his situation in Ybor, he no longer cared if it was a good deal for himself. Life without a family, without his Isabel was only part of a life for Rafael. Thirty minutes later, he was taken into Santo's office. The office looked like a typical lawyer's office with mahogany furniture and mahogany bookshelves. Two leather chairs were in front of his desk, which appeared to be raised so he would look down at his guests. "Have a seat, Rafael. You may leave us Carlos."

After the guard left and they were alone Santo looked at Rafael and studied his face before talking. "I never thought I would see you again Rafael, you have aged considerably since Ybor."

"Having one's entire family murdered by Batista and spending two years in the mountains fighting with Fidel will do that."

"You fought in the revolution?"

"Si"

"How well do you know Castro?" asked Santo.

"Fidel or Raul, both are important for Cuba?"

"Fidel"

"Very well. I fought alongside him in his column throughout the war. I also served as his interpreter during his trip to the United States."

"You weren't afraid to go back to the United States?"

"Well, let's just say I didn't go anywhere near Tampa. And as you said, I don't look anything like the kid from Ybor."

Santo laughed as he said, "Fidel must trust you a lot to have you interpret for him."

"No more than your father trusted me when I was in Ybor. I hope he is well and growing his grapes."

"I'm sorry to say he died from stomach cancer, Rafael. Yes he trusted you; I would have made sure you could not share our secrets."

"I thought that at the time. I was not in your family but I did believe in the omerta concept. I would never have disappointed your father whom I trusted and he trusted me. Your secrets were always safe because of your father, and I am sorry he is gone."

"That's what he said. I guess he was right. You didn't come here to talk about old times or my father. What's on your mind?"

Here was Rafael's opening. Without hesitation, he plunged ahead. He didn't know it at the time, but his life would never be the same after this meeting. "As you know, the casino business in Cuba is on its way out. It will never be the lucrative cash machine it once was, and the rest of your Cuban enterprises are gone for good."

Santo was irritated at Rafael for stating the obvious and for rubbing it in. Cuba, where he had invested so much, would never pay off. Santo knew his time in Cuba was limited and he didn't need any crap from a fringe player. "I don't need a history lesson. As long as Fidel is in power you are right; make your point."

"I want to propose a secret alliance between you and Fidel. One that will only be known by the three of us."

"You really think Fidel is going to remain in power long enough to make an alliance worthwhile? I hear the CIA is already on his tail; that he has become a stone in the Eisenhower shoe."

"More like the Nixon shoe but, yes, that is correct. That is what Fidel will ask of you. He will want information about what the United States government is going to do while he still has time to counter."

"You think I know that kind of information?"

"No, I know you know that kind of information just like you knew the CIA was already plotting against Fidel. And at the very least you know how to access more of that kind of information."

"Ok, maybe that's true but why should I help Fidel? I contributed to his Revolución and in return I was arrested, had my money stolen, and he has destroyed Cuba for my family."

"Yes and no. He has definitely changed the landscape but certain opportunities may be made available to a trusted friend that are more valuable than ever before."

"Stop talking in fuckin' riddles. What do you mean?"

"Cuba could be made a fail safe drug route as long as no drugs are sold in Cuba. In addition your thirteen million dollars that was confiscated, not stolen, could be returned."

"Some of my associates will not forgive Castro for taking their money when he closed the casinos. If they know I got mine back, I'm a dead man."

"That's one of the reasons you will be arrested by Fidel, and imprisoned in Trescornia Camo. You will be on the death list for drug trafficking, which by the way Fidel knows you are still doing. At the last minute, your sentence will be commuted and you will be exiled to the United States. You will appear in Ybor to be broke to complete the cover. Meanwhile your thirteen million dollars can be put into a Swiss bank. On the other hand, your arrest will happen for drug trafficking. As you are guilty, I'm sure the Cuban judicial system will find you guilty and then the only way you will be taken off the death list is when you are executed, capisce?"

Trafficante's mouth dropped open and he laughed vociferously. This son of a bitch fringe player knows how to make a deal. "Rafael you were my father's favorite and I see why. I always thought his fondness was misguided but now maybe not, as you have made me an offer I cannot refuse Italian style. You learned a lot in Ybor. Was this your idea or Castro's?"

"That doesn't matter Don Santo. It's Fidel's now and it is a win-win for both of you."

"I don't know why you choose not to join the family. You would have made a great Italian, Rafael" As he said this, he began laughing again and shaking his head. "There is just one thing, Rafael. The only way to insure this is known by only us three is for you to come back to Ybor and serve as a messenger when I have news for Fidel. To entrust anyone else is too much risk. I'm a dead man if any one else knows about this."

"I have already told Fidel that you would make that demand if you agreed to the bargain. I have no family left in Cuba. My Isabel is also dead. My family plantation is no more. I don't have any ties to Cuba that would prevent permanent residence in Ybor. There is only my agreement with you to never return. Rafael Moreno is dead."

"As you have connections in the Cuban government what name would you care to use? I can insure dual citizenship with the United States if you like. I can also bring you in as the new manager of the Fleur de Lis Cigar Factory. By the way it is now a brick building and less likely to burn."

Rafael and Fidel had discussed this probability. So far, everything was as they predicted. Rafael did not want to go back to Ybor, but he knew it was the only way to insure the deal worked. He did not trust Santo and would have to be on his guard at all times, however the arrangement just might help Fidel survive long enough to have his own intelligence service up and running. Rafael answered in the only way possible. "That would be great, I would like to stay in the cigar business and I hate fires. I will not get involved in any of your illegal activities. I will be there to deliver messages to Fidel; that is all. As far as a name, how about Alejandro Fernando Mendez Suarez? That's Alejandro after Fidel, Fernando after my oldest brother, Mendez after Isabel, and Suarez I will keep for my mother. I will go by Alejandro Mendez. Do we have a deal Don Santo?"

"We have a deal Alejandro Mendez." Both men stood and shook hands to seal the deal. Santo was very pleased, especially with the drug route and the guarantee of safety. All he had to do was provide information that he would probably know anyway.

It was a good deal indeed, he thought. Rafael's only reservation was offering the drug route up front without making Santo ask for it. He and Fidel intended to save it as a last offering and only if necessary. Fidel and Rafael had argued over the route, as Fidel didn't want drugs going through Cuba. Rafael had insisted it would be necessary to get Santo's cooperation.

"You will be arrested in the next few days; it should seem to be a surprise."

"One thing Alejandro. My daughter is getting married in Havana. If I am arrested before that, can I attend?"

"Already with the favors," Rafael said laughing "Of course. You may even receive visitors in Trescornia Camo's courtyard. It is very pleasant. And to save Cuba money why don't you have your meals brought over from the San Souci?"

"Sounds great, I can use a vacation. Will you visit there?"

"No, after you are exiled, I, Alejandro Mendez, will meet you in Ybor. You will hear nothing else from anyone until that time. The one exception will be someone will pass you a note with a number. That will be the Swiss account with thirteen million dollars. I would recommend you have the money transferred as soon as possible. If something happens to Fidel, that is yours to keep. The drug route through Cuba is only good for as long as he is alive and if your information is of value. When the information loses value, you will lose the drug route."

"Well played, Alejandro. That's motivation enough. I am surprised you are returning my money before you have any information from me."

"You may call it a good faith gesture and to make it an Italian gesture, we know where you live, capisce?"

Chapter 21
SANTO'S RELEASE CUBA 1959

Santo Trafficante Jr. was arrested two days after his meeting with Rafael and transported to Trescornia Camo.   During his stay in the Cuban prison, four assassins tried to gain access and kill him. Castro intervened, had them deported, and told them not to try that again on Cuban soil. Santo also attended his daughter's wedding in Havana along with a last minute invitee and reported friend of the bride, Alejandro Mendez.

"Thanks for coming, Alejandro. Please thank Fidel for his intervention with the four that intended to whack me. I know who they are and will deal with them and some others when I return to Ybor. That's not why you received the invitation. I have reliable information that Trujillo has raised an invasion force to attack Cuba from the Dominican Republic. They have the backing of Richard Nixon and the CIA. Trujillo has enlisted William Morgan and Gutierrez Menoyo to organize ex-pat Cubans in the US to lead the invasion as if the Cubans originated it. Gerry Droller was the CIA official who met with Trujillo on behalf of Richard Nixon. My information indicated Nixon was involved in this prior to meeting Castro in April at the US Senate Building in Washington. A priest by the name of Ricardo Velazco Ordonez is involved as well, as are at least two US Embassy officials. I only have one name, Sgt. Stanley F. Wesson, at the Embassy. The name of the group sponsored by the ex Cubans is the 'White Rose' after Marti's poem who they claim to represent. In my opinion, the weakest link is either Morgan or Menoyo. The best I could get is they plan to act sometime in late July or early August. Any word on my release?"

"It shouldn't be long. I have a set of numbers for you now. Thanks for this and I'll see you in Ybor. Give my best to the bride; she is lovely." Alejandro, as he now thought of himself, pondered over the news Santo had given him. He knew Fidel would ask if he thought it was true. He could think of no reason for Santo to make this up. He was in jail, could still be executed and had nothing that Alejandro could think of to gain by a ruse. No, he thought, it had to be true. At least Santo thought it was true.

"What do you think, Alejandro? Is he fucking with us, or is this real?" asked Fidel.

"I think it is absolutely true. Santo would not give us false information. The drug route is far too valuable for him to pull a scam. If the information is not 100% accurate, I am convinced Santo believes it is true. When do you plan to release him?"

"We will let this scenario play out and then he can go. We will put pressure on Morgan and Menoyo and see what we get. They switch sides like the wind. Perhaps we can facilitate another change in direction."

At the same time that Castro was monitoring Morgan and Menoyo, trying to pressure them by making it obvious they were being followed, the US Embassy through two of its agents, Frank Sturgis and Gerry Hemming, were arming and encouraging a small youth group to try to reinforce groups fighting in the Dominican Republic against Trujillo. The ploy was explained to Trujillo who called a meeting of the OAS (Organization of American States) to condemn Cuba for exporting revolution. This in turn could be used as his justification for invading Cuba. Fred Nelson, an associate of Meyer Lansky, informed Trujillo of Morgan's demand of a million dollars to organize and train the Cuban group 'White Rose' for the combined attack on Castro. Trujillo agreed and deposited half the amount for Morgan with the rest to be paid upon completion of the mission.

William Morgan was born in Cleveland Ohio in 1928. He had fought in the Cuban Revolutionary war with the Second Front, an organization that was organized at the same time as Castro's M-27-7. The Second Front was begun by Gutierrez Menoyo to fight against Batista's brutality of the Cuban people. In the last days of the Revolucion, they joined Che in capturing Santa Clara eleven days before Batista left the country. Morgan was nicknamed El Yanqui Comandante by the Second Front soldiers, because of his rank as a Comandante. He was quoted in *The New York Times*, where he explained his position:

"I am here because I believe that the most important thing for free men to do is to protect the freedom of others. I am here so that my son, when he is grown, will not have to fight or die in a land not his own, because one man or group of men try to take his liberty from him. I am here because I believe that free men should take up arms and stand together."

"William, I am followed everywhere I go. I think it must be Fidel," said Menoyo.

"Yes, Gutierrez; I even had a shadow on my last trip to Miami. It can only be Fidel. What should we do?" asked Morgan.

"What we always do, meet with Fidel, tell him only part of the mission and wait to see what happens. We can switch again if he is overthrown. Under no circumstances do we tell him about the money."

"That sounds good. Why don't you meet with him as soon as possible?"

"No," said Menoyo, "we will both go."

Three days later, in an apartment on 11th Street in the Velado neighborhood of Havana, Menoyo and Morgan met with Fidel. Menoyo had arranged the meeting by first going to the Presidential Palace and asking for a secret meeting. "El Jefe, muchas gracias for meeting with us on such short notice and in private. William and I have been approached to assist in an invasion by Trujillo, supported by the United States. They want us to organize the 'White Rose' and 'Second Front' counterrevolutionary groups to pose as fronts so Trujillo and the US can deny participation," blurted out Menoyo.

"Thanks for bringing me this information. Why did you wait so late?" asked Fidel.

"We did not know how serious the plans were and waited until we were sure of their intent. We did not want to bother you needlessly," answered Morgan.

A very calm Fidel said, "Please continue then. What else do you know?"

"The mercenaries will land in Trinidad. A provisional government will be set up in the Escambray Mountains and there they will ask for recognition and assistance from Trujillo. In the mean time the 'White Rose' and 'Second Front' troops led by me will cut communications and ambush any troops that respond to the invasion," said Morgan

"Who will lead this Provisionary Government?" asked Fidel.

"Former Senator Arturo Hernandez Tellahexhe will be president and Dr. Cainas Milanes will be Prime Minister," answered Menoyo.

"Where will the arms for the 'White Rose' and 'Second Front' come from?" asked Fidel.

"I will bring them from Key West on my boat just prior to the start," answered Morgan.

"And of course you will inform me when that is to occur?"

"Of course, El Jefe" answered Morgan.

"In the meantime I will have some of my security men follow you to provide protection in case your comrades become suspicious. I would not want anything to happen to such noble patrons of Cuba."

"Muchas gracias, El Jefe, that is very considerate."

After Morgan and Menoyo left, Fidel asked, "Alejandro, it still seems strange to call you that, did you hear what they said?"

As Alejandro walked out of the next room he said, "Si, Fidel, and it is still strange to be called Alejandro instead of Rafael. As to Morgan and Menoyo, they know much more than they said. They did not mention Father Velazco which we also know is involved or any of the US Embassy personnel."

"I agree. Velazco is no problem. I have arranged for his driver to be one of ours so we know everything he does in Cuba. What he does in the Dominican Republic we can pretty well guess."

On August 6, 1959, Morgan left Miami with his boat loaded with weapons. Because of bad weather, he did not land at the Regla pier in Havana Bay until August 8.

"Hola, William."

"Hola, Fidel, I didn't know you would be here personally."

"Of course, let's see what you have. Forty 30 caliber machine guns, dozens of rifles and a large quantity of ammunition. Excellent, William, this will be very useful. Let's get you to Escambray as scheduled so you can call Trujillo."

The next night as one thousand counterrevolutionaries were arrested by Cuban troops, Menoyo made his call on the communications equipment provided.

"3JK calling KJB."

"3JK, come in please. KJB here. I hear you loud and clear."

"Instructions completed. I am now in the mountains fighting the communists. The American landed at the appointed spot. Now all of the weapons are in our hands. Viva Cuba libre!"

"Excellent job, Menoyo. I just received word that Sgt. Stanly Wesson from the US Embassy was arrested while trying to organize sabotage with counterrevolutionaries on behalf of Trujillo's plan. We have the electricity off in Trinidad; it is time to complete the second report, Menoyo," instructed Fidel.

"3JK calling KJB."

"3JK come in please, this is KJB."

"The Second Front is advancing on Trinidad; and we will soon have the airport."

"Good work 3JK, I'll send the next plane with my personal envoy."

"3JK, this is KJB, come in."

KJB this is 3JK, over."

"Get me the American right now," said a furious Trujillo.

After a short pause, Morgan picked up the microphone.

"The American speaking, over."

"The press agencies are saying that everything is a disaster! They say everyone has been captured and you are about to be also. What the fuck is going on?" shouted Trujillo.

"Remember, Mr. President who we are dealing with here. The news is being fabricated by the Castro government. You know how good he is at propaganda, always has been. He's probably gambling that this news will stop the reinforcements that he assumes are on the way. Since our last transmission, we have succeeded in taking Trinidad airport and it is safe to land there. Send the next plane there and see for yourself."

"KJB out," Trujillo ended without commitment.

At 7 pm, a C-47 landed at the Trinidad airport. The door opened without shutting down its engines. When Father Velazco stepped out the peasants on the ground greeted him with shouts of "Viva Trujillo." In reality, they were Castro soldiers.

Father Velazco saluted several officials who applauded him and said, "I will report your good work and send more supplies and personnel. Viva Cuba libre!" As he departed, he could hear machine gun fire in the distance. When he returned to Trujillo he reported the good news," Presidente, we have indeed taken Trinidad. Castro's fall will not be long."

"Excellent, Father, let the flights continue on schedule," ordered Trujillo.

On August 13, another message arrived.

"3JK calling KJB."

"3JK, this is KJB."

"The troops of the Second Front have captured Manicaragua and almost had Santa Clara. Fidel still has the Soledad Sugar Mill, but we have Rio Hondo and Caonao. We must take advantage of our demoralizing victories and land your troops immediately. It should make the end inevitable. Cuba Libre is within reach!"

"I will send the troops when the situation is more favorable. Have Morgan take Santa Clara if possible. For now, I will send another plane with a personal emissary, military supplies and advisers. Great work, my friend. KJB out."

"What do you think, Alejandro?" asked Fidel.

"I think we have convinced him Morgan is winning without his troops. He is probably thinking he can save millions of dollars by not sending them and just letting Morgan win this for him."

"I think you're right. We will set up to capture this plane with its contents and call it a success. Viva Cuba Libre, Alejandro!"

"Viva Cuba Libre, Fidel! And Viva the information that made this possible," said Alejandro.

"Indeed. When this is over make arrangements to send him to the States. Trafficante will have more access to information in Ybor."

"Si, El Jefe." As Fidel walked away, his laughter was infectious and his troops joined his mini celebration with celebratory gunshots in the air.

When the plane landed, the emissary turned out to be Luis Del Pozo, a close friend of Menoyo. "I come as Trujillo's personal envoy! I bring supplies, and eight advisers to guide our victory! I bring you all greetings in Presidente Trujillo's name."

As the two friends embraced, Menoyo said, "Come friend; let us go to the airport office where I can show you our success on the maps. Our men will help you unload your supplies. They will be very helpful. Please have the advisers come also."

When the advisers and Pozo reached the building, they were conversing about old times. As they walked through the doors and sat down at the long conference table set up with maps of the area, a group of soldiers entered from the front and back doors at the same time. "Hola, Del Pozo," said Fidel with a smirk. "Viva Cuba Libre." Del Pozo looked up in astonishment at Fidel and passed out. As Fidel and his troops laughed out loud, Fidel recognized some of the advisers, "Ah Captain Betancourt, you escaped us once with Batista, you won't escape again. Roberto Perez, your padre the Constable will not like it that you are here. In addition, I see Sigfredo Rodriguez Diaz. You need to pick your friends more carefully Sigfredo, these are bad men here."

On August 14, Fidel appeared on national television, "A conspiracy between the Presidente of the Dominican Republic, Rafael Trujillo, The Organization of American States, and the United States CIA has been successfully defeated by our Army. We have arrested over 1200 participants who will stand trial for their crimes against Cuba. Two were CIA spies in the American embassy. We have documentation and irrevocable proof of their participation in the intended invasion of Cuba with the purpose of establishing a counterrevolutionary government to legitimize future aggression. This was not allowed to happen and will not be allowed in the future. Cuba is free of the imperialist yoke for the first time in hundreds of years. Viva Marti! Viva le Revolucion!"

On August 18, 1959, Santo Trafficante Jr. was sent home to Ybor via Miami. Along with him went several boxes of Cuban cigars, a new Swiss bank account, and a promise that his heroin and cocaine traffic could continue through Cuba as long as no product was distributed locally. Alejandro Alfredo Mendez Suarez, a Cuban citizen, arrived one week later to begin his next career at the Fleur de Lis Cigar Factory. His name in Ybor would be Alejandro Mendez. To his Cuban work force, he was El Jefe 'the boss.' His American friends, after hearing his staff call him El Jefe, nicknamed him Jeff.

Chapter 22
JEFF MENDEZ
YBOR
1960

The new Flor de Lis cigar factory was located between 21st and 22nd avenue, 3 blocks south of the Columbia restaurant. It was a 4-story brick building with convenient access to the railroad. Alejandro recognized some of the employees. You don't lose a good roller and Santo Jr. had been quick to retain his best after the fire in 1958. Some of the employees thought Alejandro (El Jefe as they called him) Mendez looked familiar because of his green eyes and dark complexion. He told them he was related to Manuel Suarez and that satisfied anyone that was curious about his resemblance to Rafael Moreno. Other than the eyes and complexion, Jeff Mendez no longer resembled the young Rafael. Jeff retained the beard grown in the Sierra Mountains and was hardened around the eyes. He had eyes that reflected a turbulent twenty-four years of life. His shoulders were broader and in general, he was a much stronger man. He felt and acted much older. His employer of record,

Luigi Santo Trafficante Jr., was 46 and quickly reaching the pinnacle of his career. Because the Cuban casinos were financially drying up from the constant wrath of terrorism perpetrated by the CIA, with blessings from the White House, he had transferred most of his gambling to Las Vegas. He still maintained high-stakes poker and book making and some casino type games in Ybor; but it was no longer acceptable to do this in the open. The exception, Bolita, which still created a large income in Florida.

After returning from Cuba, Santo completed two agendas. Feigning poverty, he borrowed money on his Tampa house located at 2505 Bristol Avenue. Vincent Amato, a member of the Gambino family, loaned him $200,000 on the Bristol home and then leased it back for $200 a month. The second involved his response to the four assassins that tried to whack him in Cuba. If he failed to act, he would lose respect. He knew this while still in prison and had set in motion retaliation against the two Bolita operators responsible for the attack. Joe Diaz was the first to go. Diaz had a routine. He would drive to the L'Unione Cemetery and take a cab from there to the house of Lois Nunez. As the cab driver dropped him off at his car on the return trip, a man came around a mausoleum and shot him in the face with a shotgun. The killer then calmly walked back to his car and drove off. The cab driver was so shaken he was unable to describe the killer or his car. The second involved Bennie Lazzara. Lazzara ran a produce company whose trucks were used to transport heroin. He was a well-known businessman and friend of the mayor, Nick Nuccio. As he and his wife returned home from an evening out, a man ran out of the alley next to their home and fired a shotgun directly at Lazzara, killing him instantly. Life was once again normal for Santo Trafficante Jr. As he sat at his desk in the

Columbia Restaurant he did something very unusual for him, he smiled when he was told about Lazzara. Two more stones removed, he said to himself.

The first week Alejandro was in Ybor, he met with Santo at the Columbia for dinner. They used the Vista Hermosa dining room. The Vista Hermosa was one of thirteen dining rooms in the Columbia. It had been a favorite of Santo Senior's who used it for Bolita and slots. In 1959, it was a secluded dining room used by Santo Junior for private meetings. Only trusted restaurant staff were allowed to serve this room and even then, conversations would stop or immediately turn to innocuous subjects until they left and shut the door. At times, a trusted assistant of Santo's would sit just outside the door to insure no one was listening. This was such a case.

"Alejandro, or should I call you Jeff?" asked Santo.

"Either one is fine, although I'm never going to be comfortable with El Jefe. There is only one El Jefe and that is Fidel."

"Yes, but to the employees of Fleur de Lis, you are the boss."

"I suppose, but it is still strange."

"I have already ordered dinner. We will have Caesar salad, a rare filet and red wine, if that's ok?"

"Of course, Don Santo, that is my favorite American meal."

As they started on the salad, Santo said, "The purpose of this meeting is to set ground rules. I know we talked in Cuba about you staying out of our borgata, and for the most part that's ok, but for some others it's not."

Jeff sat up straight in his chair with a stern look on his face, "What do you mean?"

"Tobacco is not the only product that goes through your factory. It is connected to our underground and cannot be taken offline. Especially now that we have guaranteed safe conduct through Cuba. We never ship everything by the same route; accidents happen. Sometimes they are accidents and sometimes they are a public show to demonstrate that progress is being made against drugs. They mean nothing. To minimize impact we split shipments by numerous routes. Some by boat, some by plane, and some by freight though the docks. The plane drops are not your problem. They go a different route. The boat and freight shipments come directly to you by either truck or underground. By truck, it will be pot, mixed in with tobacco. If underground, it will be heroin or cocaine. It will come in one day and leave the next. It will all be labeled as tobacco from a secondary distributor called Maximo Exports. It will be secured in canvas shipping bags, labeled accordingly. The Agostino brothers, Camillo and Albano, who work in your receiving area, will handle all of the Maximo product. All I need from you is to look the other way. Most but not all of their work will be at night after the factory is closed. They will come and go through the tunnels at night and through the door during the day. It shouldn't be a problem and will not interfere with your daily production schedule."

"I was clear in Cuba, I want no part of your family business."

"Hey, the guaranteed pipeline was your idea, and a good one, I might add. It has already saved Castro from Trujillo's invasion and will serve him for some time. Nixon was pissed after that failed. It wouldn't surprise me if Trujillo were taken out for the failure. The way I hear it, Eisenhower and Nixon blamed him for the failure. According to them, by not sending his troops, he left the insurgents with their pants down and doomed the operation. That, and his increased bad press about his killing civilians, has reduced Trujillo's standing with the United States.

This is not the last plot that Nixon, Eisenhower, the CIA and other Government lackeys will perpetrate. Your cooperation will insure Castro is aware of these plots in time to act."

"And the pipeline will ensure you become very rich. At least give me plausible deniability on the drugs."

Santo laughed as he said, "You sound like the fucking CIA. You can always say the Agostino brothers forced you to look the other way. They are expendable, you are not."

"I doubt they would agree."

"We won't ask."

"And should I ask how you knew what Nixon's and Eisenhower's reactions were?"

"Nope. Only family members know that. Now, do you want to be part of the family?"

"I can live with not knowing. Perhaps I can even live longer by not knowing!" Alejandro added while both men laughed. Alejandro knew this would happen. His Great Uncle had told him, they would always push and push until they get what they want, so never let them do anything for you. It was too late now; the deal was made. At least, thought Alejandro, he hadn't been asked to kill anybody. At least not yet.

"It might be wise at this time to visit Castro," said Santo. "He should know that the White House has instructed the CIA to set up a dummy company to finance terrorism against Cuba. They will attack his infrastructure, Cuban owned businesses, and terrorize the Cuban people in an attempt to get the people to revolt against his government. At the same time, the CIA will train Cuban counterrevolutionaries in the US to invade Cuba later. At least part of that training will be in Florida. Assassination attempts are sure to be part of this in some way. When I know more, I will send you again to give him the details."

"This is very good information for Fidel and that is why I am here. I will leave in the morning. The Agostino brothers can do as they please."

"Grazie, they have their own keys, so the intrusion will be minimal."

The steaks arrived and they finished their meal without further conversation. Both men were occupied with their own thoughts. Santo was thinking about a way to get Alejandro fully invested into the family business. Alejandro was thinking how it wouldn't be possible to know what Santo knew without having spies in the CIA. Both men knew they had made a deal in Cuba that would pay dividends for years to come. That is, as long as Castro remained alive.

After dinner, Santo said, "Run the Fleur de Lis any way you like. You can order any tobacco and make any kind of cigar. You make the deals for distribution and of course hire your own staff or keep the ones in place. The Factory's bank account will be completely in your control. There is a nice sum already deposited so you should never have money problems. If you need more let me know and I will arrange it. It's yours now with the exceptions already discussed. If you make a profit, we will split it fifty-fifty. If you don't, it doesn't matter, as long as it fronts the Agostino brothers' operation."

"Grazie, Don Santo. While I am in Cuba, I will look into tobacco from Pinar del Rio if it is producing. If I can get it, we can make the finest cigars in the world. I would like that." Both men looked at their Cuban made Romeo and Juliet Churchill cigars they were smoking and smiled.

"We will have fun together, El Jefe, you will see," said Santo, "Money, women of your choice, the finest cigars, and a healthy Fidel Castro; what could be better?"

Both men left the Columbia fully satiated and content with their arrangement. For Alejandro keeping Castro alive was the goal and he was willing to make the necessary sacrifices to keep it so. For Santo, he knew he would make more money than he had ever imagined. Ninety percent of organized crime drugs had come through Cuba under Batista. Now only his came that way. While the others scrambled he would flourish. He also knew change was in the air. After the heat from the Lazzara hit subsided, Santo knew business had to change. This was now the 60s, or soon would be, and it was getting harder to control the cops. Not impossible, but harder and more expensive. Those greedy buggers. Communication was getting better every day and that didn't help either. He thought it was probably better to not have the bloody headlines anymore. If bodies just disappeared without a trace, people would know but they wouldn't know. Without a body, there would be no investigation. Modern times required modern ways. On this night Santo Trafficante Jr. felt like the smartest, most modern and most successful entrepreneur in his field. "Praise Jesus, no Praise Fidel," he said as got into his car. His laughter could be heard even after he shut the door and started the car.

Chapter 23
CUBA AND YBOR EXPRESS 1959-1960

Jeff enjoyed his flight to Havana. First class service was indeed worth the price on the new DC-7 aircraft. National Airlines flew from Tampa to Miami and then on to Jose Marti International Airport in Havana. He checked in at the Hotel National and headed out to meet Fidel. As Jeff was on a business trip for his cigar factory, a cryptic message to Fidel was not necessary but was sent by Jeff anyway. He knew Fidel would be in the new office of the Minister of Trade. "Alejandro Mendez to see the Minister, por favor."

"Si, un momento Señor," answered the young and beautiful receptionist. Alejandro took a seat and waited. Within five minutes the receptionist received a buzz, "You may go in now Señor, the Minister, is waiting."

"Gracias, Señorita." As Alejandro walked into the office Fidel met him just inside the door with a bear hug.

"Hola, Alejandro, I have missed your council."

"Hola, El Jefe, I have missed being here. How are things in Cuba?"

"Bueno, we make progress everyday. In education, the push is to train more teachers and more doctors. With socialized education and medicine, we are very short of both. More than 40% of our citizens cannot read and write. This must change to become a strong nation. We have made land available to many that never dreamed they would own their own land. I have placed Che in charge of the agrarian land reform. We have limited any one land holding to 1000 acres, with the exception of industrial land that is more economical to produce with a larger tract. Any owner who has his land reduced is paid for the land taken away. The first plantation reduced was Mi Madre's in Oriente province. The Castro plantation was reduced from 2000 acres to 1000 acres.

"Was she ok with that?"

"Of course. She is a thinker and knows the benefit of workers owning their own land."

"Any news from Pinar del Rio? Are the tobacco fields producing again?"

"Si, a lot but not all of the fields have been replanted. The delay has been in the nurseries with acquiring the right seedlings. Your family's land is partially producing. A squatter family has been producing some quality plants there. Do you want to visit?"

"No, it is still too emotional for me. One day I will visit. I still miss my family and Isabel too much. It would be too painful. I feel like I have let them down with Batista's escape from justice. What is the name of this family?"

"I understand. There are many painful memories for all of Cuba from the corrupt Batista government. You must learn to move on. Fix the things that are fixable and let the others go, or the torment will never leave you. The family's name is Gomez."

"Maybe one day I will be able to do that. I think we had a Gomez family that worked for us so that is good. I hope it is the same family. For now, though, I bring you information from Trafficante. Nixon and Eisenhower have intensified their efforts to destroy Cuba after your victory over Trujillo. They are going to train Cuban counter-revolutionaries for an invasion. They have set up camps in Florida and Louisiana for that purpose. In the meantime, they have authorized terrorist acts to be perpetrated in Cuba. They plan to blow up Cuban businesses, sabotage utilities, and in general terrorize the Cuban people in an attempt to turn them away from you. They may even send some planes to drop bombs that have been painted like the Cuban Air Force and then blame you."

"Do you know where and when the invasion will occur?"

"No, but the training is just starting so it cannot be too soon. In addition, assassination plans for you and Raul have also started, but no real plan has been launched."

"Do you believe that Trafficante is giving you accurate information, Alejandro?"

"Si, I do El Jefe. He is not a man easy to trust. He kills anyone that is a threat to his family's business. He has no problem cheating his associates for a bigger personal cut of the profits. He is ruthless. However, I believe he will honor our deal for as long as you want. There seems to be a moral streak, not very wide, but one that makes it honorable to keep his word to you, because he knows he is dealing with a morally true individual in you. I don't know how else to explain it, El Jefe."

"He is an enigma, Alejandro. Take what he gives us but always watch your back. Are you happy with your work in Ybor?"

"Si, up to a point. I wanted to be completely out of his illegal businesses and I almost am but not quite. It is manageable, however, because it is a way to serve Cuba."

"Remember, Alejandro, this is a voluntary assignment. You do not have to stay. I did not want you to do this in the first place. Much work here needs to be done. Trafficante is first and foremost a member of organized crime who pillaged Cuba for many years with his vice and illegal activities. I have a moral struggle with our arrangement every day. I never wanted to play any part in allowing illegal drugs to reach their victims. For as long as we have this agreement this will be my struggle."

"Si, it is a deal with the Devil. But it may be the difference in Cuba and you surviving the attacks from the U.S. until Cuba's Intelligence system is in place."

"It is a cruel world that requires such tactics, such moral sacrifice."

"Speaking of sacrifice, have you made contact with the Soviet Union?"

"Not yet. I have decided to send Che to Cairo to meet with them discreetly. I cannot trade one imperialistic partner for another. Cuba must maintain its sovereignty, must maintain its own identity, and must be able to control its own destiny. With the Soviets this will be even harder to do than it would have been with the Americans."

"Do you think if Kennedy wins the election over Nixon that things will change with America?"

"We can hope. But if we do not have the White House against us we will still have the CIA."

"You don't think the President can control the CIA?"

"I'm not sure Alejandro. I'm just not sure if it's possible in its current form. With its secondary and illegal funding source from its association with the Organized Crime Syndicate, the CIA can operate completely independent of any oversight. The only oversight in the US is to follow the money trail. How can that be done when there is no money trail? It can't. In addition, without the oversight, unless they are caught with a hand in the cookie jar, everything is deniable. That kind of autonomy in the wrong hands is frightening not only to the rest of the world, but also for any American in the government, or private citizen that opposes them."

After leaving Fidel, Alejandro arranged with a Havana distributor to import tobacco from the Pinar del Rio farmers to Ybor. He agreed to pay more than they were paying their current supplier, but he knew the cigars would be the best. That is if the distributor sent him tobacco with his required specifications for curing.

Chapter 24
PLOTS AND COUNTER PLOTS
1960-1961

After returning from Cuba, Alejandro created a new cigar brand for his Pinar del Rio tobacco. He decided to keep his current contract to supply coronas for a wholesaler while he developed his new offering. He would designate his best torcedoras (rollers) to work with the Pinar del Rio tobacco, which he would sort and blend himself to insure the finest quality. Once he was satisfied that the quality was as expected he would allow his best sorter to assume his role. His new brand would be Flor de Pinar. The specialty would be a Churchill with a sun grown wrapper made from the finest Criollo and Corojo tobacco. The limited shade grown tobacco would be used for the Flor de Pinar Limited Edition Maduro Churchill. He would personally act as the Ligador insuring a standard blend for all future production runs. In addition to the fumigating process, Alejandro convinced Santo to add a large freezer to further insure that all Lasioderma Serricorne, including the eggs, insects, and larva were killed in the finished cigars.

Alejandro had specified the curing and fermentation processes he wanted used on the tobacco before leaving Cuba. He expected the wrappers to be fermented for 30 days with moistening and airing before bailing. The binder and filler leaves were to be air cured for 50 days. Fermentation for the upper leaves for 30 days and for the lower leaves, 20 days. A second fermentation was expected of 90 days for the Ligero leaves, 60 days for the Seco leaves, and 45 days for the Volado leaves before bailing. The aging process for the Ligero was 3 years, the Seco for 2 years, the Volado for 1 year, the binders for 1 year, and the wrappers for 1 year. For the limited edition Maduro wrappers, 5 years. The Cuban brokers initially told Alejandro that he was crazy and would never find Pinar del Rio tobacco with those requirements. "Señor, after all production is still limited and was non existent for one entire season due to the fires caused by a freak lightening storm. Fortunately the aging warehouses were located in Havana and had not burned, so some product is available, but not with your requirements."

"Freak storm my ass. It was a storm perpetrated by Batista forces that killed my family. And I know that my requirements are appropriate for Pinar del Rio tobacco. My family grew tobacco there for more than a 100 years!"

"Uh, Señor I am sorry for your loss. I ah, know nothing about Batista other than he killed many innocents and stole much money from Cuba. If I can find tobacco with your specifications and aging, it will not be at standard pricing, I am sorry. I do have tobacco from Sancti Spiritus region that would be available at standard pricing."

"I will not accept tobacco from what used to be Batista's area. I am willing to pay more for Pinar del Rio leaves, but not a whole lot more. We fought a revolution to remove extortion from Cuba, not perpetuate the previously corrupt system."

"Oh, Señor why didn't you say you fought in the Revolución! I thought you were an American since you want this shipped to Ybor in the United States. I will give you the Revolución price!"

It turned out the Revolución price was still more than standard but was within his budget so Alejandro agreed and was on his way. As he departed, he thought to himself, Revolution pricing my ass, as Santo would say 'What the fuck!'

While Alejandro was developing his Flor de Pinar Cigars, Allen Dulles was developing his 'Operation 40' for Nixon and Eisenhower.

"Charles, have Bissell set up a network of 40 undercover operatives throughout the Caribbean, including Cuba. With emphasis on Cuba. I want to know if anyone even farts communism or socialism. I also want to know what routes organized crime is using to smuggle drugs. We should be able to lean on them to pay for any black operations we need to maintain the stability required for our American companies. Castro is a bad example for all of South and Central America. We need to replace him as soon as possible. I want you to have several dummy corporations set up in south Florida to finance operations against Castro and his government. We can start with sabotage of factories and public sites. We want to demoralize the Cubans so they help rid us of this bastard. As our friends in low places say, he is a stone in my shoe! Speaking of that, have Bissell contact Roselli and see if his friends might help us assassinate Castro. He has certainly cost them enough money to motivate revenge."

"Anything else chief?" asked Charles Cabell, CIA Deputy Director.

"No, that's a good start. Ike wants Castro gone before he leaves office so we need to move fast."

"I'm on it."

That afternoon Charles Cabell met with the CIA director of plans, Richard M. Bissell Jr.

"What the fuck is Allen thinking, Charles, I can't call Roselli directly. I'll go through an FBI cutout I know and have it done that way. We will have a presence at the meeting but will imply it's an FBI deal. The agents are no problem; I already have that mapped out. We can use the Double-Chek Corporation, which is set up in Miami to handle payments. Its cover is a brokerage firm but the only thing it brokers is CIA black ops. We can recruit some additional pilots to strafe trains, firebomb cane fields, hit oil tankers, and commercial buildings as long as American companies do not own them. This should serve to demoralize the Cuban people. The Cubans should be screaming for our Marines to bail them out. They can't like that bastard Castro enough to endure the misery we will inflict. We can use surplus B-26 light bombers and paint them to look like the Cuban Air force so the people will think Castro is terrorizing his people, like a good tyrant. If Allen can keep the Brits from delivering the Hawker Siddeley jets to Castro, we will have his balls in a vice. The Soviets will be the only place left for him to get any kind of effective planes. And then he is a communist that we can eliminate, if the Cubans don't do it for us."

"Good plan, Richard. I'll remind Allen to stay on the Brits. They will comply. We can pay the pilots you recruit $10,000 a month and as always try to recruit orphans. If they happen to disappear we don't want relatives screaming for an explanation."

"We will have planes in the air before the end of the month," replied Bissell.

In the summer of 1960, Robert Maheu, a former CIA and current FBI employee had dinner at the Fontainebleau with Johnny Roselli and two guests of Johnny's. They were introduced as Sam Gold and Joe.

"We will be happy to take out Castro as our patriotic duty. We do not want your $150,000," replied Joe.

"That's very much appreciated Joe. Why would you do that?" asked Robert.

Joe looked straight at him with cold eyes and said, "Let's just say the enemy of my friend is my enemy, especially if we already dislike the rat fuck."

"By the way, who is our friend behind this Robert?" asked Sam Gold.

"Let's just say some business friends of ours that were screwed by Castro," answered Maheu. "How do you think we should do this?"

"An ambush is always good. It could be done on a street corner in Havana," responded Sam Gold.

"I don't think so Sam, Castro's security system would make it impossible to escape if someone could get that close with a machine gun," said Roselli.

"I know some people that can get close if we had poison capsules that could be put into his food. Of course, the poison should be slow acting so they can get away," offered Joe.

"We will have our guys work on the pills and get back to you say in three weeks? asked Maheu.

"Three weeks from today at this table. Good night, Mr. Maheu," answered Joe.

Robert Maheu knew he was being dismissed and left quietly.

"What do you think, Sam?" asked Santo Trafficante, aka, Joe.

"I think we do this and celebrate when this fucker is dead. I also think this is a CIA deal. Who do you have in mind?" asked Sam Giancana, aka, Sam Gold.

"I have a man in the kitchen at one of Castro's favorite restaurants. It shouldn't be a problem, and of course, it's CIA behind this. This is what they do with any government they don't like, especially one that has fucked up business."

"If we need a backup we could convince his ex girlfriend, Marita Lorenz, to return to Cuba and deliver the capsules," offered Giancana.

"Excellent, we will have both plans working at once," said Trafficante.

Johnny Roselli just listened during this exchange. He knew the two Godfathers would ask his advice if they wanted it. It was best and safest to always let them lead. The meeting ended without either one asking for his opinion.

When Maheu left the meeting, he called Bissell immediately. "Richard, I've just met with Roselli and two men identified as Sam Gold and Joe. They are very interested in taking out Castro."

"What did Gold and Joe look like?" asked Bissell.

"Joe was 5'7" to 5'8", about 150 lbs., light complexion with Roman nose and black glasses, thinning sandy air. Sam Gold was Sam Giancana I'm sure. I've seen pictures of him."

"Joe was Santo Trafficante Jr., from Tampa," replied Bissell. "With them involved we are good to go. Do you need anything?"

"Yes, I need slow acting poison pills. Santo has someone close enough to get them into his food."

"Great, I'll have Joseph Schreider get right on it. How much time do we have?"

"I need to deliver them in three weeks."

"That's no problem."

Three weeks passed and the group reconvened at the Fontainebleau in Miami. Maheu gave Trafficante five nylon bags he had taken out of his pocket.

"These are slow acting synthetic botulism pills that will dissolve in any cold liquid. There is no reaction for two to three hours after ingestion. There will be no symptomatic sign of poisoning and will leave no traces for autopsy. Just caution your people to handle with care. They are protected by the bags but direct handling is dangerous. If they do touch them they must wash their hands carefully or they could be contaminated."

As Trafficante took the bags, he gave one to a previously unidentified man at the table. "This is Tony Varona. He is one of the Cuban nationals planning the next invasion. Johnny has been helping to train his men in South Florida. He has a request."

"Sir, it would be very helpful to coordinate Castro's demise with our invasion. A time has not yet been selected but it should not be too long. What is the shelf life of these capsules?"

"They are good for five years with no degradation," answered Maheu.

"Excellent. We should launch our invasion within a few months. We have the man already in place at the Peking Restaurant. He is reliable and efficient. Do we have an agreement to coincide the poisoning with our invasion?"

"I don't think that's a problem. I will let Roselli know, if we can't wait. Otherwise, consider it an agreement to wait. There are many benefits to the timing. Having a provisional government to recognize while there is confusion over his death is perfect."

"It's done then," said Sam as he stood and shook hands.

The next day Santo had lunch with Alejandro in the Vista Hermosa dining room at the Columbia Restaurant. As usual, they were the only ones in the dining room.

"The plots are increasing everyday, Alejandro. Please tell Castro about the impending invasion. The time has not been set but I'm sure it will not occur until sometime in 1961. They are not prepared. We will let him know as soon as we know where it will be. We know it will be somewhere in the western part of the island and it will be preceded by bombing the nearest airports to decommission Castro's aircraft. Also, give him this bag of pills. It contains a synthetic botulism that is deadly after two to three hours. Tell him not to touch theses pills, because you can be contaminated by just touching. I thought he would get a kick out of seeing them however. There is a plant at the Peking Restaurant that has pills to be used at the time of the invasion. It will be planted in a cold drink, which causes the capsules to dissolve. The CIA plots have been fucking ridiculous and almost like the Keystone Cops. From the botulism capsules, to botulism-contaminated cigars, to blowing him up while scuba diving, to putting shellfish poison in aspirin, to poison handkerchiefs, it's fuckin hilarious! And now an ex-girlfriend, Marita Lorenz has a set of pills. I don't think she'll wait for the invasion."

"I'll tell him. I'll also tell him the American people have no idea what their government is doing to Cuba. The American people are still in love with the Revolución, especially Fidel, and Che."

"That is true Alejandro, but it does not stop the bombs; it does not stop the killing; and it does not stop the terrorism perpetrated by the CIA."

"I thought the government was supposed to follow the will of the people in a democracy."

"Alejandro, you can be so naive, sometimes. The government follows the will of the big companies and the power they represent. The people are there to pick up the tab."

Alejandro's trip to Cuba was without incident although there were not as many flights as before. He noticed the airport was not as crowded as it once was. It was obvious to him that the CIA bombing was having an effect. Alejandro saw several damaged buildings in Havana as he made his way to Fidel.

"Cómo estás?"

"Muy bien, gracias, Alejandro. You saw the Havana buildings. I can see the concern on your face. The CIA paints their planes to look like counterrevolutionaries. What a joke. They fool no one. They have damaged five sugar cane fields this week in Camaguey Province and three more in Oriente Province. Cuba has reached a point of no return. The hundred million dollar loan from the European banks has been sabotaged by the US and will not be allowed. In Havana Harbor, the Coubre, a French freighter loaded with Belgian arms and ammunition intended for Cuban defense, was blown up, killing 75 and wounding over 200 workers. In spite of my pleas to make peace, the US government refuses to even talk. Kennedy is no better than Nixon and Eisenhower. Their fear of Cuba becoming Communist has become a self-fulfilling prophecy. Where else can we go? What else can we do? The CIA will continue to deplete Cuban resources and Cuba's ability to manufacture the goods it needs to survive. I cannot let the people starve. Over 200,000 families now own land they never thought they would. But if they can't feed their families because the US destroys our food supply, our ability to produce oil and gasoline, and our infrastructure of roads and utilities, what good is owning your land?"

"El Jefe, I have never seen you so down. And all I bring is more bad news. How can I help Cuba?" Alejandro asked after relaying all of Santo's warnings. Alejandro had never seen Fidel so depressed.

"You are helping, Alejandro. You are maintaining contact. You are protecting Cuba in a way no one else can at this point.

The only protection against the bombing is to shoot the planes down, which we can't do now. I never intended to deal with the Soviets. I wanted to deal with the US against them. But now I must for Cuba to survive."

"I remember during the Revolution you always said that a third world country must align with one of the super powers to survive. That was true then, and it is true now. The US has given you no choice, El Jefe. The difficult task will be to remain a trade partner and not a colony of the Soviets."

"That is true, and maybe that is why the US is against us. We made it very clear from the beginning that we were not going to stay as a US colony or a US territory. We intended then and still insist that Cuba always be a sovereign nation independent of foreign rule. That will not be so easy with the Soviets, but it will be done!"

"Also, El Jefe you should know the American people see you as a romantic hero of the Revolución that gained independence by winning against overwhelming odds. They have no idea what their government is doing. I'm not sure all parts of the government even know what is being done to Cuba. The US government professes to be for liberty and freedom for all while they segregate blacks, torture prisoners, and perpetuate terrorism in Cuba and other countries too small to fight back. I've heard Santo talk about what's going on in Vietnam with the US advisors. Santo believes, with a larger US presence there, Saigon can become the heroin capital of the world. And we both know what heroin represents, money for organized crime and for the CIA."

Alejandro watched, as Fidel seemed to reenergize himself. Gone was the depressed and weary man. Present was the revolutionary fighter whose resolve never faltered no matter what the situation presented. The leader whose forces were reduced to only twelve men that never lost confidence and never doubted victory would be his.

"I hope for the sake of the US people that doesn't happen, Alejandro. It will just be another monetary debt paid for with the lives of the innocent. It happens all too often in this world. My die is cast. I will make an economic deal with the Soviets. Che has already done the preliminary talks. Formalizing a deal with the Soviet Union will escalate our troubles with the CIA. We must establish a system of collective vigilance. We must insure that every district is represented. It must be a system where everyone on the block knows his duties. Militia battalions will be set up throughout Cuba. A man for each weapon will be selected. A structure will be given to the entire mass of militiamen so that as soon as possible our combat units can be perfectly formed and perfectly trained. One must not worry, Alejandro. Let them worry. We'll conserve our serenity and solidify our resolve. It is important that all Cubans are conscious of the struggle undertaken by the Revolución. It is necessary for all of us to know that it'll be a long and hard struggle. It's important for us to realize that our revolution has gone toe to toe with the most powerful empire in the world. Of all the colonialist and imperialist countries, Yankee imperialism is the most powerful in diplomatic influence and military resources. It is also an imperialism that is not like the English, which is more mature and more experienced. It is proud imperialism, barbarous and many of its leaders are barbarous men, who have nothing to envy of the first cave dweller. Many of their leaders are men with fangs. It is the most aggressive, most warlike and most stupid imperialism. We are the frontline, Alejandro. A small country with few economic resources giving battle on the frontline for our sovereignty, destiny and right. It's necessary to be conscious that our country is facing the most fierce empire of the contemporary times. It must be resolved and of one mind, that imperialism hates us with the hatred of the masters for the rebellious slaves. And we have to defend ourselves with the fierceness of slaves who have revolted. There is nothing more fierce than the hatred of the master for the rebellious slave. And to that, we must add the fact that they see their interests endangered. Not just in Cuba, but throughout the world. For men to do this type of humanitarian wrong they must first believe they are doing right. We must have the help of world opinion to keep them in check. To do this we will bring our fight to the United Nations. But our case is the case of all underdeveloped countries in Latin America, in Africa, in the Middle East and in Asia. They are also being exploited by the monopolies. There is a universal interest in our struggle. As we wage our battle, we are being watched by those in similar situations. If we are successful, we will establish the roadmap for freedom and liberation from the imperialists of the world. The information you have given me, Alejandro, is that we have to double our efforts. We must be able to mobilize in every province to defend our freedom. So that when the next invasion comes no matter where it comes we will be ready in an instant to protect Cuba. Knowing the might of the empire we face will not discourage us, Alejandro. On the contrary, it encourages us. It is the empire that should be demoralized because of the battle being waged against it by such a small country, a small Island called Cuba. The years ahead of us will not be full of tranquility and ease. The greatest work and battles are ahead of us. But, we will be ready, the revolution will be ready, Cuba will be ready! The battles will not be fought by a small segment of the population. They'll be fought by a united front by all of the people and Cuba will persevere!"

It was a relief to Alejandro to see and hear a confident El Jefe. He knew that as Fidel goes, so goes Cuba. If Fidel were demoralized, Cuba would be demoralized and would give up. Fidel since 1957 has been the endorphin of the Cuban movement for freedom. If the CIA were to be successful in removing him, the Revolution would fall. "This cannot happen," Alejandro said to himself. But, he knew it was inevitable. Eventually, the CIA would be successful in getting one person with access to terminate Fidel. How could it not? The CIA was successful in Iran and in Guatemala in exchanging a legitimate government for one that was more favorable to US imperialism. And if that was not enough, Fidel continues to give the CIA more and more motivation, as if they needed any, by speaking out and telling the world what was happening in Cuba. It was like two protagonists in a boxing ring. One was the 250lb heavyweight champion against the 150lb newcomer that was learning to box round by round. The heavyweight trying for the knockout while the lightweight bobs and weaves, hoping to land a jab now and then without exposing too much or staying in one place too long. There were many ways for the heavyweight to win and only one way for the lightweight. The lightweight could only win if the heavyweight got tired of the fight and punched himself out. On the other hand, a moment's lack of concentration by the lightweight and it would be all over. Cuba's odds were not good.

Alejandro did not understand the United States. The country was so rich with so many natural resources, why did they have to have Cuba's? Does the government of the United States believe they should control everything in every country throughout the world? Is that the depth of their self-entitlement? If

Castro was right and men must believe they are doing right to justify so much terrorism, then it must be so. Alejandro could not believe that the Americans he knew would accept this position. It must be only the government and the companies that make money from this type of imperialism that have accepted this as truth. Alejandro thought that most Americans would agree with him that people should be free to decide for themselves what happened to the American ideal of "life, liberty and the pursuit of happiness"? Is that concept only meant to apply to white Americans and no others in the world? The United States government may think so, but Alejandro could not believe the average American thought this was only meant for them.

A few months later in September 1961, the newly formed Cuban Militia mobilized for a clean up operation in the Escambray region of Las Villas Province. They successfully crushed CIA funded counterrevolutionary groups in the region. Castro also signed a trade agreement with Moscow. On September 26, he addressed the United Nations. His speech lasted for more than four hours.

"Some people may think that we are very annoyed and upset by the treatment the Cuban delegation has received on this trip. That is not the case. We understand full well the reasons behind it. That is why we are not irritated. Nor should anybody worry that Cuba will not continue in its effort to achieve a worldwide understanding. That being so, we shall speak openly.

----------------When we were forced to leave our hotel rooms in the city and come to the United Nations headquarters while

efforts were made to find accommodations, a humble hotel of this City, a Negro hotel in Harlem, offered to rent us rooms. The reply came while we were speaking with the Secretary General. Nevertheless, an official of the State Department did all in his power to prevent us from staying there. As though by magic, hotels began appearing all over New York offering us free accommodations. Out of simple reciprocity, we accepted the Harlem hotel. Then they told the world we were staying in a brothel. Of course, since it was inhabited by Negroes it must be a brothel. Furthermore, they have tried to heap infamy upon the Cuban delegation without respect for the female members of the Cuban delegation.

-------------------The military group which tyrannized Cuba before our successful revolution was supported by the most reactionary elements of the nation, and above all by the foreign interests that dominated the economy of Cuba. Everybody knows, and the United States admits it, that is the type of government preferred by the monopolies. Why? Because by the use of force it was possible to check the demands of the people. By the use of force it was possible to suppress strikes for improvement of living conditions, to crush any movement by the peasants to own their land, and any movement detrimental to the American owned companies. That is why the ruling class of the United States favored governments of force and why they stayed in power so long. And for that government of force to stay in power they had to maintain the favor of the United States. Batista's government was such a government. But it did

not suit the Cuban people and was overthrown at a great cost in Cuban lives and sacrifices. The legacy of Batista's reign of force included 600,000 able Cubans unemployed out of six million population. Three million homes did not have electricity. Rents that required more than a third of the workers' income. Thirty seven and one half percent of the population were illiterate. Seventy percent of the rural children had no teachers. Two percent of the population suffered from tuberculosis. Ninety-five percent of the rural children were affected by parasites, and the infant mortality rate was very high. One percent of the population controlled forty-six percent of the total area of the nation. Public utilities, electricity, and telephone services were all owned by the United States monopolies. All major industries except for tobacco were owned by American companies. The balance of payments from 1950 to 1960 had been favorable to the United States by $1,000,000,000.

-------------------------------The revolutionary government began to take the first steps. The rents were lowered by fifty percent. Telephone and electricity rates, that were the highest in the world under Batista, were reduced. Now we were going against the American monopolies so we were labeled as communist. Then we adopted the Agrarian Reform Law so that 200,000 farmers would own the land they worked for the first time. And that is when we started receiving the full wrath of the United States government spearheaded by the CIA. A similar reform was initiated in the Republic of Guatemala and the democratically elected government was replaced by a government

of force that eliminated the reform and maintained the United States owned United Fruit Company's monopoly. We were not one hundred percent communist but we were becoming slightly pink. We did not confiscate land without payment, although it was in bonds over twenty years.

----------------And then one day a plane, while dropping a bomb on one of our sugar mills, exploded. We were able to collect the remains of the American pilot and his papers. His papers indicated that the plane had stopped at two American military bases before making its bombing run over Cuba. The United States government when confronted with irrefutable evidence apologized for the activities. But the bombs have not stopped. President Sukarno of Indonesia also said this happened in his country.

------------------------------The Revolutionary government of Cuba has in just twenty months created 10,000 new schools. It has built 5,000 new homes. Fifty new towns are being built. The previous military fortresses now house tens of thousands of students. In the next year, our goal is to teach every inhabitant of Cuba to read and write.

-------------------------Why is the United States Government unwilling to talk of development? It is very simple. The United

States government does not want to go against the monopolies. And the monopolies require natural resources and markets for their investments of capital. That is why the real solution to this problem is not sought. That is why planning for the development of underdeveloped countries with public funds is not done. The government of the United States cannot propose a plan for public investment because this would divorce it from the very reason it exists, namely to serve the American monopolies.

---------------------------Have colonists or imperialists ever lacked a pretext when they wanted to invade a country? Never. Somehow, they always find a pretext. And which are the colonists and imperialist countries? Four or five countries? No, the owners of the wealth of the world are four or five groups of monopolies. An outsider would say the wealth of the world has been badly distributed; the world is being exploited.

------------------------------The monopolies are against disarmament, because besides being able to defend those interest with arms, the arms race has always been good business for them. For example, it is well known that the great monopolies in the United States have doubled their capital shortly after the Second World War. Like vultures, the monopolies feed on the corpses, which are the harvest of war.

-----------------------------Do away with the philosophy of plunder and you will have done away forever with the philosophy of war. Do away with the colonies, wipe out the exploitation of countries by monopolies, and mankind will have reached a true era of progress! The warmongers and militarists who are interested in perpetuating this exploitation must be exposed and condemned by public opinion. The Cuban people condemn the exploitation of man-by-man and the exploitation of underdeveloped countries by imperialist's capital.

---------------After more than four and one half hours Castro finally ended his speech. He received a standing ovation by most countries. The United States was one exception. Soviet Premier Khrushchev was heard saying," I don't know if Fidel Castro is a communist but I'm a Fidelista!"

Following the speech, the United States government informed the Castro delegation that they were impounding the planes they flew into the country. They indicated a US company informed them Cuba owed them money. The Soviet delegation gave them a ride home.

Chapter 25
KIM-LY
1961

Alejandro's office was on the fourth floor of the cigar factory. It was a corner office with windows on the south and east side of the building. The office contained two desks, his, and the one intended for the bookkeeper. Since he arrived in 1959, the bookkeeper's job had remained open. He chose to do the work himself instead of trying to hire someone that would look the other way when the extra shipments arrived and left without any recordation. Managing the operations, inventory, books, and his new line of cigars was beginning to change his employees' nickname for him from El Jefe to El Asshole. He was short tempered and according to his employees, someone to avoid if possible. During a late night dinner at the Columbia, Santo had suggested he might have the solution. He handed Alejandro a name: K. L. Walker. Today, Walker was to come by for an interview. Santo had indicated that Walker's background included work oversees as a bookkeeper before immigrating to Tampa.

"K. L. Walker is here to see you, El Jefe," said Maria.

"Show Señor Walker in, please, Maria."

"No problem I'll show Señorita Walker in," Maria said as she left the room laughing.

"What?" Alejandro asked, but didn't get an answer.

Maria brought K. L. Walker into the office and made the introductions. "Señorita Walker, this is Alejandro Mendez our Manager, and El Jefe this is Kim-Ly Walker."

"Please have a seat, Miss Walker," Alejandro said as he shook his head. As he looked at Kim-Ly, he was awestruck by her appearance. Barely five foot tall, she was wearing black trousers and a white silk shirt with golden lions embroidered on the front and back of the shoulders. She had long black hair that extended almost to her waist. Her skin looked like porcelain and her eyes were almond shaped and very dark. The only word he knew to describe her was exotic. The most beautiful and exotic prostitute that he had ever seen. "Ok, in which casino of Don Santos do you work?" Alejandro said with a smile as he recovered from his shock.

"I'm sorry; I have never worked at a casino. Is that a requirement?" she responded with almost no accent.

"No, I just assumed you worked out of a casino and not a 'boarding house.' Santo did not tell me, because he knew I would say no."

"You think I am a whore?" she yelled. "Du me moy, buol! May den nhu cuc cut cho cho de di du may. Ngu nhu heo!" she added as she stood to go.

Alejandro had no idea what she said but he knew he had been cussed out.

"Please wait. I'm sorry; I did not mean to insult you. I just thought Santo was playing a joke on me. I meant no disrespect. Are you really a bookkeeper?"

"Yes, El Asshole, I'm a bookkeeper, not a fucking whore!"

"I deserved that, I apologize again. If you would please sit down we can start again?"

"Ngu nhu heo," she added as she sat down.

"I know I'll be sorry for asking but what does that mean?"

"It means you are dumb as a pig." They both started to laugh. "You do not want to know what else I said. That was the nicest thing."

"I will certainly take your word for it," Alejandro said with a smile. "And I really could use a good bookkeeper. If you would consider the possibility, perhaps we can talk about you and what you have done in the past."

"Very well. I am originally from Laos. My father, Neng Chu Vang, was the leader of our area. We are Hmong people, which transcend the borders of several countries. The people in the mountain areas of China, Vietnam, Laos, and Thailand are all Hmong. I was sent to Saigon for training and to work for my brother Vang Pao as his bookkeeper. My brother is a general in the Army and a businessman. The family business is opium. The family farms can sustain two consecutive years of rice farming before the land has to be rejuvenated for ten years of poppy farming before rejuvenation. Obviously, most of our land is used for opium. Our product is flown to southern Laos and to southern Vietnam to be processed. We have partners who own Air America for transport. You know the owners as the CIA. My brother's company where I worked processes the poppy into opium that is then sold to our other business partner, Santo Trafficante. He then has the opium transported to Marseilles where it is made into heroin. Obviously, my brother's books had to be handled with sensitivity, as not all of his work was legal. I assume yours is also sensitive?"

"Well, yes and no. We have a mostly legal business that occasionally receives shipments that we choose to ignore."

"Oh, that is very bad."

"You were in the heroin business. How can you say ours is bad?"

"No, it is bad you ignore the shipments. There are clear paper trails that bring the merchandise here. To not account for it is a clear giveaway that it is illegal. You must hide these shipments alongside your legal business to make them disappear. If you do not let me do this I cannot work here because you will be arrested and me along with you. Your books must be repaired."

"And you know how to do this?"

"Yes, it was my specialty with my brother."

"And how did you get to Tampa and why?"

"I met Brad Walker at an embassy function in Saigon. He was an attache in charge of visa requests. Or at least that is what he first told me."

"You don't believe that is what he did?"

"I believe that he was CIA and still is, but he won't talk about it. His business trips last from a few days to a few months. And he never tells me where he will be or when he will return. He also has an extensive weapons collection that I don't think would be typical for an Embassy employee."

"What did your family think about you seeing an American?"

"Seeing him was no problem. Marrying him was a big problem because they don't trust him. My brother thought it was best for me to work elsewhere after the marriage. Three months later Brad was sent to Ft. Lee, Virginia for 4 months and then to MacDill AFB in Tampa. I joined him here 6 months ago."

"Your English is remarkable"

"My father insisted on it. He said English was the language of money and to be a bookkeeper I needed to know it well."

"That is certainly true in Ybor. Do you have children?"

"No. I will not bring a child into a home where the father is gone so much. My father had 32 children and 8 wives. I know what it is like to not really know your father and I don't want that for my children. If I have children, they will know their mother and father."

"Your father had 8 wives, at the same time?"

"Yes, it is not uncommon for a Hmong male to have more than one wife but 8 is unusual. As long as you can provide for your wives and children, you can have as many as you want. Of course, being able to pay for them is one thing, and being able to care and nurture them as a father is a very different thing. Are you still considering me for your job?"

"I think I would like to propose a trial to see how it goes. There is just one thing. The next time you cuss me out you must do it in English or Spanish, OK?"

Kim-Ly stood up and shook Alejandro's hand, "Thank-you asshole, I'm sorry, El Asshole, I will accept. And the next time you call me a prostitute I will not cuss you out I will just shoot you, OK?"

As they both smiled Alejandro said, "That seems fair." Alejandro was not at all sure she was kidding.

It took Kim-Ly a month to reconstruct Alejandro's books. "You see El Lo Dit; they are hidden in plain sight. There will be no reason for an auditor to even notice them."

"That is very ingenious, Kim-Ly, thank-you. I am very glad you are here. Not only do you improve the scenery but you are also smart as a whip."

"Smart as whip? I don't understand smart as whip. Is a whip smart? I think it is dumb instrument of punishment. Explain please."

"Sorry, it is an American term, I don't know where it started or how but it is meant as a compliment."

"If you don't know where it came from or why it is a compliment, why use it, El Lo Dit? Use words you know, not someone else's words you don't know. That is dumb, El Lo Dit."

"Sorry, I seem to always apologize to you. It is no wonder why your husband travels so much."

"My husband does not do dumb things, El Lo Dit. He has no need to apologize."

"Ok, Ok, I stand corrected, sorry."

"That is dumb, El Lo Dit. You are sitting, not standing. May do ngu!"

"Now wait, we said you would cuss me out in English. And what does El Lo Dit mean? Is it Laotian for chief, like El Jefe?"

"No, it means asshole, and may do ngu is dumb asshole."

Even though he was shocked, he could not help but laugh at what they must look like. This diminutive woman, barely five foot, that couldn't weigh more then 90 lbs giving him hell, a six foot, 180 lb male who could crush her in a second. His laugh was infectious and she too began to smile as he said, "You are a 'cho cai' Kim-Ly."

As she laughed even harder she said," Yes I am a bitch El Lo Dit; I have no time for stupids!"

In the next few weeks, Alejandro showed Kim-Ly the cigar business and she showed him how to structure his books for maximum safety against any type of audit. She wanted to know everything. How the plants were grown, why they were fermented, how they were selected, what made one plant grown in the Pinar del Rio better than the same plant grown somewhere else. Her thirst for knowledge was limitless. She even wanted to roll a cigar, which was great amusement for the Cuban torcedoras. "No, it is not bad for your first try Kim-Ly"

"It is dung, El Jefe, pure dung!" she replied as she compared her cigar to those around her.

"No, not pure dung. The tobacco is still good quality," Alejandro added.

"I fear as a roller I could turn gold into dung. It's awful."

"Ok, Ok, the shape is not uniform, the density is off, and you used a binder for the wrapper. You are right. It is not good. But as a bookkeeper you are outstanding."

As she examined her creation and shook her head she said, "That is correct, El Jefe, now you are being truthful."

As they finished their tour and returned to the office Alejandro asked, "Would you like to smoke one of our cigars?"

"No, El Lo Dit, I don't smoke anything. I appreciate the artistry in a fine creation, but I will never smoke anything. I saw too many Laotians that became addicted to the opium pipe as a child. That is not for me."

Alejandro appreciated that in public he was El Jefe but in private, he knew he would always be El Lo Dit. "I understand Kim-Ly. Cigars and cigarettes can be almost as addicting as opium and heroin. At least they do no harm to the person. They do not ruin a person's ability to function as a human being. I see cigars as a personal reward for the individual to be savored and enjoyed to its fullest measure. It is the finished product of an excellent grower, first class fermentation, and drying, culminated by the proper mix and blend and rolled by the best Torcedoras. If any of these things do not occur at the highest level, the cigar will diminish in flavor and enjoyment for the smoker. A great cigar is truly a great work of art from start to finish."

"It is nice you love your work, Jeff. When you talk about cigars, you are the romantic, not the Lo Dit. You seem like a person that would be just as happy with only the legal end of this business. How did you get involved with Santo?"

It was not lost on Alejandro that she called him Santo, not Don Santo, or Don Trafficante. He decided to tell Kim-Ly anyway. He told her about his family, about Isabel and her family, how he came to Tampa for school, his saving of Santo Sr. and his fight in the Cuban Revolution because of Batista's butchery. In addition, he told her about Castro's deal with Santo and how Santo's information if not directly saved Castro, it certainly made it easier for him to survive.

"Your loss must be very difficult for you Jeff. I understand now why you are an asshole sometimes. You are a romantic without a center, only fringes in your life. I understand losing family. When the French thought they owned our lands, they brutalized families and killed many of my brothers, sisters, aunts and uncles that served in the resistance. You see no one can own our country except us. The French thought they did but they didn't. Even the British thought they could but they were also wrong. If the United States tries, they will also lose. No leader that is not accepted by the people will survive for long. The end is inevitable for all that try. For some they have power longer, but the end will always be the same. We are an old civilization, Jeff. We have been conquered many times but we have never surrendered to any foreigner and we never will. Cuba is relatively a young country, but your friend Castro has very old ideas about the people being in charge. That is surprising for a culture that is so young. Like you, I think he is also a romantic at heart."

Alejandro was deep in thought as he contemplated Kim-Ly's words. Such a young girl to be so worldly and wise. Then he thought about all of the things that had happened to him in the last four years. He wondered what it would have been like to live in one place all of one's life with no war and no destruction. Would it make you complacent? Would it allow you to accept tyranny to avoid having to change? What would it be like? What would his life have been if there had been no Batista and he could have managed to marry Isabel? What would it be like to marry someone like Kim-Ly, the brightest girl he had ever met? And even perhaps the prettiest girl he had ever met. Certainly, the most exotic and intriguing person he knew.

"All of this talk has made me hungry Kim-Ly. Let's go to the Columbia for lunch."

"That would be great, El Lo Dit. I'm starving."

With that, the spell was broken and Alejandro returned to his reality. At lunch, Santo invited them to dine with him in his dining room. As always, no one else was in the room. "Please excuse us a minute Kim-Ly, I must talk business with Alejandro."

"Of course. Do you mean one minute or would fifteen be better?"

"Fifteen would be great, thanks."

Santo saw that Alejandro watched her leave the room. "A pretty girl, yes?"

"Very pretty and very smart, Don Santo. She knows more than people twice her age."

"I hoped she would be a good asset for you. She comes from a very successful family that I do some business with in Asia. Alejandro, you need to make another trip to Cuba. I have word that the CIA is going to begin their invasion in four days. The plan is to bomb Castro's airports, to destroy his Air Force. Then an amphibious landing will occur to establish a foothold for a provisional government. The new government, headed by

Antonia Verona, former Cuban Prime Minister under Batista, and Manuel Artime, a wealthy owner of a Nicaraguan meatpacking plant, will ask for United States recognition to justify sending United States troops from Guantanamo Bay. They will call themselves the Movement for the Recovery of the Revolution (MRR). In addition, at that time, additional air support will be available from the US. The invaders will be Cuban counter-revolutionaries that the CIA and some of my men have trained in South Florida at Point Mary, which has been established in the Everglades. Inside Cuba, the CIA has been organizing the underground. Rafael Diaz Hanscom is in charge of the underground in Cuba so that once Castro is overthrown, the CIA will be in position to dictate the new leaders and the new form of government. Kennedy has changed the original landing sight from a daytime landing in Trinidad, a city on the southern coast, to a nighttime landing at the Bay of Pigs. Kennedy believes this will be less recognizable as a US backed invasion. Once the bay is secured, the government in exile will come ashore. After holding the beachhead for seventy-two hours, the government could be recognized under international law as a government in arms and could ask for military assistance. The US is set to provide military assistance at that time. As you only have four days, you should leave as soon as possible."

Chapter 26
PLAYA GIRON
APRIL 14-19, 1961

Fidel went to work immediately. First, he mobilized the militia. Second, he had all of his good aircraft hidden and replaced with obsolete craft and in some cases, replicas. He arranged for Khrushchev to be brought up to date with these developments, along with his congratulations for Yury Gagarin's successful flight into space. While Alejandro was in his office, he also received word of Kennedy's remarks to a *New York Times* article, which indicated the United States was training paramilitary groups in Guatemala, Florida, and Louisiana for an invasion of Cuba. "First, I want to say that there will not be, under any conditions, an intervention in Cuba by the United States Armed Forces."

"What a joke, Alejandro! I think this Kennedy is just another Nixon. He says one thing when they are only days away from doing what they proclaim they are not. Why don't you come with me, Alejandro? It will be just like old times in the battlefield. I will lead our counter-measures on the ground and you can help."

Alejandro could not keep from smiling, "I will go with you to help El Jefe, but please don't let it be like old times, with no food, no water, limited arms but great aspirations."

As he chuckled Fidel said, "No, this time we eat and we shoot back! Do you think they will try to invade at only one place, Alejandro?"

"I would not. I would have at least three landing spots so that I could reinforce the weakest resistance, and then expand from there. The goal is to maintain a foothold for 72 hours and then ask for US troops. I think this would give me the best chance."

"I agree, but we will reinforce the center around Playa Girón with our most experienced troops with a plan to converge on that area if they are really as dumb as Santo indicated."

On April 15, in a speech to the country, Fidel said, "All units should make their way to their perspective battalions. Let us face the enemy with the conviction that to die for the country is to live, and to live in chains is to live in shame and disgrace. The leaders of the Revolution will take charge of their areas: Raul Castro in Oriente Province, Che Guevara in Pinar del Rio in the West, Juan Almeida in Santa Clara at the head of the Army of the Center. Ramiro Valdes is responsible for Intelligence and Counterintelligence, and Guillermo Garcia is in charge of the tactical center of Managua, to include Havana."

Fidel and Alejandro waited for news. They slept during the day to be rested at night. With the troops mobilized and the planes as concealed as possible, they not so patiently waited for news of the invasion. Fidel had the Committee for the Defense of the Revolution detain those known to be opposed to the Revolution. In just a few hours, thousands of individuals were detained to prevent any type of internal reinforcements of the invasion.

On April 16, 1961 at 11:45pm, Marion Mustelier, the head of the militia post at Playa Girón, saw a red light at sea. He drove down to the beach and blinked his headlights in that direction. The invading force shot at the jeep. Marion turned off his lights and drove to the militia post. "The North Americans have arrived at Playa Girón," he announced over the radio.

Castro reacted immediately, "Alert the nine hundred men stationed at the Austalia Sugar Mill on the road to Playa Larga to take up defensive positions and hold fast. Send the mortar battalion from Matanzas to reinforce the other two roads leading to Playa Girón. Come Alejandro, we are off to Playa Girón, the Bay of Pigs!"

As the invasion was initiated, Radio Swan began transmitting on fourteen frequencies across Cuba. Radio Swan used the same transmitter that had been used to broadcast Radio Free Europe during WWII. Gibraltar Steamship Company, a CIA front that didn't own any steamships, for the purpose of transmitting anti-Castro propaganda across Cuba, owned the station on Swan Island. Radio Swan immediately began transmitting as the invasion began: "Take up strategic positions that control the roads and railroads. Take prisoners or shoot anyone that doesn't follow your orders. All planes must stay on the ground. See that no Fidelista plane takes off. Destroy its radios. Destroy its tail. Break all instruments. Puncture its fuel tanks. The exile force is winning. The invaders are advancing steadily on every front. Castro's forces are surrendering in droves! Raul Castro has committed suicide. Join us now!"

Castro called Captain Enrique Carreras at the San Antonio Base," At this moment a landing is taking place at Playa Girón. I want you to wait until dawn and then sink those ships. The ships must be stopped."

Fidel and Alejandro reached Playa Girón just as the sun was rising in the east. "Look, Fidel, the Houston has been hit and is aground. Captain Carreras is doing a great job attacking the ships and making reinforcements difficult. The situation on the beach and on the road leading away from the beach is not as good. Two anti tank barriers are blocking our troops."

"Come, Alejandro, we need to commandeer two tanks and drive them directly into the barriers. With heavy fire they will retreat."

As they took control of two tanks with 122mm cannons, they headed straight for the barriers, Fidel on the left, Alejandro on the right. Both tanks fired as fast as they could directly into the barrier, but they held. Both tanks crashed into the barriers and were momentarily stuck. Each desperately tried to reverse and escape but they could not do it quickly enough. As the invaders approached for the coup de grace, a massive explosion stopped them at sea. Alejandro heard one of the insurgents say as he ran back toward the beach, "God Almighty, what was that? Does Castro have atomic bombs?"

Fidel and Alejandro were able to escape the barriers and could now head toward the beach. As they exited the tanks, they were both laughing and Fidel slapped him on the back. "Well done, Alejandro."

"Gracias, El Jefe, how did you arrange the explosion that sent them back to the swamp?"

"I don't know, let's find out."

Fidel found a radioman and asked about the explosion. "El Jefe, it was the ship Rio Escondido. It must have been carrying explosives because it just disintegrated, according to Captain Carreras."

"We must keep the pressure on. The cadet battalion from Matanzas will take control of Palpite. It is the only exit from the swamp still available to the insurgents. If we can do that we have won the war."

"That is, El Jefe, if Kennedy does not reinforce the air attack and commit US troops."

"Yes, Alejandro," said a more somber Fidel. "That is exactly what would happen, what will happen if the Soviets do not interject. I had hoped our partners would have been the US but it was not to be. The Soviets were necessary for just this type of situation."

In a meeting with Vice President Lyndon Baines Johnson, US Attorney General Bobby Kennedy, National Security Advisor McGeorge Bundy, John McNamara, Dean Rusk, John Bissell, CIA Director Allen Dulles, General Lemnitzer and Joint Chiefs of Staff Commander Admiral Burke, President Kennedy said, "God damn it! I trusted you and Eisenhower to know what you were doing, Dulles! This has gone to shit in a hurry. We will not commit more US air cover and we will not commit US ships and men to this catastrophe. I don't have plausible deniability now. The Soviets have caught us in violation of Article 2 and Article 51 of the United Nations Charter as well as Articles 18 and 25 of the Organization of American States Charter and Article 1 of the Rio Treaty. The same damn things we criticize them for doing. In addition, if that's not enough I went on public TV and lied to the nation. Look at this damn letter from Khrushchev!"

Mr. President:

I send you this message in an hour of alarm, fraught with danger for the peace of the whole world. Armed aggression has begun against Cuba. It is a secret to no one that the armed bands invading this country were trained, equipped and armed in the United States of America. The planes which are bombing Cuban cities belong to the United States of America, the bombs they are dropping are being supplied by the American government. All of this evokes here in the Soviet Union an understandable feeling of indignation on the part of the Soviet government and the Soviet people. Only recently, in exchanging opinions through our respective representatives, we talked with you about the mutual desire of both sides to put forward joint efforts directed toward improving relations between our countries and eliminating the danger of war. Your statement a few days ago that the USA would not participate in military activities against Cuba created the impression that the top leaders of the United States were taking into account the consequences for general peace and for the USA itself which aggression against Cuba could have. How can what is being done by the United States in reality be understood, when an attack on Cuba has now become a fact? It is still not late to avoid the irreparable. The government of the USA still has the possibility of not allowing the flame of war ignited by interventions in Cuba to grow into an incomparable conflagration. I approach you, Mr. President, with an urgent call to put an end to aggression against the Republic of Cuba. Military armament and the world political situation are such at this time that any so-called "little war" can touch off a chain reaction in all parts of the globe. As far as the Soviet Union is concerned, there should be no mistake about our position: We will render the Cuban people and their government all necessary help to repel armed attack on Cuba. We are sincerely interested in a relaxation of international tension, but if others proceed toward sharpening, we will answer them in full measure. And in general it is hardly possible so to conduct matters that the situation is settled in one area and conflagration extinguished, while a new conflagration is ignited in another area. I hope that the Government of the USA will consider our views as dictated by the sole concern not to allow steps which could lead the world to military catastrophe.

N. Khrushchev

"And I'm sure he will go to the United Nations with a similar statement. What do you propose now?" asked President Kennedy.

"Let me take two jets and shoot down Castro's aircraft?" asked Admiral Burke.

"No, I told you and Bissell, I would not commit US forces to combat!" replied President Kennedy. "Do you realize that Castro already has the name of the US pilot, Leo Francis Berliss, of Boston, that was shot down? And you want us to do more!"

"The pilot acted on his own as a civilian Mr. President," said Admiral Burke.

"You can't even say that with a straight face, Admiral. No one will believe that, no matter who says it!"

"You will have to respond to Khrushchev's letter," added Bobby.

"I know; I'll do that now. Everybody out. Bobby you stay."

"What a goddamn mess," said Bobby. "Dad will be furious."

"I know; he will be much worse than the press."

"How are you going to respond to Khrushchev?"

"I have already responded with this, Bobby":

Washington, April 18, 1961

MR. CHAIRMAN:

You are under a serious misapprehension in regard to events in Cuba. For months there has been evident and growing resistance to the Castro dictatorship. More than 100,000 refugees have recently fled from Cuba into neighboring countries. Their urgent hope is naturally to assist their fellow Cubans in their struggle for freedom. Many of these refugees fought alongside Dr. Castro against the Batista dictatorship; among them are prominent leaders of his own original movement and government. These are unmistakable signs that Cubans find intolerable the denial of democratic liberties and the subversion of the 26th of July Movement by an alien-dominated regime. It cannot be surprising that, as resistance within Cuba grows, refugees have been using whatever means are available to return and support their countrymen in the continuing struggle for freedom. Where people are denied the right of choice, recourse to such struggle is the only means of achieving their liberties. I have previously stated, and I repeat now, that the United States intends no military intervention in Cuba. In the event of any military intervention by outside force we will immediately honor our obligations under the inter-American system to protect this hemisphere against external aggression. While refraining from military intervention in Cuba, the people of the United States do not conceal their admiration for Cuban patriots who wish to see a democratic system in an independent Cuba. The United States government can take no action to stifle the spirit of liberty. I have taken careful note of your statement that the events in Cuba might affect peace in all parts of the world. I trust that this does not mean that the Soviet government, using the situation in Cuba as a pretext, is planning to inflame other areas of the world. I would like to think that your government has too great a sense of responsibility to embark upon any enterprise so dangerous to general peace. I agree with you as to the desirability of steps to improve the international atmosphere. I continue to hope that you will cooperate in *opportunities now available to this end. A prompt cease-fire and peaceful settlement of the dangerous situation in Laos, cooperation with the United Nations in the Congo and a speedy conclusion of an acceptable treaty for the banning of nuclear tests would be constructive steps in this direction. The regime in Cuba could make a similar contribution by permitting the Cuban people freely to determine their own future by democratic processes and freely to cooperate with their Latin American neighbors. I believe, Mr. Chairman, that you should recognize that free peoples in all parts of the world do not accept the claim of historical inevitability for Communist revolution. What your government believes is its own business; what it does in the world is the world's business. The great revolution in the history of man, past, present and future, is the revolution of those determined to be free.*

John F. Kennedy

"That is excellent, brother. At least it's the best response we can give at this time."

"I asked you here to show you Khrushchev's final response and ask you what you thing he means. This concerns me a great deal."

MR. PRESIDENT:

I have received your reply of April 18. You write that the United States intends no military intervention in Cuba. But numerous facts known to the whole world — and to the Government of the United States, of course, better than to any one else — speak differently. Despite all assurances to the contrary, it has now been proved beyond doubt that it was precisely the United States which prepared the intervention, financed its arming and transported the gangs of mercenaries that invaded the territory of Cuba. United States armed forces also took a direct part in the accomplishment of the gangster attack upon Cuba. American bombers and fighters supported the operations of the mercenaries who landed on Cuban territory, and participated in the military operations against the armed forces of the lawful Government and people of Cuba. Such are the facts. They bear witness to direct United States participation in the armed aggression against Cuba.----- --- --- ---*History* records many cases in which, on the pretext of defending freedom, peoples have been drowned in blood, colonial wars waged, and one small nation after another taken by the throat. --------------- --- --- ---*You, Mr.* President, display concern for a handful of enemies who were expelled by their people and found refuge under the wing of those who want to keep the guns of their cruisers and destroyers trained on Cuba. But why are you not concerned about the fate of the six million Cuban people, why do you not wish to pay regard to their inalienable right to a free and independent life, their right to arrange their domestic affairs as they see fit? Where are the standards of international law, or even of simple human morality, that would justify such a position? They simply do not exist. --- --- --*As for* the Soviet Union, we have stated on many occasions, and I now state again, that our government does not seek any advantages *or privileges in Cuba. We have no bases in Cuba, and we do not intend to establish any. And this is well known to you, to your generals and your admirals. If, despite this, they still try to frighten the people by fabrications about "Soviet bases" on Cuba, that is obviously designed for consumption by simpletons. But there are fewer and fewer such simpletons, and that applies also, I hope, to the United States. By the way, Mr. President, I would like to express my opinion concerning the statements made by you and by certain other United States politicians to the effect that rockets and other weapons could be installed on Cuban territory for possible use against the United States. The inference from this is that the United States has some alleged right to attack Cuba, either directly or through the traitors to the Cuban people whom you arm with your weapons, train on your territory, maintain with the money of United States taxpayers and transport with the resources of your armed forces, covering them from the air and the sea while they fight against the Cuban people and their lawful government. You also refer to some United States obligations to protect the Western hemisphere against external aggression. But what obligations can possibly apply in the present case? No one can have any obligations to defend rebels against the lawful government of a sovereign State, such as Cuba is. Mr. President, you are setting out on a very dangerous road. Think of it. You speak of your rights and obligations, and, of course, anyone can claim this or that right. But then you will have to admit that other States, too, can base their actions in similar circumstances, on similar arguments and considerations. You allege that Cuba cannot lend her territory for actions against the United States. That is your supposition, but it is based on no facts. We, on the other hand, can already refer to concrete facts, not suppositions: in some countries, bordering on the Soviet Union by land and sea, there are at present governments following a policy that is far from reasonable, Governments which have concluded military agreements with the United States and have made their territory available for the establishment of American military bases. And your military say openly that these bases are spearheaded against the Soviet Union, as if this were not already sufficiently clear. So, if you consider yourself entitled to take such measures against Cuba as the United States Government has been resorting to lately, you must admit that other countries have no lesser grounds for acting in the same way with regard to States whose territories are the scene of actual preparations constituting a threat to the security of the Soviet Union. If you do not want to sin against elementary logic, you must obviously concede this right to other States. We, for our part, do not hold such views. We consider that the arguments advanced on this score in the United States constitute, not merely an extremely free interpretation of international law, but, to put it plainly, open advocacy of a treacherous policy.-- -- -------------So, Mr. President, your sympathies are one thing; but actions against the security and independence of other peoples, taken on the basis of such sympathies, are very much another. You may, of course, express your sympathy with the imperialist and colonialist countries; that does not surprise anyone. For example, you vote with them in the United Nations. This is a matter of your morality. But what has been done against Cuba is no longer morality. It is gangsterism.*

It constitutes "communism." But what right have you, what right has anyone in general, to deprive a people of the possibility of choosing their social and political system of their own free will? Have you never considered that other countries, too, might perhaps advance a demand similar to yours and might declare that you, in the United States, have a system which breeds wars and espouses an imperialist policy, the policy of threats and attacks against other countries? There is every ground for such accusations. And, proceeding from the principles, which you now proclaim, one could, apparently, demand a change in the internal system of the United States. We, as you know, do not follow that road. We favor the peaceful coexistence of all States, and non-interference in the internal affairs of other countries.

----------You allude to Budapest. But we can tell you openly, without any allusions: it is you, the United States that crushed the independence of Guatemala by sending your mercenaries there, as you are now trying to do with regard to Cuba. It is the United States, and no other country, that still mercilessly exploits and keeps in economic bondage the countries of Latin America and many other countries of the world. This is known to all. And if, Mr. President, your logic is to be followed, actions from without could apparently be organized against your country too, to put an end forever to this imperialist policy, the policy of threats, the policy of suppressing the freedom-loving peoples. As for your concern for the émigrés expelled by the Cuban people, I should like to add the following. You are of course well aware that there are, in many countries, émigrés who are dissatisfied with the situation and the system existing in the countries from which they fled. And if the abnormal practice were introduced, in relations between States, of using these émigrés, especially with arms in their hand, against the countries they had fled from, it can be openly said that this would inevitably lead to conflicts and wars. It would therefore be well to refrain from such ill-advised

actions. This is a slippery and dangerous road, which can lead to a new world war. You, Mr. President, speak often and much of your desire that Cuba should be free. But that attitude is flatly contradicted by all United States actions with regard to this small country, let alone the latest armed attack upon Cuba organized with a view to changing Cuba's internal system by force. It was the United States, which nearly 60 years ago imposed on Cuba the enslaving terms of the Havana Treaty and established its Guantanamo naval base on Cuban territory. Yet the United States is the most powerful country in the Western hemisphere, and no one in that hemisphere can threaten you with a military invasion. Consequently, if you continue to retain your naval base on Cuban territory against the clearly expressed will of the Cuban people and its Government, it is because this base is designed, not to serve as a defense against an attack by any external forces, but to suppress the will of the Latin American peoples. It was established to fulfill the functions of a gendarme, to keep the peoples of Latin America politically and economically dependent. The Government of the United States is now fulminating against Cuba. But this indicates only one thing — your lack of trust in your own system, in the policy pursued by the United States. And this is understandable, as it is a policy of exploitation, a policy for the economic enslavement of underdeveloped countries. You have no confidence in your own system, and therefore fear that Cuba's example may prove contagious for other countries. But aggressive, bandit actions cannot save your system. In the historic process of the development of human society, each people decides, and will decide, its own destiny. As for the Soviet Union, the peoples of our country settled this question finally and irrevocably over 43 years ago. We constitute a socialist state. Our social system is the most equitable of all that have so far existed, because in our country all the means of production are owned by those who work. That is indeed a contagious example, and the sooner the need to go over to this system is realized, the sooner will the whole of humankind achieve a really just society. By this very development, an end will be put, once and for all, to war. ----------------------------------- -- ---------------------------The Soviet Government's position in international affairs remains unchanged. We wish to build our relations with the United States in such a way that neither the Soviet Union nor the United States, as the two most powerful countries in the world, shall engage in saber-rattling or push their military or economic superiority to the forefront, since that would lead to an aggravation of the international situation, not to its improvement. We are sincerely desirous of reaching agreement, both with you and with other countries of the world, on disarmament and all the other questions whose solution would promote peaceful coexistence, the recognition of every people's right to the social and political systems established by it, genuine respect for the will of the peoples and non-interference in their internal affairs. Only under these conditions can one really speak of coexistence, for coexistence is possible only if States with different social systems obey international laws and recognize the maintenance of world peace as their highest aim. Only in that event will peace be based on firm foundations.

N. Khrushchev

"What worries me is his reference to missiles. Do you think he would dare send missile batteries to Cuba?" asked President Kennedy.

"I think in so many words he is saying just that. And if he does he won't remove them unless we remove ours from Europe."

"Goddamn Eisenhower and Nixon. This is their mess and we have to figure a way out."

"Jack, perhaps it's time for us to figure a way to remove Castro. After all, with him gone, the communist, the Soviet threat dies. If we kill the head, the communist snake dies."

"That's right. Only this time we do it our way under our control and with the tenacity to win."

"I like the tenacity part. Let's call it Operation Mongoose."

"Bobby, start planning Operation Mongoose but don't implement until I say. I want to investigate Cuba and Castro on our own. We inherited this mess from Eisenhower and Nixon. And Dulles has been no help and may even be part of the problem. I'm not sure we have been told the real reasons Castro is against the US and has become a friend of the Soviet Union. You remember Hondo the Doberman pincher that used to bark at us from the neighbor's yard when we played baseball in the backyard? All of us thought he was barking at us and wanted to eat us alive. That is until the ball went over the fence into his yard. All he wanted was to play fetch. He brought the ball over to the fence and barked until we threw it over the fence for him to fetch. He turned out to be a friendly and likable dog that loved to play fetch. Is Castro the menace we have been told or is he really a Hondo that has been mis-understood? Let's find out. As for missiles in Cuba, if I were Khrushchev and Castro would allow it, I'd have them there tomorrow."

Fidel and Alejandro entered Playa Girón after three days of fighting and met little resistance. The war was indeed over.

When the expected air support did not happen, the mission was doomed and the insurgents surrendered to meet their fate.

"Round up as many stranglers as possible. No one is to be hurt that does not resist capture. Get me a report as soon as possible on the casualties from both sides."

"That is just like the mountains, El Jefe. Still no mis-treatment of prisoners," said Alejandro.

"That's right. We must set ourselves apart from the imperialists that maim and torture prisoners. We will never do that. We will never execute a man without a trial either. Never."

"I have the report, El Jefe," said Lieutenant Pino, "We have 89 insurgents dead, 1,197 prisoners. More are expected as we round up the stragglers. We have lost 157."

"Gracias, Lieutenant."

"What happens to the prisoners now? asked Alejandro.

"We will tend to their wounds, feed them, and then question them. If we are lucky perhaps we can eventually trade them for things we need, like tractors, baby food, or medicines. This war is over, but the struggle of the Revolution to survive will continue until we finally have a President in the US that will be strong enough to ask, 'Why are we fighting Cuba? What is the real reason we oppose Castro and is it good enough to justify what we are doing.' Until then, Alejandro, the revolution must do everything it can to survive. Thank Santo for me. Once again, you came with much needed information that allowed us to survive another day. Our deal is a deal with the devil and I struggle with the drug traffic everyday. It wakes me up at night thinking about the children in the US using these drugs that came through Cuba. We will end this as soon as possible. I'm just not sure when that will be. I look forward to the day when I can tell you to stay in Cuba, and that we are finished with Trafficante and his drugs. But that day is not here, not yet anyway."

Chapter 27
CUBAN TOBACCO
1961-1962

"On which side did you fight?" asked Kim-Ly.

"What do you mean which side?" asked Alejandro.

"El Lo Dit, I know you were in Cuba, everyone knows about the invasion. You are not a man to sit on the side and let a fight occur and not take sides. For which side did you fight?"

"El Cho Cai, you assume a great deal. And assume means you make an 'ass' out of 'u' and 'me'."

"You have been El Lo Dit long before I assumed anything. For which side did you fight?"

"And you have been El Cho Cai for as long as I've known you! Why do you want to know?"

In a quiet demure voice, that Alejandro had never heard, Kim-Ly said, "Because El Jefe, I fear for you, and only want you to be safe. When you go to war I scared for you, scared something bad happen, and I no like that."

Laughing as hard as he could Alejandro said, "Bullshit, Kim-Ly, cut the crap. Now tell me why you want to know?"

In her normal voice Kim-Ly with a wide grin responded, "What is 'cut crap'? Crap is crap; it is not cut. You do not cut crap. Crap is shit; you do not cut shit. You talk funny El Lo Dit."

"God, you are such a pest. Wise beyond your years, and intentionally demure when you want, so you can get your way; but such a pest."

"Pest is bug right? You think little Kim-Ly is bug? Oh, I so huurrt!"

"Stop it! I fought for Cuba, OK?"

"Both sides said they were fighting for Cuba, El Lo Dit. So which side?"

"Enough, Kim-Ly. I am not mad at you but let it go at Cuba."

"Oh, I so scared you mad at me," she said grabbing each side of her face with her hands while she displayed her best look of fear.

"Ok, Ok."

"I think my husband was there also, Jeff. He left before it started and came back right after in a very bad mood. I think he was not on the winning side. And I think you were because you are in a good mood." After a pause she added," I'm happy your side won, Jeff."

Alejandro stared at this exotic beauty for a long time. What a complex individual she was. I'm glad she is here, he thought to himself. "Gracias, Kim-Ly."

"Su bienvenida, Alejandro." she said with a smile in perfect Spanish.

It was a week later before Alejandro decided to ask Kim-Ly what was on his mind. "Kim-Ly, last week you answered me in perfect Spanish. Can you speak Spanish or was that a phrase you learned?"

"I speak 7 languages fluently; Hmong, Vietnamese, Putonghua Chinese, Spanish, French, Italian, and of course English."

"Why didn't you tell me?"

"You did not ask El Lo Dit. I used those languages all the time for my brother's business. We shipped to many different places with many different languages."

"What is Putonghua Chinese?"

"It is the type of Mandarin Chinese that is considered the common language of China."

"Everyday you surprise me Kim-Ly. I'm very impressed."

In her demurred voice she responded, "Oh tanks many big guy, 'ittle Kimy mean to preesze u. Love u long time fi dol'ar!"

They both laughed and returned to their work.

The next day as both were working on separate projects, Kim Ly asked, "What are you going to do about our Pinar del Rio brand? We will run out of Cuban tobacco soon and with the embargo we can't get any more."

"Well my last trip to Cuba was not all fun and games. I've made arrangements to buy Cuban seed tobacco from the Dominican Republic."

"Do you think the quality will be the same? You have preached to me for so long that only tobacco from Pinar del Rio in Cuba is the best. How will Cuban seed grown in the Dominican Republic compare?"

"Normally, I would say not very well. However, I think what we will buy will be very good. In fact I don't think you will be able to tell any difference."

Kim-Ly's eyebrows closed together as she pondered this statement. Alejandro enjoyed making her figure out things as he thought her expressions were endearing.

"Oh, I get it. You will have Pinar del Rio tobacco sent to the Dominican Republic, re-packaged as Dominican. Very clever, and as it is 'Cuban seed' the Alcohol Tobacco and Fire Arms Inspectors will not know the difference. Flor de Pinar will be the most prized cigar outside of Cuba. Well done, Jeff!"

"Are you naturally larcenous Kim-Ly or is that something you learned from your brother?"

"Larcenous is a hard term, I think. The Hmong are simple people. If something needs to be, then we do what is required to make that happen. If it truly needs to be, then any law that forbids it is a bad law. Since simple people are not the ones who make the laws, simple people will choose to ignore bad laws. I don't know if that makes me larcenous, but it is the way my family has lived for hundreds of years. Someone else, the Chinese, the Japanese the French, or the Viet Cong are always making laws for us without our input. The Hmong believe it is our right to ignore any law that prevents us from doing what needs to be done."

"And how do you decide if something needs to de done?"

"If it helps the individual, helps the village, helps the country and does no other individual harm, then it needs to be done."

"How do you reason that your brother's opium trade is needed?"

"Without my brother's business thousands of villagers would have starved to death. He uses the money gained to provide many things for our people. The farmers can make a living growing poppy but cannot growing rice. As you know we have some big families in our country that would not make it except for the poppy."

"But the poppy, the opium made from it, and the heroin made from the opium does hurt people. Their addiction renders them non-productive human beings and overdoses kill quite a few each year."

"Yes, that is the problem with the poppy. I am sorry for the addicts, for the families of addicts that suffer. I will not use the excuse that if we didn't provide it someone else would. That is not accepting responsibility for one's actions. The simple truth is we could not find any other way to provide for our people. We made a decision knowing that it would hurt some people and help some people. As you know, the poppy also has medical value in that morphine, codeine, thebaine, and hydrocodone all come from the poppy. I cannot say if that decision was right or wrong. I can only say we chose it because we could not think of any other way. The decision was made based on the argument that the addicts have a choice to use or not to use. If they choose to use then the Japanese would say that is their karma to be an addict. Sometimes I want to believe this concept of karma. Then I think if its karma then they have no choice and they can't do anything about their plight. When the Hmong were hungry, we could have said that is our karma to be hungry and we would have starved to death. But we did not do that. We decided it was our responsibility to find a way to eat, and we did. I am proud to be Hmong and I am proud that we found a way to eat. The rest I can't judge."

"I understand your moral dilemma, Kim-Ly. I've made decisions with similar parameters. I've even convinced others to make such deals. For one part of the deal, it perpetuates something that is good and needy. On the other hand, it involves people that will suffer because of our deal. Is it ok to make a deal with the devil if it also provides a greater good? I don't know. A friend of mine likes to justify these choices by saying history will be the judge, absolve us if we did right, and condemn us if we did wrong. That sounds good to me as if something more than us will decide, but that is not true. History is written by victors. It is only treason if you lose. It is a revolution to overthrow evil if you win. Because history is written by victors, some have used this concept to say the end justifies the means. I have used this argument to justify some deals. Like you, I know this is not the right way, but I cannot find a better one.

Maybe that is our karma, Kim-Ly, to live with our choices even though they are not the choices we would have preferred. But we were not smart enough to figure out another way. I agree with the concept that for a man to do evil he must first think he is doing right."

"I think you are right, Jeff, up to a point. I think you and I have a shared karma. Where that karma will take us I have no idea but I think we will share the outcome. How we will get there, I have no idea. I think that will be our history. As for 'believing you are right before doing wrong,' this is a moral concept and only applies to a moral individual's decisions. I know this because I have seen and personally know men that will do harm to others because of the enjoyment they receive from watching suffering. For them there is no right or wrong, there is only self-gratification from others' pain. They are ruthless and will do anything to anyone to get their way. For them right and wrong do not exist, only success or failure, and failure is not acceptable."

Work was impossible after so heavy a discussion so Alejandro and Kim-Ly escaped to the Columbia for rum and coke (Cuba Libre) and Cuban sandwiches. Alejandro talked about Cuba and the Pinar del Rio and Kim-Ly talked about the mountains in Southeast Asia where the Hmong originated. Kim-Ly left at five to get home. "See you tomorrow, Jeff."

"Yes, see you tomorrow. I really enjoyed our afternoon Kim-Ly."

"So did I, Jeff," she hesitated before adding," more than I will say."

As Alejandro sat at the bar, he watched her leave. She was wearing her silk lion shirt that he had seen the first day. She had told him that Kim-Ly meant Golden Lion and that was why the shirt was one of her favorites. As he re-thought the afternoon, he knew something in him was changing. Something was happening that he thought was gone forever. He must be an idiot he thought. To always fall for a girl that either belonged to another or was promised to another is stupid. He knew that, but did he have a choice or do these things just happen. Karma maybe? He had no idea what to do. Like the first time with Isabel, he couldn't really do anything. He would just have to wait. Finally, he said to no one, "I know, I'll let history decide." He smiled as he left the bar, "or maybe karma."

The next day was business as usual for Alejandro and Kim-Ly. Neither mentioned the day before. Santo called and wanted to meet Alejandro for lunch. As both men enjoyed their 1905 salad at the Columbia, Santo said, "I've got two things for you today. One, we have an extra large package coming in tomorrow night. It seems one of our other routes has been shut down. Those fuckin' Kennedy brothers are a real pain in the ass. If our young president continues to piss off the wrong people, he will not last. Mark my word; he will not last. He won't drop Cuba either. It seems the brothers were so embarrassed by the Bay of Pigs that they have organized a new campaign of terror for Castro. They call it Operation Mongoose. More of the same, only now headed by baby Bobby and CIA General Edward Lansdale. The CIA created the Special Group Augmented

(SGA) to carry out Mongoose. William Harvey has been put in charge of Task Force W, which is under the SGA. Force W has 400 CIA agents in Miami and is trying to recruit as many Cuban exiles as possible. They have a budget of $50 million dollars a year. Their objective is to attack Cuban ships, sabotage aircraft, and to attack non-Cuban ships that trade with Cuba. They will also contaminate shipments of oil and sugar if possible. Another project is Operation Peter Pan. This involves releasing false propaganda that indicates Castro intends to send thousands of Cuban children to the Soviet Union for education and indoctrination to Communism. At the next 26th of July anniversary, the CIA will attempt to assassinate Fidel, Che and Raul. If they are successful with killing even one of the three, they will attack Guantanamo to make it look like the Cubans are retaliating for the assassination. Then there will be the pretext for US military intervention. If that doesn't work they calculate they will have created enough dissention to make a US attack by October 1962 with or without internal help."

"What fucking idiots, don't they realize they are gambling with nuclear war with the Soviets? Especially if US military are involved, no matter the pretext."

"With the latest National Intelligence Estimate on nuclear capability, I don't think they care."

"How in the hell do you get that kind of secret information? I mean I'm not complaining; all of your intel has been great for Cuba, but really top secret government reports, how?"

Santo laughed at Alejandro before answering, "Alejandro, of course I'm not going to tell you. You do know we have been partners with the CIA since WWII. More than enough time to have a man on the inside. We know what we need to know when we need to know it. It has been tricky for me to get Cuban info without creating curiosity, but I manage. Now, never ask me a question like that again, capisce?"

"My apologies, Don Santo. I overstepped. I meant no disrespect."

"I like you Alejandro, my father liked you, and I don't want anything to unnecessarily happen to you. People in our business tend to disappear if they have information they shouldn't, capisce?"

" Capisce, I understand."

"As I was saying, the latest NIE report indicated the Soviets are way behind the US in nuclear capability. The United States has 22,229 nuclear weapons and the Soviets only have 2,450. The Soviets only have ten to twenty-five ICBMs all of which are in Russia, so how much of a threat is there? You have to admit though, these Kennedys have balls, big brass balls. However, with a big enough hammer even brass balls can turn to dust. Obviously, Castro needs this info as soon as possible. Take the flight to Miami and then use the boat Castro provided. His men know the boat and will let you through. It might not be so easy if a CIA team stops you, so beware."

"Thanks, Don Santo, I'll leave in the morning."

Chapter 28
MISSILES IN CUBA
1962

The trip by boat to Cuba was actually pleasant. It was nice to be on the water and not watching it from a plane. A Cuban patrol spotted them and came close enough to read the name, wave and move on. Of course, the name was 'Miss Isabel.' Alejandro had been able to pick the name and never considered any other name.

"The assassination attempts are no longer an issue, Alejandro," said El Jefe, "my security guard can handle anything they try. The people are united and will resist the terror of their attacks, but another invasion lead by the United States military is too much for Cuba alone. Again, we will have to enlist Khrushchev who has wanted to install missile bases on Cuban soil. I didn't want that. We didn't need that before this threat. You are confident the information is accurate?"

"Unfortunately, yes, El Jefe. It seems there is no limit to Santo's access to United States secrets. At least those secrets of the CIA and FBI. It appears he has moles in both camps."

"It would seem Santo is a student of Sun Tzu. Since the first war was fought, the greatest instrument of war is intelligence.

Knowing what your enemy knows and intends to do in advance. I had hoped by now we could have ended this 'agreement' with Trafficante, but it seems we must keep it a while longer. I am sorry Alejandro. I seem to always keep you in harm's way."

"It is my duty, El Jefe. I have known for some time that the only good side of my hate for Batista has been it allowed me to serve a more noble cause, Cuba."

"And serve Cuba you have, Alejandro. But I have to admit for selfish reasons that I would like for you to be back home as soon as possible."

"I have learned a new term, El Jefe, karma. It is a Japanese term for one's fate. For example, it is my karma to serve Cuba not from home but from Ybor."

"I like that term, karma. I will have to read more about it," responded Fidel.

"Are you still reading a lot?"

"I try to read everyday for at least 4 hours. I love sports. I love the water. I love women, and I love Cuban Cigars. But the knowledge gained from reading is my passion!"

The trip back to Miami was also uneventful. Alejandro sighted a Coastguard boat near Miami but they took them to be what they were supposed to be, a fishing boat. The Captain had the boat rigged for fishing with a fighting chair in the middle of the deck. Bait and ice were always loaded with adequate tackle for up to six passengers. The fuel capacity was enlarged and when not in use as a ferryboat for Alejandro, it was rented out for fishing excursions. Whenever Alejandro called Captain Hernandez, any scheduled fishing trip was cancelled. The best part, Batista had originally owned the boat. Batista had left it behind when he fled Cuba in 1959. Fidel had it renamed when it was commissioned to transport Alejandro.

In Washington, three months later, President Kennedy was in the Oval Office with the Attorney General. "Goddamn it, Bobby did you see what Doriticos said at the UN, 'we have indeed our inevitable weapons, the weapons which we would have preferred not to acquire and which we do not wish to employ', that can only mean nuclear weapons. Did that goddamn Khrushchev give Cuba nuclear weapons?"

"Jack, we don't know that. We have the U-2 pictures which indicate missile silos are under construction but nothing is active yet."

"So they don't have them yet, but they will. We have to act now and we have to act fast. I don't want atomic weapons in the hands of Castro. Keep the U-2s flying and get me some low-level pictures as well."

"The Pentagon has no information regarding nuclear missiles in Cuba. They have advised that if we attack or destroy Cuban fortifications it will lead to WWIII."

"If the construction continues I want the Navy to implement a military blockade of Cuba no later than October 20th.

On October 22nd President Kennedy addressed the Nation:

October 22, 1962

Good evening my fellow citizens: This Government, as promised, has maintained the closest surveillance of the Soviet military buildup on the island of Cuba. Within the past week, unmistakable evidence has established the fact that a series of offensive missile sites is now in preparation on that imprisoned island. The purpose of these bases can be none other than to provide a nuclear strike capability against the Western Hemisphere. Upon receiving the first preliminary hard information of this nature last Tuesday morning at 9 a.m., I

*directed that our surveillance be stepped up. And having now
confirmed and completed our evaluation of the evidence and
our decision on a course of action, this government feels obliged
to report this new crisis to you in fullest detail. The charac-
teristics of these new missile sites indicate two distinct types of
installations. Several of them include medium range ballistic
missiles capable of carrying a nuclear warhead for a distance
of more than 1,000 nautical miles. Each of these missiles, in
short, is capable of striking Washington, D.C., the Panama
Canal, Cape Canaveral, Mexico City, or any other city in the
southeastern part of the United States, in Central America, or
in the Caribbean area. Additional sites not yet completed appear to be designed for intermediate range ballistic missiles —
capable of traveling more than twice as far — and thus capable
of striking most of the major cities in the Western Hemisphere,
ranging as far north as Hudson Bay, Canada, and as far south
as Lima, Peru. In addition, jet bombers, capable of carrying
nuclear weapons, are now being uncrated and assembled in
Cuba, while the necessary air bases are being prepared. This
urgent transformation of Cuba into an important strategic
base — by the presence of these large, long range, and clearly
offensive weapons of sudden mass destruction — constitutes an
explicit threat to the peace and security of all the Americas, in
flagrant and deliberate defiance of the Rio Pact of 1947, the
traditions of this Nation and hemisphere, the joint resolution
of the 87th Congress, the Charter of the United Nations, and
my own public warnings to the Soviets on September 4 and 13.
This action also contradicts the repeated assurances of Soviet
spokesmen, both publicly and privately delivered, that the arms
buildup in Cuba would retain its original defensive character, and that the Soviet Union had no need or desire to station*

strategic missiles on the territory of any other nation. The size of this undertaking makes clear that it has been planned for some months. Yet only last month, after I had made clear the distinction between any introduction of ground-to-ground missiles and the existence of defensive antiaircraft missiles, the Soviet Government publicly stated on September 11, and I quote, "the armaments and military equipment sent to Cuba are designed exclusively for defensive purposes," that, and I quote the Soviet Government, "there is no need for the Soviet Government to shift its weapons . . . for a retaliatory blow to any other country, for instance Cuba." And I quote their government, "the Soviet Union has so powerful rockets to carry these nuclear warheads that there is no need to search for sites for them beyond the boundaries of the Soviet Union." That statement was false. Only last Thursday, as evidence of this rapid offensive buildup was already in my hand, Soviet Foreign Minister Gromyko told me in my office that he was instructed to make it clear once again, as he said his government had already done, that Soviet assistance to Cuba, and I quote, "pursued solely the purpose of contributing to the defense capabilities of Cuba," that, and I quote him, "training by Soviet specialists of Cuban nationals in handling defensive armaments was by no means offensive, and if it were otherwise," Mr. Gromyko went on, "the Soviet Government would never become involved in rendering such assistance." That statement also was false.

Neither the United States of America nor the world community of nations can tolerate deliberate deception and offensive threats on the part of any nation, large or small. We no longer live in a world where only the actual firing of weapons represents a sufficient challenge to a nation's security to constitute maximum peril. *Nuclear weapons are so destructive and ballistic missiles are so swift, that any substantially increased possibility of their use or any sudden change in their deployment may well be regarded as a definite threat to peace. For many years both the Soviet Union and the United States, recognizing this fact, have deployed strategic nuclear weapons with great care, never upsetting the precarious status quo which insured that these weapons would not be used in the absence of some vital challenge. Our own strategic missiles have never been transferred to the territory of any other nation under a cloak of secrecy and deception; and our history — unlike that of the Soviets since the end of World War II — demonstrates that we have no desire to dominate or conquer any other nation or impose our system upon its people. Nevertheless, American citizens have become adjusted to living daily on the Bull's-eye of Soviet missiles located inside the U.S.S.R. or in submarines. In that sense, missiles in Cuba add to an already clear and present danger — although it should be noted the nations of Latin America have never previously been subjected to a potential nuclear threat. But this secret, swift, and extraordinary buildup of Communist missiles — in an area well known to have a special and historical relationship to the United States and the nations of the Western Hemisphere, in violation of Soviet assurances, and in defiance of American and hemispheric policy — this sudden, clandestine decision to station strategic weapons for the first time outside of Soviet soil — is a deliberately provocative and unjustified change in the status quo which cannot be accepted by this country, if our courage and our commitments are ever to be trusted again by either friend or foe. The 1930's taught us a clear lesson: aggressive conduct, if allowed to go unchecked and unchallenged ultimately leads to war. This nation is opposed to war. We are also true to our word. Our unswerving objective, therefore, must be to prevent the use of these missiles against this or any other country, and to secure their withdrawal or elimination from the Western Hemisphere. Our policy has been one of patience and restraint, as befits a peaceful and powerful nation, which leads a worldwide alliance. We have been determined not to be diverted from our central concerns by mere irritants and fanatics. But now further action is required — and it is under way; and these actions may only be the beginning. We will not prematurely or unnecessarily risk the costs of worldwide nuclear war in which even the fruits of victory would be ashes in our mouth — but neither will we shrink from that risk at any time it must be faced. Acting, therefore, in the defense of our own security and of the entire Western Hemisphere, and under the authority entrusted to me by the Constitution as endorsed by the resolution of the Congress, I have directed that the following initial steps be taken immediately:*

First: To halt this offensive buildup, a strict quarantine on all offensive military equipment under shipment to Cuba is being initiated. All ships of any kind bound for Cuba from whatever nation or port will, if found to contain cargoes of offensive weapons, be turned back. This quarantine will be extended, if needed, to other types of cargo and carriers. We are not at this time, however, denying the necessities of life as the Soviets attempted to do in their Berlin blockade of 1948.

Second: I have directed the continued and increased close surveillance of Cuba and its military buildup. The foreign ministers of the OAS, in their communiqué of October 6, rejected secrecy in such matters in this hemisphere. Should these offensive military preparations continue, thus increasing the threat to the hemisphere, further action will be justified. I have directed the Armed Forces to prepare for any eventualities; and I trust that in the interest of both the Cuban people and the Soviet technicians at the sites, the hazards to all concerned in continuing this threat will be recognized.

Third: *It shall be the policy of this Nation to regard any nuclear missile launched from Cuba against any nation in the Western Hemisphere as an attack by the Soviet Union on the United States, requiring a full retaliatory response upon the Soviet Union.*

Fourth: *As a necessary military precaution, I have reinforced our base at Guantanamo, evacuated today the dependents of our personnel there, and ordered additional military units to be on a standby alert basis.*

Fifth: *We are calling tonight for an immediate meeting of the Organ of Consultation under the Organization of American States, to consider this threat to hemispheric security and to invoke articles 6 and 8 of the Rio Treaty in support of all necessary action. The United Nations Charter allows for regional security arrangements — and the nations of this hemisphere decided long ago against the military presence of outside powers. Our other allies around the world have also been alerted.*

Sixth: *Under the Charter of the United Nations, we are asking tonight that an emergency meeting of the Security Council be convoked without delay to take action against this latest Soviet threat to world peace. Our resolution will call for the* *prompt dismantling and withdrawal of all offensive weapons in Cuba, under the supervision of U.N. observers, before the quarantine can be lifted.*

Seventh and finally: *I call upon Chairman Khrushchev to halt and eliminate this clandestine, reckless and provocative threat to world peace and to stable relations between our two nations. I call upon him further to abandon this course of world domination, and to join in an historic effort to end the perilous arms race and to transform the history of man. He has an opportunity now to move the world back from the abyss of destruction — by returning to his government's own words that it had no need to station missiles outside its own territory, and withdrawing these weapons from Cuba — by refraining from any action which will widen or deepen the present crisis — and then by participating in a search for peaceful and permanent solutions.*

This Nation is prepared to present its case against the Soviet threat to peace, and our own proposals for a peaceful world, at any time and in any forum — in the OAS, in the United Nations, or in any other meeting that could be useful — without limiting our freedom of action. We have in the past made strenuous efforts to limit the spread of nuclear weapons. We have proposed the elimination of all arms and military bases in a fair and effective disarmament treaty. We are prepared to discuss new proposals for the removal of tensions on both sides — including the possibility of a genuinely independent Cuba, free to determine its own destiny. We have no wish to war with the Soviet Union — for we are a peaceful people who desire to live in peace with all other peoples. But it is difficult to settle or even discuss these problems in an atmosphere of intimidation. That is why this latest Soviet threat — or any other threat, which is made either independently or in response to our actions this week — must and will be met with determination. Any hostile move anywhere in the world against the safety and freedom of peoples to whom we are committed — including in particular the brave people of West Berlin — will be met by whatever action is needed. Finally, I want to say a few words to the captive people of Cuba, to whom this speech is being directly carried by special radio facilities. I speak to you as a friend, as one who knows of your deep attachment to your fatherland, as one who shares your aspirations for liberty and justice for all. And I have watched and the American people have watched with deep sorrow how your nationalist revolution was betrayed — and how your fatherland fell under foreign domination. Now your leaders are no longer Cuban leaders inspired by Cuban ideals. They are puppets and agents of an international conspiracy which has turned Cuba against your friends and neighbors in the Americas — and turned it into the first Latin American country to become a target for nuclear war — the first Latin American country to have these weapons on its soil. These new weapons are not in your interest. They contribute nothing to your peace and well-being. They can only undermine it. But this country has no wish to cause you to suffer or to impose any system upon you. We know that your lives and land are being used as pawns by those who deny your freedom. Many times in the past, the Cuban people have risen to throw out tyrants who destroyed their liberty. And I have no doubt that most Cubans today look forward to the time when they will be truly free — free from foreign domination, free to choose their own leaders, free to select their own system, free to own their own land, free to speak and write and worship without fear or degradation. And then shall Cuba be welcomed back to the society of free nations and to the associations of this hemisphere. My fellow citizens: let no one doubt that this is a difficult and dangerous effort on which we have set out. No one can see precisely what course it will take or what costs or casualties will be incurred. Many months of sacrifice and self-discipline lie ahead — months in which our patience and our will be tested — months in which many threats and denunciations will keep us aware of our dangers. But the greatest danger of all would be to do nothing. The path we have chosen for the present is full of hazards, as all paths are — but it is the one most consistent with our character and courage as a nation and our commitments around the world. The cost of freedom is always high — and Americans have always paid it. And one path we shall never choose, and that is the path of surrender or submission. Our goal is not the victory of might, but the vindication of right- -not peace at the expense of freedom, but both peace and freedom, here in this hemisphere, and, we hope, around the world. God willing, that goal will be achieved.

Thank you and good night.

"Jack, you realize we have nuclear weapons at Guantanamo and Puerto Rico, right?"

"That's different. This is our goddamn hemisphere."

"And what about Adlai Stevenson's statements that the blockade would be similar to the Berlin Wall, and that we have offensive missiles in Turkey."

"I heard that Bobby. Sometimes I don't know which side he's on. Let's get John McCloy to help him present this correctly to the UN. We've gone to great lengths since WWII to insure the America people and the rest of our Allies see us as the good guys and the Soviet Union as the bad guys. Stevenson cannot say anything that might burst that bubble. I don't care if it's true, we cannot lose our illusion of always being on the side of freedom and doing what is in the best interest of the people. Damn him for opening that can of worms. I will not allow this. If he wants to keep his job he better only reinforce our position and nothing else."

After the news broadcast, Santo sent word for Alejandro to meet him at the Columbia. As they sat smoking cigars Santo said, "Alejandro, I think it would be wise for you to get to Castro as soon as possible, and that means tonight. This crap with the Russians has to stop before the World is but a memory. I know Kennedy wants to end this peacefully, but Khrushchev will have to meet him in the middle. I have made arrangements to get you there before morning, but you have to leave now, capisce?"

"Capisce, Don Santo. With Castro, I know reason will prevail, but I don't know Khrushchev. I will do what I can."

As Alejandro traveled, he had plenty of time to think about the situation. Was this part of Castro's plan? Did he want the Soviets and the United States to really start a War? He didn't think so. Castro had always said that to avoid war, Cuba had to be aligned with one super power or the other. "I sure hope this doesn't blow up in his face," he said to the seagull flying above the boat, "no pun intended Señor." Alejandro reached Fidel's office at five in the morning and as usual, he was already there.

"Hola, El Jefe, our friend in Ybor is worried the super powers might blow up the world just to spite Cuba."

"Hola Alejandro, as you should know I am following this very closely. We have nuclear weapons and they are armed and aimed at the United States. Kennedy and Khrushchev are writing letters back and forth. Nikita is sending me copies, so I can offer input, but I don't think he is listening. This is an opportunity to rid Cuba of the United States illegal presence at Guantanamo for good. Neither Kennedy nor Khrushchev will ever fire first. However, I am very concerned about the Russian commanders that are in charge of the Soviet submarines and the missiles that are armed and ready to fire from here. Communication is good enough on the US side to avoid mistakes. What worries me is the Soviets that are in control in Cuba. Khrushchev has assured me they already have permission to fire at will, if the Americans shoot first. He was trying to give me confidence in the situation that the Soviets would not be caught with their pants down. Instead, he has added a variable that could end the world if they act prematurely. I am glad you are here; I want to ask you if you would visit the Missile Commander and stay by his side until this is over. I know Cuba; I know the world can trust you not to let the Soviets fire first."

"And if the Commander won't listen to me?"

"Then shoot him. I know I am asking you to commit suicide, but everything depends on this. And I mean everything and probably everybody as well. Will you do this?"

"I will do this for you and for Cuba, nothing else."

"Gracias, Alejandro, before you leave read these letters from Kennedy and Khrushchev."

Washington, October 22, 1962.

Dear Mr. Chairman: A copy of the statement I am making tonight concerning developments in Cuba and the reaction of my Government thereto has been handed to your ambassador in Washington. In view of the gravity of the developments to which I refer, I want you to know immediately and accurately the position of my government in this matter. In our discussions and exchanges on Berlin and other international questions, the one thing that has most concerned me has been the possibility that your government would not correctly understand the will and determination of the United States in any given situation, since I have not assumed that you or any other sane man would, in this nuclear age, deliberately plunge the world into war which it is crystal clear no country could win and which could only result in catastrophic consequences to the whole world, including the aggressor. At our meeting in Vienna and subsequently, I expressed our readiness and desire to find, through peaceful negotiation, a solution to any and all problems that divide us. At the same time, I made clear that in view of the objectives of the ideology to which you adhere; the United States could not tolerate any action on your part, which in a major way disturbed the existing over-all balance of power in the world. I stated that an attempt to force abandonment of our responsibilities and commitments in Berlin would constitute such an action and that the United States would resist with all the power at its command. It was in order to avoid any incorrect assessment on the part of your Government with respect to Cuba that I publicly stated that if certain developments in Cuba took place, the United States would do whatever must be done to protect its own security and that of its allies. Moreover, the Congress adopted a resolution expressing its support of this declared policy. Despite this, the rapid development of long-range missile bases and other offensive weapons systems in Cuba has proceeded. I must tell you that the United States is determined that this threat to the security of this hemisphere be removed. At the same time, I wish to point out that the action we are taking is the minimum necessary to remove the threat to the security of the nations of this hemisphere. The fact of this minimum response should not be taken as a basis, however, for any misjudgment on your part. I hope that your Government will refrain from any action which would widen or deepen this already grave crisis and that we can agree to resume the path of peaceful negotiation.

Sincerely,

JFK

Mr. President:

I have just received your letter of October 22 and have acquainted myself with text of your speech of October 22 regarding Cuba. I should say frankly that the measures outlined in your statement represent a serious threat to peace and security of nations. The United States has openly taken a path of gross violations of the Charter of the United Nations, a path violating the international norms of free navigation on the high seas, a path of aggressive actions both against Cuba and against the Soviet Union. The statement of the United States Government cannot be evaluated in any other way than as naked interference in the domestic affairs of the Cuban Republic, the Soviet Union, and other states. The Charter of United Nations and international norms do not give the right to any state whatsoever to establish, in international waters, control over vessels bound for the shores of the Cuban Republic. It is self-evident that we also cannot recognize the right of United States to establish control over armaments essential to the Republic of Cuba for the strengthening of its defensive capacity. We confirm that armaments now en route to Cuba, regardless of the classification to which they belong, are intended exclusively for defensive purposes, in order to secure the Cuban Republic from attack by an aggressor. I hope that the Government of the United States will show prudence and renounce the actions pursued by you, which could lead to catastrophic consequences for peace throughout world. The viewpoint of the Soviet Government with regard to your statement of October 22 is set forth in the statement of the Soviet Government, which is being conveyed to you through your Ambassador in Moscow.

N. Khrushchev.

Dear Mr. Chairman:

I have received your letter of October twenty-third. I think you will recognize that the steps which started the current chain of events was the action of your government in secretly furnishing offensive weapons to Cuba. We will be discussing this matter in the Security Council. In the meantime, I am concerned that we both show prudence and do nothing to allow events to make the situation more difficult to control than it already is.

I hope that you will issue immediately the necessary instructions to your ships to observe the terms of the quarantine, the basis of which was established by the vote of the Organization of American States this afternoon, and which will go into effect at 1400 hours Greenwich time October twenty-four.

Sincerely,

JFK

DEAR MR. PRESIDENT:

I have received your letter of October 23, have studied it, and am answering you.------------------------------ -- -- ------------------------------Therefore, Mr. President, if you coolly weigh the situation which has developed, not giving way to passions, you will understand that the Soviet Union cannot fail to reject the arbitrary demands of the United States. When you confront us with such conditions, try to put yourself in our place and consider how the United States would react to these conditions. I do not doubt that if someone attempted to dictate similar conditions to you--the United States--you would reject such an attempt. And we also say--no. The Soviet Government considers that the violation of the freedom to use international waters and international air space is an act of aggression, which pushes humankind toward the abyss of a world nuclear-missile war. Therefore, the Soviet Government cannot instruct the captains of Soviet vessels bound for Cuba to observe the orders of American naval forces blockading that island. Our instructions to Soviet mariners are to observe strictly the universally accepted norms of navigation in international waters and not to retreat one-step from them. And if the American side violates these rules, it must realize what responsibility will rest upon it in that case. Naturally, we will not simply be bystanders with regard to piratical acts by American ships on the high seas. We will then be forced on our part to take the measures we consider necessary and adequate in order to protect our rights. We have everything necessary to do so.

Respectfully,

N. Khrushchev

Dear Mr. Chairman:

I have received your letter of October 24, and I regret very much that you still do not appear to understand what it is that has moved us in this matter. The sequence of events is clear. In August there were reports of important shipments of military equipment and technicians from the Soviet Union to Cuba. In early September I indicated very plainly that the United States would regard any shipment of offensive weapons as presenting the gravest issues. After that time, this government received the most explicit assurances from your government and its representatives, both publicly

*and privately, that no offensive weapons were being sent to Cuba.
If you will review the statement issued by Tass in September, you
will see how clearly this assurance was given. In reliance on these
solemn assurances I urged restraint upon those in this country
who were urging action in this matter at that time. And then I
learned beyond doubt what you have not denied -- namely, that
all these public assurances were false and that your military people
had set out recently to establish a set of missile bases in Cuba. I
ask you to recognize clearly, Mr. Chairman, that it was not I
who issued the first challenge in this case, and that in the light of
this record these activities in Cuba required the responses I have
announced. I repeat my regret that these events should cause a de-
terioration in our relations. I hope that your government will take
the necessary action to permit a restoration of the earlier situation.*

Sincerely yours,

JFK

Dear Mr. President:

*I have received your letter of October 25. From your letter, I
got the feeling that you have some understanding of the situation which has developed and (some) sense of responsibility.
I value this. ---

--Let   us
therefore show statesmanlike wisdom. I propose: We, for
our part, will declare that our ships, bound for Cuba, will
not carry any kind of armaments. You would declare that
the United States will not invade Cuba with its forces and*

will not support any sort of forces, which might intend to carry out an invasion of Cuba. Then the necessity for the presence of our military specialists in Cuba would disappear. Mr. President, I appeal to you to weigh well what the aggressive, piratical actions, which you have declared the USA intends to carry out in international waters, would lead to. You yourself know that any sensible man simply cannot agree with this, cannot recognize your right to such actions. If you did this as the first step towards the unleashing of war, well then, it is evident that nothing else is left to us but to accept this challenge of yours. If, however, you have not lost your self-control and sensibly conceive what this might lead to, then, Mr. President, we and you ought not now to pull on the ends of the rope in which you have tied the knot of war, because the more the two of us pull, the tighter that knot will be tied. And a moment may come when that knot will be tied so tight that even he who tied it will not have the strength to untie it, and then it will be necessary to cut that knot, and what that would mean is not for me to explain to you, because you yourself understand perfectly of what terrible forces our countries dispose. Consequently, if there is no intention to tighten that knot and thereby to doom the world to the catastrophe of thermonuclear war, then let us not only relax the forces pulling on the ends of the rope, let us take measures to untie that knot. We are ready for this. We welcome all forces, which stand on positions of peace. Consequently, I expressed gratitude to Mr. Bertrand Russell, too, who manifests alarm and concern for the fate of the world, and I readily responded to the appeal of the Acting Secretary General of the UN, U'Thant. There, Mr. President, are my thoughts, which, if you agreed with them, could put an end to that tense situation which is disturbing all peoples. These thoughts are dictated by a sincere desire to relieve the situation, to remove the threat of war.

Respectfully yours,

N. Khrushchev

Alejandro, after reading the letters, agreed with Castro's assessment that the two leaders would reach a compromise and avoid nuclear war. He was not as sure as Castro that the US military would act with the same restraint. As Colonel Beloborodov was near San Cristobal in the Pinar del Rio Province, Alejandro had no trouble finding him. Fidel had given him a jeep with Castro's identification so he had no trouble with Russian security as he traveled. Colonel Beloborodov after reading Castro's letter of introduction treated Alejandro as a superior, "Sir, the batteries are combat ready. Somehow, the bulk carrier *Aleksandrovsk* had maneuvered past the blockade and reached the Port of La Isabella with nuclear warheads for the R-14 missiles and with the tactical nuclear weapons to complete the fortifications. We are ready for anything."

"Thank-you Colonel, I have read the correspondence between Premier Khrushchev and President Kennedy, and I believe they are about to reach an accord."

"That is great news Commander. Earlier tonight seashore officers from V. A. Anastasiev's group and I were watching the flights of U.S. combat airplanes and helicopters near the U.S. warships that had approached Cuba. The U.S. forces, using their proximity to Cuba, numerical superiority in air forces and naval power and the presence of a strong group of marines, clearly demonstrated their intention to unleash a war. Therefore, we faced the question of what we would personally do in case war broke out. I, as a veteran who went all the way from Stalingrad to Prague, Colonel Anastasiev, who fought as a private miner and exploded Nazi tanks near Belgorod, as well as other officers who had fought in the Great Patriotic War, all understood that we had nowhere to retreat. After a dynamic, balanced exchange of opinions, we concluded that we would stand together with the Cuban people and their army, and repel the aggressors as part of the Group of Soviet Forces. All the generals and senior officers of the Group of Soviet Forces have combat experience. The majority of the junior officers, sergeants and soldiers were born before or during the last war, which largely determined their high patriotism, respect for nations that were victims of aggression, and confidence in the justice of internationalist ideas. We are ready for whatever comes, Comrade Commander!"

"Thank-you Colonel, El Jefe was correct in trusting the Soviets."

"El Jefe?"

"El Jefe is what we called Fidel Castro during the Revolución. It means The Chief."

"Colonel have you read Hemingway who said, *'A man is not made for defeat... a man can be destroyed but not defeated.* -------- -- ------------------------------------*The war we learned how to win, we knew what to do and how to do it; we knew how to judge the strength and capabilities of our enemy. It was clear that in the conditions of the existing balance of forces in conventional arms, which was ten to one against us, there was only one way we could repel a massive assault—by using tactical nuclear weapons against the invaders. In principle, this action would be consistent with international law on the protection of sovereignty and freedom.*

But that would be the beginning of the end. Only madmen could unleash a nuclear war. Am I such a man?'

"The two leaders are not such men, war will be avoided, I am positive Colonel."

"Thank-you Commander, your words are most welcomed. Having the autonomy to fire at will is a tremendous honor and a terrible responsibility at the same time. It will be a great relief to not exercise that responsibility."

"Have you heard from Arkhipov?"

"Not in the last few hours. He missed his last time check and we were concerned until we received your assurances that war will not start."

"Kennedy and Khrushchev" said Rafael, "will not start a war. Let's hope no one else does either."

Rafael was confident that he had convinced the missile base Commander to not fire unless he was absolutely positive that a war had started. However, the submarine commanders that were playing with the blockade also had missiles and the autonomy to fire. Since he could not reach them, he hoped they maintained a cool head in a not so cool climate.

"Dive, dive. We are being attacked!" yelled Captain Savitsky aboard the Soviet Foxtrot-Class B-59 submarine. "The block-ade ships are dropping depth-charges. We must position our sub beneath them." What are the Americans thinking, thought Savitsky. Are they trying to start WWIII? The B-59 was one of four Soviet submarines sent to assist in case of trouble at the American blockade of Cuba. Every crewmember knew the se-riousness of their mission. In case of war, the B-59 submarine had the Soviet's 'special weapon', a nuclear torpedo. After thirty minutes of maneuvering and diving deeper, the Captain believed they were safe, for now. They could not stay at this depth for too long as the air conditioner had already stopped and battery power was low. He knew they had to decide and had to decide quickly if they were to survive.

"Get the political officer, Ivan Maslennikov on deck now!" ordered Savitsky. "Ivan we do not have radio contact with Moscow and must make a decision. Does the fact we were attacked by the blockade ships mean the war has already commenced? If that is so we must fire the 'special weapon'!" Savitsky could not make himself call it a nuclear weapon. He knew the consequences that would go with any such action. He had always been taught a nuclear war meant mutual destruction for the United States, the Soviet Union, and possibly the entire world. This could be the end of the human race!

"I am sorry Captain Savitsky, what else could it mean? Why would they try to destroy us if the war had not already begun? It could have been the Americans. It could have been Colonel Beloborodov that fired a missile from Cuba, or Mother Russia may have executed a preemptive strike. We don't know. What we do know is the Americans tried to sink us! I think we must do our duty and fire the weapon."

"With reluctance I agree with you, prepare to fire," ordered Captain Savitsky.

"I do not agree," said Captain Arkhipov. Captain Arkhipov was the same rank as Captain Savitsky and was the overall Commander of the flotilla of the four Soviet submarines. As such, his approval was also needed before the nuclear weapon could be fired. Captain Arkhipov was not new to life and death situations, having served on the ill-fated K-19 when her reactor coolant was lost. Without the heroic devotion of her crew a nuclear meltdown would have occurred. As it was, 22 sailors were lost and many others including Arkhipov were afflicted with radiation poisoning.

"Captain Arkhipov, I understand your reluctance but do we have any other choice but to do our duty?" asked Captain Savitsky.

"I agree Captain we must do our duty, however that duty does not include starting WWIII!"

"It has already started, Captain, we were fired upon!" said the political officer Maslennikov. "To not fire back is treason!"

"I disagree we were fired upon. Did any of the depth charges cause any damage? And why did they stop when we went deeper? No, I do not think they fired upon us with the intent to sink us. I think they were intimidated by our presence, as they should be, I might add, and only wanted us to surface. Until we receive confirmation from Moscow that the war has started, we cannot fire. We will not start WWIII because we were too scared to wait for confirmation. We must surface to contact Moscow and that is what we should do."

"But if you are wrong that is suicide!"

"I am not wrong. This old diesel is too easy for the Americans to find. They would not have stopped if war had been initiated. Let's surface and you will see."

Captain Savitsky knew they could not fire without Arkhipov's approval nor could they sit on the bottom much longer without running out of air. He had no option but to surface. Much to his surprise WWIII had not started, only because Arkhipov would not bend to the pressure to fire the 'special weapon.'

President Kennedy and Robert Kennedy met in the Oval office over the latest U-2 pictures. "The pictures indicate three of the four SS-4 MRBM sites at San Cristobal are fully functional and the two sites at Sagua la Grande appear to be fully functional."

"Well Bobby, it's time. That damn power monger, LeMay's lackey announced in the open that we were going to DEFCON-2. In the open, without my consent!"

"That isn't all, Jack. I just had it out with that shit CIA agent William Harvey."

"What did he do?"

"He sent six teams of sixty agents into Cuba to support any conventional US military operation against Cuba because the military wanted it done."

"Who the hell authorized that?"

"He said it came from the Pentagon. The Pentagon says they know nothing about it."

"Goddamn it, Bobby, these assholes don't seem to care if they start a nuclear war! Don't they realize the slightest provocation can cause a nuclear holocaust? I thought we put Mongoose on hold pending this outcome over the missiles."

"We did. We gave them specific orders to suspend all missions until further notice."

"The CIA and the goddamn military just do whatever the hell they want! This is out of control, Bobby. A world with large quantities of nuclear armaments is an impossible world to handle. If we get through this, we must work on disarmament because this is just too much. I certainly can't control the Russians and now it seems I can't even control our CIA and military. If we approved what LeMay and some others want to do, we wouldn't live long enough to tell them they were wrong! The only sane ones in this whole mess seems to be you, Khrushchev, Castro, and me. If Khrushchev doesn't yield on this publicly I don't think you and I can stop the military from starting WWIII!"

"I'll go back to Dobrynin and see what I can do, Jack."

"Let them know that the only way I can hold the Military is to come out strong publicly."

"I will, Jack."

"And let him know in no uncertain terms the lives of millions of US and Russian citizens depend on the outcome."

On the night of October 26, the Attorney General Robert F. Kennedy had a secret meeting with the Russian ambassador, Anatoly Dobrynin. "Mr. Ambassador, our situation has reached a critical mass. Even though the President is very much against starting a war over Cuba, an irreversible chain of events could occur against his will. That is why the President is appealing directly to Chairman Khrushchev for his help in liquidating the conflict. If the situation goes on much longer, he is not sure that the military will not overthrow him and seize power. The American Army could get out of control."

"Chairman Khrushchev has been concerned about this for some time. He believes President Kennedy wants peace, but he also knows your military does not. I will tell you now that we have 20 nuclear warheads in Cuba for our R-12 Dvina missiles, which I believe you call the SS-4Sandal. As you know these can reach as far as Washington. We also have nine tactical nuclear missiles. The Chairman has also given launch capabilities to the commanders in Cuba. They will not launch unless the US invades. If, however, the US invades, I assure you they will not hesitate to fire the missiles. The Chairman understands the need for President Kennedy to appear strong in public, if for no other reason than to contain your military. The Chairman is also accountable to the Russian people and cannot be seen to acquiesce without some consideration from the US, even if that consideration is not public. What is the President willing to concede to make this happen?"

"As I indicated in our last talk, within a few months after this situation is satisfactorily resolved and the missiles are gone from Cuba, we will remove ours from Turkey and now also from Italy. He cannot do any more than that at this time. However, in the near future, he would also be open to any discussion from the Chairman concerning limiting nuclear testing and possible disarmament of some nuclear weapons. If, on the other hand, the missiles are not removed from Cuba in a timely fashion the US military will invade Cuba. It can no longer be assumed the President can keep the military from acting out this scenario that has already been formulated and poised for activation."

"Please tell the President to proceed with his public statement and request. The Chairman will respond with an acceptable compromise. It is in the world's best interest that no one invades Cuba."

"Thank-you Mr. Ambassador, I agree and will convey your message to the President."

"Thank-you Mr. Attorney General, for seeking this acceptable solution. I hope we are in time and I also hope the world never gets this close to a nuclear holocaust again."

"Me too, Mr. Ambassador, me too."

On October 27, 1961 the President publicly declared, "Mr. Chairman, as I read your letter of October 26, the key elements that seem generally acceptable, as I understand them, are as follows:

1) You would agree to remove these weapon systems from Cuba under appropriate United Nations observations and supervision.
2) Undertake, with suitable safeguards, to halt the further introduction of such weapon systems into Cuba.

3) The US would remove promptly the quarantine measures now in effect.
4) The US would give assurances against the invasion of Cuba by the US military.

The US requirements would be initiated with the establishment of suitable arrangements with the United Nations to ensure the carrying out and continuation of these commitments."

On October 27, there was a White House meeting between Robert McNamara, Robert Kennedy, and President Kennedy. "Mr. President," said McNamara "the United States had better be damned sure that we have two things ready, a government for Cuba and a response in Europe, because the Soviet Union will certainly make advances there if we invade Cuba. The CIA and the military are ready to act on your command to invade. The expectation from them is that October 29th should be the target date to launch the attack."

"And Robert, the CIA and the military don't think the response will be nuclear?" asked Bobby.

"It may well be. Then we hit them with everything. We let them launch first to appease world opinion, and then neither Cuba nor Russia will exist after the 29th."

"And this is ok with the CIA and the Pentagon?" asked the President.

"Isn't that their mission, Mr. President, to stop Communism wherever and whenever they can?"

"And millions of innocents will die. Is that ok, Mac?" asked the President.

"They are not innocent. They are Communists. Some of their missiles may get through and we may lose some but they will lose everything. But that is the price of freedom, Jack."

"But is it really, Mac? Is Cuba such a threat to our freedom that millions of innocents must die? Can the US not have freedom regardless of who runs Cuba or with what system? Are we so afraid that the communist economy is a threat to us? How can a communist economy in Russia negatively affect our freedom? It can't. Why should innocent Americans die to protect the United Fruit Company or Exxon Oil and their foreign monopolies? Their business prowess does not affect our freedom. In addition, what Castro is doing for the poor in Cuba is responsible. No country, not even ours, if it does not protect the rights of the many that are poor, cannot protect the rights of few that are rich."

"Jack, I wouldn't say those things outside this room. And Mac, you are not to repeat anything said here."

"Of course, Bobby, I understand."

Bobby added, "Jack has not slept in two days and probably won't until this is over, so be patient. We should hear from Khrushchev tomorrow."

October 28, one day before the United States military was set to invade Cuba, Khrushchev publicly declared on Radio Moscow,"The Soviet government, in addition to previously issued instructions on the cessation of further work at the building sites for the weapons, has issued a new order on the dismantling of the weapons which you describe as 'offensive,' and their crating and return to the Soviet Union. Dismantling of the missiles will begin at 5:00 p.m. in Havana."

This statement and verified action of dismantling effectivly ended the missile crisis. The details would be worked out at the United Nations. Castro had sent the following five points that he wanted addressed in the settlement:

1) End the military and economic blockade of Cuba.
2) End all subversive and covert activities by the US.
3) End all air attacks on Cuba.
4) End all US flights over Cuban airspace.
5) Return Guantanamo naval base to Cuba.

Both super powers and the United Nations ignored Castro's five points and none of them were addressed.

When Alejandro returned to Havana, he met with Fidel. "Damn it Alejandro, those two idiots were so preoccupied with their own face they forgot we were even involved! They have ignored everything we asked for. We may never get another opportunity to get Guantanamo back."

Alejandro, knowing he was furious, and rightfully so, tried to mediate El Jefe's anger, "On the good side, war was prevented, and Cuba was not invaded. It could have been much worse. Have you decided what to do with the Bay of Pigs prisoners?"

"Si, Alejandro, and stop changing the subject!"

"Of course, El Jefe, want a cigar?"

On the 24th of December, 1962, 1,113 prisoners from the Bay of Pigs invasion were released by the Cuban government along with 1000 family members in exchange for $53 million dollars in baby food and medicine from the United States.

Chapter 29
A SUNNY DAY IN DALLAS 1963

The New Year began for President Kennedy in the White House with a briefing from the CIA Director, John C. McCone. Also present was Robert Kennedy.

"Mr. President, I do not see any way to overthrow Castro except by a direct invasion by United States troops. He is too well liked and supported by the Cuban people. Operation Mongoose has been a failure. We have assets on the ground and can continue to terrorize Cuban factories and cities, but we have not been able to get anywhere close to developing a resistance that can compete with Castro. He is too well liked by too many Cubans. We've planned and attempted to assassinate him more than two hundred times without him even getting a scratch. He has now developed his G-2 intelligence agency trained by the KGB and they have proven to be damn good. It's strange though, they do not torture prisoners. Very weird thing. Our guys we just got back as part of the Bay of Pigs prisoner exchange that were captured trying to blow up the copper mine in Oriente were not tortured in any way. The G-2 in that respect is very strange."

"Who authorized General Rene Schneider's assassination in Chile?" asked the President.

"Your orders were very clear, Mr. President. You indicated another military coup in Chile was not in our best interest at this time. However, Richard Helms claims he did not receive the orders until after he had already paid the resistance group to kidnap and kill Schneider. And, as you know now that he is gone, the option of a military coup is open. It is my belief that this will not happen without direct involvement from us, which they won't receive. I have taken Chile away from Helms and am personally directing our field opps."

"Thank-you John for the report. Bobby will get back to you on what we do with Cuba."

"Good day Mr. President."

"What do you think, Bobby?"

"Jack, I think McCone is right. Cuba is the opposite of Vietnam. In Cuba, the people support the leader and in South Vietnam, the people do not support the leader. I think we've picked the wrong one to support."

"I really hate the secrecy in our government Bobby. The very word secrecy is repugnant in a free and open society, and we are as a people inherently and historically opposed to secret societies, to secret oaths and to secret proceedings."

"That's all the motivation the CIA and military intelligence need is to hear you say that, Jack. They already think you are after them."

"I am after them Bobby, I want to break the CIA into a 1000 pieces! The Constitution never intended to have any part of the government with no accountability to anyone but themselves. A part that has the power to overthrow any foreign government by assassinating its leader and handpicking the replacement. If we don't rein them in who will Bobby? The Constitution was all about the three branches serving to keep any one from getting too strong and ruling as a dictator accountable to no one. And it has done just that until now. Our forefathers never dreamed of anyone creating a secret segment with no accountability. The only way to keep them somewhat under control was the budget. So what have they done? They have created their own funding for their black ops. And that money and those opps are 100% autonomous. No president, no congress, no one can control what they do outside of the United States, and I have concerns about controlling what they do inside the United States. We think the President can control whom we appoint as Director of the CIA and Military Intelligence. But can I really? I felt the ground move under my feet when I fired Allen Dulles, Richard Bissell Jr. and General Charles Cabell after the Bay of Pigs. You should have seen Dulles' face, Bobby. It was a condescending look that I have never seen before or since. It was not just a how dare you look, I have seen that many times, it was a you have no idea what shit storm you will reap. And then he verbalized my thoughts with absolute self-confidence behind it. I tell you it was disturbing."

"You did the right thing Jack, they all needed to go."

"Yes, I know. A man does what he must in spite of personal consequences, in spite of obstacles and dangers and pressures, and that is the basis for human morality. A man may die, nations may rise and fall but an idea lives on. The idea that was the United States of our forefathers must live on, Bobby. We must protect that idea not just from the external dangers, but the internal ones as well. Let me show you a letter from President Truman concerning the CIA. Look at this, Bobby. It's a warning to us about the danger of the CIA taking over the government. He said,

'I think it has become necessary to take another look at the purpose and operation of our Central Intelligence Agency, and for some time I have been disturbed by the way the CIA has been diverted from its original assignment. It has become an operational and at times a policy making arm of the Government. This has led to trouble and may have compounded our difficulties in several explosive areas. We have grown up as a nation, respected for our free institutions and for our ability to maintain a free and open society. There is something about the way the CIA has been functioning that is casting a shadow over our historic position and I feel we need to correct it.'

This represents only one of several goals we must accomplish for the American people. We must try to take control of the United States, away from the CIA, Military Intelligence, and the Federal Reserve and return it to the People of the United States even if the effort kills us. I had no idea when I was elected that the government didn't run the country. I'm not so naive now. They will not relinquish control without a fight. And possibly a fight to the death. But it is our moral obligation to fight this fight. We are the Kennedys. We do not run from a fight no matter the danger and personal risk. I have a new empathy for Castro. In essence his fight has been against the same foes as the ones we must wage for America!"

"You have been working too hard Jack; I think you need a respite."

As both brothers laughed Jack said, "You're right, Bobby, and I know just who she is, but first let's settle on a direction for Cuba and South Vietnam. The United States needs to reverse with dignity, our direction on both fronts. For South Vietnam, I want to have our troops home before the 1964 election. For Cuba, it's trickier. We need to keep the pressure on so Castro will approach us like he has every year since we've been in the White House. When he does we will open secret and back channel dialog until we reach a settlement that will remove Russia from Cuba."

"Do you really think Castro will remove the Soviets?"

"Bobby, he would never have invited them in if Nixon had not turned his back on him. I know he will. But we can't do it until after the 1964 election. We can't carry Florida if we don't at least break even on the Cuban expatriate vote in Miami. If we lose them, we could lose Florida and if we lose Florida, we could be out of a job. And I don't know about you but I love this job. That is one thing I will not do in 1964 just to win, however. Rufus Cornpone and his little pork chop will not be our Vice Presidential candidate and wife! He's a crook and should have gone down with Billy Sol Estes, but the witnesses conveniently committed suicide, all three of them. One of them was so stiff from rigor mortis that they couldn't bend his legs behind the wheel of the car. The coroner ruled it a suicide even though no carbon monoxide was in his lungs. Sooner or later he will get in a jam he can't get out of and I don't want any association with him on any level, much less as our VP, when that happens."

"I agree Jack he is as dirty as they get. I'm sorry we needed him in '60 to beat Nixon, but we did. I would rather be out of a job and write a book than have him as VP for another four years. Any idea who you would want to replace Johnson?"

"I'm thinking the Governor of North Carolina, Terry Sanford."

"I don't know him, but I've heard good things. Speaking of good things, Hoover has a quote from King that goes something like, 'I spend 20 to 27 days a month on the road. Fucking is good exercise and a tension reliever.' Can you believe he said that?"

"Actually, yes, Bobby. For me it's medicinal. If I don't get a strange piece of ass everyday I get a migraine." Bobby was still shaking his head side to side, as he left the room.

On February 1, 1963, three men sat at Santo's table in the Columbia Restaurant. Santo Trafficante, Carlos Marcello, and Sam Giancana. "You're out of your mind Carlos! We can't kill the President. What are you thinking?" asked Santo.

"No, we can kill the President. We just can't get away with it without help. And we have help," responded Carlos.

"I don't like this, Carlos. I mean I would like him dead and his brother, but to take out the President. This is big," added Sam.

"This is early in the planning stage. Our main part will be control of the city and insuring anyone that knows too much afterwards disappears. Preferably by accident or suicide," said Carlos.

"Well, we are good at making people have amnesia, disappearing and committing assisted suicide," said Santo. "We won't actually make the hit?"

"We're not sure yet. Like I said we are early in the planning and our partners are still collecting others to assist," said Carlos.

"Who, when, where, and how Carlos?" asked Sam.

"Not sure yet. Right now we just need to commit to planning the hit and witness control. If we are in, then our partners will go ahead and get more assistance."

"Ok, cut the crap Carlos. Who is behind this? I'm not committing to anything without knowing who I 'm getting involved with," said Santo.

"Yeah, me too," added Sam.

"Ok, you remember the three CIA partners we had in the Castro hits?" asked Carlos.

"Of course, Dulles, Bissell, and Cabal," said Santo.

"They will organize and Helms will help with recruitment," said Carlos.

"Ok, that's a partial list of who that leaves when, where, and how," said Sam.

"They were thinking Sicilian style hit with a patsy. They were thinking maybe Chicago, Florida or Dallas. And when would be at the end of the year. It will take that long to plan it through and insure we have the right patsy."

"Who else are they thinking about getting Carlos?" asked Santo.

"Well, we have Hoover and the FBI along with all three cities. They are CIA, and I am sure they also have Nixon involved in some way. That leaves money people and someone in the future government and the Military Intelligence."

"Even if they get all of them that's too fucking complicated to organize all of those groups. There's no way to insure cooperation and timely execution on the ground with so many players," said Sam.

"If it's done in one of our cities where we control the cops, and the FBI, the CIA and Military Intelligence are helping either directly or indirectly, that only leaves the Secret Service and the Sheriff's department to interfere. And do you really think they will challenge the FBI and CIA?" asked Carlos.

"Well, I'll agree to listen to more but the money would have to be worth the risk," said Santo. "Do you think that scumbag Castro might contribute funds to get rid of Kennedy? He has to hate him as much as we do. After all, the enemy of my enemy is my friend. And if we do him this favor he might do us a favor."

"I don't know, Santo, I hate him almost as much as Kennedy. But his cash would be good. But can we access him?" said Sam.

"I have a lead on one of his G-2 men that we have been watching for a while. We thought we might catch him in something and force him to flip and kill Castro. But so far he's squeaky clean. When do we meet again? We can always meet here in secret since you two can come and go through the tunnels."

"Ok, done. We will commit to listen further and plan. We will meet here March 15," said Carlos. "A toast, to the end of Camelot, to the end of the Kennedys!"

"Take this stone from my shoe," added Santo.

"Salute," added Sam.

Santo caught up with Alejandro in his office with Kim-Ly. "Hola, Alejandro, xin chow Kim-Ly."

"Buon pomeriggio, Don Santo" they both replied.

"Alejandro is being Lo Dit today Don Santo." added Kim-Ly with a pout. He keeps calling me Ms Homunculus!"

"What the hell does that mean, Kim-Ly?" asked Santo.

"I don't know Don Santo I can't find it in the dictionary. He was calling me Cho cai and that was ok cause I am bitch sometimes, but I'm so frustrated with Homunculus cause I don't know what it means. I don't even know what language is homunculus," she said with a scrunched up face.

Alejandro smiled as he added, "And she is undauntedly a homunculus Don Santo if ever I have seen one."

"Ok Ms. Homunculus would you excuse us a minute?" asked Santo with a wide grin.

"Not you too, Don Santo!" she said as she stomped out. "May an long dai cham mui!" Santo, understanding her Vietnamese, laughed as he bent over. Alejandro looked first at Kim-Ly and then at Santo and couldn't help but laugh.

"I don't know what she said but it must have been something, Don Santo."

"Yes it was. What is homunculus?"

"Homunculus is a scientific term for a perfectly formed miniature human being."

"That is perfect Alejandro. She is just that, a miniature china doll."

"Ok, your turn. What did she say as she left?"

"Well, I'm sure she said it at you as she would never say it to me. She said 'you eat pubic hair with salt dip.' "

As both men laughed, Alejandro shook his head. "I have never met anyone like her before Don Santo. She is such a pleasure to have around. And she is a great bookkeeper! Thanks for sending her here."

Santo looked at Alejandro, trying to decide if this was more than a business arrangement. Since he knew her husband, he hoped not. Her husband was not a man to piss off. He was trained by the CIA and was now a contract asset. And he did very good work. More often than not, his targets would simply disappear. Santo had not thought about this developing into more than a business deal. Shit, he thought now one of them will have to go. Goddamn it, he said to himself. I'll deal with that later, if I get to deal with it.

"Alejandro, I have a very delicate mission for you. There is a group being formed to hit the President sometime this year. They are interested in whether Castro would like to be part of it. What do you think?"

After some thought Alejandro said, "I'm not sure. I don't think he likes political assassination. He never considered it during the Cuban Revolution. He knew that if Batista died, another CIA backed crook would take his place and nothing would change. He might see this differently. I don't know. It is hard if not impossible to predict his thoughts. All we can do is ask."

"Well, let him know I don't care one way or the other. We have our deal and that's enough for me. Also, let him know the CIA backed counter revolutionaries are going to hit him at a ball field or stadium sometime in the next few weeks. I don't know which one or how but it is a go. Also, they will keep up trying to sink any boats coming into Havana. I have heard Kennedy is trying to stop these terrorists from using the US as a base of operation, but the CIA is not supporting him on this. So they will probably continue. Take the same route; fly to Miami and then boat from there. I need his answer before our next meeting on March 15." After a moment's hesitation he asked Alejandro, "Do you think Kim-Ly would want to visit Cuba with you?"

Alejandro looked hard at Santo trying to read his face, but he could not. Did Santo think something was going on with Kim-Ly? This was a very dangerous question. "Of course not, Don Santo. She is married and there is no business for her to do in Cuba. There is no reason for her to go."

Don Santo knew Alejandro had figured out the purpose of the question and answered appropriately. He still didn't know what was between them. Damn he thought. I hope you don't out smart yourself, Alejandro, he thought, I do like having you around. "Of course Alejandro I don't know what I was thinking."

As Don Santo left both men knew the other was equally aware of the seriousness of the relationship between Alejandro and Kim-Ly. And, the possible consequences. The security was increased on both the US and Cuban side of the trip. The US Coast Guard apparently was trying to stop counter revolutionaries from leaving the US. The Cubans were equally vigilant in trying to intercept and prevent any nefarious activity near Cuba. The boat's prearranged cover seemed to appease both sides. Castro was delighted with the news about the impending attack at the ball field and the fact that Kennedy was trying to prevent the counter-revolutionaries from using US ports. When he told him about the Kennedy hit, his faced turned red and he became almost angry. "I have always been violently opposed to such methods. First of all from the viewpoint of political self-interest, and because as far as Cuba is concerned, if Batista had been killed he would have been replaced by some military figure who would have tried to make the revolutionists pay for the martyrdom of the dictator. But I was also opposed to it on personal grounds; assassination is repellent to me. You know these things Alejandro. You were with me in the mountains and we talked of such things. Why do you now ask if I would participate in something I am so opposed too?"

"I am but the messenger, El Jefe. I told Don Santo what I thought your response would be. He insisted that I let you know anyway."

"Very well. Do you know the writer Jean Daniel?"

"I have heard of him, I think he is French."

"Actually he was born in Algeria but he moved to France early on. He brought me a message from President Kennedy. The message read:

'I believe that there is no country in the world, including the African regions, including any and all the countries under colonial domination, where economic colonization, humiliation and exploitation were worse than in Cuba, in part owing to my country's policies during the Batista regime. I believe that we created, built and manufactured the Castro movement out of whole cloth and without realizing it. I believe that the accumulation of these mistakes has jeopardized all of Latin America. The great aim of the Alliance for Progress is to reverse this unfortunate policy. This is one of the most, if not the most, important problems in America foreign policy. I can assure you that I have understood the Cubans. I approved the proclamation, which Fidel Castro made in the Sierra Maestra,

when he justifiably called for justice and especially yearned to rid Cuba of corruption. I will go even further: to some extent, it is as though Batista was the incarnation of a number of sins on the part of the United States. Now we shall have to pay for those sins. In the matter of the Batista regime, I am in agreement with the first Cuban revolutionaries. However, we can't let Communist subversion win in the other Latin American countries. Two dikes are needed to contain Soviet expansion: the blockade on the one hand, a tremendous effort toward progress on the other. This is the problem in a nutshell. Both battles are equally difficult... The continuation of the blockade depends on the continuation of subversive activities.'

"This is the opportunity that Cuba and I have wanted since our first trip to the US, when that asshole Nixon insulted me. Socialism and Capitalism can coexist in the same hemisphere. We are Socialists not Communists. Cubans own their lands, in a communist country they do not. In Cuba workers can earn more if they work harder, in a Communist country this is not allowed. We can make a deal with Kennedy that will unite our countries and open trade. However, he will not be able to promulgate the deal until after the 1964 election. I know that Florida is too important and there are too many counter-revolutionaries and their sympathizers in Florida to win without at least part of their vote. Kennedy must not die, Alejandro. You must figure out a way to save him. The future of Cuba may depend on it. Not only will Cuba lose any chance of recognition, they will try to blame Cuba for his assassination. To stop it will be hard, Alejandro, but you must try for Cuba, for me and for all Cubans. I will have G-2 look into it from here. We must make sure no one from Cuba is implicated if they are successful. No new sympathizers will enter that we do not know. We may have to purge some CIA assets already here so they can't say we turned them. Do you know any details of the plan?"

"No, I was just told it was in the works and to see if you wanted to participate. I know the next meeting is March 15. That's all I know."

"You must find out the details. You might not be able to stop them, but you might be able to alert someone anonymously that can. That may be your only option. Is there any way for you to attend the meetings?"

"No, I don't think so. But I might be able to eavesdrop through a closed door. I 'm not sure. Ybor has a system of underground tunnels that connect different buildings. Santo and his men can come and go without being seen by using the tunnels. My building and the meeting, which I'm sure will be at the Columbia, are connected. I might be able to get to the tunnel door at the Columbia, which is in the meeting room. No one in the restaurant will see who is in the meeting if they come through the tunnels. They are Ybor's best kept secret. I don't know if I will be able to hear through the door even if I can get there unseen. The problem is there is nowhere to hide in the tunnels and your flashlight is easily seen before you are heard."

"I can help you on both accounts. G-2 has infrared night vision goggles and listening devices so you will be able to hear if you get there. I'll get them for you before you head back."

"Thanks, El Jefe, they will be very helpful. If I can see them before they see me, I will have a chance."

Alejandro sat at his Ybor desk at 10 p.m. on March 15, 1963. Everyone else had gone home at their regular time. Nothing was scheduled to come in through the tunnels tonight. He had stored his equipment in a locked cabinet along with black pants and shirt. He also blacked his face as an extra precaution. Fidel's infrared system was bulky and required him to wear a backpack that contained a battery. The viewer was about the size of a dinner plate. He had checked it out and he could see well enough in the tunnels so he did not have to use a light source. He still had one major problem, how to get from here to the Columbia via the tunnels. That he had been afraid to practice. Why take the chance on being spotted doing a trial run, he had reasoned. He thought the tunnels ran if not under the surface roads at least in a similar pattern. He remembered when he was blindfolded and escorted from the Columbia, (at least he thought it was the Columbia) to the docks, he had made only a couple of turns divided by a long straight run. This made sense. A straight run with side tunnels to individual locations would be the smartest construction method. And if they were mostly under the roads, an accidental discovery was not likely. No one was going to dig a foundation under the road. That would also explain why the roofs were made with bricks in an arched pattern for added weight bearing from above. After five minutes of walking north through a long tunnel he heard male voices from the rear. As he looked in that direction he could see a white flickering light headed his way. He immediately picked up the pace and entered the first tunnel to the right that he came across. He reasoned that the Columbia was to his north and west so taking an east bound tunnel would be safest. He went about thirty yards and stopped. He settled his breathing and waited. He had hoped all parties would already be there. Would the escorts go into the Columbia, wait at the door but inside the tunnel or return through the tunnel to another exit? He had to guess. If they reversed course and he followed he would be caught. If they remained in the tunnel but at the door, he would not be able to hear anything. Only if they went into the Columbia would his plan work. He had to try. After a reasonable time passed, he followed the noise and light. At least he would know the way now. Unless this wasn't an escort for a meeting member. Damn, he thought, how he hated not having adequate logistics to carry out his mission. He could see the change in light as the group in front changed course to the left. At least they went west he thought. That is the direction of the Columbia. And as the Columbia was on the corner, it wouldn't be a long branch. He was startled to suddenly have the light brighten. He knew he was caught, as they must be reversing course. As suddenly as the light brightened it dimmed. They had only opened the door to the Columbia and had not reversed course. At least not yet. He stopped and held his breath trying to hear any indication of their intent. He heard nothing. Maybe a good sign. Maybe they all went into the Columbia. He slowly crept to the west branch, stopping every few feet to listen for sounds. He heard nothing. As he neared the turn, he thought he heard a noise and stopped. Nothing. At least there was no light coming from the branch. Or was there? He wasn't sure. He took off his night vision and looked down the tunnel he was in and then back to the branch corner. It did seem lighter. Was light coming from under the door to the Columbia? That didn't seem likely. The most likely scenario was the escorts were waiting outside the door in the branch tunnel. He got on the floor and inched his eyes forward enough to see in that direction. He could see a faint light and now clearly heard muffled voices. Damn. Damn he thought. There was no way to spy on the meeting. The escorts were waiting in the tunnel. He would have to figure out another way. As he made his way back to his office he thought about Santo's reaction when he told him Fidel wasn't interested. As Fidel instructed he didn't tell him Fidel was opposed to it, only that he didn't wish to contribute money at this time. Santo had again watched him with a heightened sense of intensity trying to hear what was not verbalized. Alejandro had seen this intensity from Fidel when questioning prisoners or interviewing those accused of a crime. Could Santo also read minds as it seemed like

Fidel could during the Revolución? Fidel always knew when someone lied to him or when someone was not telling everything they
knew. Did Santo also have this intuition? Probably so, he thought.
Men in Santo's profession did not make it this far and survive this
long without the ability to get information and analyze it as fact or
fiction without hesitation. If Alejandro could not spy on the meetings his only option was to figure out a way to attend. He knew he
had no chance of getting the information after the meetings. He
knew he had to think of a way to be invited. He just didn't know
how. Think, Lo Dit, he said to himself.

The Kennedy Compound in Hyannis Port, Massachusetts
was a retreat for all of the Kennedys, including the President and
his brother Bobby. They often came here to escape the many
distractions of D.C. and to discuss matters of importance in a relaxed atmosphere. The compound is six acres on Cape Cod along
Nantucket Sound. On June 1, 1963 the brothers were by the pool
discussing the President's next speech. "Jack, I think that is your
greatest speech you have ever written. It's even better than your
inaugural, which many rank as the best ever given by a newly
elected President. I wouldn't change a thing." Bobby said as he
looked at the speech one last time before handing it back.

*President Anderson, members of the faculty, Board of Trustees,
distinguished guests, my old colleague, Senator Bob Byrd, who
has earned his degree through many years of attending night
law school, while I am earning mine in the next 30 minutes,
ladies and gentlemen:*

*It is with great pride that I participate in this ceremony of the
American University, sponsored by the Methodist Church, founded by Bishop John Fletcher Hurst, and first opened by President*

*Woodrow Wilson in 1914. This is a young and growing univer-
sity, but it has already fulfilled Bishop Hurst's enlightened hope
for the study of history and public affairs in a city devoted to the
making of history and to the conduct of the public's business. By
sponsoring this institution of higher learning for all who wish to
learn whatever their color or their creed, the Methodists of this
area and the nation deserve the nation's thanks, and I commend
all those who are today graduating. Professor Woodrow Wilson
once said that every man sent out from a university should be a
man of his nation as well as a man of his time, and I am confident that the men and women who carry the honor of graduating
from this institution will continue to give from their lives, from
their talents, a high measure of public service and public support.
"There are few earthly things more beautiful than a University,"
wrote John Masefield, in his tribute to the English Universities - -
and his words are equally true here. He did not refer to spires and
towers, to campus greens and ivied walls. He admired the splendid
beauty of the University, he said, because it was "a place where
those who hate ignorance may strive to know, where those who
perceive truth may strive to make others see." I have, therefore,
chosen this time and this place to discuss a topic on which ignorance
too often abounds and the truth is too rarely perceived - - yet it
is the most important topic on earth : world peace. What kind
of peace do I mean? What kind of peace do we seek? Not a Pax
Americana enforced on the world by American weapons of war.
Not the peace of the grave or the security of the slave. I am talking
about genuine peace - - the kind of peace that makes life on earth
worth living -- the kind that enables man and nations to grow and
to hope and to build a better life for their children - - not merely
peace for Americans but peace for all men and women - - not
merely peace in our time but peace for all time. I speak of peace*

because of the new face of war. Total war makes no sense in an age when great powers can maintain large and relatively invulnerable nuclear forces and refuse to surrender without resort to those forces. It makes no sense in an age when a single nuclear weapon contains almost ten times the explosive force delivered by all of the allied air forces in the Second World War. It makes no sense in an age when the deadly poisons produced by a nuclear exchange would be carried by the wind and water and soil and seed to the far corners of the globe and to generations unborn. Today the expenditure of billions of dollars every year on weapons acquired for the purpose of making sure we never need to use them is essential to keeping the peace. But surely the acquisition of such idle stockpiles - - which can only destroy and never create - - is not the only, much less the most efficient, means of assuring peace. I speak of peace, therefore, as the necessary rational end of rational men. I realize that the pursuit of peace is not as dramatic as the pursuit of war - - and frequently the words of the pursuer fall on deaf ears. But we have no more urgent task. Some say that it is useless to speak of world peace or world law or world disarmament - - and that it will be useless until the leaders of the Soviet Union adopt a more enlightened attitude. I hope they do. I believe we can help them do it. But I also believe that we must re-examine our own attitude - as individuals and as a Nation - - for our attitude is as essential as theirs. And every graduate of this school, every thoughtful citizen who despairs of war and wishes to bring peace, should begin by looking inward - - by examining his own attitude toward the possibilities of peace, toward the Soviet Union, toward the course of the Cold War and toward freedom and peace here at home. First: Let us examine our attitude toward peace itself. Too many of us think it is impossible. Too many of us think it is unreal. But that is dangerous, defeatist belief. It leads to the conclusion that war is inevitable - - that mankind is doomed - - that we are gripped by forces we cannot control. We need not accept that view. Our problems are manmade - - therefore, they can be solved by man. And man can be as big as he wants. No problem of human destiny is beyond human beings. Man's reason and spirit have often solved the seemingly unsolvable - - and we believe they can do it again. I am not referring to the absolute, infinite concept of universal peace and good will of which some fanatics dream. I do not deny the values of hopes and dreams but we merely invite discouragement and incredulity by making that our only and immediate goal.

Let us focus instead on a more practical, more attainable peace - - based not on a sudden revolution in human nature but on a gradual evolution in human institutions - -on a series of concrete actions and effective agreements which are in the interest of all concerned. There is no single, simple key to this peace - - no grand or magic formula to be adopted by one or two powers. Genuine peace must be the product of many nations, the sum of many acts. It must be dynamic, not static, changing to meet the challenge of each new generation. For peace is a process - - a way of solving problems. With such a peace, there will still be quarrels and conflicting interests, as there are within families and nations. World peace, like community peace, does not require that each man love his neighbor - - it requires only that they live together in mutual tolerance, submitting their disputes to a just and peaceful settlement. And history teaches us that enmities between nations, as between individuals, do not last forever. However fixed our likes and dislikes may seem the tide of time and events will often bring surprising changes in the relations between nations and neighbors. So let us persevere. Peace need not be impracticable - - and war need not be inevitable. By defining our goal more clearly - - by making it seem more manageable and less remote - - we can help all peoples to see it, to draw hope from it, and to move irresistibly toward it. Second: Let us re-examine our attitude toward the Soviet Union. It is discouraging to think that their leaders may actually believe what their propagandists write. It is discouraging to read a recent authoritative Soviet text on Military Strategy and find, on page after page, wholly baseless and incredible claims - - such as the allegation that "American imperialist circles are preparing to unleash different types of wars…that there is a very real threat of a preventive war being unleashed by American imperialists against the Soviet Union"…(and that) the political aims of the American imperialists are to enslave economically and politically the European and other capitalist countries…(and) to achieve world domination. Truly, as it was written long ago: "The wicked flee when no man pursueth." Yet it is sad to read these Soviet statements - - to realize the extent of the gulf between us. But it is also a warning - - a warning to the American people not to fall into the same trap as the Soviets, not to see only a distorted and desperate view of the other side, not to see conflict as inevitable, accommodations as impossible and communication as nothing more than an exchange of threats. No government or social system is so evil that its people must be considered as lacking in virtue. As Americans, we find communism profoundly repugnant as a negation of personal freedom and dignity. But we can still hail the Russian people for their many achievements - - in science and space, in economic and industrial growth, in culture and in acts of courage. Among the many traits the peoples of our two countries have in common, none is stronger than our mutual abhorrence of war. Almost unique, among the major world powers, we have never been at war with each other. And no nation in the history of battle ever suffered more than the Soviet

Union suffered in the course of the Second World War. At least 20 million lost their lives. Countless millions of homes and farms were burned or sacked. A third of the nation's territory, including nearly two thirds of its industrial base, was turned into a waste-land - - a loss equivalent to the devastation of this country east of Chicago. Today, should total war ever break out again - - no matter how - - our two countries would become the primary targets. It is an ironical but accurate fact that the two strongest powers are the two in the most danger of devastation. All we have built, all we have worked for, would be destroyed in the first 24 hours. And even in the Cold War, which brings burdens and dangers to so many countries, including this Nation's closest allies - - our two countries bear the heaviest burdens. For we are both devoting massive sums of money to weapons that could be better devoted to combating ignorance, poverty and disease. We are both caught up in a vicious and dangerous cycle in which suspicion on one side breeds suspicion on the other, and new weapons beget counter-weapons. In short, both the United States and its allies, and the Soviet Union and its allies, have a mutually deep interest in a just and genuine peace and in halting the arms race. Agreements to this end are in the interests of the Soviet Union as well as ours -- and even the most hostile nations can be relied upon to accept and keep those treaty obligations, and only those treaty obligations, which are in their own interest. So, let us not be blind to our differences - - but let us also direct attention to our common interests and to means by which those differences can be resolved. And if we cannot end now our differences, at least we can help make the world safe for diversity. For, in the final analysis, our most basic common link is that we all inhabit this planet. We all breathe the same air. We all cherish our children's future. And we are all mortal. Third: Let us re-examine our attitude toward the Cold

War, remembering that we are not engaged in a debate, seeking to pile up debating points. We are not here distributing blame or pointing the finger of judgment. We must deal with the world as it is, and not as it might have been had history of the last eighteen years been different.

We must, therefore, preserve in the search for peace in the hope that constructive changes within the Communist bloc might bring within reach solutions which now seem beyond us. We must conduct our affairs in such a way that it becomes in the Communists' interest to agree on a genuine peace. Above all, while defending our vital interest, nuclear powers must avert those confrontations which bring an adversary to a choice of either a humiliating retreat or a nuclear war. To adopt that kind of course in the nuclear age would be evidence only of the bankruptcy of our policy - - or of a collective death-wish for the world. To secure these ends, America's weapons are non-provocative, carefully controlled, designed to deter and capable of selective use. Our military forces are committed to peace and disciplines in self-restraint. Our diplomats are instructed to avoid unnecessary irritants and purely rhetorical hostility. For we can seek a relaxation of tensions without relaxing our guard. And, for our part, we do not need to use threats to prove that we are resolute. We do not need to jam foreign broadcasts out of fear our faith will be eroded. We are unwilling to impose our system on any unwilling people - - but we are willing and able to engage in peaceful competition with any people on earth. Meanwhile, we seek to strengthen the United Nations, to help solve its financial problems, to make it a more effective instrument of peace, to develop it into a genuine world security system - - a system capable of resolving disputes on the basis of law, of insuring the security of the large and the small, and of creating conditions under which arms can finally be abolished. At the same time we seek to keep peace inside the non-communist world, where many nations, all of them our friends, are divided over issues which weaken western unity, which invite communist intervention or which threaten to erupt into war. Our efforts in West New Guinea, in the Congo, in the Middle East and in the Indian subcontinent, have been persistent and patient despite criticism from both sides. We have also tried to set an example for others - - by seeking to adjust small but significant differences with our own closest neighbors in Mexico and in Canada. Speaking of other nations, I wish to make one point clear. We are bound to many nations by alliances. These alliances exist because our concern and theirs substantially overlap. Our commitment to defend Western Europe and West Berlin, for example, stands undiminished because of the identity of our vital interests. The United States will make no deal with the Soviet Union at the expense of other nations and other peoples, not merely because they are our partners, but also because their interests and ours converge. Our interests converge, however, not only in defending the frontiers of freedom, but in pursuing the paths of peace. It is our hope - - and the purpose of Allied policies - - to convince the Soviet Union that she, too, should let each nation choose its own future, so long as that choice does not interfere with the choices of others. The communist drive to impose their political and economic system on others is the primary cause of world tension today. For there can be no doubt that if all nations could refrain from interfering in the self-determination of others, then peace would be much more assured. This will require a new effort to achieve world law - - a new context for world discussions. It will require increased understanding between the Soviets and ourselves. And increased understanding will require increased contact and communications. One step in this direction is the proposed arrangement for a direct line between Moscow and Washington, to avoid on each side the dangerous delays, misunderstandings, and misreading of the other's actions which might occur at a time of crisis. We have also been talking in Geneva about other first-step measures of arms control, designed to limit the intensity of the arms race and to reduce the risks of accidental war. Our primary long-range interest in Geneva, however, is general and complete disarmament - - designed to take place by stages, permitting parallel political developments to build the new institutions of peace which would take the place of arms. The pursuit of disarmament has been an effort of this Government since the 1920's. It has been urgently sought by the past three Administrations. And however dim the prospects may be today, we intend to continue this effort - - to continue it in order that all countries, including our own, can better grasp what the problems and possibilities of disarmament are. The one major area of these negotiations where the end is in sight- - yet where a fresh start is badly needed - - is in a treaty to outlaw nuclear tests. The conclusion of such a treaty - - so near and yet so far - - would check the spiraling arms race in one of its most dangerous areas. It would place the nuclear powers in a position to deal more effectively with one of the greatest hazards which man faces in 1963, the further spread of nuclear arms. It would increase our security - - it would decrease the prospects of war. Surely this goal is sufficiently important to require our steady pursuit, yielding neither to the temptation to give up the whole effort nor the temptation to give up our insistence on vital and responsible safeguards. I am taking this opportunity, therefore, to announce two important decisions in this regard.

First: Chairman Khrushchev, Prime Minister Macmillan and I have agreed that high-level discussions will shortly begin in Moscow looking toward early agreement on a comprehensive test ban treaty. Our hopes must be tempered with the caution of history - - but with our hopes go the hopes of all mankind. Second: To make clear our good faith and solemn convictions on the matter, I now declare that the United States does not propose to conduct nuclear tests in the atmosphere so long as other states do not do so. We will not be the first to resume. Such a declaration is no substitute for a formal binding treaty - - but I hope it will help us achieve one. Nor would such a treaty be a substitute for disarmament - - but I hope it will help us achieve it. Finally, my fellow Americans, let us examine our attitude toward peace and freedom here at home. The quality and spirit of our won society must justify and support our efforts abroad. We must show it in the dedication of our own lives - - as many of you who are graduating today will have a unique opportunity to do, by serving without pay in the Peace Corps abroad or in the proposed National Service Corps here at home. But wherever we are, we must all, in our daily lives, live up to the age-old faith that peace and freedom walk together. In too many of our duties today, the peace is not secure because freedom is incomplete. It is the responsibility of the Executive Branch at all levels of government - - local, state and national - - to provide and protect that freedom for all of our citizens by all means within their authority. It is the responsibility of the Legislative Branch at all levels, wherever that authority is not now adequate, to make it adequate. And it is the responsibility of all citizens in all sections of this country to respect the rights of all others and to respect the law of the land. All this is not unrelated to world peace. "When a man's ways please the Lord," the Scriptures tell us, "he maketh even his enemies to be at peace with him." And is not peace, in the last analysis, basically a matter of human rights - - the right to live out our lives without fear of devastation - - the right to breathe air as nature provided it - - the right of future generations to a healthy existence? While we proceed to safeguard our national interests, let us also safeguard human interests. And the elimination of war and arms is clearly in the interest of both. No treaty, however much it may be to the advantage of all, however tightly it may be worded, can provide absolute security against the risks of deception and evasion. But it can - - if it is sufficiently effective in its enforcement and if it is sufficiently in the interests of its signers - - offer far more security and far fewer risks than an unabated, uncontrolled, unpredictable arms race. The United States, as the world knows, will never start a war. We do not want a war. We do not now expect a war. This generation of Americans has already had enough - - more than enough - - of war and hate and oppression. We shall be prepared if others wish it. We shall be alert to try to stop it. But we shall also do our part to build a world of peace where the weak are safe and the strong are just. We are not helpless before that task or hopeless of its success. Confident and unafraid, we labor on - - not toward a strategy of annihilation but toward a strategy of peace.'

"Great speech, brother, I wouldn't change a thing. This may be the best speech you have ever written. I think we should make sure it's broadcast to the Soviet countries as well. If this doesn't get Khrushchev to the negotiation table nothing will!

"Thanks, Bobby. I also want you to look at this Executive Order 1110. You remember our discussion about the Federal Reserve being unconstitutional?"

"Of course I remember our discussion. I believe we also said it was the main inhibitor to a balanced budget and if left without restraint would lead the United States to financial ruin."

317

"Executive Order 11110, calls for the issuance of $4,292,893,815 in United States Notes through the U.S. Treasury. The Order delegates the authority to issue silver certificates to Treasury Secretary Douglas Dillon and his successors, a power that can be exercised without the approval, ratification, or other action of the President. In essence, the Order gives the Treasury the power to issue silver certificates against any silver bullion, silver, or standard silver dollars in the Treasury. This means that for every ounce of silver in the U.S. Treasury's vault, the government can introduce new money into circulation. As a result, more than $4 billion in United States Notes will be brought into circulation in $2 and $5 denominations. The $10 and $20 United States Notes will come later. I think it is obvious that the Federal Reserve Notes being circulated as legal currency are contrary to the Constitution of the United States, which calls for issuance of United States Notes as interest free and debt free currency backed by silver reserves in the U.S. Treasury.

This is a simple matter of economics, Bobby. The Order will grant the U.S. government the power to repay past debt without further borrowing from the privately owned Federal Reserve, which charges both principle and interest on all new money it creates. The Order will also give us the ability to create our own money backed by silver, giving it real value. Since the Federal Reserve is privately owned by the investor banks, which in some cases have foreign investment, they claim they are not bound by any request for information as to their investors nor their decisions. So no one can get a complete list of who owns the Federal Reserve. When we ask them to print money the government has to give them Treasury Bonds which they sell to their banks. And with that the US Government has a debt that has to be paid with interest to these banks. They make millions off US taxpayers. It is no coincidence that the Federal Reserve and the Federal Income tax system were created in the same year, 1913. They had to have taxpayer money to pay their fees. As a result our Federal deficit has increased by 16 trillion dollars since the Federal Reserve System was created. And since the Federal Reserve has control over interest and inflation rates the dollar is destined to lose its value. I agree with Henry Ford. He thought it was stupid that for the loan of $30,000,000 of their own money the people of the United States should be compelled to pay $66,000,000 to pay it off. That is what it amounts to, with interest. People who will not turn a shovelful of dirt nor contribute a pound of material will collect more money from the United States than the people who supply the material and the people who do the work combined. That is the terrible thing about interest. In all our great bond issues, the interest is always greater than the principal. All of the great public works cost more than twice the actual cost, because of the interest. And who benefits from this subterfuge of the US taxpayer? The privately owned banks in the Federal Reserve System. Why should the US taxpayer do this? Why should they pay double for a project to a Federal Reserve System whose only job is moving paper? Under the present system of doing business we simply add 120 to 150%, to the stated cost. But here is the point: If our nation can issue a dollar bond, it can issue a dollar bill. The element that makes the bond good makes the bill good. Executive Order 1110 will end the anti-constitutional Federal Reserve System. The writers of the Constitution knew the perils of a Central Bank and eliminated it. Now its time to do it again. This act will be the best thing this Presidency can do for the American people."

"Jack, do you think it wise to do so much all at once? With this order, you will alienate the major bankers, Wall Street, and the Federal Reserve. You have already pissed off the CIA by cutting off the three headed serpent after the Bay of Pigs, not to mention Curtis LeMay and the military because you didn't let them invade Cuba."

"There isn't any time to lose. What happens if I lose in 1964 or if my back is so bad, I can't run and none of these things are in progress? I'll tell you what happens, not a damn thing!"

"I know, Jack, it's our moral responsibility to do the right thing as we know it. And it is the right thing to do, it's constitutional and in the majority of Americans' best interest. But it disturbs me that we are making so many enemies at the same time."

"You worry too much Bobby. I learned in WWII that if a soldier hides and worries about getting hurt he definitely will get hurt. But if he's like Patton and runs toward the battle with both guns blazing he never seems to get hit."

Bobby was not sure he believed in the kind of karma his brother was talking about. In this case, he thought that if a person played with fire too often, eventually he will be burned. "Don't tempt God, Jack, that's all I'm saying."

Jack appreciated his brother's concern as he too felt angst over his changes, but his duty and his responsibility to the Nation required his action, "If we are stopped, Bobby, it won't be from God's judgment."

June 1st, Ybor. Alejandro had been trying to figure a way to get into the meetings ever since the March 15 disaster. The only way he could think of was if Castro were involved, he could require Alejandro's participation in exchange for his monetary contribution. He knew it was a long shot since Fidel was so adamant against assassinations but he might agree that to pretend interest might be the only way Alejandro would be in any position to sabotage the hit. "Santo, I want to make a quick trip to see Fidel. I think he is making a mistake by not supporting your upcoming action."

"Why is that, Alejandro?" asked Santo. Alejandro's statement had surprised him. It's true he, Sam, and Marcelo had thought he might contribute some cash, but it was no big deal.

He wondered why Alejandro was suddenly more interested in Castro's participation. He wondered why Alejandro would care enough to make another trip.

"Well, I think it is in his best interest to have Kennedy gone. The next President cannot treat Cuba any worse. And it's payback for all of the assassins Kennedy has sent his way. It may lead to a trade agreement with the US that would help Cuba rid herself of the Soviet Union. That is something Castro wants. However, without US trade and protection he has to keep them in place."

Santo had never questioned Alejandro's motives before but something was up. He didn't buy this newfound change of heart. Alejandro had been matter of fact after the first trip that Castro wasn't interested. Why now? And for what reason? "What do you think he would contribute?"

"I don't know Santo, what did you have in mind when you sent me to ask him the first time?"

"We thought money would be needed. Now we don't. Kennedy pissed off the financial world with his silver certificates that could eliminate the need for a Federal Reserve. The powers in the Federal Reserve System will not let any President diminish their power. They have agreed to finance the whole operation no matter what it costs. It's nice to have a blank check. Especially one written from someone else's account. We don't need Castro now. In fact, at this point it's better if he doesn't participate."

Alejandro knew for Santo to turn down money needed or not, meant he wasn't buying his reasoning. He also knew to carry it further would jeopardize his current role. When Santo lost confidence in someone, that person tended to disappear from Ybor. That usually meant 'they slept with the fishes' as Santo would say. Alejandro did not want to be a stone in Santo's shoe, nor did he want to sleep with the fishes.

"No problem Santo, it was just a thought. I thought it might be mutually beneficial but if it's better to leave it alone that's fine. I don't care either way. I don't have a dog in this fight."

What the fuck are you up to Alejandro? Santo asked himself. *You can't lie worth a shit! I don't know what your motives are but I know what they are not. Fuck, I've always liked having you around. You are the one guy I know I can talk to that doesn't want my job. God damn it. Your tit's caught in the ringer now boy. I will definitely have to watch you from now on. Fuck it!* "Good, Alejandro. Enough said."

After Alejandro left, Santo contemplated everything they had said. It had something to do with the Kennedy thing but he could not figure out what. Was it Alejandro's or Castro's thing? He didn't know. Castro would be better off or at least no worse off with Kennedy gone, right? He asked himself. Fuck, he couldn't think of any angle that indicated otherwise. *If you have become my enemy, Alejandro you will die, if not we can continue.* Santo could think of only one way to find out. *I have to know. If you were anyone else you would just disappear, but you are necessary to maintain our drug route through Cuba. Because of that I have to know, not guess. Don't tempt me, Alejandro, don't be a Lo Dit!*

If Alejandro is now an enemy, the best way to watch him is to keep him close. Keep your friends close and enemies closer. If it involved the Kennedy hit, then he should be part of our meetings. He can't lie, so he will tip his hand. Santo told Carlos and Sam he was bringing a mercenary to the next meeting. A mercenary that had fought for Castro in the Revolution migrated to the US and then returned to fight in the Bay of Pigs invasion. He just wouldn't tell them he fought for Castro in the Bay of Pigs. He didn't tell Alejandro he was coming to the meeting until the afternoon of the meeting. "We could use your military perspective, Alejandro. This is more of a sniper operation than a street hit. We want to know what a soldier or mercenary would think. Be at the Columbia at 11pm."

Alejandro did not like the new development. Yes, he thought, he would get into the meetings but he didn't like the fact that Santo told him to be there and didn't ask him to be there. He was under the microscope and knew it. You fucked up this one, he said to himself. His Great Uncle told him not to get involved with these people, why didn't he listen?

"Carlos, Sam, this is Alejandro Gomez, the expatriate from Cuba I told you about." Everyone shook hands and sat at the table. As usual, Santo had ordered food and wine. The group ate in silence, each watching the other. As the silence grew, Alejandro became more and more apprehensive. "Don Santo said you did some work for him Alejandro, what kind of work?" asked Sam.

Alejandro knew this was the beginning of his test, "I did this and that Don Giancana, whatever needed doing."

"And what would that be?" asked Carlos.

"I was in the Revolución and I fought at the Bay of Pigs. He has had me do the things I do best, Don Marcello."

Sam liked the fact Alejandro would not talk frankly about his work. He also liked to play things close to the vest. "Have you been back to Cuba since the Bay of Pigs?" asked Sam.

"Yes, I've had a couple of missions in Cuba since the failed invasion. One was successful, one was not."

"Ok, fair enough Alejandro, Santo has told us you have been helpful. We will see if you can help with our Bay of Pigs. Did Santo tell you that was our code name for this job?" asked Carlos.

"No he didn't. The name has certain symmetry doesn't it? The first Bay of Pigs was a disaster for Kennedy, and this one will be also, yes?"

As all four men smiled, Carlos said, "That's the plan. This motherfucker has caused too much trouble for too many people."

Santo saw that both Sam and Carlos accepted Alejandro. His less than straightforward answers were only an attempt to not lie about his work. However, for Sam and Carlos it represented that he was close mouthed even in a safe room. They both appreciated that type of caution. They obviously thought his main function was wet work, which was just fine. "Alejandro, if you were going to plan to take this stone from my shoe how would you do it?"

"Well, he's too well guarded for an accident to happen. And if we were to poison him it would reek of an inside job and smell like CIA. Therefore, I assume that's out. The best way to maintain anonymity is to take him out in a military style hit. Probably during one of his motorcades that he likes. Obviously, we will want to make it look like someone else did it, and that will take a lot of coordination before and after the fact."

"If you were to take him in a motorcade, how many shooters would you want?" asked Carlos.

"The way we did it was to have three teams in a triangular surround of the kill zone. You would have one shooter in each group, one spotter in each group, and one communicator in each group, to insure all three fired at the same time. If the kill zone is properly selected this method will take out the target. The hard part is getting away without anyone knowing we did it."

"If need be, can you be a shooter?" asked Sam Santo knew this was a trap if Alejandro answered, so he interjected, "Alejandro is more hands on in his work, Sam, if you know what I mean. He certainly could be part of the ground team but we have better long-range shooters than him. No offense Alejandro, you do good work, but this is not what you do best. "

"I agree, Don Trafficante. Of course I'll do whatever is asked."

Carlos thought Alejandro was a good addition and that Santo was right to bring him in with his military concepts. "We have four possible kill zones to work with. We know that he'll visit Chicago, Tampa, Miami and then Dallas, all in November. Those are our choices. Dallas is our fall back. If we haven't been successful at any of the other three we have to make Dallas work. There will be motorcades in all four locations. As we get closer, we will have exact dates and routes. We have fall guys being prepared in Chicago and Dallas. Both ex-CIA men that we can paint as Communist and possibly with Castro ties. Best case we get rid of Kennedy and have an excuse to invade Cuba and get our casinos back. Then we can reestablish our southern drug route through Cuba."

As Carlos continued to talk, Alejandro realized that Santo had not told them he still had the drug route through Cuba. He glanced at Santo who was looking in his direction. Neither man's facial expression changed but they knew what the other was thinking. Damn thought Alejandro, I didn't need to hear that. Now I represent more liability to Santo.

As Carlos finished, he asked, "Any thoughts on the best location as far as city?"

Santo said, "If it is in Florida, I would prefer Miami over Tampa. Easier to escape and control the ground there than Tampa. And I can get us a fall guy there but he will be a Cuban expatriate, so that's not ideal."

Alejandro, in an attempt to increase his credibility, added, "Couldn't we swing it to indicate Castro had flipped him or that he was Cuban G-2?"

"Yeah, I like the way you think Ale. That's perfect. Ok, we have our man in three spots. That's enough. Any ideas on shooters?"

Santo responded, "Sure we can bring in three from Sicily. We can have them follow the same route so we don't need three different ones in three different locations. I can get them."

"How many partners do we have in this?" asked Alejandro.

"Why do you want to know, kid?" asked Sam, not liking the question.

"Well, you need three, three-man teams. Why not have every partner supply some to insure equal participation and therefore equal liability and equal determination to maintain the cover story? If everyone is fully vested no one can rat the others out."

Satisfied that Alejandro's point was well made, Carlos said, "You trained him well Santo, I like that. This way no one but us really knows who will actually shoot. I like that a lot.

Nixon, Johnson and Hoover are no problem. We own them. But the CIA, Military Intelligence and the Texas oilmen are slippery. If they contribute possible shooters, they can't weasel at the last minute. I'll see to it that they contribute shooters and weapons."

Sam, thinking that most everyone else had some Texas connection, said, "Since Texas is the home state for most of our partners should we just concentrate on Dallas?"

"No, I don't think so," said Santo, "I think Chicago and Miami will give us an opportunity to cancel at the last minute if something is wrong. We only go in Chicago and Miami if everything leading up to the hit is perfect. If not, we reload at the next stop, with Dallas as the go at all costs location. The Mayor of Dallas, Cabell, is the brother of General Cabell that Kennedy fired so Dallas is our last and best chance for lots of reasons. We also need ground teams to control the immediate scenes. When we are successful, it will be chaos. If pictures are taken, we must get the cameras. If witnesses see the wrong thing, they must be neutralized as soon as possible. We have to have multiple escape routes for the shooters. They can't all leave the same way. Between Johnson and Hoover the investigations can be somewhat controlled if we insure only the right witnesses testify. We also need a plan to take out the patsy as soon as possible. Best case, the police shoot him when arrested. If not we need a fall back to insure he doesn't have time to convince anyone he didn't do the shooting. That also means we need to control the autopsy. And plant some evidence that implicates the patsy's weapon as the rifle that was used."

"How about some false IDs for some of the ground team to help collect evidence," suggested Alejandro.

"That's no problem. We can get CIA, FBI, and local police uniforms and IDs as needed," added Sam. "I think we have a good basic outline. We have three target cities, Chicago, where I will select the best location for the kill zone; Miami, where you, Santo, will select the kill zone; and Dallas where you select the kill zone, Carlos. Santo gets three shooters from Sicily. And Carlos you line up the rest from our partners. Santo, you line up the patsy in Miami. The fall guys in Chicago and Dallas have already been identified. Police IDs can be a local thing with CIA and FBI coming from Carlos through his contacts. Anything else?"

Alejandro asked, " What about the weapons. Will they be the same in all three locations?"

Carlos thought this was a good question and said," In Dallas, we have already selected the weapon type for the patsy. We can use those in Chicago and Miami unless we need something else."

"I like all being the same." said Santo, "One less variable, you know."

"Fine with me," said Sam.

"The ground team and mix should probably be left up to each of us to determine based on the needs of the location. The Chicago ground crew can also work in Dallas but in Miami, we probably need a different team on the ground. The crew can drive from Chicago to Dallas but not to Miami. I don't want an entire plane filled with our guys all going to one place."

"I can get my own," said Santo. "If that's it, we'll meet again in four weeks."

As everyone stood to leave, Alejandro was not included in the obligatory handshakes and cheek kisses. He was not an equal and didn't expect to be treated as anything other than Santo's man. Carlos and Sam left via the tunnel with escorts for both. Alejandro and Santo left through the front. As both lit cigars Santo said," Thanks for your input, Alejandro; I think they appreciated your views."

Alejandro knew he was still not righteous in Santo's eyes and responded, "I'm glad to help, Santo. But you know my experience is limited."

"Yes I know. But you do have a mind for details and that's helpful. After all whacking a president is new for us all."

Yes, it is, thought Alejandro. And for some it's newer than it is for others. For someone that wanted to stay away from crime, this is a real peach of a way to break in to the game. For Sam, Carlos and Santo this was just that, a game. Maybe their World Series but still a game. They were enjoying the challenge of putting it all together. It seemed to be a test of their skill and manhood. For Alejandro, it was life and death. For them, it was ball and strikes. He said to no one, "Well, I got what I asked for, I wanted in the meetings."

The next four weeks passed with Alejandro dealing with personnel issues at the factory. Kim-Ly noticed an irregularity in tobacco consumption for the new line. It appeared to her that an employee was stealing part of the Pinar del Rio tobacco. When Alejandro compared the cigar manufacture rate and the consumption rate of the unrolled tobacco, he had to agree.

"Why would someone steal our tobacco?" asked Kim-Ly.

"What makes you think it's tobacco they are stealing and not finished cigars before they are inventoried?" asked Alejandro. "The cigars are much more valuable than the tobacco."

Kim-Ly looked at Alejandro with a wide smile, "Ah, El Lo Dit, you are so smart sometimes."

Alejandro looked straight at her and raised his eyebrows, "Sometimes?"

"Ok, if you are so smart who is stealing?"

"The second shift floor leader, Alvise Bifano."

Kim-Ly's face became very serious, "Why him? He's one of Santo's men. Surely not him."

"That's why it's him. As Santo's man, he thinks he is bullet-proof. He'll learn otherwise. As the second shift leader, he's the last to inspect the production. He certifies how many cigars each roller has made to determine their pay. If he shorts them, one or two a day they would not notice and he would set the extras aside or put them in his satchel to take home each day. No individual roller could account for the amount of shortage reflected in your numbers. He thinks either we would not notice the shortage or does not realize he would be the only candidate for the theft. That, or he thinks we won't say anything because of Santo. He is wrong on all counts."

At lunch the next day with Santo, Alejandro explained his reasoning. Santo stopped eating and listened quietly until Alejandro finished. "That makes sense. If he steals from you, he steels from me. This we will not allow. Meet me tonight at nine in our warehouse by the docks. Use the tunnels."

Before Alejandro could say anything about not knowing the way, Santo raised his hand to stop him, "Please, I know you have used the tunnels recently and you know the way so don't say anything. Besides, I don't want you to embarrass yourself. We both know you can't lie worth a damn."

Alejandro and Santo looked at each other, both with serious expressions. Was Santo fishing or did he know something about his JFK motive? It was impossible to read his face. Santo did not become Boss of Florida, Boss of the Havana Casinos, without the ability to keep his thoughts off his face. "I will be there," was all he said.

As Alejandro walked down the tunnel toward the dock, he was very uncomfortable. His earlier thoughts about what Santo knew or didn't know made him very uneasy. If Santo could be this mad about the theft of a few cigars, what would he do if he knew about his trying to block the JFK hit? He knew he felt uneasy about tonight because of Santo telling, not asking him, to use the tunnels. He knew he could never be traced to the warehouse and if he disappeared, no one would know from where. His last known whereabouts were the factory and no one saw him leave. Another Ybor mystery. When he reached the warehouse, the door was already opened. The first person he saw was Santo's bodyguard, Adamo Castinetti. "Ciao, Alejandro"

"Buona sera, Adamo."

He heard Santo from across the room, "Ah, Alejandro right on time. Come over here."

Alejandro passed two open barrels as he walked over to Santo. Next to the barrels were several cement blocks. As Adamo guided him with one hand on his back, he saw Santo was sitting in a chair smoking a cigar. He could not see what Santo was facing as two large containers blocked that area of the warehouse. As Alejandro approached, Santo removed the cigar from his mouth and looked at it with admiration. "Care for a cigar Alejandro, these are just like the ones you gave my father. I cannot tell the difference between these and the Cubans you used to make. That Dominican grown Cuban seed tobacco is amazing."

Alejandro was filled with trepidation, "There will never be a substitute for the real thing, Don Santo." As Alejandro neared Santo's chair the hidden area came into view. Alvise Bifano was sitting in a chair facing Santo. His hands were tied behind his back and his face had been rearranged, probably by Adamo. He was gagged but his eyes indicated he was still aware of what was going on around him. As Alejandro digested the scene, Santo was the next to speak. "Alvise has been kind enough to give me a couple hundred of these amazing cigars, Alejandro. He just happened to have them in his car. We have had a nice talk. He said he had only borrowed them from you to see if he could get you a higher price. I thought that was very kind. He said he didn't have a buyer yet. I'm not sure if I believe that, do you?"

Alejandro didn't believe for a minute that Alvise hadn't told Santo everything he knew. Alejandro looked at Alvise who was struggling against his bonds and was trying to speak. Alejandro's first thought was that Alvise must have been stealing them for Santo. The only reason Alvise wouldn't tell Santo the buyer's name was if Santo already knew the name. Alejandro received 40% of the factory's profits, Santo the rest. Would he steal from himself for 40%? Alejandro knew the answer. "Does it matter,

Don Santo, who the buyer was? To me it only matters who stole our property."

"Very wise, Alejandro, I agree. Now what do we do with Alvise."

Alejandro knew that was already decided. The barrels and concrete were evidence enough. He just had to make sure the second one did not have his name on it. Alvise would die tonight, probably not for stealing but for being caught, and almost causing Santo to lose face. "He is a stone in my shoe, Don Santo."

"And mine, Alejandro. Will you take this stone from my shoe?"

Alejandro looked at Santo who was holding a gun as if handing it to him. He knew if he did not take it and shoot Alvise his corpse would be in the second barrel. This was another test to insure he could be trusted. And if Santo didn't trust you, you didn't live in his world past your ability to be useful. Alvise was going to die for probably following orders. But he was caught and Santo was going to insure omerta was not violated. The only thing Alejandro could do was insure Alvise died quickly and did not suffer. "Of course, Don Santo."

Alejandro took the gun from Don Santo walked quickly over to Alvise put the muzzle to his head and pulled the trigger.

"Grazie, Alejandro. I knew you would not disappoint. I have another job for you. I need you to go to Philadelphia and meet a friend of ours. He's an excellent planner like you. Kennedy will have a short motorcade trip while you are there. Look at the security and help plan the how of our Big Job. We have also changed from Miami to Tampa for Florida. Therefore, we'll have separate plans for Chicago, Tampa and Dallas. You will stay at the Ben Franklin Hotel under the name Al Martinez. Our friend will be using the name Lou Conner. His real name is Lucien Conein. He's an operational scenario expert for the CIA. Listen to what he comes up with and you'll report it to us at the next meeting. You were not invited to our last meeting so let's have lunch tomorrow and I will bring you up to date. Go back the way you came and leave from your office. See you tomorrow."

As Alejandro and Santo had lunch in the Columbia, Santo explained the plan. "As I told you yesterday, the Florida effort will be in Tampa, not Miami. We want to do this when he is in a motorcade on streets we can control. We have in this order Chicago, Tampa and Dallas to make this happen. If our Chicago and Tampa plans fail, then Dallas will be the last chance to complete our deadline."

"Is there a reason Dallas is the last chance? I would think many more opportunities will be available in 1964 since it is an election year. And with Kennedy traveling so much and with his propensity for good looking females we could probably accomplish this with less splash than a daytime hit using a well trained female. And possibly make it look like an accident in the throws of illicit sex. It would certainly be easy then to keep it quiet even if it looked a little suspicious. Everyone tends to wink at his love affairs anyway."

"That's a very good thought, Alejandro. We have discussed this with our partners and the headman does not have the time to wait. If it does not happen this year he will likely wind up in jail. Without him in the picture, his friends won't participate. And our other partners would probably get cold feet without the main guy to control the aftermath. I would like for this to happen in Chicago. Then the street control is Sam's to worry about. If that doesn't happen then we will do our best to make Tampa happen, if it looks like at least a 90% chance of success. What we can't do is try and fail. Then we are done, as the security will be impossible to control after a failed attempt. We have a patsy set up for each location. In Chicago, it is Thomas Arthur Vallee; in Tampa, it is Gilberto Policarpo Lopez; and in

Dallas, it is Lee Harvey Oswald. Vallee and Oswald are ex marines with CIA and Russian ties. Lopez is a Cuban that we will link to Castro. All of them think they will be part of the attempt but none will actually shoot. They do not have the skill. We have selected the shooters for each location with some possible overlap between Chicago and Dallas. However, the timing is so tight we have separate teams for each location just in case. We have been told that preparations for a motorcade begin weeks before the event so you will go two weeks ahead of time. We will be waiting on you the day you fly back to Tampa on October 30. We will meet here at 9pm. Any questions?"

Alejandro had a lot of questions but he knew better than to ask. Evidently putting his fingerprints on the weapon and shooting Alvise had been enough to be trusted, at least for now. He wanted to ask who was the headman. Was it Hoover? He didn't think so. He was not in legal trouble. Was it a CIA guy? Kennedy said he was going to smash it into a thousand pieces. The new CIA Director McCone? On the other hand, maybe it was one of the three ex CIA men Kennedy fired, Allen Dulles, Richard M. Bissell, Jr. or General Charles Cabell. All hated Kennedy but none of them could really help control the aftermath except Hoover and then only in a limited fashion. "No, Don Santo I have it. I will be in Philadelphia on October 15 and will return with a plan on October 30. I just hope Lou is as good as you think."

With a wry smile Santo said, "Oh, he is, Alejandro, he may even be better."

On his walk back to the factory Alejandro stopped. *Oh my God*, he thought, *I know who it is*. He had been implicated in the Billy Sol Estes case, but the three witnesses against him all committed suicide. *Yeah right, suicide my ass*. Now he had another problem with Bobby Baker and payoffs. If Baker talks he will definitely go to prison, if *Life* magazine had it right. And the only way to fix that is if he is President. And what better person to control the aftermath than the next President, Lyndon Baines Johnson. Oh my God, he thought, this is a coup d'etat. A coup d'etat in the United States of America! How can this happen here? This isn't a third world country. This isn't Cuba. But Alejandro knew it could happen and would happen if he didn't stop it. He would now certainly know the plans but he also knew he would have to rely on others to stop it. The majority of Americans seemed to respect Kennedy. But were they the ones with the ability to stop the coup? He hoped so. He would know for sure by the end of the year.

The Ben Franklin Hotel covered one block on Crawford Street in downtown Philadelphia. The first two floors were devoted to the commerce of the hotel with three towers that contained the rooms. The second floor was nothing more than a balcony that extended around the floor that overlooked the first floor. Along the balcony in the back left hand corner was the Betsy Ross room. The Betsy Ross room was a small bar with limited seating and a view of the balcony on the west side. It was in this room that Lucien felt most at home and where he talked the most. During the day when we walked the motorcade route, Lucien was all business. No smiles, only professional considerations of the surroundings. The professional demeanor changed after a few drinks and the eccentric and boisterous persona took over. Lucien was born in France but moved to the US when he was five. He was fluent in at least three languages, including French, English and Vietnamese. Once he knew Kim-Ly worked with Alejandro, he felt free to talk shop. "I've heard a lot about Kim-Ly, although I have never met her. Is she as beautiful as I have heard? Her husband, Brad Walker, couldn't stop talking about her. It was most annoying."

"In my opinion, she is the second most beautiful woman I have ever seen."

"Let me guess, the most beautiful was your first love, right?"

"Yes, Isabel was her name. She was killed by Batista's troops in 1958."

"I'm sorry Al; it's difficult to lose one's first love, especially to death. Even if she marries someone else as long as she is alive, it doesn't hurt as much. Are you married?"

"No, I have been too busy and have not met the right girl. Are you married?"

"Oui, I have two sons, Laurent and Philippe. I agree with you on Kim-Ly, she is the second most beautiful woman I've ever met, next to my wife, Elyette."

"I thought you had never seen her"

"Ah Al, don't believe a thing I tell you. I'm an expert liar. Or should I call you Alejandro?"

As Lucien enjoyed his inside joke, he added, "I've known Santo for a while now. I met him through Kim-Ly's brother, Vang Pao, and have done a few things for him. I like working for the Sicilians. If you do a job for them, it is always in the US, Canada, or maybe Mexico. The Corsican Brotherhood, now that's a different story. They could send you anywhere in the world. Now this is the double truth. There's an old Corsican proverb that if you want revenge and you act within 20 years, you're acting in haste! I suppose you're curious about my missing two fingers. Don't deny it, I saw you looking at my hand. Well, I'll tell you, I lost them when I was on a mission with the French Foreign Legion. I was in a knife fight and only received a scratch but I was undercover and couldn't get medical attention without losing my cover. So when the fingers became infected I had to amputate them myself to save my hand. It was very messy as they bled a lot until I cauterized them with a heated knife."

"You are dedicated to lose two fingers rather than blow the mission. Was it worth it?"

Laughing as he slapped Alejandro on the back, "You're so funny. I'm glad you liked that story. The truth is I was driving a good friend's wife to a motel when the car broke down. In trying to fix it so we weren't caught, the fan cut them off. It was terrible. I didn't even get laid! I like the other story better, don't you?"

Alejandro didn't know how to take Lucien. He was deadly serious when they toured the motorcade route, but now he didn't know what was true, "Yeah, the first one is much better. I would stick with it."

Smiling from ear to ear Lucien said, "No, Alejandro you wouldn't, because you can't lie."

"So I've been told. Mi Madre would say that is a good thing."

"Probably, but in this world if you can't lie, you don't live long. My suggestion to you would be to get out as soon as possible. Find you an Isabel or a Kim-Ly of your own and retire to a tobacco plantation."

"I wish it were that simple, Lucien. My situation is complicated."

"All situations are complicated until you break them down to the simple elements that make them seem complicated. Even this job may seem complex but it really is just a maze of simple elements. If each element is accounted for, the project becomes a piece of cake. And, like I told you, I am the best at knowing how to identify all of the simple elements so nothing is left to chance. That's the key to success. And after we have finished this job you will know all of my trade secrets, so of course I will have to kill you, cause I don't want the competition!"

Alejandro was so startled all he could say was, "W-What?"

Laughing, Lucien slapped him on the back again, "Just kidding mon ami, just kidding. I was just checking to see if you were paying attention."

"Yes, I'm paying attention and no I don't think it would be wise to compete with you in anything!"

"That's wise, Alejandro, and I believe you. Your face would tell me if you thought otherwise. Now impress me. What has changed since we started making our daily walks along the motorcade route?"

"Well, the traffic is heavier some days. Barricades have been located on the side streets, to block access from that direction. The police patrols have also increased. I think that's all."

"What you noticed was good, but you missed the most important element. On our first walk, there were open windows in some buildings. Now all windows have been secured and sealed shut. The military always sends in an advance team to insure this is done. This makes our job harder. We can relocate to a rooftop but we risk being seen from above. With enough advance work, adequate camouflage can be added to the selected roofs to avoid detection from above. Santo said you had an eye for details and you saw most things."

"What else did Santo tell you?"

"I forgot. What should he have told me?"

"Well, I know he should have told me not to trust you."

"Oh, contraire Mon ami! When it comes to business, I am very serious and the very best at what I do. When I celebrate, I like to share a good tale. In addition, I'm celebrating completing my last mission in Saigon. I just completed the coup d'etat that took out Ngo Dinh Diem and replaced him with Nguyan Van Thiev."

"Is that a true story or another lie?"

Laughing Lucien said, "Oui, Oui it is Alejandro tres bon!"

"Santo should have told me you were an enigma."

Lucien's smile vanished and his face was instantly very serious, "Yes I am an enigma. I am inscrutable, obscure, and deliberately obtuse. However, I am the best, so deal with it. When you are planning to take someone out, someone very well known and to do it in the open and in daylight, it is wise to show some levity so the situation does not overwhelm and disorient you. This is a very short route as motorcades go and does not offer many location options. I'm glad the mission is not here. Can we control the advance military team?"

"I don't know."

"Well, find out. If we can our options expand. If not we'll have to deal with the roofs. The best option is to select a turn in the route to triangulate the field of fire. This insures that at least one angle should have a clear shot unless his protection is too heavy. Again, see what we can control. Police, Sheriffs, Secret Service and the military are all charged with protection of our target. The less available the better. Once the killing zone is selected, a diversion is always advisable. Something that requires an ambulance. All potential witnesses will be drawn to the diversion and will not see what is behind them. If another ambulance can be called at the right time, the siren can cover the shots especially if silencers are used. Are we using the Sicilian patsy system?"

"Yes, we have them in all three potential locations."

"Good, if everyone except the patsy uses silencers the shot directions can be camouflaged. All we need are mixed reports to discredit the accurate witnesses. Sometimes, and I mean sometimes, we can plant a witness. It's hard to find a reliable and unknown witness that cannot be traced back to us to report what we want reported. But if we have them, then that also helps to get our story out as the credible one. Immediately after the event is the most important time to control in order to direct the investigation. A troublesome witness can be made to disappear or influenced to the point they are no longer sure what they saw or heard. But this cannot always be done immediately. Some time needs to pass before it becomes easily doable. It is always best if the patsy dies during the event or shortly thereafter. If it can be arranged for a cop to be killed during the event and pinned to the patsy, chances are good the police will take him out during his arrest. Who is supplying the patsies?

"The CIA."

"Excellent. It's what we do best. Misdirection is our specialty. If only one story comes out people believe it as the truth. If five stories come out, people believe the one they want to believe. And if the truth is the most difficult to accept, very few will want to go there. A coup d'etat is such a story for the American public. The one thing we must avoid at all costs is a trial. Without a trial everything is speculation and impossible to prove."

"Does it bother you that our target is the President of the United States?"

"Of course not. We have removed many presidents from office in other countries, so now it's here. The challenge may be enhanced because it's the US but the goal to remove the president is the same in one country as it is in another."

"But you work for this government. It's like taking out your boss?"

"Are you serious? I work for the CI-fucking-A. We do not answer to any government. We have complete autonomy to do what we feel is best for this country whether it's in this country or in any other country in the world. The US is a capitalist country. Don't ever forget that. Two presidents have lost sight of that fact, Abraham Lincoln and John F. Kennedy. What happened to the first will happen to the second. A capitalist country is all about the money. He who has the money rules, not some government official. The government officials are in place to remove any and all obstacles that block this process. Santo knows and lives by this rule. Do you think with all the murders he has committed or ordered done or for all the future murders he will commit that he will ever spend a day in jail? I promise you he won't, because he has the money. Money buys influence and enough influence gives you autonomy of action. Even if you shot the Pope on film in front of thousands of witnesses, enough influence gives you a chance to escape justice. And in a capitalist world, no one is allowed to interfere with the big money people who will continue to increase their share. Personally, I don't care what Kennedy did to impede this process of making money, but he did something and that's why you and I are here. Like with Lincoln, it is sometimes necessary to impeach a government official because they have become too socialist or too idealistic. Kennedy crossed the line somewhere and pissed off the big money people. And now he will be impeached permanently. C'est la vie! And now more wine, Mon ami, the night is young!"

On October 30, Alejandro watched the motorcade with Lucein from a room in the Bellevue Stratford Hotel. Alejandro had no idea when Lucien had rented the room but he had the key. The room was on the 15th floor of the hotel with a large window facing the parade route. The limousine would be visible for several blocks using the two pair of binoculars that Lucien provided. After the motorcade ended, Lucein drove Alejandro to the airport for his Tampa flight. Lucien was on his way to Chicago to finalize the first attempt, which he had already planned.

That night when Alejandro came through the tunnel into the Columbia, Sam, Carlos and Santo were already there. A Cuban sandwich and a bowl of black beans and rice were waiting for Alejandro. As he ate, the other three smoked their cigars and commented on the high quality of Alejandro's Flor de Pinar brand. As he admired the cigar from the side Sam said, "Santo, I think these are just as good as my Romeo and Juliet Churchill's that I normally smoke."

Between bites Alejandro added, "They're better, Don Giancana. Our wrappers are superior to theirs in every way possible."

All three smokers laughed together. Santo looked at Alejandro before he said, "You can take that to the bank, gentlemen. Alejandro told me he would make me the finest cigar in the world, and I believe he has done it!"

Carlos raised his Sambuca Nero toward Alejandro, "Salute, Alejandro, these are perfetto!"

After Alejandro finished his sandwich, beans and rice, he also lit a cigar while he told the men everything he and Lucien had discussed prior to the motorcade that concerned the 'Bay of Pigs.' He had been told that was the code word adopted for this operation. Evidently, one of the major players involved thought the Bay of Pigs was not over until restitution had been paid. Restitution for the lack of US air support that many Cubans blamed for the plan's failure, and led to the incarceration of so many combatants. Alejandro continued explaining the day of the motorcade. "The Secret Service rode the entire way on the back of the limo. This would impede any shot from behind. To complicate matters motorcycle cops rode on each tire and would alternate being just in front to just behind the target.

Lucian believes we can still be successful with taking out the target but we could not predict the direction of the successful shots. In other words, we can surround the selected kill zone to insure we have a shooter to access the target but we cannot predict from which direction he will be exposed. This would make it very difficult to use our patsy if we don't know where to place him. Lucian knows we control the FBI, and our top man will be responsible for controlling the subsequent investigation. What he doesn't know, and of course, I couldn't tell him, is if we can control the military advance team, the Secret Service and the local police that provide the escort. He asked me to make it clear that a negative answer does not mean he can't be hit but it might complicate the Sicilian patsy scheme. He told me he already had selected a kill zone for Chicago and that these things were not important there but may be vital if Tampa and Dallas are used. The difference is in Chicago he has an overpass that is available that will negate most of the security precautions."

The three Godfathers looked at each other before speaking. They seemed to share a concern before Santo said, "We control things differently in the three cities. The military and police are the easiest to control. Although the military may be the hardest in Tampa with McDill Air Force Base right here. But we can work on it. It may be Dallas before we have something in place for the Secrete Service. They have just never been a concern before this job. Lucien has already done his preliminary in Chicago. Philly was to confirm and identify protection issues. Hopefully, it will end in Chicago. At the same time, we want you to scout Tampa for an appropriate kill zone. You have the route in front of you. Let us know if you have problems. We will need the location right away to insure the patsy is in the right location. Sam, you have a contact for Lucien in Chicago, right?"

"He is already waiting on him."

"Carlos, what about Dallas?"

"We have two waiting, Ruby and Roselli. The CIA has also given us Hunt. Everyone knows if we get to Dallas, it has to happen there no matter what. Why don't you also send us Alejandro if Tampa doesn't work?"

"Good idea, Carlos consider it done."

Carlos looked at Alejandro before adding. "And bring some of these cigars, too."

Alejandro did not want to go to Dallas under any circumstance, "Certainly, Don Marcello, it will be my pleasure," was all he said. Alejandro knew he was in way over his head. He also knew that many participants would not survive long after the job. Many would cross the line where risk outweighed their value. He felt uneasy about his potential risk outweighing his value. Maybe they had already decided his fate and it really didn't matter what he knew. If he were lucky enough to survive this operation long enough to get back to Cuba, he would stay and never leave home again. All he ever wanted to do was grow tobacco and make cigars, not this.

As Alejandro made his way back to his factory, he contemplated how to stop the attempts. Three dates, three plans and three patsies were already in place: Chicago, 11/2 Thomas Arthur Vallee, patsy; Tampa, 11/18, Giberto Policarpo Lopez, patsy; and Dallas, 11/22, Lee Harvey Oswald, patsy. In all three locations, the weapons would be the same, rifles with scopes and there would be at least three shooters, maybe four. He also knew an overpass above the motorcade route was Lucien's kill zone. Or at least it was before Philadelphia. He thought about using Lucien's name but thought that was too risky. He didn't know how many people actually knew his name. He decided he would call the Chicago FBI and give them the patsy's name and that an overpass would be used.

He would also mention three shooters and the rifles with scopes. If that worked, he would do the same for Tampa and Dallas. He found a suitable payphone on Nebraska Ave. in Tampa and made the call. After the call, he was not very optimistic. The male that answered the phone at the FBI office in Chicago treated the call with less interest than a pizza joint when you called in a pick-up order. Alejandro was not optimistic.

Three days later Santo sent a runner to invite him for lunch at the Columbia. Alejandro had never seen Santo so angry. His face was beet red and he was pacing the floor. His lunch was untouched on the table. When Alejandro arrived, Santo told him to sit and eat, which he was doing. "Goddamn it Alejandro we have a fucking rat! Somebody tipped off the FBI and Kennedy cancelled Chicago. Fuck! And two of our guys were arrested along with Vallee. Of course, Sam got them out but we were ratted out! A mother-fucking rat! There is no lower scum than that! But we know who, Alejandro, we know who!"

Alejandro lost his appetite as he watched Santo pace. He could try and run but he could not get away. He knew that he would be taken out through the tunnels and would never be seen again. At least his call had worked. He wouldn't be around for the next two but it had worked this time. At least he had served Castro well. He had no regrets. "What now, Don Santo?"

"Sam's already taken him out. And I sent the bastard to Chicago. What I don't know is if Lucien knew. Fuck no, he didn't know. He's a professional and would have taken him out himself. Can you believe it, a CIA guy that had a problem with taking out this scumbag of a president? You don't know do you? Of course you don't, how could you. Brad fucking Walker tipped off the FBI from Tampa before he went to Chicago. He called anonymously from a pay phone on Nebraska. He told one of Sam's guys that he didn't like this idea of taking out the President and was only there out of friendship for Lucien. A fucking rat! There is nothing I hate more than a fucking mother fucking two-faced fucking rat! And now I owe Sam for this."

Alejandro, still in shock from the news, was not sure he would be able to stand up if he had too. As he watched Santo pace back and forth, he was finally able to say, "Wait, Don Santo, you didn't send him. Lucien Conein asked for him and he's CIA, not one of your crew."

Santo stopped and looked at Alejandro for the first time since he sat down. He looked flushed and visibly upset about something. Poor bastard can't lie worth a shit. He's got a guilty conscience over this. The son of a bitch probably wished Kim-Ly's husband dead and now he feels guilty. What a sap. "Kim-Ly has not been told about this, so say nothing to her, capisce?"

"Of course Don Santo."

Santo seemed to visibly relax as he contemplated Alejandro's words. He changed the subject. "Have you selected a kill zone for Tampa?"

"Not yet but the area around the Floridan Hotel looks promising."

"Just between you and me, Alejandro I don't want this to occur here. It should happen in Dallas. Carlos's base is a long way from Dallas and the fallout will not affect him as severely as it would us if he is hit in Tampa. This is where we eat; you don't shit where you eat. I want to find a reason to not do it here. Even if you don't pull the plug until the day of, that's ok but it must look legit."

"Me?"

"Yes, you. I'm going to use you as the signal to shoot. You'll be in the area and will decide go or no go."

"This'll never work unless I have a real reason to pull the plug. Carlos and Sam will see right through me when I get to Dallas."

"Well, it'll only be Carlos, Sam and I will not be in Dallas. And you'll have to be ready to leave for Dallas on the 18th if it's a no go here."

"The only problem with the Floridan location is if the Secret Service are still on the President's limo. They will block the shot from the patsy's location. That will blow our Sicilian scheme."

"That's it then! The Secret Service will not get the word to stay off the limo until after they pass the Floridan. You will call out abort on the radio and we move on to Dallas. A good plan, Alejandro. That will work. We all agreed if anything was wrong with the plan we abort and move on to Dallas. And when you tell Carlos what happened here you won't be lying and that's good cause you are the worst motherfucking liar I know."

The next week with Kim-Ly was very difficult for Alejandro. If she knew anything, she didn't show it. She had said before that Brad would leave without her knowing when he would return. Maybe this was such a time. Whatever she was thinking it did not show in her body language. He even took her to lunch and she seemed perfectly normal. He finalized his placement of the teams around and on top of the Floridian Hotel well in advance of the 18th. Everyone knew to not shoot until he gave the order. Santo promised there would be no air surveillance, but some camouflage had been erected anyway. The motorcade came by the Floridan with two Secret Service men on the limo's back platform. Alejandro was audibly upset when he announced the abort over the radio. "Abort, Abort, do not fire. Why is the fucking Secret Service on the back of his limo.? Goddamn it!"

Alejandro smiled as he thought he was getting better at deception. Not good, but he was better. It was a bright, sunny day in Tampa.

That night Alejandro arrived in Dallas not knowing what to expect. Santo had told him he would be picked up at the airport. When he asked how he would know by whom, he was told not to worry; they will know him. As he walked toward the exit with his luggage, he heard a familiar voice, "Mon ami, it's good to see you again."

"Thanks Lou."

Nothing else was said until they were in the car. Lucien sat in the front and Alejandro sat in the back with Carlos. "Don Marcello, I don't know what to say. I didn't expect you to pick me up."

"It was very important, Alejandro, for you to tell me exactly what went wrong in Tampa so it does not happen here. Tell us what went down and why you aborted the shot."

"Of course. I selected a location, the Floridan Hotel based on the criteria Lucien taught me in Philadelphia. We were ready and in place when the motorcade went by. Evidently, the Secret Service agents did not get the word to stay off the limo until after the motorcade passed our location. How this happened or why I don't know because I left almost immediately after we shut down. I didn't even debrief with Don Trafficante, but I am sure he is distressed over not being successful in Tampa."

"Ah, bullshit, Alejandro. He didn't want it to happen in Tampa from the beginning. First, he wanted Miami and when the Miami motorcade was cancelled he had to choose Tampa, but he didn't want to."

"That's ok, Don Marcello," said Lucien, "we knew Dallas was the best place anyway. We have everything we need for success here. Since I didn't go to Tampa, I've had plenty of time to cover every nuance of this job. It won't fail to give us the desired result."

Lucien glanced at Alejandro and added, "Not your fault Mon ami, aborting was the right choice in Tampa, but it was a good exercise and we will insure the same mistake does not happen here. The Secret Service will not be on the back of the limo except on long straight runs."

"Don Marcello, I did not forget your cigars. I have three dozen in my suitcase."

"Good man Alejandro! You will be staying at the safe house with Lucien and some others. Lucien will fill you in on the details of your job. Like Tampa, we are going to use you to signal. The only difference, you will give a visual signal not the auditory signal. On the 21st, you will go with me to a party. You need a tuxedo. One of my guys will help you get one as I'm sure you didn't bring one."

"Grazie, Don Marcello."

Leaning over the back seat Lucien said, "I have a tux for him, Don Marcello, I knew his size from our Philadelphia trip. If we need to we can have it altered, but I think it will fit."

Lucien and Alejandro were dropped off at the safe house. Since Alejandro had never been to Dallas he had no idea were he was. He would learn that this section of Dallas was called Oak Lawn. It was on Congress Avenue a few blocks from the Parkway and about 10 blocks from Dealey Plaza, Lucien's kill zone. After settling into the house, Lucien and Alejandro took the Rambler station wagon, which belonged to one of the other occupants in the Congress Avenue house, and drove to Dealey Plaza. "This is where you will be positioned. We will have a team on the second floor of the Dal-Tex building over there. Two other teams will be on the sixth floor of the Texas Book Depository, another behind that fence, and a fifth underground, that will shoot from that drain. All five can see you from here. In addition to my verbal command, you will have an umbrella that you will raise up and down as a second signal to fire."

"Is there a chance of rain on the 22nd?"

"No, but no one will say anything to you about the umbrella. There will be no military presence in Dallas. The 112th Military Intelligence Group stationed at Fort Sam Houston has been told to stand down rather than report to Dallas." Lucien grinned his knowing way. "And boy was that Commander Col. Reich pissed! Also, no Secret Service agents will be assigned to Dealey Plaza. Secret Service or I should say men with Secret Service identification, will be here but they will all be ours, as will any police officers immediately on the scene and on the overpass there. You may look out of place but you will also be easily visible to all shooters. In case our communications are compromised, you will be the back up. You will signal even if you do not hear the order through your earpieces. Timing is critical here. There will be five shots, one from each location. The overlap should allow for a lone gunman firing three shoots to get the credit. We will plant the patsy's gun and shells in a prearranged location. We will have two diversions set up. One, before the shooters are in place, is over on Houston. We will time the response and call in another to coincide with the hit. The siren will also mask the shots. Only the rifles in the Book Depository will not have silencers and one of them will fire two shots. This will make six shots in play that will sound like three. After the hit, I want you to sit down on the ground. Chaos will be everywhere. I will come over to you and sit beside you. At the right time, I will say move. You will go right and I will go left. The car we came in today will be parked just behind the Book Depository on the right side as you look at the building. You will walk slowly to the car and get in. You will have a driver already there and when his riders all get there he will bring you back to the safe house. He may have another stop after the safe house. Don't say anything to anyone, that is not professional. Once inside the house every-one will debrief. Any questions?"

"No questions, but I assume the umbrella is already at the safe house, yes."

"That's correct. Let's get back."

Once they were in the Rambler, Lucien, who was driving, glanced over to Alejandro, "Did you know Brad?"

"No I never met him. I only knew of him through Kim-Ly and she never said much."

"I just don't figure it the way Sam did. He may have bitched about the job but he would never rat. Sam thought he was one that would purposely get himself arrested so he wouldn't have to do the job. But that's not Brad. I don't think he made the call from Tampa, do you?"

Alejandro felt like he was on center stage with a million people watching. Did Lucien know something or was he just guessing or fishing? Alejandro knew he had to change his fear to anger. If he were angry, he might be able to convince Lucien. If he felt fear, Lucien would know without him saying a word. "How in the hell should I know Lucien, I didn't know the fuck-ing guy!"

After a pause Lucien said, "Ok mon ami............ I was just checking."

The rest of the trip was in silence as both men contemplated their next move.

On the night of the 21st, Carlos Marcello arrived in a stretch limo. Two men were in the front and he was in the back. Alejandro did not know it until the last minute but he and Lucien were going on this trip. His tuxedo had fit fine and didn't need any alterations. Lucien had said of course it didn't, he was trained to size men up and laughed at his own joke. "At this meeting neither of you speak unless I ask you a question. Otherwise, just listen. We'll debrief on the ride back. This will be a meeting with most of our partners present or with a representative present. When we arrive, the party will be in progress. We'll get something to eat and drink, then withdraw to the meeting room. When everyone is present, we'll begin. We're going to the home of Clint Murchison. Not everyone there will be part of our meeting. The party is the cover. A number of girlfriends, goomahs, and assorted reporters will be there so watch what you say if you say anything. Once in the meeting only I'll talk." Lucien and Alejandro just nodded and looked at each other. Alejandro could not read anything on Lucien's face. He knew Lucien had suspected that he had made the Tampa call, not Walker, and that was behind the question he asked earlier, and Alejandro had to assume he was still Lucien's prime suspect. The Murchison's estate, called Glen Abby was in north Dallas. At this time of night, it only took 30 minutes to get there. After Carlos presented the invitation, his group was ushered into the main house. The host and Carlos made eye contact and nodded at each other. Carlos obviously knew his way around the house and led his men to the dining area where a prime rib carving station had been set up. Assorted fish entrées were also available, but all three men opted for the prime rib, caesar salad, asparagus, and baked potato. An

Italian Brunello de Montalcino red wine was the drink of choice. Carlos told the servers to bring the food into the meeting room. The server started to object but thought better of it as he and Carlos made eye contact. Carlos had a presence that warned others not to question him. The so-called meeting room looked like another dining room except for the wood-paneled walls. It had a fireplace in the center of the back wall with a rectangular table in the center that would seat at least 50. Tonight there were 25 chairs with two at the head of the table and one at the foot. There were no nameplates. Carlos selected three chairs in the middle of the backside that faced the window. Carlos wanted his back to the wall so no one could approach him from the rear unseen.

"There'll be no introductions. If you don't know someone you don't need to know them, so don't ask," said Carlos. "And remember no talking unless I ask you a question."

A few others chose to eat in the meeting room but no one spoke. Everyone was constantly checking the door to see if any one else came into the room. The meeting room was away from the entrance to the house and insulated so that no noise escaped or entered the room. Through the large window, Alejandro could see an illuminated waterfall and large water feature. A fountain sprayed what appeared to be different colored water but it was actually different colored lights that created the illusion. He could see it but he couldn't hear it. How appropriate, thought Alejandro, Kennedy's safety was also an illusion. No noise from the water reached the room. From that, Alejandro assumed that the meeting would not be heard by anyone not in the room. All three men declined dessert. Instead, it was Flor de Pinar cigars from Ybor and Sambuca from Italy. Around eleven, a group of meeting guests entered the room led by Richard Nixon. Alejandro watched as the others took their seats. Next to Nixon was J. Edgar Hoover. Next to him was a man he didn't know but guessed it was Tolson. Many of the others Alejandro didn't know. Without exception, every one of them acknowledged Carlos with a nod that he reciprocated. If anyone spoke, it was in silent whispers to their neighbor and no one else. Cigars and cigarettes seemed to be the vice of choice to ease the tension that was obvious on all of the faces. Even Nixon was tapping his fingers on the table as he impatiently waited. At first Alejandro thought he had been wrong, maybe the big man was Nixon. However, that didn't fit. No, he was big, but not the big man. He was in no position to add much after the fact, much less control things as Santo indicated the big man could.

As they waited Hoover leaned over to Nixon and asked, "Dick, why are you here?"

With a smirk Nixon replied, "Some people think I'm paranoid Herbert, but you know who is even worse than me? I'll tell you George Bush. Now don't get me wrong I'm a friend of the light weight, but he thinks he'll be President one day and doesn't want to be any where near Dallas today or tomorrow. He is afraid someone will find out he's CIA and it will hurt him at the polls. What a fucking joke, he can't even win a Texas Senate race. So he asked me to be here, since I had the Pepsi meeting, it was ok for me to be in town, but not him. You know what else Herbert, the son-of-a-bitch is going to call in a tip tomorrow to establish a record that he wasn't here."

"Don't underestimate him Dick, he is crafty and knows his business and is a genius with counter information and deception. However, I agree he will never be President with his personality. He comes across as a buffoon when he makes speeches. But he was the manager that gave us Oswald as the patsy so it isn't all bad."

Both men laughed at their joke, not knowing that the room was so quiet Alejandro and several others heard every word.

It was around midnight before the big man arrived. "Gentleman, it's late so I will get to the point. Our host will be with us shortly. He is dismissing the rest of his guests, except for our chosen ladies for tonight." Laughing at his own joke, Johnson actually smiled. "I know I will make use of mine tonight and I'm sure you will yours as well. Carlos do you have another cigar? That smells great!"

As he handed Johnson a cigar, he said, "Of course, Mr. President."

Johnson paused as he lit the offered cigar and winked at Carlos, "This is nice, Carlos, thanks." As he looked at the label, he said, "Flor de Pinar, I never heard of it."

"You will," was all Carlos said.

Chuckling, Johnson said, "I bet I will. Can we special order any with a White House label?"

"We can send you some to the White House Lyndon, but they will have the Flor de Pinar label."

Now Lyndon was smiling, "Don't do business with this man folks, he will always win. Wait a minute, we are doing business with this man and we will all win." Johnson raised his glass in the direction of Carlos. "Thanks for being here, my friend."

"Thank-you, Mr. President, I wouldn't dream of letting you do this without me."

"Mr. President has a nice ring to it doesn't it?"

With that, everyone stood up and said, "Here! Here!"

"I wanted to have this meeting that, of course, never happened, to insure you all that everything is in place to take the stone from our shoe. Mayor Cabell, is the city ready for the last day of the Bay of Pigs?"

"We are, sir. The motorcade route has been altered to fit our needs."

"Excellent, are the shooters here Mac?"

Mac Wallace stood and said, "Yes sir. We have six, three man teams that are ready and well trained. I will be one of the six and in the book depository at the patsy's location."

"Thank-you. Speaking of the patsy, is he ready Jack?"

Jack Ruby stood and answered, "The patsy has been completely controlled for the last three months. The only thing we were not able to do was get him into Cuba. That however is of little consequence. Oh, you didn't ask but nine Secret Service agents are at the Carousel Club tonight and probably will see the sun come up before they leave."

Lyndon looked at Carlos," How many Secret Service and police will be stationed at the kill zone, Carlos?"

Carlos Marcello did not stand, "The only actual Secret Service and actual police will be the ones in the motorcade. We will have twenty agents on the ground with either police uniforms or Secret Service identification to control the crowd and to address the unexpected. In addition, there will be eighteen men on the hit teams including spotters and lookouts. We have two diversions planned, one before the hit, and one at the same time. We have calculated a way to have our patsy killed during arrest so he cannot answer questions. If on the off chance he is arrested alive we have a fail safe method to take him out."

J. Edgar pondered that for a second, "Uh, that may not be possible to hit him after he is arrested and be able to get away."

Disgusted by the interruption, Carlos said, "The shooter will not try to get away. We don't want a Valentine's Day event. However, we are committed to making this work and for the patsy to get the blame. I'm sure you are all good at what you do, and so are we. Tomorrow's event has been planned by the best in the world. Even so, things happen. The key is anticipating as many as possible, and controlling the other ones as quickly as possible. The stone will be removed from our shoe tomorrow as planned. Does anyone have any concerns?"

Richard Nixon asked, "What about getting the teams out after the event?"

"We expect most of the civilians present to be hysterical and run. A few may go toward our shooters but they will be intercepted by our police and/or Secret Service."

"We have six routes for escape. Even so, we can't be sure some won't be stopped and taken in for questioning. The weapons will be broken down and hidden within 60 seconds of the event. They will not be discovered. If one of the teams is picked up, they'll be released at the station having given false names with clean records. They'll have no weapons. I'm confident there is little to no risk of our men being held for more than a few minutes."

Still, Richard Nixon looked worried. "Where do you see the biggest risk?"

"As always in these public events, there will be witnesses we can't control immediately. We will also have witnesses at the event that will report what we want reported. Some of the witnesses will not be confident of exactly what they saw the next day because of the shock. Some credible witnesses will have accidents, but not right away. There is no need."

"A full investigation will have to be conducted, right Edgar?" asked Nixon.

With a smile, Hoover said, "Of course, by only my best men. They will find what they are supposed to find. However, politically, Lyndon, you may have to appoint a federal team to oversee the investigation and to reach the right conclusion. Will that be a problem?"

Now it was Johnson's turn to smile, "Of course not. What American citizen would not volunteer for such a task? I imagine even some of you would volunteer for that assignment, would you not?"

With mutual agreement and a shared smile, most everyone in the room acknowledged what Allen Dulles said next, "Of course we will do our civic duty and serve our country's needs. After all to serve our country is the least we can do in such a tragic time as this."

Now Lyndon stood and raised his glass. "Thank-you gentleman. Does anyone doubt that we're ready and that the Bay of Pigs will officially end tomorrow?" No one said a word. "I thought not. A toast gentlemen. Here's to the end of Communism in the White House and a return to American business as usual!"

Everyone at the table except for Carlos and his two companions stood and said in unison "Here! Here!"

Carlos, Alejandro and Lucien stood and said, "Salute!"

"Lucien, you and Alejandro go on out to the car, I want to talk to the Sheriff."

"Sure, Don Marcello."

Carlos went over to Sheriff Bill Decker, "Bill you got a second?"

"Sure Carlos what's up?"

"Can you still put Weatherford on the roof of the jail with his rifle and silencer?"

"Sure thing. I told you he was a crack shot and could be counted on."

"Well, here's what I want. I want him to have the umbrella man in his scope prior to the event. If he does not give the signal by raising his umbrella up and down, have Weatherford take him out."

"That's his target, the umbrella man?"

"That's his target if he doesn't signal when he should. If he gives the signal, he can shoot at the main target if it's clean, otherwise have him stand down. Understood?"

"Sure, Carlos, he will be in place with those specific instructions. Should I ask why?"

As he walked away Carlos said, "No."

The motorcade left Love Field at 11:55 Dallas Time. As the president's limousine began to roll, Secret Service Agent Henry J. Rybka was called back by Agent Emory P. Roberts from running along the car as per normal protocol. Roberts explained to Rybka who was obviously confused, "The President told Boring in Tampa he didn't want any Ivy League charlatans riding on the car today. According to Boring the President said, 'If I don't get out and shake hands with the people, I couldn't get elected dog catcher.'

That's also why the motorcycles have been limited to four instead of eight. You are assigned here at Love Field to assist agents Lawton, Paterson and Warner in making sure Love Field is secure for the return flight. You will also have a group of Dallas police to help."

Later, Agent Rybka would tell anyone that would listen he had no idea why these rules were put into place. It obviously reduced Kennedy's safety, as he was not needed at the airport. However, of course no one of importance listened.

Alejandro arrived at Dealey Plaza in the same Rambler station wagon that he and Lucien had driven to Dealey Plaza on the day he arrived. Beside the driver was another man from the safe house that had introduced himself to Alejandro as Lucien Sarti. He said to call him Sarti so he would not confuse him with Conein. Alejandro felt the same queasiness in his belly that he used to get just before a major battle during Cuba's Revolución. He had been trying to figure out how to stop the hit since he arrived. He had nothing and time was running out. He had no doubt Lucien's plan would work. And, with the ability to control the investigation in place, they would get away with it. How could they not? He had never been part of a plan this complex and detailed. They had contingency plans for the backup plans. They even had a plan to take care of any pictures that were taken that might show the wrong thing. If that happened, the negatives would be either destroyed or flown overnight to the CIA lab in Maryland to be reprocessed. Alejandro knew that the first diversion had already occurred before he arrived. This was a planned medical emergency by a spectator on Houston Street. While everyone would be watching the incident and ambulance, the shooters could enter their buildings unseen. The second diversion was to happen at about 12:19 at the front of the book depository building so that the ambulance siren would obscure the rifle shots. He thought this was the weakest part of the plan as timing the arrival and the shots was unlikely even though Lucien had called in several false alarms in order to time the response. He had not been able to call anyone since his arrival in Dallas. He had to think of another way to stop the hit. His only hope, and it was a small one, was if he did not hear Lucien's verbal order to shoot in his ear piece he would not give his physical response of pumping the umbrella up and down. Lucien had told him either way he was to pump the umbrella up and down when Kennedy's car was even with him. As this was a go no matter what, the signal was merely to organize the shots, not as a go, no go signal. Not organizing the shots might blow the patsy cover but it probably wouldn't save Kennedy. Alejandro's sense of pending loss was close to what he had experienced when Batista killed his family and Isabel. He thought about rushing the limo but then he would be stopped and he and Kennedy would both die. At 12:25, he could see the motorcade begin to turn onto Elm Street in front of Dealey Plaza and the Book Depository. Another few minutes passed before Kennedy's car made the turn. Alejandro was almost in a trance as the limo approached his location. With or without out Lucien's verbal he was supposed to be pumping the umbrella. He stood frozen in time.

"Now!" reverberated in his ear and he began to slowly pump the umbrella up and down.

Almost immediately, he heard shots and saw the result. As the first shot echoed, he saw the limo slow down. The driver had reacted to the shot not by accelerating out of trouble but by hitting the brakes and turning around to look at Kennedy. Almost simultaneously, Sarti's fragmentation round hit the side of Kennedy's head, causing it to explode. He knew the President was dead or would be shortly. Alejandro sat down on the ground still in shock. Lucien sat beside him, "Get it together mon ami. When I get up you walk to the Rambler, and I'll walk in the other direction. Ready?"

Alejandro knew he had to come out of his daze or he would not leave Texas alive. "I'm ready. Great plan, Lucien, well done."

With a smirk on his face he said, "But of course, mon ami. Now the hard part, retention. You're done here, go."

As they stood, people were running in all directions. Some to get away, some to check out what they thought they had seen. The only calm people were Marcello's team, some in police uniforms, and others in suits with FBI or Secret Service identifications.

When Alejandro reached the Rambler, the driver and one of the shooters were in the front. As he got into the back the driver said, "It'll be just a minute. We're waiting for Oswald."

It was closer to ten minutes before Oswald reached the car. He immediately got in and said, "Get me to the Carousel Club now! God damn it. I was told it was off and they go ahead without me, what the fuck!"

Alejandro knew the plan for Lee Harvey Oswald was not to take him to Ruby's Carousel Club. There was not to be any connection between the two of them as far as the public was to know. Jack Ruby was his Dallas handler, which he now knew had been assigned by a CIA operative named George Bush, but they were to have no contact in public. The plan was for Oswald to go to the movie theatre and be arrested and taken out there. Roscoe White was to hit J.D. Tippet, another cop, plant Oswald's wallet, and the police were to kill the cop killer in the theatre. That wouldn't happen if he went to the Carousel Club.

"It wasn't us. We didn't do it. I think the fucking Cubans really did take him out for all the threats and attempts on Castro. I know it wasn't us or the CIA. Why the Carousel Club? I saw Jack here."

"I don't know, fuck. We really didn't hit him?" asked Lee Harvey Oswald.

"No, I'm telling you, we were called off and told to stand down. We're heading to our fall back location to await orders. Is the Carousel Club where you're supposed to go? What a cluster fuck. We're all set to do this, we're told to stand down and bam someone else does it."

"No, I'm supposed to go somewhere else but I want answers from Ruby. I know Ruby is here, he gave me this pistol." As Oswald said that, he pulled a revolver out from his waist and showed it to Alejandro. "If Ruby thinks he can set me up as the fall guy, he's fucking wrong!"

Knowing that things were getting out of hand, Alejandro tried to redirect Oswald's thoughts, "Whoa there, Oswald.

We're not setting anybody up for anything. We are all just as confused as you are. That's why we are headed for our fallback position, so the boss will know how to contact us. If anybody's being set up, it's all of us because we were all called off at the last minute. I've never had this happen before, have you Oswald?"

"No, but I'm no one's patsy!"

"I'm with you there. Are you sure you want to break protocol like this?"

Oswald pondered for a moment before answering, "No, take me back to the apartment, I'll change clothes and meet them at my fall-back location."

The trip to the apartment was in silence as everyone pondered their own fate. Alejandro knew he might still be in trouble because he waited to give the signal until after he heard Lucien. He had already decided if he got out of Dallas alive, he was never coming back. The plan was to wait at the safe house for three days and then drive to New Orleans and fly home from there. Lucien would come by and debrief each one separately and then they could leave, but not before.

The driver and the Rambler station wagon left on the second day. After three days, only four were left in the safe house and none of them knew when Lucien would return. Alejandro, Lucien Sarti, Felipe Santiago, and Paul Mandilone all took turns pacing the floor. They had been following the coverage on the television, just like the rest of the world. Except, this group knew how to interpret what they were seeing. Several contingencies had already been used. They knew Oswald had been arrested and not killed as expected. They watched in surprise as Ruby killed Oswald. As they heard witnesses say many different things, they knew some had been planted.

On the morning of the fourth day, Lucien Conein arrived in a new Pontiac Bonneville. He was followed by an older Chevy

Impala. "Good morning gentlemen, I've arrived with your transportation. I've brought you a new Bonneville for your trip to New Orleans and first class tickets from there. We have some very happy clients. We will dispense with the usual debriefing except for you Alejandro. I want to talk for just a minute then you all can leave. Lucien, Felipe, Paul is there anything that you need to say to me?" They all shook their heads side to side. "Very well, Alejandro come with me," he said as he went into a side room and shut the door. Looking straight at Alejandro he said, "Mon ami, you are a man to read, in spite of the fact you can't lie. In Philadelphia, I thought you were a professional with a good eye. Green, yes, but with potential. Then we had the problems in Chicago and you called off the hit in Tampa at the last minute. I was sure you were the rat. And, you hesitated in Dallas with the signal, but only for a second, but it was enough for me to question your motives. I was sure we would remove you after calm was restored. You sensed this didn't you?"

"I knew I was being tested at times, yes," Alejandro said without emotion. The last few days had changed his perception of life. As he did after his family and Isabel were murdered, he was overcome with sadness and no longer cared if he stayed in this world. He looked directly at Lucien and for the first time he answered without emotion on his face or in his eyes. Instead, he spoke as someone that was hardened by life's cruel lessons. "If I did something wrong or if I jeopardized the mission, do what you have to do, but do it now!"

Lucien stopped for a moment and then continued without acknowledging Alejandro's statement, "Yet you did not try to run nor get out of what you were asked to do. You knew you were a dead man if we caught you. Why didn't you run?"

Again Alejandro answered without emotion," I knew I was a dead man if I did not do as requested just like every other member of this assassination team. I also knew you would not waste an asset if he didn't do anything wrong or didn't pose any kind of threat. I didn't do anything wrong and I pose no threat to you or anyone else involved. It's true that if any of us are now on the official radar, it will be the 'umbrella man.' The umbrella man will not be located as I assume he is already dead, and I can go back to serving Santo as before." With a conviction born of not caring about the outcome he asked," Am I wrong, Lucien?"

The two men stared at one another trying to read the meaning of the words they had heard. Finally, Lucian asked. "Why did you talk Oswald into going to the theatre?"

Looking at Lucien with disgust he answered, "You have to ask? If he doesn't go there, the patsy scenario may not have worked. He had to go there."

Finally, Alejandro's fate was decided. "Mon ami you were right it would not have worked if he deviated and went to Ruby's Club. We all owe you for your quick thinking and your ability to convince him to stay with the plan. I will make sure Santo has a full report. Have a safe trip home and maybe we will work together again. It was fun, no?"

Without smiling and as he was walking to the door, Alejandro answered, "No, it was not fun. I hate umbrellas, especially on a sunny day in Dallas."

Chapter 30
HOME
1964

Alejandro's flight to Tampa gave him time to reflect on Dallas. Even though he had escaped the trap, he knew part of him died with Kennedy. He had seen men die before, he had even been responsible for some of their deaths, but Dallas was different. The men he killed in the Revolución were trying to kill him, Kennedy wasn't. It could even be argued that Kennedy was trying to save lives by getting out of Vietnam. Did it really just come down to the fact that Kennedy was bad for business and therefore had to be fired in the only immediate way possible? And how could the same people that had been trying to kill Castro in Cuba without success, be successful in taking out Kennedy in the United States? Moreover, why did it feel like a personal loss to him with Kennedy? He had not met him, didn't know him, had little cause or opportunity to really have a strong opinion of him. However, it was a loss. According to Castro, he would have been good for Cuba. He may have made it possible for Cuba to disassociate with the Soviet Union if not totally, at least partially. It also felt like part of his soul died in Dallas. Fidel certainly admired him. Not at first, of course, when they were fighting against each other. Fidel had said Kennedy inherited that war from Eisenhower and Nixon and that once he was there long enough to think for himself, he saw Cuba was not the enemy. That's why Fidel did not want him to die. He thought that Kennedy would normalize relations between the two countries and both would benefit. It was much too early to know what direction Johnson would take.

His first night in Ybor was spent telling Santo everything that had happened in Dallas. The people he did not know at the meeting in Dallas he had to describe until Santo was satisfied that he knew them or that it was someone he had never met. They talked until three in the morning. An exhausted Alejandro finally fell asleep just before the sun came up.

On the flight back to Tampa, he had decided to continue with his plans to have a company New Year's Eve party. Last August he had reserved one of the large ballrooms on the second floor of the Columbia for that purpose. He had hired entertainment complete with flamenco dancers to help ring in the New Year. Since everything had been arranged well in advance, there was no reason to cancel. Besides, he thought, it was good for employee morale. It might even help his. He had wanted to see Kim-Ly but he had not gone to the factory since his return. He somehow felt it was wrong to return so soon to the daily routine as if the world was still the same as it was before the assassination. He could not figure out why his sense of loss was so profound, but it was. He was deep in thought as he entered the ballroom and was shocked that everyone stood up and clapped for him as he walked to his table. His face turned red when he realized his first thought had been, are they this happy Kennedy was dead and that he had been part of it? He quickly recovered and blushingly realized they were clapping for their host and this party.

"Hola, please be seated. Eat, drink and be merry. Tonight we say goodbye to 1963, and bienvenida to 1964! Feliz Año Nuevo."

"Welcome back, El Jefe. We have missed you."

"Gracias, gracias. I have missed being here these past few weeks. Please sit down, have fun. Let's be happy as we welcome the New Year and all that it means. A toast. To Flor de Pinar, the most successful new cigar line in Ybor since 1909 and to all of you that made it happen!"

Alejandro stood up and as he raised his glass up said," Arriba"

He lowered his glass and said, "Abajo"

He centered his glass and said," Al Centro"

He moved the glass to his mouth and said," Adentro."

Everyone stood with him and moved their glasses in the same manner. After everyone drank they joined him in laughing as he said, "It's good to be here!"

The rest of the evening passed quickly. The dancers were great, the music was excellent. As always, the Columbia's food was superb. The only missing element had been that Kim-Ly had not come. He was afraid she might not as Santo had told him she knew she was a widow. As the time approached midnight, many of the folks had left. Even though the factory was closed tomorrow, they were not used to staying up so late, even on New Year's. The ones that remained were dancing. The lights had been lowered and only the dance floor was well lit. A good atmosphere for his mood, he thought.

"Hola, El Jefe, or should I say Lo Dit?"

Alejandro turned to see Kim-Ly standing behind him dressed in all black except for the golden dragons on her shirt, "Kim-Ly, it's good to see you! Did you just get here? I didn't see you when I came in." He wanted to hug her but thought better of it. Instead, he said "And Homunculus, you can call me whatever you want as long as we talk." Looking at her, some of the immense weight he had felt since Dallas began to lift, if only for a brief moment.

"I was here. But I left for a while to think before we talked. You know I am a widow, yes?"

As the weight returned he said," Yes, Santo told me. I'm very sorry."

"Did he also tell you he was a traitor, a rat as they call it?"

Alejandro could see the pain in her eyes and with empathy said," Yes, but I'm .....sure he was not."

She looked at him with sad eyes and wrinkled eyebrows, "I knew you would know he was not a rat. Castro did not want Kennedy dead did he?"

Alejandro was immediately on guard. Was this a trap? Was this conversation for her, or Santo? As he stared into her dark eyes, they enveloped him and he no longer cared." If you tell anyone I'm also a dead man, Kim-Ly, but no, he did not want him dead."

"I saw the pain on your face when you walked in tonight, and knew you had a part in it. I also saw a picture of the umbrella man on TV. If others recognize you, you may be a dead man anyway. You may become a threat if sought after for questioning."

"I'm not surprised that you recognized me. You have amazing perception. Lucien has a diversion set up for that. I will not be identified as the umbrella man. If sought after, which is doubtful, Louie Steven Witt will come forward as the umbrella man. He'll say he was heckling the Nazi appeasing Kennedy with the black umbrella used as a symbol of the Nazi appeasing Neville Chamberlain."

"Lucien is very good at what he does. I'm surprised you got away with fooling him as to your intent. He is not easy to fool.

I would have said impossible, but you being alive disproves that. You've evidently learned to lie."

"Evidently something inside you has to die to be a good liar. After the assassination, part of me died. I am not proud of that, Kim-Ly. I do not feel I am as worthy a human being because of it. Somehow, it shames me. In addition, I cannot shake the feeling that mankind has taken a step backward because of Dallas. It was so well done no one that was involved will ever be held accountable."

"Alejandro, I have never known an occidental to be so oriental before. The village monk would be proud of your untrained insights into the frailty that is the human conscience. The monk would also tell you that part of you is not dead, but badly tarnished, and that only good deeds for others will make it whole again. But what do monks know, eh?"

"I'm sure they know more than I. Right now I feel very stupid and very defeated."

Taking his right hand into her left, she then placed her right on top of his, "I will help you. I will help you heal your soul."

As he looked into her dark eyes, the room, the world, seem to shrink away. All he could see was this beautiful creature holding his hand and inviting him to kiss her. The desire was strong as he bent over to kiss her for the first time. The world was suspended for Alejandro. He did not even hear the Prospero Ano Nuevo chant that enveloped the room. Their kiss went unnoticed as the New Year's revelers were caught in their own revelry. If anyone saw them, it would have looked like a New Year's celebration and not the life-changing event that it would be for both of them. They were momentarily stunned by the depth and warmth of their kiss. For Alejandro, it reminded him of the first kiss he shared with Isabel. The chemistry he noticed with her was also evident in his kiss with Kim-Ly. He didn't think he would ever experience that same connection again, but here it was. They decided to leave together as the party was ending.

To their surprise, Santo was in the bar on the first floor of the Columbia and waved them over. "Hola, Alejandro, Kim-Ly, I 'm glad I found you together. We need to talk and it can't wait. Let's go into my room so we can have privacy."

Both were somewhat startled to find Santo apparently waiting for them to come down, "Of course, Don Santo. It must be important for you to interrupt your New Year's to be here," said Alejandro.

As the three sat down at the table, Santo began. "Alejandro, I have news for Castro that can't wait. You must leave tomorrow."

Surprised that Santo would say this in front of Kim-Ly, Alejandro glanced at her before he said, "Of course." Then he asked," Does this somehow involve Kim-Ly?"

"No, not directly. It seems that our friends are in extreme clean up mode since Dallas. All, and I mean all, possible leaks are to be sealed. Some believe that Kim-Ly may have assisted her husband in preventing the Chicago hit. For her safety, she should return to Vietnam. It is too risky for her to stay here and too risky for me if she goes directly to Vietnam from Tampa. That is why I want you to take her to Cuba and she can safely leave from there."

Looking in Santo's eyes, which were dark and cold, Kim-Ly asked," Thank-you for looking out for me Santo, but you really don't believe my husband was a rat, do you?"

Santo returned her intensity as he said, "It no longer matters what I personally believe." Changing his gaze to Alejandro, he added, "Or what Lucien Conein believes. People are nervous after Dallas and all possibilities are being addressed." Looking back toward Kim-Ly the tension in Santo's eyes relaxed, "My business is headed for a very prosperous time during the next four to eight years and nothing and no one can get in the way. We have assisted some very powerful people in solving a major problem. They now owe us and we will get what we want at least for the immediate future. That is, as long as we complete our job and the loose ends and possible loose ends are eliminated. Vietnam will play a big role in our future and so will your brother, Kim-Ly. Your brother will be a major part of that future because of his opium distribution network, which you helped create. You can help him in a big way, Kim-Ly, and it would be a shame to take you away from him when you can help with the increasing demand for his product. Your value as an asset outweighs your risk as a loose end. However, you will have to disappear from Tampa tomorrow. Do you understand me?"

Looking down at her feet she answered, "Yes, Santo I understand."

As Santo passed a sealed envelope to Alejandro he said, "I have this letter Alejandro, for you to give Fidel. It explains Kim-Ly's situation. Now for the news, it seems one of Fidel's confidants has been planning to take him out for a while. Rolando Cubela was given a Papermate pen in France that will inject poison. Of course the CIA is behind this."

As usual, Santo dismissed the two without asking either if they were ok with his plans. That was not his way. If he said it, he expected others to carry out his wishes without question. This was not just ego for Santo Trafficante Jr.; it was more a reflection of the real world and his time management and conservation of words. To waste time asking if others were ok with his plans was a massive waste of his time and would never happen. Time was money, money was power, and power was king and would be respected without question. The undisputed King in Tampa, in Florida, and soon to be in Vietnam was Santo Trafficante Jr., and as always his wishes, his orders would be followed. Kim-Ly and Alejandro made their way to their respective homes. Each pondering how the end of 1963 and the beginning of 1964 was not at all what they thought it was only one hour before. Alejandro also knew Don Santo was not sparing Kim-Ly because he liked her; He was sparing her because she could help him in Vietnam. It was just business as usual.

That night neither one could sleep. Alejandro was deep into his thoughts of Kim-Ly and his first love Isabel. Thinking of Isabel always brought pain. He never knew if she suffered or exactly how she died in 1958. It hurt him deeply to think she may have been raped, but he knew the probability was strong. And he couldn't imagine a worse death than to be burned alive as so many were by Batista's troops. That's what Batista's troops did. Especially to young and beautiful girls like Isabel. She was a fighter and would not have gone quietly. He had loved her completely and never even considered that he might find a love that strong, that whole, that encompassing, ever again. Now he wasn't so sure. He hadn't really thought about being alone for the rest of his life but he didn't think he would love anyone the way he had Isabel. Kim-Ly was an enigma. So complex, so very smart, so exotic and with the promise of passion the like of which he could only imagine. But how could she really love him? He had been responsible for her husband's death.

At the same time Alejandro was having his internal dialogue, Kim-Ly was having her own. She had always respected Alejandro ever since they moved passed his thinking she was a whore. That made her angry, but now she thought it was funny. She was all set to hate him for his involvement in her husband's death but she knew that was never his intent. The intrigue that was her husband's everyday life would be intolerable to Alejandro. Mark had fooled her too. She did not know he was an assassin until after they were married. She would never have married him if she had known. An assassin is a different type of person. Cold as ice, really. They play at love and passion but they do not value human beings. She had always thought it was strange that Mark had thought more of the life of an animal than he did the life of a person. He did not hunt animals but he would hunt human beings without a second thought. He had been damaged goods. She knew she had loved him when they were married. However, that love was never the same after she learned what he did for a living. He had worked for the CIA and then as a freelance killer. She shuddered as she thought about what he would have done to her if she had betrayed him. She knew he wouldn't hesitate to make her suffer for that betrayal before he killed her. Maybe Alejandro had done her a favor. Even though he didn't know what the outcome of his actions would be, they had ended her marriage in the only way it could have ended with her still alive. On the other hand, maybe she was trying to ease her conscience because she had strong feelings for him. She didn't know the answer to that question. She knew she could easily fall in love with Alejandro. His bout with his own guilt was refreshing. She knew he had killed in war, but he valued life and especially the life of innocents. He would never see an innocent's death as acceptable collateral damage in completing a mission. She thought the tenderness of his kiss probably indicated he was already in love with her. But, what did she really want? Did she want to return to her family and her brother in Vietnam or did she want to live in Cuba with Alejandro? Or maybe neither at this time. For now, she decided not to commit to anything past leaving Tampa at this point. Let her karma become self-evident. After all karma is karma and cannot be changed.

Both were quietly consumed with their own thoughts as they flew to Miami. It was not until they boarded the boat that they began to address their respective futures. The weather had improved since they left Tampa. In Tampa, it was raining and 55 degrees. On the boat, it was sunny and 75 degrees. They had settled into the chairs on the back of the boat. The only other person aboard was the captain and he was on the flying bridge and could not hear their conversation.

"How long do you think you will stay in Cuba, Kim-Ly?"

This was the question she knew he would ask. And she had just not decided, "At least until you have to go back. I assume you are going back, aren't you?"

Just like Alejandro's question, Kim-Ly's had been equally direct. "I have no choice, Kim-Ly. I made a pact in 1959 to be the conduit between Fidel and Santo. Secrecy was a prime concern for both and until you became aware of it, only the three of us knew it existed. Santo got out of prison with his money and Fidel gets inside information about what the CIA is planning which is usually not good. Well, actually, it's never good. Like this Cubela thing, it usually involves an assassination attempt. If not that it's another invasion plot or just basic terrorism against the Cuban people."

"Why would the CIA terrorize the Cuban people?"

"To make Castro look bad, or to just blame it on him. It is hard to believe some of the misinformation the CIA has planted to discredit him. They keep trying but it never works. The United States has always underestimated the love of the Cuban people for Castro. The ones that didn't love him, the very rich who didn't want to share with the poor and the crooks like Santo have all moved to Miami or other parts of the United States. The reason I wanted to stop the Kennedy hit was that finally a president of the United States saw through the propaganda against Fidel and was going to normalize relations. The United States and Cuba were already having back channel discussions on how to accomplish this and save face for everyone involved when Kennedy was shot."

"Why was he killed, Alejandro? Was it over Cuba?"

"No, not really, but I think that was a factor. I was part of a meeting in Dallas with Marcello and at least some of the major players in the hit. They were a mix of oilmen, bankers, politicians, organized crime, CIA, and assassins. The one thing they all had in common was a hatred of all things Kennedy. Maybe Castro will know how or why this hatred infected so many seemingly different people. The man in charge at the meeting was Lyndon Johnson, the new president of the United States."

Kim-Ly made a whistling sound through her lips as she said, "The new president is a killer. Wow! If the American people only knew."

"They will never know. Lucien Conein and his plan made sure that Johnson could control the outcome of the investigation. The so-called Warren Commission has members that were part of the plan. Can you imagine the killers investigating themselves? What a sad commentary for this country."

"It truly is sad. A coup has occurred and the people don't even know it. From a planning perspective, a masterpiece will go unrecognized by everyone not directly involved. I hate what he does but Conein is the best at his job. Mark had often verbally admired his work. Did Santo recruit him?"

"Yes, he did."

For the rest of the trip the two were mostly quiet, captivated by their own thoughts. Kim-Ly marveled at the complexity of a plan that could pull off such an accomplishment. She was always intrigued by intellectual challenges no matter what they involved. Alejandro could not help but notice that Kim-Ly was more intrigued by the ability to successfully pull off the secretive coup than she was by the fact an innocent president was killed in his own country by his own people that he had trusted to protect him. He wondered was that a product of being married to an assassin.

Before meeting with Castro, they had decided to get two adjoining rooms at the Hotel Nacional. They unpacked, changed clothes, and prepared for their meeting with Fidel Castro. When they met, Fidel was already aware that Alejandro had brought a girl with him. Ah ha, Fidel thought, Alejandro has a girl. That is very good and long overdue. He has mourned enough and is due some good fortune.

When they walked into his office, he was not prepared for just how beautiful and exotic she was. For a non-Cuban that is. No other woman can compare to a beautiful Cuban princess. She was close though. "Hola, Señorita, hola, Alejandro. Señorita, I am Fidel Castro and as a friend of Alejandro's you are most welcome in Cuba. Would you like something to drink?"

Alejandro smiled at Fidel's reaction to Kim-Ly. He had never offered him a drink! "Fidel this is Kim-Ly. She is from South East Asia. I met her in Ybor. She has been working with me at the Ybor factory as our bookkeeper."

Si, thought Fidel, *I bet that is not the only work she has done for you! You lucky dog.*

"Her husband is recently deceased and she is no longer welcome in Ybor. I have this letter from Santo that explains everything." With that, Alejandro handed Fidel the letter. Fidel noticed it was still sealed.

My trusted friend,

As you read this letter, I know Kim-Ly and Alejandro are with you. They must not return to the United States for any reason. I would ask that you allow Kim-Ly to stay in Cuba until she wishes to return to Vietnam. Her husband was suspected of betraying an action in Chicago and was removed by my associates. Some have even suggested Alejandro was involved in trying to sabotage the Kennedy hit, but I know that could not be true. He would never act in disagreement with my plans and I know we both hated Kennedy for different reasons. Because of this apparent distrust of Alejandro by some of my associates and the desire of those associates to purge any and all perceived threats there is some risk for Alejandro should he return to Ybor. He is not aware of this and I thought you should decide. If you wish to replace him with another conduit, I would like to continue our association.

With Respect,

Santo'

Fidel digested these statements before glancing at Alejandro and Kim-Ly who were patiently anticipating his comments. "I am sorry for your loss, Kim-Ly. Santo has explained what happened to your husband in Chicago and why you cannot return to the United States. You are of course welcome in Cuba for as long as you like. As I said earlier, any friend of Alejandro's is a friend of mine and all of Cuba. I owe him my life many times over."

"El Jefe, you are too kind and you exaggerate. It's true we fought together in the revolution, but it is I who owe you. I was a damaged person in those days and could only see my own revenge. You helped me to become a man and to see that Cuba was the important thing in the revolution, not revenge."

Both men were shocked out of their reminiscing when Kim-Ly said, "It's nice that you boys share a mutual admiration, but I'm hungry. Could we finish business and have something to eat? It's been a long day."

As Alejandro and Fidel laughed at her comment, Fidel replied," Of course, Kim-Ly. I would like for you and Alejandro to join me for dinner tonight."

Another first, thought Alejandro, drinks and dinner! "Of course Fidel, but first I must tell you about Rolando Cubela and the CIA."

After dinner, the two men walked in the garden outside the restaurant and waited for Kim-Ly to return from the ladies room. They walked in silence with a Cuban cigar in one hand and a Cubata in the other, until Fidel asked, "Do you know what Santo wrote in his letter?"

"I haven't read it because it was sealed. Santo said it was about Kim-Ly and her situation. Was it not?"

"Si, Si, It was that. I have made a decision Alejandro. I want to end the heroin traffic through Cuba. Ultimately, it hurts too many innocent people for us to be part of it."

Alejandro stopped walking and looked at Fidel, "That will mean an end to Santo's help. Is that safe?"

"Si, I believe it is Alejandro. We now have a section of our G2 unit that does nothing but watch the United States. We have men planted in most expatriate organizations in the United States. We also have a source in the CIA. The work you have done for Cuba and for me has allowed us time to develop these resources. Without that, I don't know if we could have survived this long. I will forever be grateful to you and your service."

"And Santo's?"

"No, not really. What he did was for money. He has been well compensated for his information. You on the other hand have never asked for anything in return. You have risked your life for Cuba and for me. Cuba and I owe you much Alejandro. As I told you before, I have put your family's property in your name. I have saved the land adjoining it for the squatters that are still working your land. I don't know why they don't want to move to their own land and still prefer to work yours, but that is the case. When you get there, you can decide what to do with them. Obviously, with me breaking our arrangement with Santo you cannot go back there even for a visit. Besides, it is time you took your place in Cuba. We need your guidance in the tobacco and cigar business. I think I will develop a new ministry for Cuban cigars and tobacco. I have noticed the quality of some that are being made and labeled as Cuban are not good enough to be called a Cuban cigar. As I want to ensure Cuba's preeminence in cigar manufacturing, I need an experienced Minister who could standardize quality. After everything you have already done for Cuba, I have no right to ask you, but would you consider doing this as a favor to me?"

"I don't know what to say, El Jefe, other than of course I will do this. There is nothing I love more than tobacco growing and cigar making. This is so unexpected. I thought I would be returning to Ybor. I wanted to stay a while here first, but I thought I would be returning."

"Perhaps my young friend, this will give you the opportunity to convince our dinner guest to stay in Cuba. I saw the way you two looked at each other. I am very happy for you, Alejandro. I think she will make you a very happy man."

"Thank-you, El Jefe. We are in the process of defining our relationship and this definitely presents possibilities that would not have been practical if I had returned to Ybor."

As Kim-Ly approached she could see that the two men were engaged in a very serious conversation. "And why have you two men become so serious all of a sudden? I thought you were here to wait on me and cater to my every need. Is that not so?"

All three could not contain their laughter. "I have always heard that the Oriental woman is shy and demure. Is that not the case?" asked Fidel.

"The Oriental woman is shy and demure when that fits her needs or if the man's ego needs stroking, but this Oriental woman has also learned to be the master of her universe and the center of attention when that meets her needs."

"Ole, Alejandro what a catch she is! said Fidel. She has mi Madre's spirit and strength. She is a match for any man and then some!"

Alejandro, all smiles at the exchange, replied, "I have truly never seen her be shy and demure except in jest. Sometime I will tell you about our first meeting. It was something. She was something."

Taking Alejandro's arm she added, "Oh El Lo Dit, you bad boy. You tell on poor Kim-Ly. I so hurt. I be shy. I be demure. Just the way you likey, k, k? You furgib little Kimmy, I love you long time, No?"

Fidel was hysterical as Alejandro smiled at Kim-Ly. Finally Fidel was able to say, "I have not laughed that hard since I was a kid. Thank-you, Kim-Ly. Was does Lo Dit mean?"

"Asshole," answered Alejandro and Fidel was laughing again.

"Please you two have lunch with me tomorrow, bien?"

Kim-Ly was looking up at Fidel still holding Alejandro's arm. "K, K, Fedil we be dare. We start reboluchen soon but we wait affer lunch K, K? No good fit war wit empy belwie."

As Fidel left, he was still laughing and shaking his head. What a creature, he thought. "I am very happy for Alejandro," he said to no one or should he say" Berry hapie!"

Alejandro and Kim-Ly walked to their rooms with little conversation. Both were wondering how the evening would end and more importantly how did they want the evening to end. They kissed goodnight, which promised anything was possible on both sides. It also said, *I'm not sure what I want.* Kim-Ly because of Mark, and Alejandro because of Isabel. They went to their separate rooms with only one thin unlocked door between them. What to do? Alejandro asked himself as he lay in bed. *What to do? Should I open the door or should I wait to see if she will open the door? Do I dare open the door?* Then the look on his face changed from wonder to want and desire. *The important question is do I dare not open the door?*

With that, he got up and put on a shirt and slacks. He was barefoot when he opened the door. Immediately on the other side stood Kim-Ly, in her nightgown looking as if she had just reached for the doorknob. Startled she said, "Oh!" She recovered quickly and said "Hola, sailor, fancy meeting you here!" Alejandro was holding her and bending to kiss her before she said the last words. The passion was urgent for both and their breathing was already short and rapid before they hit the bed.

The first lovemaking was over very quickly for both, as they climaxed together. The second time was slower and more passionate. The first was animalistic and met the needs of their bodies, the second was full of passion and desire to please the other, and met the needs of their souls. As they lay side by side, they each thought about what had just occurred. Alejandro was amazed at her body. It really was a perfectly formed small woman's body. Her breasts and hips were joined by the smallest waist he had ever seen. He was getting aroused again just thinking about her. Kim-Ly was surprised at how physically fit Alejandro was. His stomach muscles were well defined and he had the cutest round and hard butt she had every seen and grabbed. He was also bigger than Mark had been. She was afraid he might be too big for her but that fear was short lived. She felt herself getting wet again as she thought about his body. She turned to face him. "One more time for the road, sailor?"

He responded immediately. She smiled when she reached for him and found he was already hard.

Fidel came to the Nacional for lunch as arranged. He noticed a change in the two lovers and smiled to himself, and thought. Isn't love wonderful? These two are very deserving. At least he knew Alejandro was; he could only hope Kim-Ly was as she presented herself. "So you want to know why Kennedy was killed?"

"Si, El Jefe, I know who, I was there, but I don't know why. Can you answer that?"

"Well, I can give you the KGB answer to that. They immediately did their own investigation in case they were accused. As you suspected, Lyndon Johnson was the ringleader. I don't know if he was the first to propose such a thing but I know he was happy to do it. And for good reason, at least from his perspective. If Kennedy had lived, Johnson would probably have gone to jail. He certainly would not have been part of the 1964 election. He was up to his ass in dirty politics, and kickbacks for contracts. To cover up his nefarious actions in Texas he had people murdered. Kennedy was just the last to be murdered. The KGB estimates seven others in Texas were murdered at his request. As president, he has been able to cover all of that up as well as cover up the Kennedy assassination. Those were his reasons. Kennedy also made some political decisions that were diametrically opposed by the major capitalists in the United States and around the world. The United States Federal Reserve System, which is owned by private for profit banks around the world, not just United States banks, was created in 1913 the same year as the Federal Income Tax system, which was needed to fund it. It also placed the American taxpayer as the guarantor of its profit margins. Kennedy knew the system was unconstitutional. The Constitution requires the Congress to be responsible for the United States money system and dictates that the right to control the money supply cannot be farmed out to anyone else. That's why he issued Executive Order 11110 creating the silver certificate. That simple act would have ended the Federal Reserve's ability to loan money to the United States at interest. It would have been dissolved because it would no longer have a purpose or guarantee that the US taxpayer would bail them out. After the assassination that order was immediately reversed by Johnson. Kennedy also eliminated the oil depreciation allowance, which would have cost oilmen billions in taxes. Johnson also reversed that. Kennedy signed the Nuclear Test Ban Treaty with the Soviet Union. This did not help the Military Industrial Complex, which makes millions from military weapons contracts. He also began withdrawing troops from Vietnam with a promise to have all of them out by 1965. If Cuba taught the

United States a lesson, it was that a ruler could survive anything if he has the support of the people, and without the will of the people, the leader is vulnerable. He knew the South Vietnamese government did not have the support of the people. It was time to get out. Again, that meant smaller military budgets and fewer no-bid contracts for companies like Brown and Root. Good for the taxpayer, not so good for the military which would have suffered a reduction in troop strength, and not so good for the Military Industrial Complex. They would lose millions in profit from bombs and equipment if the US withdrew from Vietnam. Johnson has already reversed this decision. Kennedy said he wanted to "break the CIA into a thousand pieces". He started by firing three: the Mayor of Dallas's brother, General Cabal; Alan Dulles; and Richard Bissell. Now, the CIA is in firm control once again with no threat of interference from Johnson. Lastly, Kennedy denied Operation Northwoods to the Pentagon. Operation Northwoods was a series of terrorist attacks against innocent United States citizens. The blame was going to be put on Cuba in order to justify an invasion. It would have started World War III, as the Soviets would have come to our defense. In the process, Cuba would have been destroyed. What all of these things did was to unite the Military Industrial Complex, the US military, international bankers, desperate politicians, oil tycoons, certain CIA and former CIA operatives, along with organized crime who will do anything, if the price is right, into a cohesive force impossible to survive. Normalizing relations with Cuba was not a big element in the overall scheme of things here. The coup was possible because the American people were ignorant of these facts and will be kept ignorant for as long as possible. They don't understand because they have never been taught how their financial system, especially the Federal Reserve

System, works. This is a prime example that any economic system, whether it's socialism or capitalism, cannot be taken to the extreme without dire consequences. If you take socialism too far you get Communism, which I will not ever support, and if you take capitalism too far, you get a system controlled by only the wealthiest. In that system, a democracy cannot survive. It may be dressed up to look like a democracy or a republic but it won't be. The country, its government, will be controlled by the few that are the richest. This is a sad thing for the United States. They may never again have a president that even tries to represent the masses. Enough of this sadness, life will go on at least here in Cuba." Shaking his head Fidel changed the subject, "Do you really speak nine languages, Kim-Ly?"

"Si. It was necessary for one of my jobs. I am rusty in some of them now but they will come back with practice."

"What's on your agenda today, Alejandro?"

"I want to show Kim-Ly our country. I am hoping she will decide to stay with us, but that is her decision."

Fidel looked at Kim-Ly and asked, "And when will you make your decision?"

"When it is time to make that decision. It is not yet time."

"She may not be shy and demure, Alejandro, but she is her own woman and a woman of mystery."

They both looked at her as Alejandro said, "I couldn't agree more, El Jefe."

She raised her glass toward both of them, "A toast, gentlemen. Here's to the most interesting men I have ever met."

As Alejandro and Kim-Ly left for their fishing trip, Fidel stayed behind and enjoyed his cigar. He also pondered his friend's future. *Oh, Alejandro, I want this to work out for you in the worst way but I fear it will not. I cannot tell you but I had her investigated. Her past life is more city than anything else. If you love the farm and want to grow tobacco, you will not do it with her. She is city, not farm. Her sophistication will be lost on the farm and she will wither. However, she is smart enough to know that and will never go there in the first place. Then you will have to choose her or the farm. Life can be so cruel.* Fidel walked away slowly after he finished his cigar. Fidel knew Cuba had lost a friend in Kennedy. When would Cuba have another friend as President of the United States? Johnson would not be that friend. Fidel knew enough about US politics to understand the importance of Florida in any presidential election. He also knew Florida had a large number of Cuban dissidents who would make it impossible to normalize relations unless it was from a lame duck president who did not have to worry about reelection. He hoped it would not take too many years but he was not confident. Until that day, he knew he could not safely hold open elections in Cuba. Cuba was too valuable to American business interests. They would buy a candidate, and swamp him in money and propaganda in order to win. Fidel still thought he would probably win, but to take the chance would put Cuba at risk of another Batista. Could he risk it and jeopardize everything good that was happening in Cuba? Some day this would happen, but not now.

Chapter 31
PINAR DEL RIO
1964

After two weeks of unabashed lovemaking, site seeing, and general tourist activities, it was time to set out for Alejandro's farm in Pinar del Rio. Another agrarian reform had been enacted so the maximum acreage of land that any one family could own was now 168. As Minister of Tobacco, Alejandro could create co-operatives, if desirable, and work as large a plantation as he wanted to maximize production and maintain quality controls. His dream was to unite all of the top growing areas of the Pinar Province into one co-operative that would represent Cuba's standard of excellence in tobacco and cigar production. If successful, he could expand into the other tobacco areas of Cuba. First, he wanted to organize the Pinar Del Rio Province. Fidel had explained to Alejandro that the Ministry of Tobacco would not be a Cabinet level Ministry but would be under the cabinet level Ministry of Agriculture. Fidel was very interested in organizing Cuba's tobacco and cigar industry to maximize quality and production. He thought Alejandro was the perfect man for the job. To Alejandro, cigars were his passion and his birthright as a Cuban. He also wanted to have a family. He had not realized how much he wanted a family until his relationship with Kim-Ly started to bloom. Having a partner to share ambitions and desires was a great way to live. Having children was a responsibility; they don't come with an owner's manual or a set of instructions on how to be a good parent, but he knew they would be good parents, if Kim-Ly wanted kids and a family. They had not talked about kids so he really didn't know, but he couldn't imagine her not wanting the same dream.

They got a room at the Hotel Pinar Del Rio, which was in the capital city of Pinar Del Rio. He only got one room this time. Why get two? He reasoned one was all they would use. After unpacking, they set out to explore the province. Most areas were at least partially planted, but when he inspected the plants, he could see some degradation in the quality. He reasoned this was probably caused by improper seedling production. His theory of a co-operative would solve that. Especially if he personally established the quality control measures he envisioned. Yes, he thought one central location where he would only use disease resistant seeds to insure a resilient as well as great smoking tobacco. That was his dream. In addition, to accomplish his dream he would have to live on the farm to handle the entire production from start to finish. He wanted to oversee the drying, curing and fermentation of all Pinar del Rio tobacco. His tour confirmed what he already suspected; the quality was in a decline in the entire Province. The quality of the last few shipments he had received for his Flor de Pinar cigars had not been an anomaly but a reflection of the poor standard that was now produced in his beloved Pinar Del Rio. He had thought that maybe someone was manipulating his tobacco and he wasn't receiving Pinar del Rio stock. Now he could see and feel the truth as he inspected the plants. Quality control and the pride in producing only the finest tobacco was nowhere to be found. The farmers he talked to seemed to be confused as to the solution. They meant well, but they didn't have the knowledge it took to produce the best. Moreover, Alejandro knew why. In a word Batista. Not only did his raid destroy the best crops, but he also killed the men with the knowledge necessary to produce what had been accepted as the best cigar tobacco in the world. Alejandro felt it was his mission in life to restore Pinar Del Rio Province to that pre-eminent state. The province had been blessed by God to grow the best and his goal was to reaffirm that blessing. Until this day he had not realized everything else he had done in his life was a preamble for this work, for this mission.

Now it was time to visit his father's land. He had been putting it off until last. He still dreaded the memories that would be attached to seeing his home. Or at least to the land that had been his home. The house had been burned down and he didn't have any idea if any structure was there. He knew a family had started growing on the land but that was all he knew. That, and their name, Gomez. His father had a family with that name working for him at the time of the Batista attack. It could be them. It was time to find out. As Alejandro and Kim-Ly neared the Moreno homestead, Kim-Ly asked about the name, "Why do you call it the Moreno Plantation and not the Mendez Plantation? Isn't that your family name?"

"It's the name you know but it's not the name I was given at birth. As I was just finishing my classes at the University of Tampa, Trafficante deported me with the threat that Rafael Diego Moreno Suarez, my real name, was no longer welcomed in the United States. I'll tell you the details later. When Fidel and I arranged with Santo to let him out of prison with his money intact and allow him to continue running heroin through

Cuba in exchange for information, Santo insisted that I be the conduit. As my old name was well known and not welcomed in Ybor, I picked a new one for my second venture to Ybor. Fidel handled all of the paperwork necessary for me to legally use the new name. And as Alejandro, the bearded Factory Manager, did not resemble the clean shaven college student Rafael, no one recognized me as the outcast."

"Which name are you going to use now?"

"Oh, Alejandro of course. I am used to it, and everyone important to me knows me by that name." As he said this, he and Kim-Ly exchanged glances and they both smiled, inside and out.

"I like being important to you Alejandro. It seems fair, as you are equally important to me. Where do you want to live in Cuba?"

Before Alejandro could answer, he began slowing the jeep. As Kim-Ly looked at him to see why, she saw his mouth was open, "What is it Alejandro?"

He glanced at her and closed his mouth, "Look at that! This is the center land of the plantation. Do you see those buildings there?"

"If you mean those huts with the thatch roofs, yes."

"That's where the house used to be. They've built next to the very foundations of the original structures. The big one would be the main house, the next would be the nursery, and the last would be for curing. But look at the plants. Can you see the difference?"

Trying to see as Alejandro saw was impossible for Kim-Ly. Her only experience had been in his factory and today was the first time she had ever seen any tobacco plants that had not been cured and fermented. These looked just like all the other fields to her. Most were in the sun but some were also covered to grow in the shade. She knew that could not be it. "No, sorry, I don't see the difference."

"Look at the color, the richness in that color. These are darker, more uniform in shape. Someone has been using the nursery to maintain a higher quality plant stock. I guarantee this tobacco will be better than anything we have seen today. The squatter's family must be the Gomez family that worked for Mi Padre. That's how they knew what to do in the nursery to maintain this quality. Come, let's go to the house and meet them, I should recognize them if they are the same family!"

Kim-Ly could see the excitement on Alejandro's face. She had never seen him this animated. He was more excited today than she had ever seen him. Maybe in her bed there was more passion but it was damn close. She knew she would never be challenged by another woman for his affection, but she wasn't so sure about this damned tobacco. He was a man possessed!

Alejandro did not see anyone in the fields so he knocked on the front door. "Hola, anyone there?"

"Si, un minuto."

As the door opened there stood a woman Alejandro did not recognize, "Hola."

"Hola, Señora, is this the Gomez farm?"

"Si, Señor, I am Ana Gomez." As she said this a man approached from around the building, "Hola, I am Juan Gomez. May I help you?"

"Si, Señor Gomez. May we come inside to talk? I am the owner of this property. It had belonged to Mi Padre, Señor Moreno, before Batista's soldiers wiped out the valley. My name is Alejandro and this is Kim-Ly." Alejandro did not care to explain his relationship to Kim-Ly.

The man and wife exchanged glances before Señor Gomez answered, "Of course, Señor, we knew this day would arrive. We thought we were ready but we are still shocked. We've been left alone on this land for almost five years now. Please come in."

As they entered the house, it was just as rustic inside as it was on the outside. They had constructed a wooden floor and had wooden chairs and a table in the large room. The kitchen was off one side and a loft had been constructed upstairs for sleeping. They did not appear to have electricity and Alejandro guessed they probably didn't have a telephone. "Please tell me, did you know Mi Padre, Señor Moreno?"

"No, Señor."

As Señor Gomez talked, a young girl about sixteen came out of the kitchen area.

"Ah, this is my daughter Carolina, her sister Maria is in the nursery. She usually stays there until time to eat. Our two sons are at a boarding school in the city of Pinar Del Rio that Fidel has provided for all children in Cuba. Would you care for something to eat or drink?"

Alejandro glanced at Kim-Ly who shook her head. " Gracias, Señor, no. We can't stay long. I noticed your fields before we came in. The quality is superior to what we have seen today in the other fields. You must know how to select seeds and seedlings for planting to achieve what you have here that is not evident elsewhere. If you didn't learn from Mi Padre, who taught you about tobacco and how to run a nursery? I have been under the impression that Batista had killed everyone in the province that would have this knowledge."

"My oldest daughter is the one that knew how to grow tobacco and cultivate seedlings in the nursery. At the time of Batista's raid, we did not know tobacco; we grew sugarcane and raised pigs. We were in the Vuelta Abajo region around San Juan Y Martinez. We were near the river Guyaguateje close to the Cordillera de Guaniguanico mountains. Marie wanted to grow tobacco and move here so we did."

"Isn't that a bit unusual to let your oldest daughter make those decisions, Señor?"

"Si, but our whole family was in agreement. Maria had special needs at the time and we all felt this would help her recover."

Thinking Maria must be retarded, Alejandro changed the subject. "And where did she learn about tobacco? Was she married to a grower?"

"Señor that is something you need to ask her."

"Very well, I will go out to the nursery and talk to her."

"No, Señor you wait here. I will go and explain why you are here. Un minuto."

After a few minutes, Juan came back in with his daughter behind him, "This is my daughter Maria, Maria, this is Señor Moreno and Kim-Ly."

Kim-Ly looking at the shy woman as she came in said, "Hola, Maria."

"Hola, Señorita." Maria looked at Kim-Ly for a long time. What an unusual looking person she thought. So beautiful, and she moved with grace and projected dignity. The man with this creature was staring at Maria with his mouth open. His look was frightening to her, "Hola, Señor Moreno."

Forcing himself to come out of his stupor he said, "Señorita, it is Mendez, not Moreno now."

"Oh, sorry, Señor Mendez."

Watching her he saw no sign of recognition on her part, so he assumed, he must have been mistaken. He knew Isabel was dead but this girl could be Isabel's sister. "Is Señorita correct or is it Señora?"

"Señorita is correct. Mi Padre said you had a question for me?"

"Uh, yes. Where did you learn about tobacco and how to run a nursery?"

Kim-Ly was watching Alejandro with concern. He was stuttering some of his words and was obviously awestruck by this girl. She was pretty in a homespun sort of way but she didn't merit his reaction. Very curious.

"That's two questions, Señor, and I wish I could answer you but sadly I cannot."

Now Alejandro's curiosity turned to irritation. "You mean you settled on my family's farm and don't have the decency to tell me how you learned the tobacco business. That seems rather rude, Señorita!"

"Señor, you do not come into my home, even if it is on your land and talk to my family like that. Either show respect or leave!"

"It's ok Padre, he didn't understand me. Señor it is not that I know and won't tell you, I honestly don't know. You see I had an accident a few years ago, you can still see the scar on the left side of my head, see?" As she said this, she pulled back her hair and reveled a three-inch scar. "Following the accident I lost all memory, except how to grow tobacco and harvest seeds and seedlings."

As she said these words, she saw Señor Mendez lose all of the color in his face. She thought he might pass out. What a strange man.

Recovering, Alejandro stuttered, "Señor Gomez, I apologize for my rudeness. It was not appropriate." Turning to Maria he asked, "Did you also forget your name?"

Turning red Señor Gomez said, "That's enough Señor Mendez. We do not go into that with Maria. It distresses her to talk about the accident and her memory loss. You have met my family and explained your ownership of this land. What are your intentions? Should we move?"

Alarmed, Maria could not be quiet, "No, Señor Mendez please don't ask us to leave this land. I, I, I somehow feel connected here. It is the only place I feel connected!"

Alejandro was so moved by this, his eyes began to water. He brushed his face before replying to the anxious family. "Please don't worry. You may stay here for as long as you like. You have done a great job here and you can stay."

The family rushed to Alejandro, thanked him profusely, and insisted he and Kim-Ly stay for dinner. It was not much, Cuban bread, a pork dish he didn't recognize and frijoles negro with rice. Kim-Ly only ate a little rice saying she was not hungry. Alejandro barely noticed as his gaze hardly left Maria all evening. After the meal, Alejandro and Juan walked outside with their Cubre Libres and cigars. When they were out of hearing range, Alejandro stopped Juan, " She is not your biological daughter is she Juan?"

"She is just as much my daughter as Carolina, Alejandro."

"Yes, I believe you have taken very good care of her, but she is not your biological daughter is she?"

"Do you think you know her name? Others have thought that and it only caused more anguish for her. She should not go through that again."

"What did the doctors say?"

"Only that with a head blow and the possible trauma that came before she may never regain her memory. Then again, he said with love and security she might wake up and remember everything or maybe just parts. The doctors just couldn't say. That is why the family wanted to move where she felt comfortable and if growing tobacco pleased her, it pleased us. We all love her. I saw the way you looked at her all evening. You know her, don't you?"

"Maybe, I think so, but there is no way to know for sure. She looks, walks and talks like my childhood friend and neighbor Isabel Mendez. When I had to change my name, I used her family name in tribute. I loved her but she was to marry my older brother on the day of the Batista massacre. As kids, we would spend hours and hours talking about tobacco and how to grow the best seedlings. But then I don't see how it could be. Isabel and every other member of our families were killed and burned in their houses along with all of the other families in the San Juan Y Martinez area. The resemblance is so strong she must be a distant relative."

Both men walked on in silence smoking their cigars. "I better get back, Juan; I need to get Kim-Ly back to the hotel in Pinar del Rio."

The ride back to the hotel was very quiet as Alejandro and Kim-Ly were absorbed by their own thoughts. That night for the first time, since they had been in Cuba they did not make love. They held each other until Kim-Ly fell asleep. Alejandro got up and sat in the chair facing the window. Kim-Ly silently watched him.

How could he think this girl was Isabel, he chided himself. Isabel was dead and he was just wishing it were she. But why would he wish it? He had the most beautiful woman in the world in his bed; why was he thinking of someone else? Why does life play these fucking mind games? He wanted to pace the room but that might wake Kim-Ly and he didn't want to disturb her sleep.

As he sat in the chair and looked out the window, he tried to turn his melancholy into anger. That always works, he thought. Maybe this family was just conning him to keep his land. Maybe Juan and the daughter thought up this amnesia in the nursery before they came in to get him to feel sorry for them and let them stay, and it was just a coincidence that she looked like Isabel. In addition, he fell for it, what a sap he was! Yes, he was a sap. This is not Ybor. Their name isn't Trafficante. They are hard working farmers; they wouldn't know how to con anyone. Would they? More fucking life mind games. He got up, went to the bathroom, then back into bed. He inched over to Kim-Ly who was facing away from him. He eased his arm around her and assumed the spoon position. This had become their favorite way to sleep. Go to sleep idiot, he told himself, all will be much clearer in the daylight.

As Kim-Ly watched Alejandro sit in the chair, she began to cry without noise. Her eyes watered and the tears wet her pillow. This was not like her to be so emotional, she scolded herself. However, the eyes kept tearing. Were they all for Alejandro or were some for Mark? She didn't know. She had not cried when Santo told her that Mark was dead. She was strong. Why was she being so weak now? She could not answer that question, it was just happening. Was she crying because she didn't like this province of Cuba that Alejandro thought was so great? It was dirty and poor. Some of the landscape around the mountains and river were nice but so poor. She had enjoyed Havana, but this was not Havana. It was like being in another country; it was so different. Or was it because of the way he couldn't take his eyes off that peasant girl? No, it wasn't her. She knew she could compete with any woman, even a dead one. She had ways. In addition, it wasn't just because this was in the country. She was born in the country. Yes, she thought, but her country was clean and beautiful; this country was dusty and did not feel clean. No, she thought that wasn't why she cried, she was only fooling herself because she did not want to hurt him. She knew she loved Alejandro in the city. She also knew that their love would not last in this country, especially on a tobacco farm. In Havana, maybe, but even there, she would become bored. This was not her life. This was not her karma. Alejandro was not her karma. And she was not his karma. She now knew why she was crying. She was crying because it was time.

The next morning Kim-Ly had control over her emotions and told Alejandro, "Alejandro do you remember when you, me and Fidel were talking about when I should go to Vietnam and I said I would tell you when it was time?"

Alejandro stopped eating, "Yes"

"Well, it's time."

Startled by this sudden revelation, Alejandro asked, "Is this for a short visit or long?"

"I'm not sure, but I think a long visit. The Americans have escalated the war and there is much for my brother and family to do. My brother could use my help. In his last letter that I received before we left Ybor he told me of a new Pepsi factory that was being built in Laos."

"What does a Pepsi factory in Laos have to do with your family? Your brother sells opium, not soft drinks."

"That's true, and this Pepsi factory will not sell soft drinks either. The only product coming out of this factory will be heroin produced from our opium. He said some tricky dick was behind it, whatever that means."

"Does this trip have anything to do with yesterday Kim-Ly?"

"Yes and no. I love you Alejandro and I always will. I know you love me but you also love tobacco, cigars, and have a strong desire for a family. That was more than evident last night. Those things are necessary to make you whole. They are your passion along with me. Buddha teaches that a person must strive to be whole. That one's passions must be part of their lives or they are not complete. Without them, the holes in their lives will bring them down and they will not be happy. In Ybor, your factory completed you and you were whole. That's when I fell in love with you. In Cuba for you to be the man I love you must have these other passions that come from the land."

"Are you saying these passions of mine, as you call them, are not shared by you, not even for a family?"

"Alejandro, I have never had anyone touch me, caress me and posses me the way you do. It excites me to make love with you. You can unleash a great passion that I feel in my soul. A tobacco farm, cigars, Pinar del Rio Province, and children do nothing for me. I feel whole when I live on the edge doing something slightly illegal and sometimes more than slightly illegal. The things you liked least about Ybor, the tunnel deliveries and trying to figure out how to hide them in plain sight, smuggling Cuban tobacco into the factory and all of the other fringe areas of Santo's world excited me. They made me whole. The adrenalin that the excitement creates is a rush for me. I am addicted to it. I must have it to be nourished. It is time I went back to my element in Vietnam. A year from now if you invite me I will visit Cuba. But I do not expect it."

"Kim-Ly, I don't know what to say. How can I argue with Buddha? I do love you and want you to be part of my life. I don't want you to go, especially to Vietnam with Johnson escalating the United States involvement. I thought we would share Cuba and help to make it whole. I thought we would get married, have children a home and a family. It never occurred to me you might not share that dream."

"Excitement is my passion, Alejandro. It always has been and always will be. You once called me your exotic Asian flower. Excitement is my nectar and without it I will wither and have no appeal to you or anyone. I should go back to Havana and take the first plane out that will connect with Saigon."

"Kim-Ly isn't this too soon for such a decision? A little rash even."

"Alejandro you know I am right. We cannot change who we are. We are the lucky ones; we know what makes us whole. It's the ones that don't know that I feel sorry for. They go through life in circles not knowing where to go or what to do to make them complete human beings. We are not like that, we know what it is and we must not resist our karma. We must embrace it, and always let it lead. I should leave today."

"Karma is the law of cause and effect, Kim-Ly. Nothing ever happens to us that we do not deserve. Buddha said if we do good things, good things will happen to us. If we do bad things, in the future bad things will happen to us. Karma should be our friend and teach us to do good things."

"That is true Alejandro, Buddha said those things. We have been building our karmas for more than twenty-five years. And we will continue, each of us in our own way. Buddha also said if we search the entire world for someone more deserving of our love and affection than ourselves, that person is not to be found anywhere in the world. We must love ourselves Alejandro and here, in Cuba on a farm, I cannot love myself. It will never happen."

Alejandro knew there was nothing else to be said. How could he expect anyone with her thoughts to make a different decision? "I will drive you."

Alejandro knew that to argue with Kim-Ly was useless. Actually less than useless, it could make it worse. He had always assumed she wanted kids and a family. He had never known any woman that didn't. He fought it but he knew everything she had said was true. They loved each other, but they couldn't make love all day every day. Beyond that, they had very different values, very different goals, very different desires in life. Simply put, different karmas that did not overlap except for sexual desires, and that was not enough. The first flight was not until tomorrow at noon so he checked them into the Hotel National in the same two adjoining rooms they had before. After dinner, he lay in bed and remembered their first night in these rooms. How he nervously walked to the adjoining door only to open it and have her standing just on the other side. He wondered should he go to the door now? Would she be waiting just on the other side? Or would it be locked? No, he thought, that door is now closed, never to be opened again. For the second time in his life he felt a sadness rooted in loss. He hoped it didn't last as long as the first time.

After taking her to the airport and waving goodbye as the plane left, he could not keep his eyes from tearing. Would he ever see her again? He didn't know and that was very sad. With a heavy heart, he knew he must do something to distract his thoughts. He decided to go see Fidel. Fidel was not available and wouldn't be that day so he talked with Celia Sanchez. He had known Celia since the revolution. She had been a main conduit for supplies until it became unsafe and so she fought alongside Fidel all the way to Havana. She was now Fidel's gatekeeper. You did not see El Jefe without her clearance. He had always liked Celia and the way she watched over Fidel. She took the role of his caretaker and mother in the field and Fidel fully embraced her in that role. He had always appreciated a strong woman like his mother. Alejandro had already explained to Celia about Maria and her memory loss.

"Alejandro, we can send you a doctor that specializes in memory issues. When would you like him to be there?"

"Muchas gracias, Celia but I first must ask the family if they want this. According to Señor Gomez there have been some problems with trying to regain her memory in the past, and I don't want to upset them."

"Surely they will want her to remember, if she can, don't you think?"

"I do, yes, but it should be their decision, not mine."

"Bueno, just call and let me know."

"Gracias Celia, I just have one other thing. Fidel had arranged for me to have the deed of the main 168 acres of my family's plantation, and for the Gomez family that has been working it to have the main 168 acres of the Mendez family plantation. I would like to reverse that. "

"You want the Gomez family to have your family's property? Why?"

"It's a long story Celia, but I am sincere about making the change. Can you please do this?"

"Bueno, I'll have Hectar make the changes while you take me to lunch and you can tell me your long story, bueno?"

"Bueno, gracias Celia."

"And while I work on the deeds, you can tell me about this exotic non-Spanish vixen Fidel said you brought with you."

After lunch, deeds in hand, he drove back to the Hotel Pinar del Rio. He tried to eat but could not. He realized that nether he nor Kim-Ly said anything about writing to each other. He knew it was not an accident on her part. He also wondered just how long she had been planning this or did it happen all of a sudden. No, too much thought was behind her decision. She may even have known the outcome before they arrived in Cuba. Maybe he was just her way of getting over Mark and she never intended their relationship to last any longer. He felt she did love him and he knew he loved her. To be honest with himself, he had to admit he had never considered how she would like Cuba or tobacco farming or having a family. If he had not been fixated on his own desires and goals, he may have realized that this was no place for her. Could he give up Cuba and tobacco to go with her to Vietnam? Kim-Ly knew not to ask that of him because she knew the answer. If she had asked and if he had said yes, he would not be able to love himself in Vietnam. There he would wither and there his soul would die. Kim-Ly was wise not to ask. She was as smart as she was beautiful, and would always be his Exotic Asian Flower. She was now compelled to return home to Vietnam and her karma as he had been compelled to return home to Cuba and his karma. He wished her a good life, a good karma, and much happiness. All of the things he had thought they would have and share in Cuba, he now knew they were never meant to be. They were never a shared karma.

After a lonely and sleepless night, Alejandro drove to San Juan y Martinez. He located an empty space for rent that would serve as his headquarters. From here, he would organize the to-bacco farmers in the region. At least he thought he would. After the revelation with Kim-Ly, his confidence had taken a hit. Just because he thought it was a good idea to organize, the other farmers in the region might not. In addition, to make it more difficult he didn't even have a farm of his own to show them what he could do. He wanted to concentrate on this region, as it was the best tobacco area of the best tobacco province in Cuba. Tobacco needed the sunny days, cool nights, and the rich sandy soil of the Pinar Province that to him smelled like vanilla and leather. The soil's flavor was the only smell that instantly triggered his salivary glands. He made a deal with the local paper to print flyers of his meeting in seven days. He contacted a builder to start on a house next to where the Mendez house had originally stood. He thought about having it built as a copy of the Mendez house, but decided on one that replicated his family's instead. He added a large nursery and an even larger curing and packaging barn. When he and Fidel had discussed his deed, Alejandro offered to manage the State owned lands in San Juan y Martinez for a fee and profit sharing. Fidel was more than happy to agree. Alejandro wanted to share this fee and profit with all of the members of his San Juan y Martinez Tobacco Guild, of which he was currently the president and only member.

The next day, flyers in hand, he cruised the area, stopping whenever he saw activity. He gave every person he saw several copies to pass around, telling them he was Cuba's new Minister of Tobacco and wanted as many farmers as possible to attend his meeting. He promised nothing more than a chance to discuss any problem they were having from product acquisition, growing issues, quality control, necessary supplies and distribution. Everyone he talked to seemed excited about the opportunity to voice their opinion of the current system and some had to tell him immediately rather than wait for the meeting. The main issues seemed to be lack of quality control with the seedlings, lack of fuel for their tractors, lack of fertilizers, lack of pesticides, degradation of the soil, and lack of transportation to the Havana warehouses for curing and distribution. Alejandro realized that these issues explained why he had noticed a dip in quality in the product he purchased for Flor de Pinar Cigar line. The quality was well below the expected from Pinar del Rio, especially from San Juan y Martinez. "That God damned Batista!" he said to know one as he drove back to the hotel. "I didn't kill you but I will undo the travesty you inflicted on this land I love."

For the next week, Alejandro's sleep was interrupted by dreams of Kim-Ly. He had nightmares of her being attacked in Saigon by the North Vietnamese. He dreamt of her being arrested and brutalized in jail. He envisioned her being accosted by US sailors looking for a good time. By the end of the week he realized not once did he dream about her being in Cuba or him being in Vietnam. Karma is Karma.

For the meeting he had membership papers printed for the San Juan y Martinez Tobacco Guild, whose membership was free but required a commitment to only use seedlings approved by the guild and to allow the guild to arrange distribution. He also had a declaration or plan for the valley's production methods. He had reserved the large town hall for the event that started at 6pm. By 5:30, he saw that it was standing room only and many people were still outside. The farmers brought their entire families instead of coming alone. Outside the hall was a town square with a fountain in the center. He decided to move the meeting there. It was a perfect night, no chance of rain and about 70 degrees. It was at least 85 in the crowded town hall. He positioned himself at the fountain and the farmers with their families gathered around. "My name is Alejandro Fernando Mendez Suarez. I am the new Minister of Tobacco for Cuba. My residence will be in this valley where the Mendez plantation was located prior to the Batista massacre. I am here to listen to you and to offer suggestions to relieve as many of your issues as possible. I will be living with you, farming with you, eating the same food as you, receiving the same, and nothing more, in the way of assistance and allocation from the government. All I ask is that you speak one at a time. Everyone that wants to speak will be heard. Nothing is off-limits. Please wait until I recognize you before you begin." Pointing at the man who had his hand up the longest Alejandro said, "Si, Señor, you may go first."

"I do not think this revolution has improved the life of the tobacco farmer. We have no fuel for the tractors; it all goes to the farmers growing food products like rice and sugarcane. We are last on the list. It wouldn't be this way in the United States."

Alejandro was shocked at the statements made by this black farmer. He had not expected anyone to voice any negativity about the revolution or Fidel's government.

"Well, thank-you for speaking up. Let me first tell you about the United States for a minute as I have lived there on and off for about six years. Part of the time, I was in school and the other part in a cigar factory. In Cuba everyone is treated the same regardless of where you came from or the color of your skin. You all know this, we are all the same. In the United States a black man whether he is a farmer, a baseball player like Jackie Robinson or the manager of a cigar factory is not treated the same as his white counterparts. You, for instance, would not be allowed to use the same restroom that I used; you could not eat at the best restaurants as I could, and you would be subjected to racial slurs and personal degradation if you talked back or challenged something a white man said. If that is the life you want, I am sure I can get you an exit permit. If, however you want to help me as an equal to improve Cuba for all citizens, not just the rich, then stay and help because Cuba and I need you. We need each and every one of you. You can let me know anytime you want to leave and I will make sure you get an exit permit without hassle or questioning for you and your entire family, if that is what you want. Next speaker, you Señorita, please tell me what's on your mind?"

"It's Señora but gracias, Señor." After the laughter she continued, "For my family it's food. We have to plant every available acre in tobacco because the yield is not as good as it used to be, and we are always hungry. Our allotments are just not enough. Can you help with that?"

"Yes I can, I will explain after everyone that wants to talk has had their opportunity."

Alejandro did not expect the meeting to last well into the night but it did. At one in the morning, it did not seem that anyone had left. The problems he had been told about in the fields were repeated many times over during the night. Finally, it was his turn. "First, I want to thank you all coming here esta tarde, uh sorry, I meant esta noche. Every concern you have voiced must be addressed if we are to regain our pre-eminent status as the best tobacco growers in the world. This we can do, just not the way you might think. How did our grandfathers deal with insects prior to the invention of petroleum-based insecticides? How did our grandfathers till the land before they had tractors? How did our grandfathers get enough to eat when food was not given to them? How did our grandfathers fertilize their crops without petroleum-based fertilizers? And the final question, how did our grandfathers get high yields year after year? Have any of you used animal manure to fertilize your fields?"

"A lot of us have but it's not enough."

"Have you supplemented with green manure?"

"What's that?' asked one farmer. "We don't have any animals that shit green!"

"Well, let me ask you this, what do you do with your fields after the season?"

"We let them rest and let the sun and rain heal them."

"Green manure is planting your tobacco fields in the summer months with maize or jack beans and then plowing it under before the start of the next tobacco season. This is called green manure. We stopped doing this many years ago when the United States chemical fertilizer companies convinced us it was easier to use their products. Now this generation has forgotten how. So-called progress sometimes does more harm than good. I think that is what has happened to us. Tractors certainly make the farmer's job easier. But did they improve plant quality or diminish it?"

"Improve it unless you drive like Jose," someone shouted and everyone laughed.

Glad for the break in tension, Alejandro continued, "I know it's late but tomorrow I will be in my office all day. The address and what I propose are on this flyer. Please take it and come by to see me at the office if it makes sense. I will be there at 6 am until 6pm tomorrow. Simply put, I propose we form a guild with the sole purpose of improving our lives, by returning this province to its heritage as the top producer of the best tobacco in the world."

As Alejandro handed out his flyers, he realized how tired he was. With poor sleep, the late hour and the mental stress of wanting this to go well, he could hardly stand. As he drove to the hotel, he realized he had less than four hours to sleep and get back to his office by 6am. "Damn, what was I thinking? I guess I wasn't. I'm sure no one will show up until later anyway," he said to no one as he drove.

At 5:45, Alejandro approached his office. His cafe con leche and morning bread with cheese were still in his hands. Surprisingly he didn't feel that bad. No dreams of Kim-Ly for the first time since she left. Of course not, he thought, he only slept for 2 hours. He was excited with the anticipation that by tonight he might not be the only member of the guild. He knew he needed a good turn out. Would the farmers consider the old ways? Some, he knew, would not change. They had been trapped by the modern conveniences of tractors and petroleum based products. Products that made money for the companies that sell them, made the life of the farmer easier but lead to inferior tobacco and low yields. This was not sustainable in today's Cuba. As soon as he turned the corner, he saw the crowd of farmers in front of his office. He no longer felt tired. The excitement that his plan might work, and the adrenalin that followed, were energizing. "Hola, Buenos Dias."

"Hola, Alejandro, we have come to talk and maybe join your guild."

"If you join it will no longer be my guild, but ours." He said as he opened the door and everyone walked in. At least as many that could fit. The others gathered around the door to listen.

"We have one major problem with your plan. It's not the hard work, we are farmers, and we are used to that. Giving up the tractor would be possible if we had oxen and plows. Most of us have neither, some one or the other. How do we solve that problem? Secondly, we have reduced our livestock population as the yields have decreased. They required land that we had to plant in tobacco to make up for the reduced yield."

410

"Let me ask you this, would you trade your tractors for oxen, plows and livestock? The livestock would be pigs, cows and chickens. Would you give up the tractor, the petroleum fertilizers and insecticides? And in exchange return to the oxen plow, to green manure, to animal manure and reduce our need for petroleum?"

"We could do those things. Most of us have not slept. We have been talking since you left. Our families have gone home and hopefully, are still asleep. Without fuel for the tractors, without more food for our families, without higher yields and cheaper production costs, we are not going to survive. We could convert to sugarcane because that is a plant that you can eat if you are starving. However, we all love tobacco and the cigars we produce. There is much pride in doing something better than anyone else in the world. This is the heritage of San Juan y Martinez and we want to regain that pride. Are you the man that can lead us to that end?"

"Señor, if you want an ironclad guarantee of success I cannot give it. No man can predict what nature may bring us. What rains may fall, what storms may come. These we have to endure because we cannot fight them. We are farmers. We all know nature's fury. What I know is the plan outlined in the flyer was the plan successfully used for hundreds of years by our predecessors, and by my relatives. I believe in the plan enough to spend all of my funds to develop the Mendez property as my own and to live this process with you. If it does not work, I will be penniless. Fidel will have misjudged my talents and Cuba will lose its signature product, the Cuban cigar. I will do everything in my power to insure that does not happen. That I can promise you, success I cannot."

"That's good enough for me, I, Philippe Rodriguez would like to be the first to give my pledge to the San Juan y Martinez

Guild. I will offer you my tractor to trade for the animals we need. And could we get a horse or two?"

"Certainly, Señor Rodriguez, but know that horse manure is not suitable for fertilizer."

"Why not?"

"Horses eat grass and weeds. The seeds are not processed and will germinate if planted as fertilizer. You would be very mad at me if I let you use horse manure as fertilizer."

Philippe's pledge was only the first. Two hundred and sixty-three farmers signed up that day. Philippe's son Jesus was also there and Alejandro hired him to help the farmers sign the guild pledge. Some could not read but they were learning as part of Fidel's literacy campaign. One farmer that Alejandro had hoped would come by but did not was Señor Gomez. He decided to pay him a visit tomorrow if Jesus would open the office for others that might come by. This was a great start. He had 150 tractors that were pledged to help him trade for oxen, plows and farm animals. He asked Jesus to staff the office for the next few days as he traveled to Havana and back to arrange the trade.

"Señor Mendez do you really think this will work? Everyone is so excited now. Mi Madre could not stop grinning last night when Mi Padre told her he signed up. I think everyone in the Valley is encouraged and willing to do any amount of work to see this succeed. If you fail us, the Cuban cigar of San Juan y Martinez will be no more. People will leave. I think they will give up. Please make it work Señor."

"Jesus, it will work if Mother Nature allows it. No farmer can be successful without her blessing. We are nearing harvest time. We will have all summer to organize our farms, plant the green manure and grow our seedlings. We will be prepared for next season, and if Mother Nature allows, we will be successful."

"That's great, Señor. I think Mother Nature would miss her Cuban cigars too much to not allow us to succeed."

"Let's hope, Jesus, the next season is critical. I'll return in a few days. You have a key and plenty of blank pledges until I return. Be safe."

"Vaya con dios, Señor."

No dreams that night. The first restful night since Kim-Ly left. Alejandro knew it was because he was busy with all of his plans, the guild and the farm. Today's agenda, meet with the Gomez family and then on to Havana to convince Fidel to trade. The trip gave him time to second-guess himself and what he had promised the farmers. "Now I think about discussing it with Fidel. Why didn't I do that before I promised them I could do it? What if he says no? Oh, fuck! I will be run out of the valley! Maybe alive, maybe not. Damn it. I always do this to myself. I think because I came up with a plan that makes sense to me, everyone else will see it that way. Didn't I learn anything from Kim-Ly?"

Alejandro finished his internal dialog just as he arrived at the Gomez farm. Señor Gomez was in the fields checking his plants, probably for disease or infestation. It was too close to harvest to allow anything to go wrong now. "Hola, Señor Gomez."

"Hola, Señor Mendez. How did your meeting go?"

"It was tremendous. The San Juan y Martinez Guild has 263 new members. I am sorry you were not able to be there. Would you care to talk about it now?"

"No, I don't think so Señor. Our farm is doing well. We will have a good yield from our healthy plants, and I don't see why we should change anything. We have been thrifty with our fertilizer and have enough for next year. With minimum fuel, our tractor will be enough to see us through next season. Maria is confidant she will have the right seeds to germinate and our seedlings next year will be even better than this year. Why do we need a guild?"

"It could be that the guild needs you more than you need the guild. The guild will insure that we return our valley to the preeminent stature as the best valley for tobacco. We will transition away from tractors to oxen and plow. We will transition away from petroleum based fertilizers and insecticides and use a combination of animal and green manure. We will consolidate nurseries into one central location with quality control measures in place to insure maximum yield, and resistance to disease and insects. I believe Maria can be a major factor in developing this type of plant year after year."

"Señor, I know you mean well, but we already have a stable system that we know works, not one we think will work. Again I ask you why should we risk it?"

"With Maria in charge of the guild nursery what is the risk? You know her success in the nursery, and with my help we can eliminate the downturn in quality that happens every fourth year."

Señor Gomez looked directly at Alejandro wondering how he knew about the fourth year problems. Maria had been trying to figure out why that happened but had not. How could this stranger know about that? "What makes you think we have a downturn every four years?"

Alejandro knew his guess had been right. Maria was using a system similar to the one his family had used for years. He had learned at the University of Tampa why the problem occurred, and how to fix it. "I don't think it happens, Señor. I know it happens. Let's visit Maria in the nursery and I will tell you both how to solve it."

"If you can do that Señor to Maria's satisfaction, I will join your guild."

"It's no longer my guild, Señor it is the San Juan y Martinez Guild."

Alejandro greeted Maria and explained why her methodology produced the fourth year stunted crop. He explained that once a hybrid was developed that was acceptable it would only last three years before it began to degrade. The solution was to develop multiple strains that could be continually cross-pollinated for an ever developing and improving strain that would not degrade. She listened intently to every word he said like the protégé listens to the admired professor. "Padre, this makes sense to me. I believe him and want to try his method." Alejandro noticed a young boy had walked into the nursery. "Ah, come here Fernando," said Maria. "Señor Mendez, this is my son Fernando."

Alejandro thought the youth looked strong for his age and walked with a style that indicated coordination and strength. He looked directly at Alejandro without any indication of shyness or intimidation. As Alejandro returned his gaze, he was surprised to see the eyes he saw every morning in the mirror. He saw the Suarez family green eyes that he shared with his great uncle. Until now, he and his great uncle were the only two people he had ever seen with those green eyes. His face flushed as he said, "Hola Fernando, do you share your Madre's fondness for tobacco plants."

"Some, but my passion is baseball. I want to be a pitcher like Señor Castro."

"Si, Fidel is a good pitcher. Have you ever met him?"

"Oh no, Señor, Mi Madre and I saw him once in Pinar del Rio when he visited and gave a speech at the University. But we have never met him. He is a great man and very busy. He would not have time for farmers."

"Fidel always has time for farmers. Did you know that he was raised on a farm?"

"Truly Señor, Señor Castro was a farmer?"

"Not exactly. His Padre was a farmer, his childhood friends were farmers' children. He studied law and is a lawyer, but he has affection for the farm and the people that work the land. If you would like to meet him, I could take you and your Madre with me to Havana. I have an appointment with him tomorrow morning. We would stay at the Hotel Nacional de Cuba, and of course you and your Madre would have your own room,"

"May we go por favor?"

"No, I don't think so Fernando. We cannot impose on Señor Mendez like that."

"Señorita it would be my pleasure to show you Havana and to introduce you and Fernando to Fidel. I know he would enjoy meeting you. In addition, of course, the cost of the trip would be my pleasure. We would only be gone four days."

"Padre, what do you think? I have never seen Havana."

"Maria, if you would like to go, I think it would be ok. I trust a man that would give us the secret to the tobacco plant without forcing us to first join his guild. He has my respect and my trust. I think it would safe to go with him. But only if you want to."

Por favor, Madre, por favor!" said Fernando.

Marie looked from her son to Alejandro, "Si, let's go inside and pack."

Fernando screamed and embraced his Madre and jumped up and down as they made their way to the house. When they returned Alejandro and Señor Gomez were smoking cigars and telling stories like old friends. Alejandro was relieved that the Gomez farm would be part of the guild. As they talked Alejandro said as he handed Señor Gomez the deed he had Celia execute, legally giving the land to the Gomez family, "I want you to have this land. You and your family have earned it and it should be yours forever."

At first, he was dumbfounded by this gesture. Then his expression turned to concern, "Thank-you Señor, why did you not give this to me when you first arrived? The obligation would have compelled me to join the guild."

"I was afraid that might be so and I didn't want that to be the reason you joined. Either it felt like the right thing to do or not. However, to join because you felt obligated would be the wrong reason. I did not want you forced into the Guild."

"Thank-you for that. I know my daughter and grandson will be safe with you"

As they prepared to leave, Fernando sat in the right front bucket seat next to Alejandro with Maria in the back. Alejandro suggested she wrap her hair in a scarf to keep the wind from blowing it around. She thanked him as they left for Havana. For Fernando it was a big adventure. He had never been farther north than the city of Pinar del Rio. Alejandro took a small detour to show him the Cuyaguateje River, which excited him almost as much as the Cordillera de Guaniguanico mountain range that divided the Pinar del Rio Province into the Sierra del Rosario and the Sierra de los Órganos. They searched for a few minutes until Alejandro found a cave. "Come, let's explore this cave." The cave had a small opening into a large cavity, not unlike the cave of his youth that he and Isabel had named Alcazar. He watched Maria closely but she offered no indication that it looked familiar or that she had ever been in a cave before. She walked crouched over even though the roof was at least 15 feet away. "Have you ever been in a cave before, Maria?"

"No Señor, this is a first for Fernando and for me."

"Please call me Alejandro."

"Si, Alejandro."

As they walked back to the jeep Maria asked, "Why are you doing this for us Alejandro? Is it because you think you know me from before?"

"Maria, I promised your Padre to not talk about maybe knowing you from before. He said it upsets you, especially when others have been wrong about knowing you. I don't want to do anything that would upset you. As for why, I've been very impressed by what you have done in the nursery. It's not easy to do it as well you obviously can. And Fernando! Who could not like him?"

"Yes, he is a joy. He is the joy of my life. The doctors were amazed that I did not miscarry him. You see I was hurt and in the hospital for a while before I even knew I was pregnant. The doctors said that because I was in bed for so long it helped make the pregnancy successful. You may think badly of me, but when they told me I was pregnant, it upset me a great deal. I didn't know why it upset me but it did. I even told them I didn't want the baby. Can you imagine what a bad Madre that is to not want her baby? I cried and cried because I was pregnant and no one could figure out why, including me. I am so lucky to have him. I know that now, but it almost never happened. I have a bad side, an evil side that I hope never comes back."

"No Maria, I don't believe you are capable of having evil or bad thoughts. There had to be a reason even if it was not known at that time."

"You are very kind Alejandro, gracias."

When Alejandro checked in at the hotel, the same clerk waited on him that had waited on him when he and Kim-Ly had checked in. He asked for adjoining rooms and the clerk winked at him and gave him the same two rooms. It wasn't until he got to the room that Alejandro realized what the clerk saw. He saw a husband, a wife and a son checking in when it had been the husband and mistress checking in before. His initial reaction was to get mad, and then he laughed when he thought about what Kim-Ly would have done to the clerk for that mistake. He knew he missed her, but thankfully, there were no new nightmares.

Before dinner, Alejandro went looking for a store that sold baseball equipment. After asking several people, he finally found the store. He bought two gloves, one for Fernando and one for him, and a ball. Before dinner, he took Fernando's glove, oiled it, and placed the ball inside in the pocket. He wrapped a handkerchief around it and tied it tight to form the pocket.

At dinner, Fernando and Maria seemed very uncomfortable. Alejandro realized they had never been in a restaurant before. "Would you like me to order for you?"

"Si, Alejandro that would be nice."

"Would you like wine with dinner?"

"Si," said Fernando.

Maria looked at Fernando. "None for you Fernando".

"Ah Madre, I'm five years old!"

"Si, and that's too young!"

"Cola for me, gee."

Alejandro ordered chicken and yellow rice for everyone and a white wine for him and Maria and a cola for Fernando. After dinner, they walked over to the two-foot wall that looked over the water. They sat on the wall facing the water, looking at the boats. "Have you ever seen the *Granma*, Señor Mendez? I hear it is enormous and the most famous boat in all of Cuba"

"Si, Fernando, I was on the *Granma* from Mexico to Cuba that began the revolution. And it is not that big, especially with 82 soldiers on it."

"Are you a hero of the Revolución?"

Alejandro chuckled as he answered, "No, Fernando, I was just a soldier, Che Guevara, Celia Sanchez, Fidel and his brother Raul are the heroes."

Maria looked at Alejandro, "It seems you have done many things in your life Alejandro. What else have you done?"

Alejandro talked for hours about his growing up on the farm, his work in the nursery, his life in Ybor and then his return to Cuba. He did not talk about his mission for Fidel, his near death experience with Santo Trafficante Sr. or Santo Trafficante Junior and the Kennedy assassination. The only omission that created guilt was Kim-Ly.

"Why did you come back from the United States, Señor? Didn't you want to stay?" asked Fernando.

"No, Fernando, I always knew I would return to Cuba, to my home. The reason I was away was revenge and then business, and when the business was over, I wanted nothing more than to come home. I think Cubans are the luckiest people in the world because we have a government that serves all of the people, not just a few rich ones. It's late Fernando; don't you think we should get some sleep so we can be fresh for our meeting with Fidel?"

"Is he a nice man like you?"

"He is the best man I know Fernando. He is honest, smart, and a leader of men. And if that's not enough he throws a mean curve!"

"Si, I want to pitch just like him someday!"

As Alejandro lay in his bed, he realized how happy he was. He thought this must be what it's like to have a family, except for the separate rooms of course. He thought about the first night with Kim-Ly and how different that was. That night was excitement and he was thrilled by it. Tonight, he was thrilled by it, without the sexual excitement. Was it asking too much of his karma to think he could have both? How could Isabel have survived? Why can't she remember? Does she see Fernando's eyes when she looks at him? What does she think if she does see them? And why would she have been so unhappy when she learned she was pregnant? If her memory loss were caused by an emotional trauma as well as her physical trauma, would it be safe for her to remember? He fell asleep with so many questions and no answers. However, he slept through the night.

The three waited in Celia Sanchez's office for Fidel to finish. She had greeted Alejandro as a friend and asked many questions about his work. Now as they waited she kept looking back and forth between Fernando who was playing with his new glove and ball and Alejandro. She glanced at Maria who was watching her look at the two males. He must know Fernando is his son, she thought. They are the only two people she had ever seen with those green eyes. He must be his son. However, the woman and Fernando had different names and he introduced her as Señorita so she was not married. She would ask Fidel when they left, he would know.

When Fidel was ready, the three guests walked in. Alejandro introduced his guests to Fidel, who was delighted to see them. "Fernando, you are a baseball player, si?"

"Si, Señor Castro, I want to a pitcher just like you."

Shaking his head and extending his index finger at Fernando, Fidel said, "No Fernando, you want to be better than me. You want to take my records and smash them!"

Full of excitement he answered, "Si, I can do that."

"After we have finished talking and I meet with Alejandro, we will go outside and play catch."

"You will play catch with me!"

"Si, but only if you do not throw too hard and hurt my hand. Promise?"

"Si, I promise. I will not hurt your hand."

"Maria you have a fine son."

"Muchas gracias, El Jefe, if I may call you that, Alejandro told us it was a sign of respect."

"Of course, a Señorita as pretty as you may call me anything she wants."

Fidel smiled as Maria blushed. He looked at Alejandro with a curious frown on his face.

"Maria, would you and Fernando wait for us in Celia's office? Alejandro and I have some state business to discuss."

As they got up and walked to the door she said, "Gracias El Jefe."

After the door was shut Fidel looked at Alejandro and raised both of his arms in the air. "She knows Fernando is your son right?"

"I don't know, she has not said."

Alejandro explained to Fidel everything he knew, including her sensitivity to dead ends.

"There are some doctors at the University who are doing some excellent work with memory loss. Do you think she would let them look at her?"

"I don't know, El Jefe. Celia offered to send a doctor to see her at home, but the opportunity to suggest it did not happen."

"When we bring them back, I will ask her. Now tell me Alejandro, how are you going to fix the Cuban cigar business?"

"First, return to ox and plow, as the hooves are better for tobacco soil than tractor tires that compact it too much. Animal and green manure are the only fertilizers used. The nursery process will be consolidated, so the seedling quality can be controlled. The state owned land in Juan y Martinez will be converted to individual owners, because tobacco thrives on individual attention not mass production like sugarcane. The farmers just north of the San Juan Valley should have the first option on the newly available land, so that their current land can be consolidated into a large state plantation. This newly created plantation will contain the nursery for the entire San Juan Valley, an animal farm to replenish stock, the fermentation warehouse for the valley, and a cigar factory that will be the only recipient of the San Juan y Martinez Guild's tobacco. The cigars will be made under a newly created state brand and will be the finest in the world. In order to start this project we, the guild members, which number over three hundred as of this morning, will trade our 180 tractors to the state in exchange for oxen, plows, pigs, cows, chickens, and horses with the necessary tack. When this is done we will have created a sustainable agriculture system for tobacco that will not be dependent on petroleum products for any facet of the production."

When Alejandro had finished, he noticed Fidel had a solemn face and was shaking his head. He immediately felt deflated and defeated. Fidel got up from behind his desk and walked over to Alejandro who stood up as he approached. Fidel grabbed him around his shoulders and kissed both of his cheeks. "Alejandro, what would Cuba be without you? I would probably be dead, the victim of a CIA assassination and who knows what would happen then."

"El Jefe, I di...."

Fidel interrupted, "Be quiet a minute, I gave you an impossible job, no resources, and no vision of a plan and in less than a month you have created a system that will carry Cuba successfully into the twenty-first century. I promise you this! Anything you tell Celia you need, you will get. I know you are someone that I can trust to do what is best for Cuba."

"Thank-you El Jefe, I will do my best. By the way, I have an initial list of needs already prepared."

Fidel's mouth dropped open and both men roared with laughter. "I should have expected that. Leave it with Celia; she will get everything to you as soon as possible. Now let's not keep our guests waiting.

As Fernando and Maria returned, Fidel said, "Fernando did you know Alejandro was a hero of the revolution?"

Fernando looked at Alejandro, "You told me you weren't!"

"And do you know why he didn't tell you, Fernando?"

"No."

"He didn't tell you because he is the truest kind of hero. He does his duty without asking for anything in return. He has saved my life many times and yet he says he was just doing his duty. He is a true hero Fernando, and I am proud to call him my friend. Maria, could I ask you a favor?"

"Si, El Jefe."

"This is a big favor Maria, one that you might want to think about before you answer. Alejandro has told me about your memory issue." Maria looked at Alejandro with a scowl and pointed her finger at him. Before she could speak Fidel continued, "Please don't be mad at Alejandro, I forced him to tell me and no one can refuse El Jefe, especially in his own office, right? I was sorry to hear of your unfortunate condition, but not too sorry to try and take advantage of it." Now she looked at Fidel not understanding what he meant. "You see, we have several doctors at the University of Havana that are working with the kind of memory loss you suffered. It is not common and they only have a few patients to examine and treat. The favor, and I mean this, it is a favor for Cuba, would be if you would consent for them to examine you. It would not take long and if they suggested any treatment, it would be up to you if you decided to take their treatment. Would you do this for Cuba?"

Maria did not want to do this. She was afraid of the outcome and the depression that would probably follow, as it had before. She looked at Alejandro and some of her trepidation disappeared. "El Jefe, how does anyone tell you no? I want to so bad but I cannot. If any citizen can do something to benefit Cuba, they must do it. And I can do no less even though it scares me very much."

"That is so brave Maria. Fernando, I think your Madre is a hero too, don't you."

Beaming with pride and smiling at his Madre who was looking at him he said, "Si, she is the best and bravest Madre in the entire world."

"Well said, hombre joven. Isn't it time to play ball?"

The next day Maria, Fernando and Alejandro visited the University Medical Center. They were expected as Fidel had Celia call while they played catch. The three doctors that examined Maria were Alessandro Garci, Gaetano Forlan and Rafael Cardenas. They were very professional and did tests on Maria for five hours. At the end of the day Alejandro, Maria and Fernando waited for the doctors to make their assessment. Doctor Cardenas was the representative for the group.

"Maria we believe you have had co-morbid pathologies that have affected your memory loss. We believe the first was a traumatic event that resulted in Post Traumatic Stress disorder and the second is a TBI or Traumatic Brain Injury, or as a non-professional might describe it, a blow to your head. The result has been a prolonged dissociative amnesia that has lasted for more than five years. The good news is we can find no neurobiological abnormalities caused by the blow to the head. That leaves only the dissociative amnesia. The prognosis in your case is mixed. Your memory of things that have happened since the incident is excellent. Your IQ is above average and your motor skills are unblemished. Your only issue is the retrograde memory loss. You can lead a normal unimpeded life without that memory, so we will not recommend any type of hypnosis or other means of stimulating your past memories, as they could be harmful to you at this time. Your mind has suppressed the memories to protect you. If recovery of these memories is artificially induced, you could go into a coma and never awaken. You could suffer permanent damage to your current excellent brain functions. The reality of your situation is you may never recover your memory. However, if you do, it will be at a time when you feel safe and ready to talk about what happened and process the occurrence. If this happens, we would very much like to know when and the circumstances that led to this epiphany. The information you provide could help us greatly in understanding more about memory loss pathologies. On behalf of the University, I want to thank you and your family for coming in and sharing your situation with us. Your case has already been a benefit for us, mucho gracias. Do you have any questions?"

Maria seemed despondent over the news, even though Alejandro did not think it was bad. She shook her head to indicate she didn't have any questions. Alejandro asked, "Doctor is there any chance the memories could hurt her even if they come back on her terms?"

"We don't believe so, but if they induce too much stress she should come back here as soon as possible. Otherwise, she should come here at her convenience to process the event with a psychologist. There's still the chance that a failure to adequately process the event could cause problems but they'll be treatable at that time. She may not need treatment but she might. It will depend on how much the memories affect her ability to conduct her normal activities. Does this make sense to you?"

Maria shook her head that she understood. Alejandro said, "Si, Doctor, muchas gracias for your time and explanation."

The next day was spent showing Maria and Fernando the sights around Havana. It passed too quickly for all, and the next day they headed back to the Gomez farm. The jeep was quiet on the ride back. All three were tired from the excitement of the Havana trip. Alejandro was contemplating what he should do about Maria. He was convinced that she was Isabel. He also felt that Fernando was his son, conceived in their cave Alcazar the night before Batista's attack and decimation of the Valley. He could only guess at the horrible events that must have happened to Isabel. Rape, sodomy, torture, all the despicable things that soldiers do in war without the discipline required by leaders like Fidel Castro, were not only possible but probable. At the very least, some of these things had to be what she was not prepared to remember. It would also explain why she did not want to be pregnant. She must have thought, at least subconsciously, that the pregnancy was from being raped and not from their night in Alcazar. About half way back he decided. He would win her love and affection now and not rely on her memory for assistance.

She had fallen in love with him once, and he would do anything to make it happen again. Her memory he could leave to karma.

Maria was saddened by the doctors' report. She wanted her memory back. She wanted to know her real name, her real family, if they still lived. Could Fernando be Alejandro's son? They have the same eyes and facial structure but how could she forget that? It would have been a special night when he was conceived instead of the horror she fears it must have been. He cannot be, she thought, she would have remembered. But wouldn't it be grand if somehow he were. Alejandro is the most remarkable person she had ever met, including Fidel. He has done so many amazing things and he is just a little older than she is. Fernando may not be his son she thought, but she thought he knew her from before. *And, I think we must have liked each other a lot for him to care enough to take us with him this week.* She thought nothing was more important than regaining her memory, but now she wasn't so sure. Maybe it just didn't matter. *If we were not lovers and just liked each other before it would be ok. We both enjoy each other's company now.* She decided she would no longer worry about regaining her memory. If she did, ok; if not, ok. Fate would decide.

Just before they reached the farm, she leaned forward and put her hand on Alejandro's shoulder, "Mucho gracias for this trip, Alejandro. I loved every minute of it." She sat back and smiled. Life was good again.

One year later, they were married in Havana. As a wedding present, Alejandro asked Fidel to make Fernando his legal son, which he was glad to do. At the time of the wedding, the guild included every tobacco farmer in the San Juan y Martinez Valley and was a bigger success than he ever imagined. The next season he planned to start another guild for other tobacco farmers outside Pinar del Rio province. He gave lectures at the University on his sustainable agriculture system.

To celebrate their one-year anniversary, Alejandro took Maria on an overnight camping trip to Alcazar. They slept by the fire, made love by the fire, and held each other the rest of the night as they slept until mid morning. When they awoke, Maria looked into Alejandro's eyes and wept. Alejandro was immediately alarmed and feared he had done something wrong, "What did I do? Please don't cry."

"It's ok Rafael, these are happy tears. Your Isabel is back."

Epilog
FACT, FICTION, FEASIBLE 2015

Resources:
Inside The Company, CIA DIARY, by Philip Agee, Stonehill Publishing Company 1975

CIGAR CITY MAFIA, by Scott M. Deitche, Barricade Books Inc. 2004
Reminiscences of the Cuban Revolutionary War, by Che Guevara, Monthly Review Press 1968
The Cuban Connection Nixon, Castro, and the Mob, by William Weyand Turner (former FBI) Prometheus Books 2013
Fidel Castro Handbook, by George Galloway
The Trafficantes Godfathers from Tampa, The Mafia, CIA, and the JFK Assassination, by Ron Chepesiuk, Strategic Media Books 2010
Fidel Castro My Life, by Fidel Castro & Ignacio Ramonet, Scribner 2007
The Real "Mr. X": Colonel Fletcher Prouty interview by EIR 2013

The Man Who Killed Kennedy The Case Against LBJ by Roger Stone 2013

Family Of Secretes: The Bush Dynasty By Russ Baker 2009 Bloomsbury Press New York

Robert J. Groden interviewed by Richard Burk at Dealey Plaza in Dallas 2013

Texas in the Morning: The Love Story of Madeleine Duncan Brown and President Lyndon Baines Johnson, by Madeleine Duncan Brown Conservatory Press 1997

JFK ASSASSINATION CHRONOLOGY compiled by Ira David Woods III Edited and Adapted for the Web by Bernard Wilds Dealey Plaza UK

Every attempt has been made to portray all historic events and characters according to the above research. For example, during the Cuban Revolution the three men who were executed following an in-the-field trial for crimes against the compensinos were executed by Castro's troops as described. The names of the Russian missile battery Commander and the Russian Submarine Commander are accurate and the events are described as reported. The JFK Conspiracy in this book, while impossible to prove without a trial, is shared by the French DGSE and the Russian KGB who did independent investigations following the assassination. The French investigated following a request by Jacqueline Kennedy and the Russians investigated in case they were accused. Both indicated that LBJ was behind the assassination. Rafael and Isabel as well as their family trees were invented. Manuel Suarez, however, was the individual that brought Bolita from Cuba to the United States. The Organized crime events and names are consistent with the above research. How Santo Trafficante left Cuba after being arrested with his money intact (he did fain poverty to conceal this fact) is a mystery and the scenario used is speculation. Santo Trafficante Jr.'s assistance to Castro, however, has been promulgated by several of the above sources. And last but not least, the Ybor tunnels are real and to this day have not been mapped or explored to determine their magnitude. On July 24, 2011, the outside World received a glimpse of the tunnels following a rain storm that caused a minor collapse on 7th Avenue (the address of the Columbia Restaurant) and exposed a section of tunnel. The next day the tunnel was again concealed. Although Trafficante owned part of the Columbia Restaurant, the tunnel connection is speculation by this author. After all, very few people know exactly where the Ybor tunnels connect and this author is not one of them. If I claimed to be, I might become The Stone in Someone's Shoe.

www.ingramcontent.com/pod-product-compliance
Lightning Source LLC
Chambersburg PA
CBHW051434260626
47162CB00001B/90